HAVOC

HAVOC OF SINS

To anyone who needs a little pep talk. This moment in time is not forever. Things will change if you just wait.

CHARACTER GUIDE

Gates Family

Jim Gates: Grim's father and owner of Indulge Hotel

Laurel Gates: Grim's mother

Grim Gates: Owner of Secrets and oldest of the brothers

Leo Gates: Middle of the three brothers

Knox Gates: Youngest of the three brothers

Leal and Zhar: Grim's Doberman Pinschers

Darcy: Dog walker

Extras to the Gates Family

Jesse: Grim's right-hand man

Cartwright: Grim's main driver

Louis: Grim trusts him to ride his bike

Janelle: In love with Grim

Deborah: Real estate advisor

Tayla Canos: Cartel daughter (Dark Water Series)

Jerry and Elva Canos: Tayla's parents (Grim lived with them for 10 years when in Mexico)

Tame Family

Cameron Tame: Kenna's father, Lawyer to Jim Gates

Claudine Tame: Kenna's mother, travels the world for work

Kenna Tame: Goes by Lodge to keep her job separate from her family

Calli Tame: Kenna's younger sister, doesn't get along with Kenna

Extras to the Tame Family

Simon Gable: Private Investigator, works for Cameron

Zara: Cameron's secretary

Extras

Jayden Wallace: Manager to super hosts

Mr. Salazar: Client of Kenna's

Yen Hong: Client of Kenna's

Elio Capri: Head of the Capri mafia family in Italy (Quiet Wealth Series) and friend of Grim

Vinni and Niccola Capri: Elio's cousins

Martin Castillo: Head of Cartel (Dark Water Series)

Hannah: Kenna's old friend

Gavin: Elevator operator at Indulge Hotel

Shore: Kenna's favorite driver at Indulge Hotel

<u>Devil's Reach Motorcycle Club</u>

Location of official clubhouse: Santa Monica, California

Trigger: President, married to Tess

Brick: Vice President, Minnie's longtime boyfriend

Tess: Married to Trigger, best friend to Brick and Minnie and owner of Dirty Deeds Club

Minnie: Kenna's best friend and owner of a sex house and Dirty Demons strip club.

Rail: Good friend of Kenna's and dates whoever he can

Morgan: Good friend of Kenna's. Holds the rank of Sergeant of Arms

<u>Stripe Backs Motorcycle Club</u>

Rival club to Devil's Reach

Location of official clubhouse: Venice, California.

Club weak and scattered as many members were killed over the years. Power struggle within the membership as they try to rebuild.

ONE

GRIM

"Kill him! Kill him! Kill him!" fans chanted as New Jersey's Dominque Wiser came down the ramp with his hands high in the air. I rolled my eyes at the TV screen that showed him playing up to the cameras as I jumped back and forth on the balls of my feet.

"Speed is everything," Ricky yelled in my ear. He got in my face as we saw the cameras zoom in on a guy who shouted for Dominque to crush my skull. "When that bell rings, nothing matters but that first move. Bring him down, break what you need to, so he won't get up." He grinned his stained, yellow teeth at me. "Do what you do best." He slapped the side of my head. "Ready?" I nodded. "Good." I knew Ricky was the best, and the crowd sounds diminished as I homed in on what he said.

A few seconds later, Ricky pulled back the curtain and I stepped into the brightly lit arena. The place was packed to the rim with crazy-ass fans who paid good money for Dominque to kick my ass.

"Hey, Grim." I turned back to look at Ricky. "Live up to your name." He pointed to the screen that wrapped around the place, and I saw my stage name flash in black. It had a scythe ripping between the two words, Vegas Reaper.

I grinned at the cameras and jogged down the ramp with Ricky behind me. The banner above the ring read Lost Lives Fight Club. This was my first fight here, and we all fought for the last open place in the official Lost Lives annual tournament. I was a nobody in the underground fighting ring in the US, but I was determined to become a name they'd fear. I'd been fighting since I tossed my first punch in second grade, and I hadn't stopped since.

I trained in Singapore through my high school years then skipped the Ivy League dream to feed my fighting addiction. I was lucky my family had the money and supported my need to fight. As long as I attended my classes and got the marks necessary to pass, they were behind me. I continued to train while I worked for my family's business after I graduated. I didn't need a degree to tell me what I could do. My parents knew I was quick, and I proved my worth to them early. Besides, at nineteen, I could land a hit no one saw coming, and I was determined to make a name for myself.

I had to hand it to Ricky. He had been my coach from the start and got me a slot for this night's fight. Apparently,

Kevin Hawthorne, the owner of the property where the tournament was being held, saw me fight the previous year and extended an invitation for me to fight sometime. Ricky made sure Hawthorne knew I was ready, and here I was.

I dipped under the ropes and breathed in the excitement that poured off the crowd.

"Bust his spleen, Dom!" someone shouted, and I grinned inside. These people were about to know my name.

"Hey, rich boy," Dominque yelled, "Daddy pay your way so I can kick your face in?" Laughter from the crowd joined the hoots and hollers, and I nodded at Ricky to give the green light to hit the bell.

We slapped hands, stepped back, and the crowd became deafening as the bell rang twice. It was almost like things went quiet for me as I marked my moves before I even made them.

Just as the second ring faded out, I reached forward and snapped his wrist backward. I felt the bone break. He screamed, and with his defenses down, I dipped, loaded my weight on my back leg, and jolted forward. My back knee went to the mat, I grabbed both of his legs, and slammed my shoulder into his pelvic bone. My front knee went down, I connected my hands behind his knees, stepped up on my foot, and drove him down to the floor. Within a second, he was on his back, I chopped his windpipe when he gasped for a breath, then punched his lung and cracked his temple, and he was unconscious. I popped to my feet as the bell rang and glanced at the clock as the crowd went quiet.

Five seconds, that was all it took. I paced the ring as everyone around me caught up to what I'd just done. The cheers for Dominque instantly switched to cheers for me.

"Reaper! Reaper! Reaper!" Ricky clapped with the crowd and winked at me. I was fast, smart, and hit like a cannon. That was what I was known for.

"Another!" Ricky shouted, and I waited for the next opponent to enter the ring as Dominque was carried away. I rolled my neck and shook my arms, prepared for the next round. A sheen of sweat had broken out over my body and made my tattoos more vibrant. My father introduced me to the world of ink at sixteen, and I'd been adding to them ever since. Every tattoo meant something, and when I needed to focus, I focused on them. The crowd cheered, and I saw a man hold up a Halloween prop. I rolled my eyes. This wasn't the WWE.

Next came The Slammer, as they called him. He was twice my size and clearly could use his weight as a weapon. I knew to stay away from any kind of hold. I was six-two and solid, but he could crush me with one blow. Maybe he could, but I wasn't going to chance it.

I calculated my moves, and when the bell rang, I jammed my fingers in his eyes to blind him. On instinct, he covered his eyes, and that was when I used his own weight against him. I kicked the outside of his knee, and as he fell, I twisted his elbow, breaking the bone with a snap. The sound and vibration sent a thrill through me and woke that part of me I lived for. He screamed into the mat as saliva spewed. I wrapped my arms around his neck and squeezed hard, cutting the blood flow to the brain. His face turned red, and he tried to swing at me, but I bent him backward, bowing his spine, and his hands flailed in the air. His body relaxed, and he passed out. I jumped to my feet and saw it was just over five seconds. I wasn't pleased with that, but it had to do.

"Wow, Vegas Reaper for the win again!" the announcer yelled over the speaker. "Let's see what else you got."

One by one, they'd enter the ring. I'd break a bone or two at lightning speed, disabling them, then knock them out within five seconds. I walked the ring each time and let the adrenaline rush feed my body. Then I'd get my head on straight and prepare for the next one. I wasn't cocky; I barely registered the crowd. I broke bones for me. It wasn't a cry from a bad childhood. It was a need from deep within, something that gave me the release I needed. I didn't question it; it was who I was. I slammed my fist into the man's head, and he went down.

"We have our winner!" I barely heard the words as I tried to clear my head and focus on the cheering crowd.

Ricky was screaming and grinning and jumped into the ring and slapped me on the back. He grabbed a towel and tossed it at me.

"You sure got people's attention!" he yelled. "The Vegas Reaper is here!"

I walked the ring and nodded at the crowd. Then my attention was caught as a man approached Ricky and they talked. I focused on the man; he wore a leather cut. Then I realized there were other guys behind him who wore the same cut.

The Devil's Reach MC.

I'd seen bikers roll through town before who had worn that cut. It had a reaper holding a skull on it, I'd never paid much attention to them except to admire their bikes.

I left the ring and started up the ramp. I lost sight of the guy as he disappeared into the crowd. Ricky caught up with me.

"Who were you talking to?"

"Some biker dude wanting to know where you trained."

"Did you tell him?"

"Of course. Gave him my card, too."

"Mm." I pushed open the door to the dressing room and downed a bottle of water.

"You got the spot, Grim. How's it feel?" He grinned and leaned his hip into the doorway as I stripped down and grabbed the soap.

"Makes all the training worth it." I turned on the shower and stepped into the cold spray. "Do we have the schedule yet?"

"I'm gonna zip out and get it."

When he left, I cooled my body down with icy water, washed up, and got changed. Just as I fastened my watch around my wrist, the door swung open.

"Grim Gates?" a man asked.

"Who's asking?" I eyed my security guys who stood behind him. One had his hand on his gun. He mouthed the word "sponsor," and I made a note to kill Ricky for not locking the door behind him. I'd deal with Trevor, my head of security, later for allowing this guy to get in. Ricky may have left the door unlocked, but it was Trevor's responsibility to watch my back. Since our arrival back in the States, I noticed he'd slipped more than once when it came to my protection.

"Congratulations on your win. That fills the last spot for contenders."

"Thanks."

"One of the sponsors of the tournament would like to have a word with you if you have a sec."

"I suppose I could do that. Just give me a moment." I quickly sent a text to Ricky to let him know what was going on, then told one of my guys to follow us and make sure Ricky would know where we'd gone. I followed the man down a hallway and into a large room.

A well-dressed man sat in a chair and studied me as I came into the room. He had maybe ten years on me, and from the look of him, I guessed he was European.

"Mr. Gates?" His Italian accent confirmed my suspicions.

"I am."

"Please have a seat."

"All right." I glanced at a couple other men in the room then looked over my shoulder to see Ricky pleading with one of the men to let him through the door.

"He's with me." I lifted a brow, unimpressed that once

again Trevor hadn't stepped in and made sure Ricky was able to join me. At a look from me, the Italian gave a nod to let him through.

"Thanks a lot." Ricky looked pissed.

"You were impressive between the ropes." The Italian smiled, but there was a hint of something much darker there, something I could identify with.

"Thank you."

"Do you think you can win this tournament?"

"I know I can." I held his gaze.

"I see." He tilted his head slightly. "You didn't come across as cocky—"

"I'm not," I assured him. "I've just trained with the best, and trained hard. I take my time to make my moves."

"But you win in five seconds or less," one of the men chimed in. "Where's the time to plan your moves?"

"I'm quick." I pointed to my head.

"I would like you to throw the next fight." The Italian man in the chair brought my attention immediately back to him. He rubbed a finger over his lips as I gathered myself. I couldn't help but notice the large black ring he wore.

"Excuse me?" I needed him to repeat that.

"When you signed up for this tournament, you gave a stage name, nothing more. So, no one knows you. You came into the ring and beat every opponent. You turned the crowd in your favor. Rumors will spread and bets will be made." He adjusted a cufflink and looked directly into my eyes. "So, I want you to throw the next fight then come back swinging

in the next and take it. Let's give people something to talk about, a reason to come, to bet even more on you in the next round."

"Grim." Ricky handed me the official invitation to fight. It was outlined in gold. I'd wanted that. It was something I'd worked hard for and something I could be incredibly proud of.

"I'll make it worth your while, of course. I'll double whatever you'd make if you had won."

"Why?" I'd dealt with plenty of shady people before, but this somehow really bothered me.

"It's just business." He shrugged and watched me carefully. "I'll have your name put on the door, and 'Vegas Reaper' will be on everyone's lips."

I eyed the card as the light caught the gold on its edges. I stood and handed it to him.

"Not interested."

"For what it's worth," Ricky folded his arms, "I agree with Grim. I'm his trainer, and he's worked hard for this. If you loved this sport like he does, you'd never ask him to throw a fight."

"Sorry, Mr....?" I waited for his name.

"Capri."

"Sorry, Mr. Capri, but I fight to win, every time. I'm not the guy for you." He studied the card then looked at the man who had spoken earlier, and something passed between them. Then he returned his gaze to me. "If that costs me my spot in the tournament, then so be it." I stared him down.

He nodded then held the card out to me.

"It will cost you nothing." He waited for me to take it back, then he called to his men, and they walked out. Confused, I watched them leave as I wondered if I'd made the right choice coming here.

"Gentlemen." I turned to address my security detail.

"Yes, Mr. Gates?" Trevor replied.

"You're all fired."

"Grim." A voice said from far away. "Hellooo, Grim." I blinked and saw my brother's confused expression. "Where the hell were you?"

That was odd. I'd let my mind slip far back. Those days were long gone.

I shook my head and glanced at my phone. It showed I had a missed message and two calls from Morgan.

"Sorry. Give me a sec, Leo."

I tapped Morgan's number and waited for the call to connect.

"I hope I didn't wake you," Morgan yawned.

"No, I was just dealing with something," I lied. "Well?"

"I followed her to her house, she slept, and now looks to be awake." I heard him grunt as he moved around. "No company so far."

"Good."

"I'm not spending another night in the truck. I'm going inside and see what's up."

"Stay in touch."

"Yeah." I hung up, and Leo eased into the chair.

"She, okay?"

"Yeah. Morgan's going in to check on her."

"Good." He rubbed his tired face. It had been a long last few hours. "I still can't believe she wouldn't stay. The doctor should have looked her over."

"I know. She has a bad habit of not listening to me." I moved over to the window as he laughed, and I let my mind drift back to when we found her in the elevator.

"Leo! Shut down the floor!" I boomed. "Steven, find out exactly where she came from," I ordered the security guard who already had his radio in his hand. "You," I pointed to Freddy the second guard on duty, "find me a fucking head!" His eyes went wide, then he whirled and ran.

Kenna's gaze latched on to mine, and I saw the moment she let go. I jolted forward and caught her, then lowered her to the floor.

Someone was going to fucking die before the night was done, or blood would spray across the city of Vegas until the truth showed its ugly face.

"Grim," she whispered, and I looked down at her, "I'm so sorry."

"Shit." Leo turned around as he lowered his phone.

"She just passed out." I lifted Kenna in my arms and hurried into the elevator with Leo right behind me. He pressed the button for her floor, and I wanted to argue that

she should come to mine, but I kept my mouth shut. He unlocked her door, and we whisked into her suite.

I carried her past her horrendous white couch and into her bedroom. I noticed her makeup was strewn all over her vanity. I laid her down and studied her for a moment. Blood was on her face from her nose and a swollen lip, but I couldn't find any other obvious injuries. I just hoped there wasn't any internal bleeding. Sometimes what didn't show was worse.

"Here." Leo handed me an open bottle of tequila and waved it under her nose to draw her awake. Her eyes fluttered open as she moved away from the smell.

"Hey," I shook her arm gently, "look at me. Do you know where you are?" She looked around and flinched in pain.

"My room." Her expression registered with me. Fear was there, but also anger.

"Where are you hurt?"

"My side, mostly." She tried to move, but I stopped her.

"Who did this to you?" I barely recognized my own voice as I took the warm facecloth from Leo and cleaned up her face.

"I don't know."

"Don't lie!" I felt heat flash through me as I fought to control my temper.

"Grim," Leo warned, and I tried to curb my tone.

"How do you not know?"

"He wore a fucking mask!" She tried to pull away, but I wasn't allowing it. She took a breath and winced. "Also, his voice was altered." She evened out her breathing. "Look, Grim." She put a hand to her head as if it hurt.

"Why are you sorry?" I wanted an answer to that. She squinted at me then seemed to remember, and a look of panic came over her face.

"You need to go. B-both of you need to go."

"You need to see a doctor first."

"No."

"That wasn't a question," I shot back and chucked the facecloth in the direction of the table.

"Kenna." Leo came at her softer, and I fought not to roll my eyes in frustration. She was seeing a doctor with or without her consent. "Can I have a look at your side?" He held up his hands and waited for her to nod.

"Let me." I released her arm and undid one of the panels on her dress. Her skin was already turning a nasty purple. Anger seeped into my bloodstream. "Does this hurt?" I slid my hand along the damage and felt her flinch.

"I don't think anything's broken." I did her dress back up and noticed a rip in the fabric.

"Did he try to—"

"No." Her voice was firm. "Grim, can you guys go now? I really want to rest." She pleaded this time.

"For now," I replied through clenched teeth. I hesitated as I saw her eyes gloss over.

"Grim," she sniffed, "I can take care of myself."

Against my better judgement, I gave in.

"I'll check in on you later." I turned to go and nearly

knocked into Leo. He'd gone to get her some water and a painkiller.

Good, he could fuss over her, while I hunted down the fucker who dared hurt one of our own.

"Holy shit," Leo's voice brought me back to the present, and I went to see what he looked at.

"What?"

"Just this," he pressed play on the screen, and Kenna popped up.

"Is this it?"

"Yeah," he stood next to me as we both leaned close to the TV, "she gets a call here." He pointed at the screen. "Then…" His words trailed off as we watched the horror unfold.

"Jesus."

TWO

KENNA

I wiped the mirror free of steam and blinked through the tears that blurred my vision. In a pair of shorts and a t-shirt, I limped to my bedroom. I hadn't wanted to stay in my suite at the hotel. I needed to be in my own space, my real space. Once everyone stopped hovering, I left. I'd decided to do the fifteen-minute drive to my house. It was pretty late when I got there, but I was glad I did. I slept like the dead, got up and managed to eat, then called in sick.

I had shared everything with Minnie when she came to my suite that morning. Grim had called her and told her. He probably wanted her to report back. Her mouth hung open when I got to the part where I was being blackmailed. I stopped her rant about how I needed to share the truth with everyone, and I told her I would. I convinced her I needed a little time to heal before the wrath of Grim was set upon me. She was horrified at the idea of me leaving the hotel, but she also understood my need to be in my own space to recover. She made me promise I'd check in, and I called her as soon as I arrived.

Feeling only slightly better, I checked the locks on my windows, closed the blinds, then pulled out the metal box from my vanity drawer. I removed the small gun, loaded it, and put the safety on.

The floor-length mirror I stood in front of showed no mercy when I pulled up my shirt to reveal a massive, deep blue bruise on my right side and several scattered scrapes and nicks around my back. It was the first time I'd examined the damage. Even my arm was sore from where I was grabbed and hauled into that nightmare.

"So, he was right," came from the door, and I whirled and wildly pointed the pistol at him.

"What the hell are you doing here, Morgan?" I winced at the pain that went through me with the unexpected movement. I thought about offering myself over to the reaper featured on the leather Devil's Reach cut he wore. It sure would make things easier at this point. "I could have killed you." I carefully put the gun down and shifted my shirt back in place to cover the bruises.

"Not with the safety on, you wouldn't've." He stepped into the room and came close. He lifted my shirt and made a noise of disapproval. "You take anything for that?"

"Yeah." I pointed to the pain relievers by the bed. "Hopefully, they'll help. They're expired."

"Those won't touch that, anyway." He handed me a joint. "Take this for now, and I'll get you something else in the morning."

"'K." I sniffed, and he studied my face.

"Wanna tell me what happened?"

"No."

"All right." He leaned against the desk while I lit the joint. "Grim found me that night at the fundraiser, said you left. He wanted me to check in on you."

"Is that so?" Sweet smoke rose from my lips. "Seems he is telling everyone my business."

He ignored my words. "I thought maybe you had it out with Jayden again, but I saw him at the bar. He was talking to that bartender Dale slept with last week. Then I thought, what did your dad do now? But he looked happy as a pig in shit entertaining his clients with your mother on his arm." He took the joint from me, drew in a hit, and passed it back.

"Then Minnie told me you went to her club, so I

went lookin' for you there." He paused and watched me for a moment. "Guess I just missed you, according to the bouncer. I called Shore, your all-time favorite driver, and he said you got a text just when you stepped out of his car at the hotel. Said your face went pale. Then fifteen minutes later, you show up on the twentieth, with wet hair, red eyes, lookin' like shit. What happened in that fifteen minutes, Kenna?" He crossed his arms and waited for me to speak. I took another much-needed draw.

"Someone watches too much true crime with Rail." I coughed and my eyes watered.

"Kenna." His tone told me he wasn't having it.

"Fine." I dropped my arms. "I pissed off some people and had to deal with the consequences." That wasn't a lie. I certainly had pissed someone off; I just wasn't sure who or why.

"Who?"

"I don't know." I slowly moved across the room. "Now," I swiped at my eyes again and pulled back the covers on the bed. "I've had a shitty last forty hours, and all I want to do is sleep, so, if you don't mind."

"You have a concussion? Because you slept all day."

"No, and how do you know that?"

"Minnie told me, plus Grim saw you leave. I slept in the van last night. Figured I'd break in once I knew you were up."

"That's reassuring," I muttered.

"I found Grim out on the rooftop after I looked for you." I glanced away and carefully slid under the covers. "Yeah." He gave me a look with raised eyebrows. "He thought you left the fundraiser because you were upset about him and that girl he fucks sometimes." He rolled his eyes, and I gave a sarcastic huff. He waited for an answer, but I didn't offer one. His gaze flicked to my side. "He watched the video from the parking lot."

"I figured he would."

He snagged my phone off the table and held it up. "So, who'd you call when you were getting' in your car to come here?" I went still, and I knew he saw me swallow. "Whoever it was," he unlocked my phone, "made you look over your shoulder while you talked."

"Natural reaction for what I'd just been through."

"Maybe," he looked at the number without a name attached to it, "but what did you mean by 'I'll do it?'"

I wished the drug would hit me now. I hated the attention this whole terrible situation had brought me. I didn't like to feel so vulnerable.

"Grim knows you made a phone call," he repeated. "He's gonna ask you about it. Who was it, Kenna? Who upset you like that?" I rolled on my back and hoped the weed would hurry and take the throb out of my side and help to numb my thoughts. "Kenna—"

"Morgan," I fought hard not to tell my friend,

"please, don't ask." I sniffed then dabbed out the joint. "This entire thing is so much." I rubbed my chest. "It's like dominos, you know? I'm just trying to keep them from all crashing down." I paused to catch my breath. "I'm just trying to keep it all together."

"Fuck! Okay." He sighed heavily, toed off his boots, and laid his cut on a chair then crawled into bed with me. He was careful to tuck the covers in around me, then he settled and lay there quietly on top of the covers. I could hear his slow breaths as we both stared at the ceiling and listened to the house sounds. I matched the rhythm of his breathing, and it helped slow the panic I held inside. I relished that he was with me, and I wasn't alone.

"Make me laugh," I begged. He was always so good at that.

"Rail crashed a wedding at Indulge couple nights ago. Thought he went back to the room with the maid of honor, but it was actually the bride's grandmother." Morgan said it in a deadpan voice, and I started to laugh despite the stabbing pain in my side. "I'm unsure how he made that mix-up."

"Do you think he noticed before or after she took out her false teeth?"

"I think it was after he helped her into her fluffy floral dressing gown." He made me laugh harder, but soon the humor faded away and we were left in silence again. "Can I ask you something?" He got up on his elbow.

"Depends." I used the back of my hand to clear the tears that insisted on outing my nerves.

"Are you really okay?"

I huffed out a long breath and craned my neck to look up at him, but I couldn't find the words. I just shook my head. My chin quivered, and I put my hand on my mouth.

"Okay." He pulled the blanket tighter around me, and I curled into his side. After a few minutes, he pulled out his phone and I saw he had a text. He waited a few minutes, most likely hoping I'd fallen asleep.

He unlocked his phone, and I read the screen.

Grim: Update.

Morgan: I'm spending the night.

Grim: Is she okay?

Morgan's thumb hovered over the letters, and as my eyes grew heavy, I saw him text.

Morgan: Far from it.

As much as I wanted to go to work the next day, I spent the night staring at the wall. The day after that, I still found myself ready to spin out over my own shadow. I knew it wasn't healthy to stay so secluded, but I was internally trying to process the attack and who knew what.

Minnie came by, and I filled her in on everything again and made sure I left nothing out. I felt terrible about dumping another secret on her, but I promised I'd make it right, or at least that I'd tell one of the guys. She agreed not to say a word but only because she saw I was hanging on by a thread. She insisted I get myself back to work the next day so she could keep an eye on me. I kept my promise and headed to the hotel first thing in the morning.

I spent a couple hours with my client Yen Hong before he had to leave for the airport. He had to be back in Hong Kong for business. He'd gotten to know me fairly well, and I saw him glance at me a few times. I knew he could tell I was off, but he was too polite to probe.

"Have you thought any further about my offer of a job?" He shrugged on his jacket, and the tailor got to work. Yen's offer for me to come work for him in Hong Kong would have tempted me a few years back. He basically gave me the go-ahead to write anything into the contract that I wanted. I was flattered, but my roots were now firmly planted in Vegas.

"I have, a lot, actually," I crossed my legs and leaned back in the chair, easing some of the pain in my side, "but right now I see myself here."

"My hotel needs you, Kenna. I don't take refusal easily." He grinned, but it morphed into work mode when he suddenly got a call. "Hello?"

I checked the time and knew he'd have to leave for the airport soon. Once he left, I'd be free for the rest of the day. Sadly, the idea of being alone upstairs in my suite wasn't as appealing as I hoped.

"Kenna, I'm sorry. I have to go. Keep thinking of that offer." Yen blew me a kiss, and we said our good-byes as I snagged my bag and headed for the lobby.

Once I was back in the lobby, I spotted Rail with a group of young women. He made them all laugh loudly. *Oh, the Rail charm.*

"I didn't see you as a Paul Anka fan." A security guard chuckled, and I blinked at him.

"Pardon?"

"*Put Your Head on My Shoulder*, that's a classic." He pointed to my purse where my phone was playing that song.

"Oh." I forced a smile and pulled it free, curious as to who the hell it was. "Please excuse me for a moment." I stepped away and answered the now silenced call.

"Hello?"

"Walk over to Rail and ask what his meeting with

Trigger was about last night." The automated voice made my blood run cold. I couldn't forget that voice if I tried.

"I can't." Somehow, I found my voice and scanned the crowd to see if I could spot someone watching me. "I would never ask him a thing like that. It would be too risky. He'd know something was up."

"I don't recall you having a choice in the matter," the voice said loudly. "Why did Simon Gable call you that night?"

My head spun. How did he know so much?

"He, ahh…" I tried to put my thoughts together, but this call had frozen my brain. "The night I was attacked by you?" I tried to show some guts.

"Don't be smart, Kenna. Remember what I told you. You want the cops at your door for murder?"

"He wanted to talk to me, but we didn't get very far. I had to hang up because that woman you were with interrupted us."

"Look to your left." I slowly turned and saw Grim talking to Jenelle. "Always got a woman on his arm," he pointed out to me. "Grim had a meeting with his father early this morning. I want to know what was said."

"How am I supposed to do that?"

"You were supposed to be at it." Wait, how did he know that? How did he know any of this?

"Get the details on what I asked and wait for my

call." He paused, and I caught Grim's eye. "Remember, Kenna, I got to you once. I can get to you again." He paused. "That color looks good on you, by the way." The line went dead.

I lowered the phone and felt the massive room tilt as panic waved through me. How was I going to pull this off? *Breathe, Kenna, breathe.* A cold prickle went up my back when my mind finally slowed down.

He was watching me. He told me where to look, he knew where Rail and Grim were, and that meant he was close by. The thought terrified me.

I scanned the busy lobby, but no one stood out, then I looked toward the cameras, and my stomach sank. *What if…?*

Rail caught my attention. He was headed toward me, so I turned on my heel and went quickly in the opposite direction. I wouldn't ask him about Trigger's meeting; I could never cross that line. The less I knew, the better, anyway.

I wanted to see those cameras. I used my ID card and hurried through the locked doors, wove my way through the shift change of dealers, then ran up the stairs. I paused at the door and raised my hand to knock then thought better of it. I held up Grim's black keycard he'd left with me and held it to the security pad. The light turned green. There was Leo watching the craps table. He didn't glance up because at the top of the screen it read Grim's name for who entered the room. It was so you didn't have to take your eyes off the screen.

"How's Jenelle? Ya married yet?" He snickered, and I sighed at his comment as I stood there and watched the bird's eye view of the hotel. I had been here before but never without Jim or my father.

"Kenna?" He had turned and eyed me oddly. Then he saw Grim's black card in my hand. "I see." He didn't question it, and I didn't offer any explanation. He knew I would never cause any harm or trouble to the hotel. "How's your side?"

"Still hurts a lot, but it's getting better each day." I kept my eyes on the monitors.

"I saw the tape of what happened, and we'll get the animals who did that to you."

"No doubt." I wanted to talk about the problem I had now and keep the conversation off what happened before. "I need a favor." I hated to put myself on Leo's radar, but I had to figure this out fast. "Can you rewind the video on the lobby?"

I felt Leo study me for a moment. Then he spoke quietly into a mic and had another guy keep an eye on the man he'd been watching at the craps table.

"How far back?" He switched to the lobby camera.

"Ten, maybe twelve minutes ago."

"Okay." He started to tap on the keyboard, then the picture jumped to that timeline. "Anything I can search for? A color of a shirt, jeans, height?"

"A man on a phone." I spotted myself on the screen and moved closer to study the footage. Multiple green boxes outlined several men on their phones.

"Can you help narrow them down?" he asked.

"Are any of them watching me?" I knew it was a longshot, but to my surprise, he moved the camera angle, so it was from my point of view looking around the lobby. He did a compete circle and the green boxes followed the men.

"Two of them were." He brought their faces to the side of the screen.

"Can you see if they were watching Grim too?" I pointed to Grim across the way.

"Yeah." He tapped away, and the green boxes around the two guys turned red. "No, they didn't look in his direction." I rubbed my head and ran multiple scenarios of what was happening.

"Can you tell me approximately how tall they are?"

"This guy," Leo brought up the guy on the left, "given by what he's standing next to, is roughly five-five." He tapped again. "This one is about five-eight." I thought about the man who attacked me; he was much taller. "What's this about, Kenna?"

"Can anyone access these cameras?" He laughed but stopped when he saw my face. "I'm serious, Leo. You hear about hackers, so could these be hacked right now, and you wouldn't know?"

"Not with how much we pay to keep people out.

You'd have to be the best of the best, and those guys work for us."

"Who has access to this room?"

"A select few and, apparently, you."

I looked at the phone and sucked in a deep breath.

"What about my phone?" I tossed in on the desk like it might bite me. "Could my phone be bugged?"

"Highly unlikely, but," he moved to a different computer and plugged in my phone, "I can run it through here and see if anything pops up." I stood over his shoulder, then he pulled out a chair next to him. "This will take a moment."

"Maybe I'm losing my mind," I confessed but knew I wasn't.

"Maybe it's because you were attacked, and you haven't dealt with it yet." He shrugged sympathetically. "I wasn't aware you had one of those." He pointed at the black key card.

"Grim knows."

"I figured, considering it's his."

"Are you okay with that?"

"If my brother gave you his black key card, I'm fine with it."

"He didn't exactly give it to me, more of he didn't take it back when I tried to give it to him."

"I see."

"Strange, right? I mean, does this get me anywhere?

I'm still trying to understand why he hasn't asked for it back."

"He must really trust you." The corners of his mouth went up, but he focused back on the computer.

"I don't think Grim trusts most people. Well, the ones who aren't in his direct bloodline or have four legs."

"He does love his dogs. Did he ever tell you about how he came to own them?"

"I just figured they were a gift from the Devil for all his hard work." I didn't mean to be so sarcastic, but I was dealing with a lot. "No, he never told me."

"Grim's dark, there's no question about it." Leo smiled. He loved to talk about his older brother. "He knew Leal and Zhar when they were just babies. They belonged to someone else back then. Then when they were about two, something bad happened and he took them. It's a long story, but ask him about it sometime." The computer made a noise and drew our attention. "Just as I guessed, it's clean."

"Can people hack into your phone and change a ringtone?" I knew I sounded crazy.

He tried to pry. "Only if they have access to your account online or know the passcode to your phone. Did that happen?" I ran a frustrated hand through my hair and closed my eyes, confused how this person knew so many things. "You seem very spooked, so what do you think happened?"

"Spooked doesn't even describe what's going on inside me," I huffed. "Look, I really appreciate your help. Wish I could say I'm just overreacting, but…" I shrugged. "Thanks, Leo." I patted his arm and stood. "As always, I appreciate that you're so ready to help."

"Any time." He nodded and handed me my phone. "Are you staying at your house or in your suite tonight?"

"My suite, via Jim's request."

"I think that's a smart idea." He leaned back and looked at me. "Have you slept?"

"At first, I did. Slept like the dead."

"And now?"

"I don't know." I leaned my hip into the desk and pressed my lips together. "It's like I'm scared to shut my eyes. Afraid they might come into my room at night. I'm afraid of where my mind will go when I'm not in control of it."

"Sounds—"

"Exhausting, overwhelming, the list is endless." I smiled apologetically. "Sorry. It's just been a hard last few days."

"Don't be sorry. I'm glad I'm someone you feel you can share stuff with."

"You are." I loved Leo. He had such a warm heart. "Well, I'm off to go lie in bed and count the minutes until tomorrow."

"Remember, that card opens any door," he called as

I left. I wasn't sure exactly what he meant, but my head was too tired to figure it out. I almost ran into Simon as I headed for the elevator.

"Whoa. Everything okay?" he asked as he looked at me.

"Yeah." I was sure my lie was written all over my face.

"I'd like to finish that conversation we started the other day on the phone." My stomach rolled, and he appeared to read my mood. "Perhaps a little later, then."

"Thanks. That'd be better." I could barely make eye contact, I felt so out of sorts.

"No problem." He studied me for another beat then smiled warmly and let me pass. I hurried into the elevator and was glad when the two steel doors closed.

I showered and changed into an oversized t-shirt I'd stolen from Dale before we broke up. It had his name on the sleeve and the culinary school where he'd graduated. I only wore it because it was soft, and maybe it reminded me of a time where I hadn't slept alone.

The glow from the flameless candles on the living room table provided just enough light to move about comfortably in my suite. I missed my house, but I didn't miss the ground floor windows or doors. Sounds were different here. It was quieter way up in the sky, and even though there was only one way into the place, I found myself staring at the door. Scared the handle would turn.

The time ticked by, and I never moved from the couch. My heart was in my throat, and tears streamed down my cheeks. I was such a strong person, and it bothered me that I couldn't hold it together that now I was alone.

The sound of the gunshot and the jolt of his body played out in front of me for the first time since that night at Minnie's. I clenched my jaw and pushed the image back inside where I kept it. With all that had happened lately, I felt like I was losing control.

The sound of the elevator motor slowing caught my attention, and I sprang to my feet and grabbed a knife from the chopping block. My heart pounded so hard it made it difficult to hear if there was anyone outside my door. With my phone in one hand and the knife in the other, I slowly moved over to the door and pressed against it to listen. Just as I did, my phone buzzed in my hand and my heart went into my mouth. Any bravery I had left inside me fizzled out. I silenced the alert then unlocked the screen to see a text message.

> Unknown: Your suite can't protect you from me.

A tremor tore through me, and I fought to turn the phone off. I grabbed my purse and, without another thought, ran into the hall and, with shaky hands, held

Grim's card up to the screen and bolted inside the elevator the moment the doors opened. It took forever for them to close again. When they opened, I stepped out to meet two sets of pissed-off eyes.

"Oh, shit." I took a couple of involuntary steps then froze. "Grim?" I called hopefully as a wave of terror washed over me. "Hi, puppies." I tried to keep myself calm.

Leal, the moodier of the two Doberman brothers, let out a low growl and bared his teeth as a warning.

"Okay, boy." I turned to find Zhar had now blocked my way to the elevator. He just stood there in an intimidating stance while his brother did all the talking. "Yeah, this is great. Shit." Without warning, I hit my emotional limit and broke. I slumped down until my butt hit the floor, unable to hold my weight any longer, and sobbed. Both dogs moved to stand in front of me. I was sure neither had any idea what the hell was happening. I drew my knees to my chest and wrapped my arms around myself.

"I'm sorry," I whispered through a hiccup. "It's like things are snowballing, and I can't stop it." Zhar looked at his brother, who had a death stare on me, then he sat down. Almost like he knew I just needed someone. "Have you ever been so scared that your own mind works against you? I don't know if I can do this." A pair of black loafers stepped into view, and I looked up into eyes colder than Leal's.

"Go on," Grim commanded the dogs then bent down in front of me. "You're lucky they didn't hurt you."

"Wouldn't be the first time this week." I gave a small shrug, and his face remained like stone as he helped me to my feet. "We need to talk."

He looked down at the t-shirt I had on, and I saw he registered there was nothing else under it. He lifted an eyebrow.

"Seriously, Grim, I'm not okay, and if I don't share this now, I don't know if I can."

"Then let's talk." He walked into his living room and took a seat on the couch. I couldn't sit. I needed to stand as the panic of what I was about to do started to kick in. I just let my mouth run. "I need to tell you about the night I was attacked. Your dad knows the version I gave him, but there was more." With a deep breath, I began to tell him my story.

Thanks. Shore. I appreciate you dropping me off here and not out front." I snapped my compact mirror closed, *pleased my makeup was on point. Now if only I could say the same about my wet hair. But when the hotel owner, Jim Gates, summoned you to the twentieth floor, you hauled ass.*

"Anytime, Kenna." He held up his phone. "Duty calls. It's Mr. Salazar. Gotta go."

My own phone rang as I gathered my things.

"Hello?"

"Kenna, it's Simon. I need to tell you something." He hesitated. "Is now a good time?"

"Oh, hey, yes, just give me two seconds." I pulled the phone away from my mouth as Shore opened my door.

"Be sure to let Salazar know I say safe travels."

"Happy to." Shore smiled as I stepped out into the parking area. Then he rushed off to go pick up an actual paying client.

"Sorry, Simon. I was letting my driver go. What is it that you needed to tell me?"

"The deal with Trigger and your father just got more complicated."

"How so?"

"Luis Aguilar is dead."

I couldn't understand why this was being brought up to me, and not Trigger.

"I didn't know the man, but I'm sorry to hear he's dead."

"No, you don't understand, Kenna—"

"Kenna Lodge?" a woman's voice interrupted from somewhere nearby. I squinted into the dark corner of the car port. I knew Jim had some construction going on for the level five employees after a couple of the battery charging ports had been vandalized, but I didn't see anyone. "Yes, that's you." Heels clicked on the pavement while I stayed put and waited for whomever it was to show themselves.

"Simon, there's someone here who wants to talk to me. Can I call you back?"

"Yes, okay, but make sure you do. We really need to

talk." I hung up and saw a brown-haired woman, about my size, give me a coy wave. She looked oddly familiar, but I couldn't place her. I took in her hair cut and her freckled face as she got closer, but nothing rang a bell.

"This all feels very Deep Throat, doesn't it?" She chuckled. Something about the way she held her bag told me she was nervous.

"Do I know you?"

"No, but your friend Hanna Hudson does." Oh. "Look, I'm sorry to come at you here where you work, but I'm Linda Pestle, and Hanna and I used to work together."

Okay, I must have seen Linda in a couple of Hanna's photos over the years, and that was why she seemed familiar. It came to me then.

"Oh, yes, Hanna's mentioned you." Apparently, they were pretty good friends. I'd left before Linda came. If I remembered correctly, she worked for Markle Hotel.

"Good, I was hoping she'd mentioned me." She let out a small breath of relief, and I felt my defenses come down a bit.

"She seemed to be upset the last time we talked. Do you know what kind of trouble she's having?" I took a couple steps toward her, dying to know how my friend was. "Have you spoken to her? She called me the other day, but I never heard back from her."

"See, that's the thing." Linda licked her lips nervously. "One moment she was rambling to me about some guy, and the next she gets a call and races out. That was two days ago."

"Why did you come here?" Curiosity nipped at my core.

"Because you were the one who called her that night." Her mouth twisted. "Is there any chance she said something to you?"

"Like what?"

"Like who the guy was or if she was in some kind trouble?" Her eyes darted around.

"She wanted to tell me, but…" My words fell away like my mind put a stop to them. Something wasn't right here. Tiny sparks of fear prickled my veins as my brain tried to process something I was unable see.

A surge suddenly connected those sparks together, and my heart jolted as a leather hand slapped over my mouth. I was lifted off the ground and swallowed up by the shadows.

Fear consumed me as I was slammed into a wall. I struggled to see, but his face was covered by a dark mask that only showed his weird white eyes. Then something flashed by my face.

"You scream, and I'll slit your throat." I felt the cold steel against my windpipe. Then he pulled it back so I could see the ugly switchblade he held to make his point. I nodded and couldn't control the heavy, hot tears that burned as they ran over the suddenly hypersensitive skin on my cheeks. He lowered his hand, and I desperately tried to make out his features through the covering. I realized he wore white contacts, and his voice was altered by some sort of device. It sounded mechanical and deep. "What did Hanna say when she called you?" his weird voice demanded. A faint whiff of body odor mixed with spice and something else found its way to my nose. It may have been my fear, but it wasn't pleasant, and I felt myself gag.

Focus.

Linda, or whoever she was, stayed back, and her head kept going back and forth as she watched. So many terrifying thoughts went through my head, but I willed myself to fight my nausea and stay in the present.

"She told me." I shook my head to get my thoughts straight. "She thought she was in trouble, but she never said what it was." An unexpected explosion of pain in my side took my breath away, and I doubled over and felt sick. I'd never experienced anything like that before. I fought to breathe as I was pulled up by my hair and the knife stuck in my face again. I could hear whimpers and realized the sound came from my own throat.

"Try again." The hand with the knife waved around, and I desperately swallowed back the vomit that threatened.

"She, she got another call. Said she had to call me back." The man hit me again in the same spot, and I blacked out for a moment. I was on the cold concrete and felt him move my skirt around. I came to with so much fight that I managed to kick him square in the balls. He fell, and I raced around him, but the woman snagged my arm and yanked me back with such force she knocked me right off my feet. My back hit the ground hard, and I was dragged back out of the light.

The man breathed heavily in my ear. "Fucking whore! I

should fuck you right here and see what the Gateses think of that."

It's strange how some humans handle a life-threatening experience. I switched into survival mode. I kicked, scratched, tried to bite, and flailed around like a crazy person. Sadly, he held on, and I was soon exhausted.

"Are you done?" He punched me hard in the side again, and I lost my will to fight back as the pain blinded me.

"Come on, hurry up!" The Linda woman's voice found me. Was someone coming? "You're taking too long. Just tell her."

What? I struggled to stand. My battered body hurt everywhere.

"I told you to shut up!" he snapped at her, and she gave him the finger. I saw her cower at his words. The guy loosened his hold and put his face to mine.

"Here's what you're going to do. You're going to be my own personal little spy. So, when I call you, you answer. When I tell you to do something, you do it." He held up a piece of paper with a number on it. "Memorize it."

"Spy?" I looked at him. "I'm not going to spy for you. What are you talking about?" My lips trembled as I looked at him in amazement.

"Oh, you'll do it," his weird voice threatened.

"Why should I?" I felt anger replace the fear, and I raised my chin at him.

"Oh, you wanna know why?" He smirked, and I waited for another blow that might finally burst my kidney.

"Because I know." He leaned so close to my face I almost choked on his breath. "I know what you did."

I froze in pure fear. How could he?

"Hey, bitch, bring it here," he called to the Linda woman. She glanced at me and kept her distance as she reached way out to hand him a pink phone case. Hello Kitties waved at me from their liquid home on the back. He turned it around, and I felt my knees give out as I watched.

"This is my favorite part right here." He pointed at the phone, and I watched in horror. "When will people learn that there's always someone with a phone, watching?"

"Like right now?" the woman huffed, but he ignored her. He tossed the phone at her, and she cursed when she missed the catch and it clattered under a car. "All I need to do is leak that tape, and the world as you know it is over."

"Please, I won't do it." I gasped. "You can't."

"Oh, can't I?" He gave a crazy, mechanical laugh. "That little tidbit all by itself would make Daddio see his little girl in a whole new light. That his own daughter is a murderer." As he let that settle into my consciousness, I stared into his eyes through the cutouts in the mask. The creepy white contacts he wore made my mouth go dry. "You got balls, baby girl. I'll give you that."

"Let's get out of here," the woman begged as she looked around.

"Listen for that call, Kenna, or kiss your world goodbye." He suddenly dropped me like a rag doll, and I watched helplessly as he and the woman hopped in a car. As it peeled out *of the parking lot, I tried to see a plate, but there wasn't one. I sagged into the wall. The pain in my side helped to ground me as my world spun.*

I heard a car door slam and knew I had to get out of there. My phone pinged in my purse, and I somehow dug it out.

> Unknown: Get inside, Kenna. There's a lot of dangerous people out here tonight.

I snapped out of the vivid memory and stared at Grim, who seemed to be stuck in his own trance.

"Say something," I whispered.

"Was that why you've been avoiding the meetings?"

"Yes."

"Why you've been avoiding me?"

"If I don't know anything, how can I share anything?"

"And the call you made at the car? Was that to him?"

"Yes. I had to make a decision to do it, or…"

"What are they blackmailing you with?" His angry gaze held mine. I knew he was a breath away from losing his shit. "Is it the same thing you've been keeping from everyone, even your friends in the DR?"

"Grim, please, it's so much more complicated—"

"No, it's not!" he yelled, and I nearly jumped out of

my skin. He stood and pointed a finger at me. "Stop lying!"

"I'm not lying!" I matched his temper because it felt good to be mad. "I just shared all this with you, and now you're here yelling at me—no, demanding I tell you something that I just can't share."

"Why?" He stepped closer. "You've seen things I've done. Shit, you watched me kill a man in front of you. So why can't I know this?"

"Grim, stop!"

"Why can't you tell me?"

"Because! Because I'm starting to see what I did is connected to so much more than I thought. I'm terrified to see the truth, and now someone else is holding it over my head. I'm totally fucked." I dropped my heavy arms and head. "God knows what will happen now that I've told you. I'll probably end up in some ditch somewhere." Shit, I'd welcome a ditch right now.

"I just want to sleep, but when I'm alone, I relive that moment. If I so much as close my eyes, that moment comes to my mind. I came up here because he just called and mentioned I wasn't safe in my suite."

"He knew you were home alone tonight?"

"Yes. I panicked and thought what was worse, the ditch or being the Cujo duo's midnight snack." I looked around for the dogs.

"Okay." He cleared his throat, and I looked at him.

"That's it? No more scary Grim?"

"Not tonight." He shrugged out of his jacket and tossed it over the chair.

"Good." I felt like it was a trap but was pleased not to waste any more energy I didn't have. The yelling took its toll. "I'll let you get back to your night."

"No." He waved for me to follow him to his bedroom. Leal glared at me as I made my way behind Grim. He disappeared into his closet and returned a moment later with a t-shirt. "Put that on and get into bed."

Huh?

"I'm confused," I said as I held it. Then he reached down and tugged the t-shirt I wore over my head. He made a show of reading what was written on it as I stood there in bare feet and my panties. I didn't cover myself up. He'd seen everything and been everywhere on my body anyway, so I just stood. He homed in on the bruises on my side.

"Jesus." He shook his head then tossed my t-shirt in his hamper, and then he went into the bathroom and slammed the door.

I shrugged and slid his shirt on and pulled back the covers to his massive bed. I hesitated when a strange feeling came over me. I tried not to think of when Jenelle was there last, or God knew who else. The bathroom door finally opened. He'd stripped down to his boxer briefs, and it wasn't lost on either of us that he was aroused.

"Aren't their guest rooms in this penthouse?"

"Three."

"Should I be in one of them?"

"No." He pulled back the covers and slid between them. He ordered the dogs to their beds on the far side of the room. "Go to bed, boys." I heard a low growl, but the click of their nails told me they did as they were told.

"Why?"

"Goodnight, Kenna." He turned off the light.

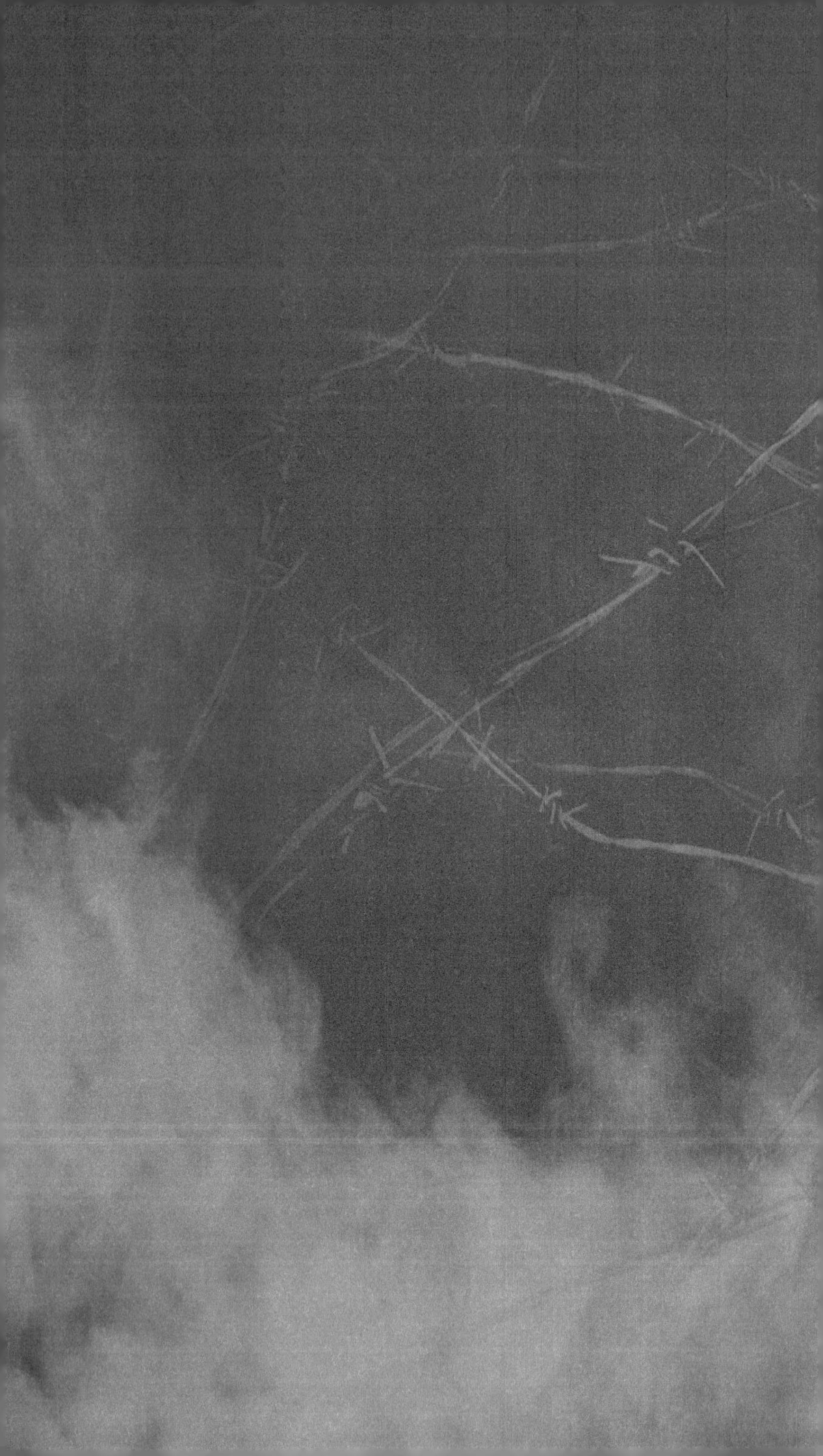

THREE

"It's a rumor, but you know Kenna. Anything for attention." Calli had just finished her story about how Kenna had been attacked. Her father never mentioned it, but leave it to her sister to make Kenna sound like a crazy person. "Hopefully, your old friend," she waved her hand around, "you know…"

"Kurt?"

"Yes, that's his name. Hopefully, he can get the truth on what happened."

Kenna hadn't called me back because she had been attacked. Made sense.

"So, what's it like being in a room with him?" She nodded at Trigger, who had just arrived. I'd asked him to meet me here for a quick chat.

"Intense." We watched him stop and talk to Minnie, who had intercepted him at the entrance. She seemed upset, by the way her hands moved about in front of her as she talked. Trigger nodded and looked around and caught my look. His face wore the same murderous expression he always seemed to have whenever I was around. Maybe he always looked that way.

"Just intense?" Calli wanted more, so I moved my attention to her before she started to pout.

"Picture being in a room with someone after you just watched them slaughter a bunch of people, then you have to share a meal with him. Your mind spins with the horror of it, your nerves are shot, and your stomach begs to turn inside out."

"I'm really glad I asked." She made a disgusted face. "Well, on that note, I'm going to let you and that," she looked at Trigger, "get to your meeting. I need sleep. See you later?" She blinked down at me, and I nodded. "Kiss, kiss." She made the motion and left as Trigger arrived.

Here we go.

I stood and gave a polite nod, remembering he didn't like to be touched.

"Thank you for meeting me so late." I glanced at the time on my watch. It was well past three in the morning, but it was Vegas, after all, and no one here ever thought much about the time. The Devil's Reach were basically nocturnal, anyway.

"You said this had to do with Brick's brother?"

"Yes and no." I swallowed hard when his green eyes pierced mine.

"I don't like being blindsided." He rested his elbows heavily on the table, and I saw his knuckles were battered. I wondered where the body was hidden. "You have two minutes." He raised a hand to the waitress, and she rushed right over. "Whiskey, neat."

"Yes, sir." She batted her eyes at him, and he turned to look at me. He only had eyes for his wife. That was the only part I admired about him.

"We have a problem." I don't know why I started so aggressively. "I did some digging on the name you gave me, and it turns out Luis Aquilar is dead."

"One less, more for the rest." He shrugged and handed the waitress too much money. She grinned when he waved off his change.

"Trouble is he died a month before Martin Castillo." I waited, but Trigger didn't react or miss a beat. He just sipped his drink slowly and continued to stare at me. Christ, he was intense. "So, how did he kill Castillo from the grave?"

"I've seen it happen," he muttered, and I wondered what he meant.

"So, you realize he couldn't have killed him? Do

you have any thoughts on what might have happened that day?"

"No." He still held eye contact, and my body started to overheat. This was not a man to go up against. My hand shook slightly when I pulled out a photo and slid it over to him.

"I find that interesting because you guys were there."

Trigger plucked the photo up and squinted at the background where a man stood in a Devil's Reach cut.

"Give me a day. I'll see what I can find out." He downed the rest of his drink, giving me nothing to go on. "And Brick's brother?" I should have known he'd still ask.

"I got word he's living in Washington, but I don't know for sure. Here is the last known address." I handed him a piece of paper.

"Tell me somethin'." He took the paper and put it in the breast pocket of his cut. "Where's the hothead lawyer? Somethin' tells me he wouldn't like you talkin' to me without him."

"I thought we should talk before he got involved." I went with the truth. "We all know Cameron has a temper. I thought it best we met first before he did something we might regret."

He smirked, and I found myself leaning back in my chair for distance. "I'll be in touch." He stood and left without so much as a look over his shoulder. For a man with so many enemies, he sure was confident with his back to an open room.

I slept in Cameron's office that night. A part of me was worried Trigger would have me killed, and being up here with the security guys made me feel better. Plus, Cameron would kill me if he heard about my late-night talk with Trigger without him. It would look better if I was here when he arrived.

The light turned on, and I squinted and adjusted to the beam of light. Cameron looked at me with a twisted expression as he tossed his briefcase on a chair.

"Don't you have your own place?"

"Yes, with a mattress," I stretched and felt my back crack, "but I need to talk to you."

"Talk fast. I have a meeting in five with Jim."

"Cancel it. You're going to want to hear this."

"Fuck." He picked up his phone and made the call to Jim. "So, talk."

"Not here."

We headed downstairs, and I led the way to a small breakfast place I knew about on the Strip. We didn't have much time, and we needed to figure this out. The café overlooked a man-made lake where you could rent little rowboats and pretend that you were in Louisiana or some shit. God, people paid a lot of money to pretend.

"What's this about?" I felt my heart jump when I

thought I spotted Trigger in the distance. Was he following me?

I handed Cameron another copy of the photo since Trigger took the last one and explained what I'd discovered. That Trigger's information on who killed Castillo couldn't have happened. His face got more and more red as I went on.

"That fucking prick lied to my face."

"It seems that way, yes."

"Seems that way?" He didn't like that I wasn't completely on his side, pissed off as he was.

"I only say that because there's a small chance his guy could have lied to him. Gave him bad information."

"You think," Cameron leaned in close, "that Trigger, the president of the DR, a major motorcycle club whose territory spreads through the U.S.—fuck that, all over the world," he paused for a breath, "has people in place who aren't a hundred and twenty-two percent correct before they hand over information?" He raised his hands. "I think not, Simon. You know them. You know what they're capable of."

"All right." I shook my head and knew he had a valid point. As much as Cameron was all temper and aggression, there was a reason he was such a good lawyer. He could spot a criminal's mannerisms a mile away. I had to admit he was probably spot on about Trigger. "So, the question is why did he lie to us?"

I pointed out the window as Trigger came into view. He was on the phone but lowered it when something caught his attention. Grim walked toward him with his two identical dogs slightly in front of him. Neither of them was on a leash. As the dogs reached Trigger, they looked behind them at Grim, then both sat as if on command. It made an impressive sight.

"Maybe the question is who is he lying for." Cameron's tone made the hair on my neck stand up.

FOUR

GRIM

Her scent found its way into my dream, and one minute I was pointing a gun at a Stripe Back and the next he pointed one at Kenna. Everything inside of me hurt when the bullet drove through her chest.

My eyes opened, and I slid a hand under my pillow to check for my handgun. I blinked a few times and brushed the odd feeling aside.

Kenna was on her side facing me, her breaths even and deep. Her face looked stressed even in sleep, and I could only imagine what went through her mind when she rested. The brain was a tricky tool when not exercised correctly.

I studied her nose, her lips, her jawbone, her neck,

and now I kicked myself that I'd given her something to wear. I just couldn't stand seeing her in Dale's old shirt. At least I'd given her a shirt with thin fabric so I could study the outline of her breasts. Kenna Lodge was gorgeous and fed my sexual appetite in just the right way. She was rare. She was dangerous. And she had just what I needed right now. I knew I had to be careful. Her warm hand brushed mine, and I felt myself respond. There was no way to hide how turned on I was that she was in my bed.

I ripped my gaze away and focused on the ceiling to control myself. It wasn't easy, but I wasn't totally insensitive. It was obvious she needed sleep, and I wasn't about to be the one who woke her. Even if everything inside of me begged me to take her. This was new territory for me.

I'd never had a woman spend the night unless sex was involved, and if I woke in the middle of the night, I sent them packing. I didn't like people in my space. I guessed that was where the boys got it.

Zhar sensed I was awake and lifted his head, and his eyes glowed in the red lighting along the base of the wall. A moment later, he let out a low whine, and I strained to hear what he'd tuned in to. I'd locked the elevator and wasn't concerned, as I was on the top floor and there was zero way anyone could break in through the elevator doors. They only opened if you had the right card.

"No!" Kenna shot straight up in bed, and both dogs leapt to their feet. She sucked in a breath.

I gave a command for the boys to stand down. They listened, but both kept their eyes on her. Kenna looked around then slowly turned to see me awake. It was dark, but I could sense her fear.

"Sorry," she whispered as she rubbed her head like it hurt.

"I was awake, anyway." I turned the low lighting up a bit so she could take in her surroundings.

"Maybe it's best if I go."

"No." I yawned uninterested in the idea.

"And if I wanted to?" She raised her chin, and I saw a tiny spark in her eye. I missed that spark.

"I'd chain you to the bed."

"Right." I reached over and pulled a chain from the bedpost and let the cuff dangle from it. "Why does that bring me comfort?" She rubbed her arms uneasily, and I could tell it wasn't from the idea of being bound but from what was weighing on her. She slowly lowered herself to the pillow.

"Reach out and feel the back of the nightstand." I felt her reach over, and when she did, I rolled over and put my hand over hers. "Feel that buckle?"

"Yeah." Her glossy eyes blinked up at me. I could see the nightmare still clinging to her mind.

"Unsnap, pull down, and it's ready to fire." She nodded. I moved her hand up and under the headboard. "That's a Talon knife, sharp as hell. Just pull forward and it will release." She nodded again, and I stared down at her worried expression. "You're safe."

"Okay." She nodded a bunch of times, then I ran my hand down her extended arm, across her collarbone, and up her neck. I brushed her jawbone, and her gaze dropped to my lips. I pushed my interest into her hip.

I leaned down and caught her mouth with mine. It was a slow kiss, just lips at first, then my tongue danced with hers. Her hand moved up my side and into my hair while my hand was under her chin gently holding her in place. It felt different. She tasted just as she smelled, fresh but fruity, and it was fucking with my head. My normal instinct was to ravish, to consume, flood her body with pleasure and take whatever I wanted at the same time. But I felt an unusual need to be careful. Her body still needed time to heal, and her head was in a bad place. I couldn't shake the feeling of being split down the center. I pulled back and studied her. Her confusion on what just happened mirrored my own.

"You should sleep," I said quietly.

"Yeah, I guess we should." She waited for me to roll back, then she pulled the covers up to her chin. When my head hit the pillow, I came nose to nose with Leal.

"Jesus!" I mouthed then glared at him. He stared just as hard back. I swore he cocked a brow at me. I wondered what went through his brain in that moment. "Go." I pointed. He waited for a beat then did what he was told. His typical huff as he plunked back down in his bed was louder than usual.

We lay in silence. I heard Leal growl at Zhar. Leal hated it when Zhar touched his feet. I chewed on the inside of my cheek as I mulled over this odd situation. After a bit, I felt her body relax and her breaths came slowly. She'd fallen asleep. I forced myself to block out what had just happened between us. I didn't like things I couldn't explain, and I sure as hell couldn't explain that. I needed control of my life. Fuck this. I got out of bed.

My phone lit up in my hand, and I read the screen.

Trigger: We need to talk. Meet me at the diner.

Grim: Give me fifteen.

I showered and changed, and as I entered the elevator, I called the boys. We made our way down to the lobby. They were well trained and didn't need a leash when they were with me. They only used them when they were with Jesse or their dog walker, Darcy.

I'm sure we looked intimating to most, a fully tattooed businessman with two knee-high Doberman pinschers. My dogs watched and listened for things I couldn't, and I liked having them with me as much as I could.

I let the dogs take the lead as I walked toward where Trigger said we should meet. His expression might look the same as usual to other people but to me, I knew something bad was up. The boys looked back at me, and I told them to sit.

"How bad is it?"

"Bad enough."

"Hey." Brick's voice came from behind me. He must have followed me out of the hotel. "Trig, I heard you met with Simon? Did he find out anything on...?" Brick rarely spoke about his brother, but we all knew he would move mountains to spend even one day with him.

"Last known address." Trigger handed him a piece of paper. "Call Lu. He'll do a drive-by for you."

"Yeah, okay." He looked at us. "Everything okay?"

"No," Trigger drawled, "but go do your thing."

"Okay." He didn't ask anything else; he just held up the paper and left.

"Let's walk." Trigger pointed with his chin.

We headed out to the Strip toward Secrets. I needed to check on the progress of the kitchen, and the boys needed the walk.

"They know Luis is dead," he drawled.

"That's impossible." I kept my head straight. No

need to give anyone following us a reason to watch. "We covered all our bases on that one."

"They fuckin' know he was dead a month before Castillo went down."

"Shit."

"They got proof the DR were there."

"What kind of proof?"

"A photo, maybe more."

Fuck, this was bad.

"Okay, you guys were there. That doesn't mean you know anything." Trigger gave me a look, and I knew he was right. Trigger knew everything.

"Same city in Mexico as you were in and a rival drug lord of yours. It won't take 'em long to put two and two together. It was either you or me."

We went into Secrets in silence. It was coming together much faster than I'd hoped. Tupot, the owner of the construction company, finally got his act together after our persuasion tactics in the desert. Now his men worked twenty-four-seven.

As we approached the bar, the workmen scattered after one look at Leal and Zhar. Once we were totally alone, he took a seat, and I walked over to the bar and poured us a coffee from a big stainless coffeemaker.

"How's Kenna?" Trigger sipped the drink I handed him.

"Struggling." I shrugged. "She shared with me some of what really happened."

"Oh?"

"Someone's blackmailing her into spying on my family and yours." I gave Trigger a wry look as he absorbed that information.

"Huh." He stroked his chin, deep in thought.

"It explains why she's been avoiding everyone. Even skipped a mandatory meeting."

"Do you trust her?" His question caught me off guard.

"Do you?"

"I don't judge based on havin' a shit father." Trigger still carried his heavy past. "When Minnie brought her around, I was skeptical, so I tested her, and she's loyal as hell to us. Morgan and her are tight. He's a good judge of people."

"Agreed." I thought about how scared she was last night. She even risked the dogs to talk to me.

"You never answered my question."

"I know," I huffed then shook my head and went with the truth. "I do trust her."

"Good." He seemed pleased by that. "The fuck are they blackmailing her with?"

"Minnie knows." I shrugged. "Whatever the fuck it is, she won't share it with anyone else."

"We could take her to my slaughter room." Trigger chuckled, and I joined in.

"Tempting." I rubbed my head. "How bad could it be? Can't be half as bad as the shit we've done."

"My favorite was Tampa two years ago." Trigger smirked.

"It's amazing how quickly someone can swim when they're floating with chum in shark infested water."

"I was referrin' to when we drag raced the owners of that night club on the Formula One track."

"Bodies and asphalt are a delightful combo. Those were some good times." I laughed.

"Fuckin' right. So," Trigger leaned back, and his cut flexed against the chair, "we got two shit situations on our hands. What to do?" I looked pointedly at my mug.

"Switch to whiskey?" We both grinned.

Later that afternoon, after Trigger left and Jesse arrived with some of my security, I got a bit of paper-work out of the way. I liked the quiet of my new office and was glad it was almost finished. While I sifted through some emails, one caught my eye. It was from one of my contacts in Mexico. Jerry Cano was a mafia drug lord in Rosarito. I stayed with him from time to time, posing as his daughter Talya's boyfriend. We had a good thing going, Talya and I. We even had Martin Castillo fooled. Jerry was the one who asked me to do him the favor of killing Castillo. I clicked on the email and scanned it.

Grim,

Since you left without notice, things haven't gone to

plan. I understand and respect why you had to leave, but I need you back to help us continue our original plan. – Jerry.

I cursed and quickly called him. On the second ring, he answered, and I could already feel the tension in his voice.

"I guess you got my email?"

"I did."

"Things are bad, Grim." He paused, and I heard a door click shut on his end. "We weren't able to step into Castillo's position and merge our businesses. Someone was ready for it, and now we're at war for territory. There's a new player."

"Who?"

"I'm not sure yet, but I thought you might be interested in who the middleman is."

"I'm listening."

"That Italian guy."

"Who?" My mind raced with who the hell that could be. The only Italian that came to mind was my friend Elio Capri, but I knew it wouldn't be him.

"You know, Rosa Coppola's right-hand man, Tieri." Rosa Coppola was one of the last remaining heirs to the Rome syndicate, and Tieri was someone who had a lot of information about Elio. He was a threat not easily dismissed.

I blinked a few times while I absorbed the information. Rosa Coppola… The last I heard of her guy Tieri, he was in Canada.

"What proof do you have?" I felt my phone vibrate and pulled it away to see Jerry had texted me. A bunch of photos popped up. I clicked on the first one and saw Tieri having dinner with a man I knew all too well. I swiped through the others. All were of Tieri with family members of those we'd killed when we took out Martin Castillo's empire several months ago.

"Shit."

"So, you can imagine my concern when I recently got these photos, then add in that my business partner up and left for America without so much as a warning. I'm not a happy man."

"You know why I left. I won't explain a second time, Jerry." I tried to curb my temper. I'd been honest with him about my father once I found out he was sick.

"I'm sympathetic as to why you left, Grim. I am. You know me, I appreciate the importance of family. Where my concern lies is in how hard it's been to reach you."

"I have a lot going on here."

"As do I here, and I try not to point out that we still have eight months left on our contract. Your role was important here, Grim. We were building an invisible empire right under his nose. We waited until the time was right, we made our move, then you left. Now things are falling apart, and I need you. No one can see things the way you can."

I rubbed my face. I certainly didn't need this right

now, but I had to admit he was right in everything he said. "I've been knee deep in shit here. Our contract was to move the drugs from you to Vegas. You make top dollar on all our deals. Yes, it benefits us both, but I stepped in and helped you out when you needed it, and also dealt with Castillo as a favor to your family. But let me remind you, I don't work for you. My business is here."

"You left us vulnerable, Grim. I thought you'd see this all the way through until we were on top."

"And I had every intention of doing that, but my family takes precedence over everything. That being said, I know Elio Capri will be very interested to hear Tieri is back. Let me make some calls and see what I can do."

"I'd appreciate that," he huffed.

"Leo will be there soon. He'll fill in for me."

"Right." Sarcasm dripped from his voice, but I chose to ignore his rudeness.

I knew what they'd sacrificed in order to make their plan happen, but it wasn't on me to fix. It was their show, and I'd helped in whatever way I could. I also knew I needed their drugs to keep my clients happy.

"I'll be in touch." I hung up and thumbed over to Elio's name.

The foreman knocked on my door, and I held up a hand for him to hold on. He stepped back, but I could see his shadow under the door. It must be important.

"And to what do I owe the pleasure of hearing from you, Mr. Gates?" Elio's thick accent purred over the phone.

"I'm going to jump right into this, Elio. Are you still in Los Angeles?"

"I am." His voice sharpened as he took in my tone.

"Call your pilot, because Tieri's in Rosarito, and he looks to be planning some kind of retaliation for what we did."

Silence.

"Send me what you have."

"Already have. Keep me in the know. Jerry's losing it over there."

"*Grazie.* I'll look into it." He hung up.

"Jesse, I need to get back to Indulge." I grabbed my things and called for the dogs to follow us to the elevator. The foreman seemed to have disappeared. Once we were on the lobby floor and the doors parted, I was faced with the last fucking person I wanted to see in my new hotel or anywhere else.

"Grim! It's been a minute." Sonny Conti gave me a big fake smile. "I've got someone I'd like you to meet. This is a friend of Cameron's."

Who the fuck allowed them in here?

Jesse moved with me as I stepped out, and I heard the doors close behind us. He tensed with his hand on his gun, and the dogs were ready. I knew any of them just needed my command. It was tempting. I looked at my security team hovering uncertainly near the entrance.

"Sasha Landry." The man held out his hand. "Nice to meet you, Mr. Gates. Cameron was just telling me you're looking for a chef for your new hotel."

I didn't offer him my hand. "You don't look like you cook, Mr. Landry."

"Ha! Me, no, no. My cousin just left his job in Paris and is looking to relocate here in Vegas. Sonny overheard and offered for me to tour your new hotel, take some pictures, and send them to him."

"Did he, now?" I glared at Sonny, who had zero fucking business telling him he could do that. "Well, just now, I have somewhere to be. If you don't mind, we're still under construction." I pointed at the entrance then snapped my fingers, and the dogs moved closer to my legs. I hit the screen to lock the elevator doors. Not that anyone could get off on my office floor, but I felt it made a point. "If you leave your information with my men, I'll be in touch."

"Ah, sure." He stepped back as Sonny pushed by him and made a move to go around the dogs.

"Do say hello to Kenna for me." He laughed, and I whirled around so fast Leal let out a loud snarl. "Easy there, Grim. We're just due for another dinner. She is, after all, my hostess, and I do love that she'll do *anything* for her clients."

"She's not your hostess," I corrected him, "as I'm

sure you remember the conversation my father had with your father, Victor. Ms. Lodge has a number of clients, and although she brought you to us, she can't personally handle every one of them."

"We'll see about that."

Jesse put a hand on the back of my shoulder and spoke quietly. "You're only putting a target on her back. Sonny didn't give a shit about Kenna until you stepped in. The guys'll watch them."

The urge to rip through that asshole's chest and snap his rib bones made my fingers itch. I spun around and walked toward the doors. Jesse was right; he was just baiting me.

Jesse went to speak to the security team, as he knew I was furious and might fire the whole lot of them.

"Sonny told them they had permission to come look. They won't fall for that again."

We drove back to Indulge in silence. I stared out the window and thought about what Trigger had told me, what Kenna shared last night, how I needed to deal with Jerry in Mexico. Sonny hovering around added fuel to the fire.

"You okay, boss?" Jesse pulled me from my thoughts. I nodded slowly, the need to break things building. "Elio's plane just took off. He said he'll touch base once he's in Mexico. He should be here within the hour."

"Good." My mind slipped away.

"*Winner, winner, winner!*" The announcer tossed my hand in the air, and I heaved to catch my breath. My opponent, who'd taken seven and half minutes to bring down, lay in a blood pool on the mat. "*Ladies and gentlemen, the winner of the Lost Lives Tournament iiissss, The Vegas Reaper!*"

I dodged between the ropes and jumped to the floor and caught the towel Ricky tossed at me. He slapped my shoulders in pure joy. "I knew you'd be a champion. You're a born fighter, Grim. There's magic in those fists of yours." We pushed through the doors and almost into the arms of a woman in a bright blue dress.

"Whoa, there, Mr. Gates." She laughed and held up her hands, palms out. "Claire Cost. Congratulations on your big win. If you'd please follow me, we'll get the paperwork out of the way."

I followed her down the hall where she opened a door, stepped through, and waited for me.

"Nice to see you again, Mr. Gates." The Italian, Mr. Capri, sat at a table and waved at a chair. "So, we meet again. I'm not surprised." He chuckled.

I stayed standing. I didn't want to have another conversation about any plans he might have for me to throw a fight. Claire handed me a check, and I took it with a nod. Then I turned and shook my head at the well-dressed Italian.

"I told you once, I won't throw any fight. I respect and appreciate the opportunity you gave me here, but I'm in it to win. It's why I do it." I set the check on the table.

"You don't want the twenty grand?" He studied me.

"I didn't do it for the money."

"So, why do you do it?"

"Let's just say I like to inflect pain without consequences." Mr. Capri looked over my shoulder, and his face morphed into a satisfied smile.

"Well?" A deep voice came from behind me.

"You were right on this one, Trigger." He laughed. I turned to find the now familiar tatted-up biker who had talked to Ricky at the start of the tournament. He'd had front row seats at every fight. "Grim Gates, please meet the owner of the Lost Lives competition, and the president of the Devil's Reach motorcycle club, Trigger."

"Nice to meet you." I reached out for a handshake, but he nodded instead, and I dropped my hand. I turned to Mr. Capri. "What was he right about?"

"We're looking for someone we can trust, someone who can fight but not be bought or swayed in some way. So far, we haven't been disappointed."

"You didn't bite when I offered you information on your competitors." Another guy in a leather cut stepped up. The name Brick was stitched on it. "Even Rail couldn't get 'em." He pointed to a guy who puffed away on a cigarette. "He tried to bribe your trainer."

"He's smarter than that," Ricky chimed in. "I trained him to fight here," he held up his fists, "and here." He tapped his head.

"We've established you're here for the right reasons, so why do I feel like there's more?" I cocked my head at them.

"We're looking for a full-time fighter, a ringer, if you will." Mr. Capri moved around the table and leaned against it. "Someone who will fight once a week against any challengers. It's a way for us to make some money, of course, and to keep the tournament out there in front of people. It sounds like it could be a good fit for you. A way for you to have an outlet for inflicting pain without consequences." He smiled.

"And one that won't land you behind bars either," the president of the Devil's Reach MC drawled.

That piqued my interest, and I took a moment to study the guy. Trigger. Then it hit me. I remembered that name. I'd heard about his days in the ring. He was a ruthless fighter. It was rumored he'd black out when he fought and often didn't even remember the fight.

"Trigger will work with you when you train here, and when you're in Vegas, Ricky can take over."

"So, what do you say?" Brick grinned. "Wanna come play in the Devil's playground?"

"When do we start?" I felt my addiction takeover.

FIVE

Sleep, a long shower, and a good breakfast perked me back up. I pushed down all the nervousness that was rooted deep in my stomach, because what choice did I have?

I hated to admit it, but I was pleased Grim wasn't there when I woke. It gave me the chance to slip out after making the bed. We'd had a moment in the night that played over and over in my sleep, and though it was a nice distraction from the nightmares, it left me feeling strange. Like something had shifted slightly inside me. It was a foreign feeling and one I wasn't sure I wanted to explore.

I was still a bit sore but felt much better, and that was good because people had started to notice my absence. It wasn't like me to take time off, and I didn't want to call any more attention to myself.

"You look better." Minnie appeared next to me and made a show to check my outfit. "Nice to see the girls again. They needed some sunlight." Her gaze went up and down my short, skin-colored dress. "I thought you were naked when I spotted you across the way." She made a sad face. "But I see I was mistaken."

"God, we'd make an excellent couple, wouldn't we?" I smiled and threaded an arm through hers. I turned her so we could see our reflection in the glass. Then she turned so we could both admire her ass in her leather pants.

"Your tits and my ability to bend like a pretzel at almost forty would make us unstoppable."

A blur of color and a sudden waft of weed came to us.

"It's like every man's fantasy." Rail puffed out a cloud of smoke as he draped an arm around our shoulders. "Min, your man's lookin' for ya."

"Duty calls." She winked at me. "I want to talk later."

"You know where I'll be."

"Fuck, all these gorgeous women." Rail grinned. "I'm always sportin' a hard-on."

"How are you?" I swatted his shoulder as he patted his crotch.

"Nope, that's my line." He shoved his hand in his

pocket and pulled out a fat joint. "Tess wanted you to have this. It's her favorite. Called Dragon Butter."

"Thanks," I slipped it into my cleavage before anyone saw it, "and to answer your question, I'm fine. Rattled, a little sore, but better."

"Grim told Trigger," he whispered loudly. I reached out and pressed my fingers against his lips to stop his words.

"Rail, you can't say that stuff. Whoever it is, they have people everywhere. They seem to know what I'm doing—hell, where we all are." I forced myself not to look around.

"Fine, but that means now we all know," he lowered his voice and held up a hand to stop my mini freakout, "which means Trigger wants to meet up tonight and make a plan and flush this fucker out."

It wouldn't work, but I didn't have time to argue. I had to meet Mr. Harris to make up for not being there when he signed the contracts.

"When and where?"

"Ten." He looked up at the roof.

"Here?" My eyes bugged out. "He's like big brother. No, it can't be here."

"It's actually perfect. A big meeting on the roof will make him call you and ask what it's about, then you'll apply the plan."

"The plan? All I can say is it better be a damn good plan."

"Remember Allen and the airplane hangar story?" He took a moment to remind me of a huge takedown Trigger had orchestrated years back.

"Fine." I nodded but felt that nervousness threaten again. I knew the roof was rented out for a birthday party of twenty or so people, so it wouldn't be overly crowed. I also knew we would blend in, given that it had been booked by a nephew of one of the Harley Davidson club members. "I have to go. We can talk later." I kissed his cheek and hurried off.

The rest of morning went by fast, and just as I was saying my goodbyes to Mr. Harris, I felt someone come up and slide a hand around my waist.

"Kenna, you look gorgeous as ever," Sonny cooed, and my face instantly heated. When the hell had he arrived?

"Mr. Conti," I eyed Mr. Harris, who didn't look impressed, "I didn't know you were back in town." I slid out of his hold and almost tripped but righted myself and flashed him what I hoped was a mega-watt smile. I was totally blindsided by his sudden appearance and knew Mr. Harris could see my discomfort.

"Yes, I'm back. I was trying to get Sasha a tour of Secrets. As usual, Grim made things difficult. You know what a good friend he is of your father's. I'm gonna have to tell him Grim refused to cooperate."

He looked over at Mr. Harris, who just stood there watching. He looked at me with worry on his face.

"Well, Kenna, I'll see you a bit later, then." He stumbled, and I felt badly for him. It was obvious he wasn't sure how to handle my discomfort. "Thanks for this morning."

"Anytime, and I'll see you soon."

Please don't leave.

"So," Sonny stepped forward and blocked my view of Mr. Harris, "I need you to bring us over to Secrets."

"Wait," I just caught what he was saying, "how do you know Sasha Landry?" Hanna's warning that Sasha was dangerous made my heart race.

"Your father introduced us the last time I was here. He's a great guy."

My phone buzzed, and I welcomed the distraction.

Grim: Walk away from Sonny.

I looked around but couldn't spot Grim.

Kenna: I'm trying.

Grim: Try harder.

"Um," I thought about a way out, "I'm sorry, Sonny, but I have so much on my plate right now."

"Oh, please, I just so happen to know that your week is lighter than usual."

"And how would you know that?"

"Your father."

"I see." I ran my tongue along my teeth to curb my anger. My father hadn't checked in with me since he was told I'd been late for the contract signing. My guess was he had no idea what had happened to me. I could live with that, but I didn't need to hear his "what did you do?" speech.

"Kenna," he stepped toward me, and I felt my phone alert me again, "I'm trying not to get a complex here, but I signed on with the understanding that I'd get you as my hostess, but then I was told you don't have room for me on your roster." He reached out and took my hand, and it was everything I could do not to lash out at him. "Now I come here and ask for some help, and you can't even spare me an hour?"

I felt my fight return in a rush.

"Mr. Conti."

"Sonny," he corrected me. "Please, Kenna, we're closer than that." His other hand brushed down my arm.

"That's exactly my concern." I slipped into a mocking tone as I ripped my hand away. "You say we're close, yet you slipped a drug in my drink." He held my gaze, and I saw no emotion flicker there. That concerned me more than if he'd lied. "You tried to get me up to your room that night. To do what, Sonny?"

"First, it was just a party drug. It's Vegas, Kenna." Obviously, he didn't see how fucked up that was. "Second, you seem like a girl who enjoys a good time."

"Well, you'll never know, now, will you? After that stunt, you won't ever see that side of me."

His hand hit his chest like he was in pain. "Kenna, your words hurt."

My phone buzzed again.

Grim: Walk the hell away.

Grim: Read my texts, Kenna!

I looked up at the camera and knew he was watching me from there.

Kenna: I can handle it.

"Hey," Sonny covered my phone with his hand, "why don't we start over, fresh?"

"Sure. Why don't you walk over to the entrance and wait for me there?" I turned on my heel, only to hear him chuckle. I got three steps before Sasha stepped in my way.

"Can I steal two minutes of your time?"

"It's not a good time." I went to move, but he caught my arm.

"Your father said you could help me, and I'm running out of time."

"Despite," I looked down at his hold, "what my father thinks, he's not in charge of my time."

A hand suddenly reached forward and fastened

itself around Sasha's wrist. Sasha grunted in pain, and I broke free.

"Wrist, nose, and three ribs, that's what I can break before your next blink," Grim snarled, and I stepped away from them.

"Mr. Gates, I was just hoping—"

"Like I explained earlier, my hotel isn't ready to be toured yet. Miss Lodge has a job to do, and you and your friend," he tossed a look at Sonny, "are keeping her from it."

Sasha looked down at me with unreadable eyes then nodded a few times, and that alone sent a chill down my spine.

"Understood, Mr. Gates." Grim let him go. "Sorry for the inconvenience. Let's go, Sonny." Sonny didn't say anything else, which surprised me. They both walked away as we watched. "I'll see you tonight, Kenna," Sasha called over his shoulder.

"What the fuck does that mean?" Grim turned his temper on me.

"It means I get to relive my teens all over again." I rolled my eyes. Apparently, Dad's entourage was back. "He's invited Sasha to a family dinner." I watched as the two men went into a bar. "How'd you know he was here, anyway?"

"We've been watching Sonny since he bombarded me at my hotel and made a comment about you. I didn't trust he wouldn't go looking for you. Seems I was right."

"Well, thanks, but I had it under control."

"Clearly." He snickered.

"Meaning?"

"I told you to walk away, and you didn't listen. If you had, this wouldn't have happened, and I wouldn't have had to come down here."

The hell?

"I'm confused, Grim. At what point did I ask for your help?"

"Excuse me." He stepped closer.

"You're coming down on me because I didn't jump when you said so, but I was perfectly fine handling things myself."

"Was that before or after Sasha had his hands on you?"

Oh, shit, he was pushing my buttons today.

"His hands have been in a lot more places than on my wrist." The words sprung unwanted from my mouth, and I wanted to bite off my tongue.

His face went to stone and his chest rose as he dragged in a deep breath. If we weren't in the middle of the lobby at Indulge, I bet he'd have me thrown in a trunk and dumped me somewhere.

"For the sake of your safety, Kenna, I'm going to walk away, but hear me when I say this. You will not be attending that dinner tonight."

He did not just threaten me. Oh! I felt my inner Minnie rise to the surface, and I licked my lips, ready for the kill.

"Small problem with that, Mr. Gates." I pressed my toes into the floor to gain some height, leaned in, and pressed my hands flat against his vibrating chest. I let my perfume invade his nostrils for a moment and slowly licked my lips as I peeked at him from under my lashes. "I know exactly what you're capable of."

His eyes flashed something wicked as I stepped away, aware of where we were and who might be around. It had been a daring move on my part. It felt good to know he had no option to display his feelings here in the middle of his father's hotel lobby. I turned and marched away before he could gather himself. The one good thing about Grim pushing my buttons was that the feeling of being scared in my own skin was replaced with hot flames. It fueled my fire and made me think I could handle everything, at least for a while.

As much as I wanted to skip out on dinner, I couldn't. I'd received a short text early that morning that left me with a haunted feeling. Did he have eyes *everywhere*?

Unknown: Be at the dinner tonight.

The text wasn't the only reason I'd be at that dinner. I sure as hell wasn't about to let Grim tell me what I was or wasn't allowed to do. He might feel he could tell me what to do at work, but I had to set some ground rules when it came to my personal life.

"More wine, miss?" The waiter held the bottle, and at my nod, he poured it. I used the tip of my finger to tilt the bottom to add more to my glass. He chuckled and left the bottle behind.

My nerves were incredibly shot, and the dinner didn't help. Mom announced she was about to leave on another job, and I wasn't sure how I would be able to navigate my family without her.

"Thank you." I smiled, but it dropped when I realized Calli had focused on me.

"So, is it true?"

"Is what true?" I knew better than to play into her games, but I'd been silent through most of the dinner, so I figured I'd entertain her for a moment.

"The rumor."

"Calli, maybe not here." Simon threw a pointed look at our guest, Sasha. Of course, that caught Dad's attention.

"It's fine." She dismissed him. "Is it true you got jumped in the parking lot?"

"I'm sure that's just gossip." Dad attempted to wave her off, but Mom caught it and threw a worried expression at me. Dad's face went tight, and he glared at Calli as the table went quiet.

"I heard it from the staff." She shrugged at my parents and picked up a glass.

"I did have an altercation the other evening, but it was taken care of." I glanced at my father.

"Are you okay, sweetheart?" Mom put a hand to her chest.

"Don't overreact." Dad patted her hand. "Look at her. She's fine."

"Kenna?" She raised her tone, ignoring dad.

"Yes, Mom, thank you. I'm fine." She eyed me then nodded, but I knew she'd bring it up again when we were alone. At least she cared enough to.

"I'm glad to hear that." Simon nodded politely, bringing a glare from my sister.

"It wasn't a client of mine, was it?" Dad peered over at me as he cut into his steak.

"No, Dad."

"Good, because if it was and you didn't tell me about it, I wouldn't know to do damage control with that client."

"Right." I shook my head and tossed back some more wine. Simon changed the topic, and when the conversation picked up, he gave me a quick glance and I mouthed a thank you.

Sasha, who had made it a point to sit next to me, leaned over. "Are you really all right?"

"Oh, you care?" I laughed and thought how ridiculous he was. I'd been young and naive when we dated years ago, but seriously. He'd never cared then. That seemed to be a job I'd done solo. Whyever would he care now? There was a time when my heart had been invested in Sasha; he'd been my first love. I was older and wiser now with a lot of experience in how people worked.

"I do, actually." He cleared his throat. "I just find it interesting that the very busy owner of the hotel with much more important things to do just happens to come up on us while we we're having a conversation."

"You mean when you had your hand on me?" I tried to redirect his comment.

"You didn't seem to mind when we were up on the cliff watching the sunset," he purred. I felt a wave of nausea come over me.

"It's really sad that you're referring to something that happened in my teens. It's way past time to move on."

"Or maybe we could go somewhere and talk?" Suddenly, Hanna's warning about him crept into my head. She said I needed to be careful of him.

My phone vibrated in my purse, and I tapped the screen to see who it was.

Unknown: Lean in and tell Sasha you'll get him a tour of Secrets tomorrow.

My skin went cold. The thought of constantly being watched by God knew who creeped me out. On cue, I scanned the restaurant and wondered where he could be. I could be looking right at him and not know it. I decided to make a mental note of who was around me at all times so I could do a process of elimination. Simon turned his phone over to read something but didn't text; he just flipped it back over and took a sip of his water. I pushed that thought off, Simon was like a lap dog, sweet and kind. He seemed to only want to please those around him, almost to a fault.

"Look, Sasha," I sighed, "if you want a tour of Secrets, I can arrange it."

"You'd do that for me?"

"I would."

"Why?" He studied my face as he asked.

"Because."

"Because?" He leaned in, and I held up a hand.

"Because it's my job, actually."

"Well, I won't question that because I really want to see the place." He seemed to think for a bit. "Thank you, Kenna. I really appreciate it because something tells me your boss wouldn't agree."

I took a deep swallow of wine. "Just know that this," I waved between us, "will never be anything but friends. You had your chance." I couldn't resist the dig, but as normal, he let it roll off his back.

"We'll see about that." He gave me a cocky smile, and I shook my head, thinking how juvenile he was.

"Don't look now, but that boss I just mentioned, he's at the bar." Sasha slid an arm around the back of my chair as he said it.

"He's here for me." I ignored his arm and excused myself from the table. I tossed my napkin on my chair and went to meet Grim before he decided to come to our table. Grim pushed off from the bar top he leaned against as I drew close.

"I see you went to dinner?" He cocked a brow.

"I did," we both began to walk toward the elevators, "but I need to tell you something."

"It'll have to wait." I could tell he didn't want to take the call. "What's up, Dad?"

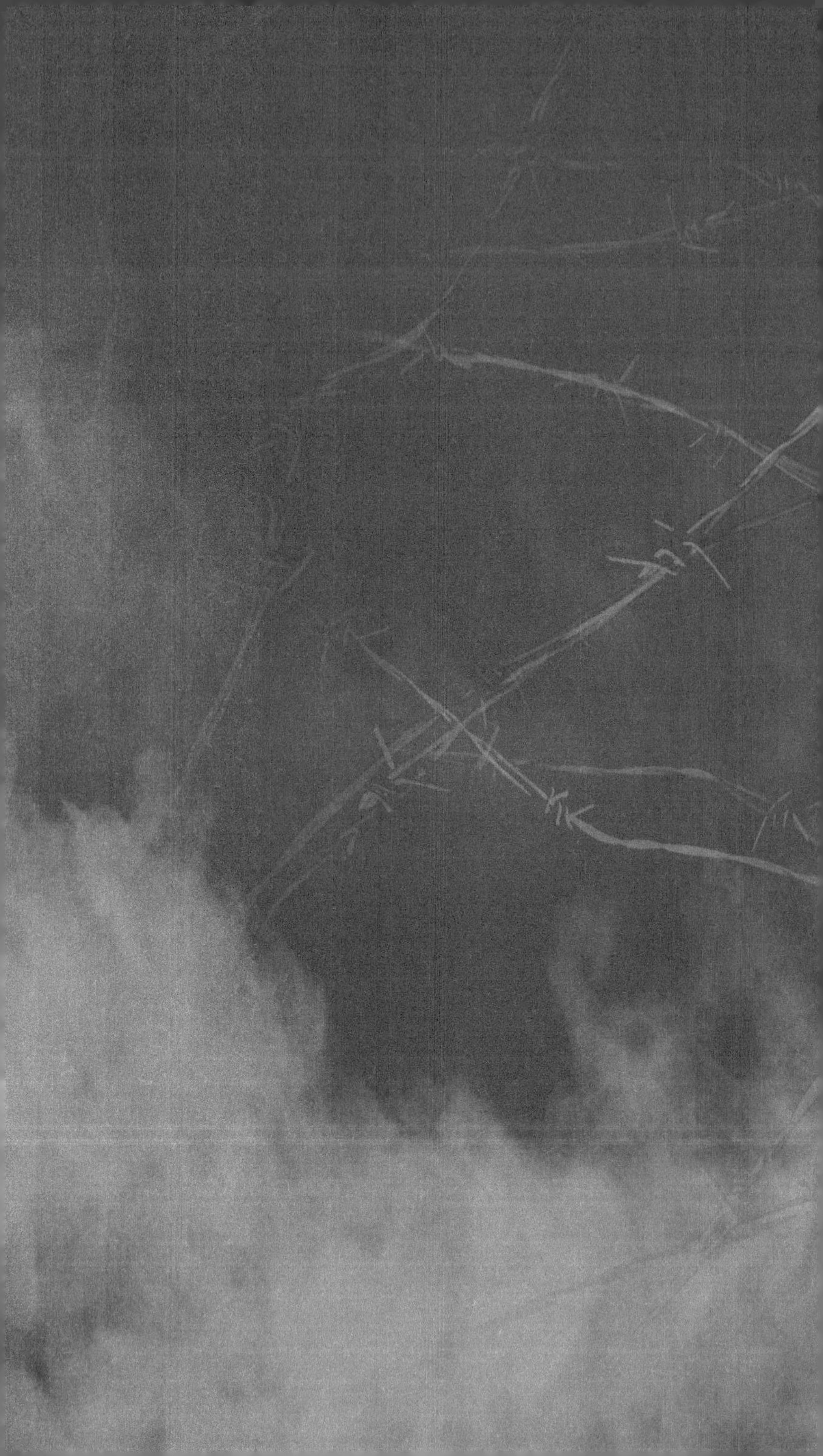

SIX

SIMON

I brushed the steam away from the mirror and stared into it as I scratched my beard. I really missed a clean-shaven face. Squeezing the beard cream into my hand, I rubbed it through the short hairs and hoped the moisturizer would help the itch.

> Calli: Will I see you later?

I quickly washed my hands then removed a contact.

> Calli: Knox is just about to leave. Let
> me shower, then I'll be ready for you.

I stared at my eyes, now one brown and one blue, and shook my head. I should be disgusted by what she implied, but I knew Calli had an expiration date with Knox, and it was soon. Then we'd see where we were.

> Calli: I'll wear the little pink nightie
> you love so much.

She was fishing for a response, but I found myself thinking about Kenna. Of course, the Gateses would keep her attack quiet. It would be swept under the rug. The reputation of the hotel came first, above all else. Kenna would know that better than anyone and would totally agree in spite of the danger she was in.

I swiped the screen on my phone and studied the photo I'd secretly taken of Kenna at dinner. She certainly was gorgeous. She was a very strong woman and could handle herself; that was incredibly sexy in itself. She certainly caught the attention of men, even the waiter had drooled over her at dinner, but somehow, I didn't think she took it in, or if she did, she ignored it. I wondered if Grim saw what I did, and that was why he hovered around her. He was her boss, but I wondered if there was some sort of fatal attraction there.

I popped out the other contact and leaned back to apply some moisturizing eyedrops to clear the sting. Vegas in the summer was dry and dusty, so I changed my contacts every twelve hours or so.

My phone buzzed and I huffed, as I knew Calli would hate it if I didn't respond immediately.

"Hello, dear."

"Hello, darling," my buddy Kurt purred into the phone than let out a rough cough. "Meet me at the Mac." He hung up.

I repeated his words, confused why Kurt was here. He didn't often show his face, so I knew something was up. I dressed quickly and headed toward Mac. Suddenly, I remembered Calli's text.

> Simon: I just need to meet up with a client first but keep that nightie warm.

I checked in at reception and was given the key that waited for me. The carpet was being updated, and the horrible swirly pattern many of the older Vegas hotels had were being ripped out and hopefully burned.

I inserted the key and stepped inside the darkened room.

"We have a problem," he grunted from behind his surveillance equipment. "Matt Myers is dead."

Oh, shit.

"What?" I looked at him like he was crazy, and then the panic started to heat the back of my neck. "What? How? Wait, when?" My head spun. "Does anyone know?" I lowered my voice, unsure if anyone could hear me. This was bad for a few different reasons. Matt Myers was a close friend of Sonny's. They were in business together, and their families were close. When Sonny discovered Matt was dead, he'd probably lose it.

I wasn't sure we were ready for that kind of wrath with all that was going on.

"Just me, you, and the off-roader who found him in the desert." He looked into the telescope and continued to watch the rooftop across the way. "No idea what killed him. His body was too mangled, what with the vultures feeding off his flesh."

Ew.

"And you're sure it was him?"

"Yeah, looks as though he'd been out there a while. The vultures did a good job of destroying the evidence. I'm sure they weren't the only animals that had a taste of him either. He had the tattoo, and there was just enough to trace it back to Matt."

"Shit." I sank into the chair and thought about what that would mean for our case. "Cameron's going to lose it."

"No kidding, and wait until Sonny hears the news. He'll tear the city apart until he finds who's responsible for Matt's death." He turned and faced me with tight lips, and I knew there was more. "Just to add insult to injury, Morey Ines is getting cold feet again."

"How do you know?"

"I've had my guys on him, and he mentioned to a colleague that he felt he'd gotten himself in a bad situation and wasn't sure if he could go through with it. Apparently, one of his clients knew of the Devil's

Reach and warned him of the repercussions of going up against them."

"Fuck," I pinched the bridge of my nose, "this is bad."

"I know," he glanced at me, "so you better get his testimony fast or you're up Shit Creek."

I sat in silence while I let everything absorb. Normally, I could pivot and come up with a solution to things fairly quickly, but in that moment all I could envision was Vegas dripping in blood, with chaos and destruction at every turn.

"Now there's one sexy woman." Kurt whistled, now back behind his telescope. "How you haven't hit that at least once is some self-control, my friend." He handed me a pair of binoculars so I could look. I sat in front of the window and focused the lens on Kenna. "Did she mention anything at dinner about her attack?"

"No, but she wouldn't say much with Cameron there." I shook my head and felt bad for her.

"I'm sure in her line of work, she's bound to piss someone off."

"Not Kenna." I lowered the binoculars. "She's not like that."

"You sound kinda sweet on her." He gave me a pointed look.

"No, I generally just care about her well-being." I cleared my throat. "I did call in a favor to Johnny.

Hopefully, he can find me something from that night. You know he's amazing at tracking phones, even if they are burners."

"I see," he grunted. I knew he didn't like it when I worked outside the two of us. "Well, I'm sure if there was something to find, he'll find it."

"Let's hope." I gave a tight nod and focused back on the task at hand.

"Here, I got ears too." He handed me an extra set of headphones. "There's a lot of noise, but he's working on it."

I spotted him and watched as *he* moved closer to Minnie.

"Careful," I said into the mic. "Where Minnie is..." I stopped talking as Brick came up and wrapped an arm around her shoulders. "They're very protective," I reminded our ears and eyes at the party.

"What Harley Davidson drinks a damn mojito? At least in public?" I muttered to Kurt as I took in the drink our informant sipped on. "Jesus, at least lose the straw."

I focused my binoculars on Kenna, who had changed into a tight leather dress with ties holding the garment together on the sides so you could see her skin. She definitely was off the clock as she made her way toward the bar. Grim didn't hide the fact that he watched her. If Kenna was trying to blend in at a biker party, she did anything but. I was sure there wasn't anyone there who hadn't noticed her.

"You think Grim and Kenna—"

"They're like oil and water." I cut him off, but the more and more I watched them interact, I was starting to second guess myself.

"You sure about that?"

"Kenna wouldn't risk her career for someone like Grim Gates. She's smarter than that."

"Right." He smirked. "Oh, look who's arrived." He turned up the volume as Trigger walked over to Grim and they seemed to look toward us.

"Anything?" Grim asked.

"We have another problem," Trigger grunted.

"Oh?" Trigger handed him his phone, and his face fell as he looked at it.

I was amazed at how clearly I could see what was going on. The sound wasn't the best, but I could make out what they said.

"What's on that phone?" Kurt yelled into his mic. "Get me eyes on that phone!"

"And risk my throat getting slashed?" the informant immediately snickered back. "No, thanks!" Grim handed the phone back to Trigger. I knew we were out of luck.

"I knew this was going to be bad," we could hear Grim say. I stared through the binoculars at him. His posture was that of a powerful, majorly pissed off man.

"This," he pointed to the phone, "is about to change everything."

"Fuck," Kurt hit the table, "we only have so many opportunities!"

"There'll be more," I assured him. "We've got all night."

"For fuck's sake," Kurt yelled into the radio, "lose the damn drink, Olly!"

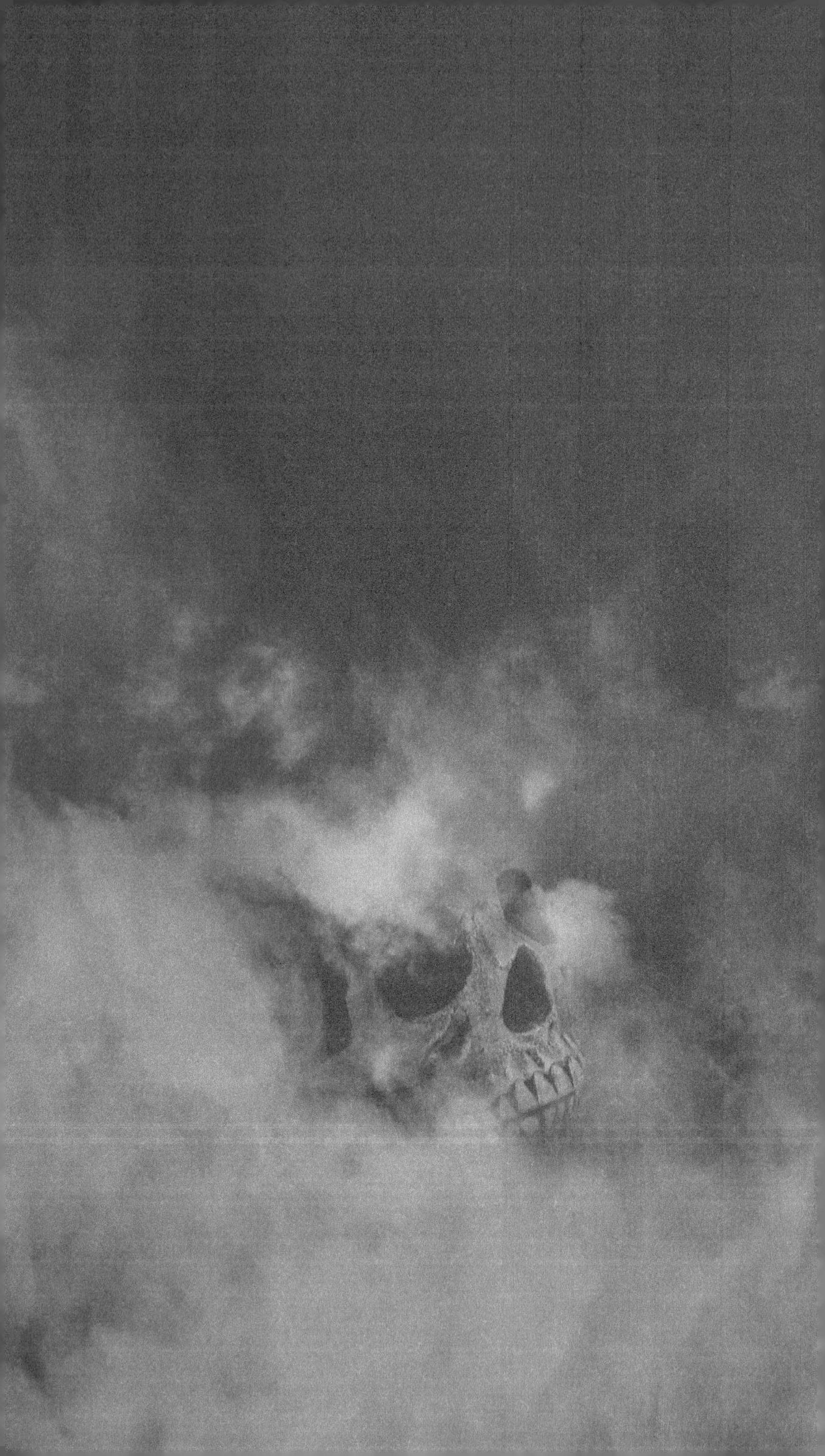

SEVEN

GRIM

"Here ya go, Uncle Trig," Denton handed him a glass of whiskey. "This place is insane, Grim." The young man's face showed his excitement. I knew for the first half of his life he'd been raised by his father, Trigger's Uncle Gus, and his junkie mother. After Gus's death, Trigger and Tess had done their best to parent him and his younger brother. Denton was being groomed to run Devil's Reach someday. I knew he'd make a good president down the road, but now all the kid was interested in was women.

"Mm," I halfheartedly answered as I continued to scan the rooftop party for anyone who shouldn't be there.

"Did I interrupt something?"

"No, just looking." I turned my eyes on him. When he shifted, I noticed he wore his gun on his hip. I glanced at Trigger, who shook his head and hitched a shoulder like it had been an ongoing battle.

"Why are you wearing your gun like a fucking fanny pack?" I gave him shit. "Are you waiting for the bureau to issue you a holster?"

"No, I just like wearin' it there." He pulled his cut to the side and studied it. "The ladies seem to like it."

"What ladies?" Trigger joined in and Denton made a face. "I ain't seen any fuckin' ladies hanging off you at the club."

The kid stuck out his chin. "I can get ladies."

"That, I'd like to see." I laughed into my glass. My mind wandered a bit as I looked around again. I still had a hard time digesting that Matt Myers was dead. I hated the guy, but I'd tolerated him. With Sonny's attention on Kenna and me, I couldn't be sure where he'd spew his anger once he heard, if he hadn't already.

"Let's get this plan moving, Grim." Trigger brushed past me and waved for the others to gather on the far back couches.

I headed to the bar where Kenna was. The dress she wore burned all kinds of dark fantasies into my brain, and a guy I didn't recognize was too close to her. I cleared my throat and eyed the mojito in his hand as I forced my way between them.

"Hey, man," the guy complained, "I was just going to buy the lady a drink."

"No," I tossed over my shoulder.

"Thank you, but I'm fine getting my own." Kenna tried to smooth the situation over. I waved at the bartender, and he knew to put hers on my tab.

"Here you are, Kenna." The bartender leaned over. "On your tab, Mr. Gates."

Kenna's angry expression found mine. "You love swinging that big dick around, don't you?" She pushed off the bar, and I licked along my teeth. Christ, she had a set of balls.

We made our way over to the others and sat on the couch next to Minnie and Brick. Kenna leaned over and gave Denton a hug. He smirked at me as he rubbed her back.

"It's great to see ya again, Kenna." The kid practically salivated as he nestled against her.

"You too." I noticed her dress rode up her thighs, and I forced myself to look away.

"Let's get this started." I nodded at Trigger, whose smirk morphed into a serious face.

Trigger kept it short and to the point. We all had a role to play, and because they seemed to be after information on both my family and Trigger's, it needed to be flawless.

"Kenna," Trigger swung his gaze over to her, and I

felt her shift, "I'm going to ask you this one time. What is this person blackmailing you with?"

"What? No," I watched the pulse in her neck quicken, "I can't do that." She looked at me for help, and I studied her panic without reacting. "What if he's here?" She lowered her voice as I remained emotionless. "Look, just give me a few days. Let me get hold of Hanna and figure out something." She stopped talking when she realized what she'd said.

"Wanna expand on that?" Trigger glared at her.

"Wait, I mean…" Her gaze went from me to Trigger and back again with wide eyes. I was curious to know what that was about as well. Trigger was right. She held back secrets, and the only way we could move forward with everything was if she told us the whole truth.

"Let's not do this here." I gave Trigger a quick glance, and Kenna looked at me in silent thanks. Both Trigger and I had left Kenna out of this part of the plan.

"Fine." Trigger nodded, pleased Kenna knew she had to share what she was holding. It had gone on long enough. "If any of you hear anything, come to me."

Everyone agreed, and the tension eased slightly as we ordered more drinks and continued to play our parts of the plan.

"Mom's in the lobby." Denton looked up from his phone. Trigger nodded, and I saw Rail smirk like something hit him.

"Is it weird that when you were younger you used to hit on your mom?"

"It was only weird when you hit on her," he shot back, and we all broke into laughter. "I don't have any problems with the ladies, right, Kenna?" Denton winked, and Kenna shrugged.

"You're cute even if you do wear your gun like a *murse*." Kenna laughed.

"Thank you," Minnie called. "I keep telling the kid to tuck it away."

"The ladies like a piece." He stood. "I just stand like this," everyone laughed as he drew his arm back to reveal the weapon, "and the lady's eyes are drawn there, then they move here," he pointed to crotch, "and the rest is history."

"You might catch *girls* that way," Kenna shook her head, "but you won't catch a woman." She leaned forward seductively and plucked her drink off the table. "See, Denton, a woman is what you really want."

"Fuckin' right it is," Trigger pulled Tess onto his lap and kissed her. Kenna pointed at them and nodded at Denton.

"All right, all right, you're a woman, Kenna." Denton lifted his ball cap and threaded his hands through his shoulder length hair before he returned his cap backward. "You're somewhat closer to my age than these old folks. Teach me your ways."

"This should be good." Rail kicked his feet up on

the table, and I draped my arm along the back of the couch and got comfortable. This was a side of Kenna I hadn't seen, and it intrigued me. I wondered how many parties I'd missed with her in the group.

Kenna flipped her hair out of her face, and I caught a whiff of her shampoo. It went right to my groin, and when she leaned forward and I got a view of her breasts, I had an instant flashback of my face buried between them. I had to rein myself in before everyone saw how much she affected me.

"Girls are young," she started, "and inexperienced. You could blow through twenty of them and never get the rush you're looking for."

"I'm not looking to get married." He grimaced and pretended to put a gun to his head.

"Neither am I," she laughed, "but a woman comes with experience, maturity, craft."

"I just want sex." He made the others laugh, showing his age.

"Well, there's sex, and then there's," she paused, and air quoted, "sex."

"You have my attention now." He sat forward.

Mine, too.

"All right, stand up." She tugged him to a spot where they could face one another. "Show me how you approach a girl."

"You don't have to ask me twice." He grabbed her by the waist and jerked her toward him. "I've got a bike with a big engine." He wiggled his hips. "Wanna see how powerful it is?"

"Fuck," Tess groaned and put her head in her hands. Kenna peeled herself out of Denton's hold.

"Can you tell he's been raised by bikers?" Minnie rolled her eyes. "Kid, have we taught you nothing?"

"Well, Rail said it works," he shot back.

"He's still single!" all three girls yelled.

"Why keep all this," Rail waved his hand down his body, "for just one person when there's so much Rail to nail?"

"I see your point." Denton nodded at Kenna. "Continue." I laughed at Rail as he pretended to be hurt.

"It's all about your approach. Let's pretend we're at the bar." Kenna pushed her hair off her bare shoulder and grinned at us. She seemed to be getting into it. "You study the liquor on the back wall, wait a beat for her to notice you standing there, you order, then turn to look at her."

"Okay."

"You could offer to buy her a drink, or if she's already got one say you'll get the next round. By doing that, you're ensuring a chance to talk with her again."

"Oh, that's a good one," Minnie whispered.

"Then," her movements were slow and fluid, "you turn your body to face her dead on. You've got a good frame," she touched his shoulders, "so use it. Not to intimidate, just to show confidence and maybe a little dominance." I chuckled to show how true that was, and she glanced over at me and arched a sexy brow. "If," her attention moved back to Denton, "she smiles, there's an eighty percent chance she's what you want, but if she gives you a sexy smirk, well, you might just have a keeper."

"Okay, now what?"

"Now," she stepped closer to him, "you hold her gaze." Denton followed what she said. "If her gaze drops to your lips, she's interested. Do it back and see her reaction. For me, I lick my bottom lip, imagining what you'll taste like. Some bite." She mimicked the action. "Maybe she'll part for you, but if there's some kind of tell, then you move in for the touch."

"Go for the ass?" Denton was like a boy with his first porn magazine.

"No, not the ass. That's way too soon." She took his hand and directed it. "Brush your fingers over my heart like this." She moved his hand, and his eyes widened. "Skim the collarbone, and slide up the neck, until you're under her chin." Denton nodded when she moved in even closer. My body coiled as I watched. "Use the tip of your thumb to tilt her chin up and stare into her eyes. Savor the moment, go slow. Watch for cues." Her lips hovered beneath his, and I gripped the side of the couch. "Then just when she thinks you aren't going to make a move, dive down and catch her lips."

He made a move to kiss her, but Trigger reached out a big hand and quickly hauled him back.

"Don't play with fire," Trigger grunted. Everyone shouted and booed, and I took the moment to force myself to relax. I sank back into the cushions and readjusted.

"Kenna, I might need some more lessons." Denton's face was flushed. "What are ya doin' tonight?"

"Not you." She laughed and winked. She sat down next to me, and Minnie pulled her attention.

"Hey, boss?" Jesse approached me. He'd been watching from the opposite roof. He leaned down to speak in my ear. "We've got a situation." I followed his gaze and saw Jenelle had just appeared. I didn't think to add her to the list to keep out. In what world did she ever associate with bikers? "Say the word, and I'll have her removed, Grim."

"Her father just brought in a big fucking client this morning," I hissed impatiently. "We need to play this nice."

"I'll leave." Kenna stood. I hadn't realized she'd heard. She reached for her purse, but I snagged her arm.

"No." I pulled her down to sit next to me.

"I'm maxed out on tolerance, Grim. It's for the best if I go." My hand clamped down on her leg, and I glared at her.

"What did I say?"

"Heads up, twat approaching," Minnie hissed. "I knew I smelled seafood." Kenna gave a huff.

Jenelle whispered something to her friend, and they both looked over at us. Jenelle gave us a wicked grin. Daddy's girls with money were a deadly combo. They both wore designer dresses, and it made them stand out against the leather, jeans, and boots crowd.

She immediately homed in on my hand on Kenna's thigh. "You know, Kenna, I'm trying to remember a time when you weren't hanging off Grim." She gave a fake smile.

"And I'm trying to remember when you weren't such a passive aggressive narcissist." Kenna didn't miss a beat.

"Jenelle," I warned, "what do you want?"

"Not that I ever imagined myself as a delivery girl, but I was handed this and asked to come up here to give it to you. I was just curious enough to do it." She held up a piece of folded paper. I held out my hand, but she smirked and held it just out of reach. She was delighted to know she had something she thought I wanted. I dropped my hand and looked disinterested.

"Who gave it to you?" Minnie asked, and Jenelle looked around at the group of us.

"Some woman." She shrugged. "Grim, can we speak?"

"I'm in the middle of something." I stayed in my relaxed position and waved at everyone around me.

"You know where to find me." She dropped the paper on my lap and walked away.

I opened the paper to read the words *hands off*. I had no doubt Jenelle would have looked at what was on the paper. That alone would have enticed her up here.

"Shit." Kenna's voice pulled my focus, and she tilted her phone so I could see the screen. Her eyes darted everywhere. It was a picture of us sitting together on the rooftop.

"He's here," she whispered, then her gaze dropped to the open paper in my hand. "Oh, my God."

"We knew he was watching," I reminded her. "It's why we're here, remember?"

"It's one thing for us to be seen together. It's quite another to look like we're together." She pulled her leg away and quickly stood. "I need another." She pointed to her drink, but I could see she was about to run. She whisked off toward the exit. I waited a beat then followed.

"Hey," I caught her arm as she entered the hall, "our plan worked. We got his attention."

"The wrong kind!" She pushed her hands through her hair.

"No one will dictate what I do and who I do it with—"

"Grim," she whirled around and sucked in a deep breath, "when he attacked me that night, he said...he said maybe I should fuck you and let's see how much that will hurt the Gates family. On top of everything else, he seems jealous of something that's not even there." She waved between us.

"Or the coward's just proving he's watching," I countered.

"Either way, he makes me want to slither right out of my skin." She quivered and ran her hands up and down her arms. "Oh," she looked as if she remembered something, "I was told," she eyed her phone, "to take Sasha on a tour of Secrets tomorrow."

"No." No fucking way that was happening.

"I don't really have a choice, do I?"

"Fuck." I hated that I had to bend for this guy, but it was only a matter of time. "What time?"

"Eight."

"Jesse will join you."

"Okay. Thanks." She looked drained. "I should go."

"Go to my penthouse. I'll meet you there."

"What?" Her face dropped. "Are you crazy?"

I smiled at her words; I was a little crazy. "At times, yes."

"I'm not laughing, Grim." She pushed her hair back with both hands, clearly stressed, so I backed off. A little.

"No one can get in without one of these, remember." I held up my keycard. "You'll be safest there."

"What if he has one?"

"He doesn't."

"I have one." She looked away, and I decided not to get into that. "Look, Grim, I appreciate the offer, but let's not forget your two moody pups. You know they hate company, especially when you're not there."

"I'll take you up."

"No," she shook her head and stepped back, "not together. Just call me when you're heading up to your place, and I'll meet you there."

"Fine." I looked over my shoulder. The bikers were getting noisier as the party went on. "Keep your phone close."

I spent the next hour watching every face that came in and out. To anyone else, I seemed engaged in conversation, but my mind was elsewhere. I had to know who the hell this fucker was, and I itched to break every bone in his body for thinking he could use one of my people to spy on me.

Minnie and Tess got up and grabbed their things. They said the real fun started the next day for them, and they'd need some sleep. Most of the guys left with them, including Denton.

Since everyone had decided to turn in, I made my way to the bar. I tipped the bartender well, as I knew what the rest of the night would look like for him. The place was definitely amping up as I left. I tapped my phone and sent a message off to Kenna.

Grim: Headed up.

I pressed my keycard to the box, and Jesse joined me with two other security guards.

> Kenna: Already in bed. I'll meet Jesse
> in the lobby tomorrow.

Anger flashed through me, but as I was about to jab my finger at her floor number, Jesse cursed.

"What?"

"Shit, boss, we've got a fucking problem."

EIGHT

"This is the main bar." I pointed out various things in the massive room so Sasha could envision what it would look like. "Mr. Gates just signed DJ Clay, who'll be on stage there." I tried to sound upbeat, but I hated the way Sonny kept watching me.

Jesse kept a close eye on me. I was glad Grim sent him. He was in a meeting, but I knew he would be here in a flash if Jesse so much as texted. Two security guys walked the perimeter of the newly built walls of the hotel and watched for anything out of place. I noticed Jesse was extra edgy and made motions for the guards to keep their eyes peeled. I wondered if it was just my situation or if something else was going on.

"I love the fabric he chose for the dining room chairs." I ran my fingers over the dark velvet swirls embedded into the deep red fabric. "It's rich but carries a hint of darkness, don't you think?" I let my mouth go to try to hide my nerves.

"Kind of like your dress." Sonny gave me a smile that was more like a leer and moved next to me. "I have to wonder what kind of secrets you have underneath this." He pressed his hand into my lower back. I shrugged out of his reach and made a show of describing the custom taps that Grim had brought in from Italy.

"And this," I went on, "is one of the kitchens." I moved through the doors so Sasha could admire what I was sure would be one of the busiest kitchens on the strip. I saw Jesse take a call, and he pulled back.

Sasha nodded. "Impressive." He'd been rather quiet during the tour but seemed interested in the kitchen. He moved to get a better look at the walk-in fridge. "What will this be?" He popped his head out and pointed at something inside.

"Let's see." I stepped inside, and he suddenly pushed me back against the wall, one hand slapped over my mouth, as he pressed an arm hard against my chest.

"Where's Hanna?" he hissed at me, and I shook my head in confusion. He pushed harder on my chest, and I struggled to think straight. "I know she knows something. What does she know? What did she see?" I fought to breathe against his hold. Finally, he let my mouth go, and I sucked in a deep breath. "Don't lie to me, Kenna. She's your friend. I know she called you!" His arm eased a little.

"She did, but we got interrupted by Leo. She never told me anything."

"Call her." Saliva pooled in the corner of his mouth. His behavior shook me; I couldn't believe I'd once been intimate with this man. I thought I at least knew who he was as a person. I couldn't get my head around the fact that I felt threatened by him. He couldn't possibly be as scary as my mind was now playing him up to be. I straightened my back and raised my chin as I felt my fight kick in. It was either that, or I was just a little insane in that moment.

"No." I stared him straight in the eye.

"Kenna," he blinked a few times, "call her, now."

Was that desperation I saw in his eyes? "What is it that you think she knows, Sasha?"

"This goes way deeper than you think. Shit's getting real." He shoved me back into the wall, and suddenly Jesse stepped through the door with his gun drawn. Sasha ignored his gun and ran past him. Jesse grabbed my arm and pulled me with him out the door. The security guards stood in the kitchen; both had their guns on Sasha.

"Did he hurt you?" Jesse quickly gave me a onceover.

"I swear to God, Kenna, if you so much as—" Sasha sputtered as Jesse cracked his face with the butt of his gun. Sasha's hands flew to his face as he yelped in pain.

"Get 'im out of here." Jesse shoved Sasha to get him moving then turned back to look at me. "Kenna, what the hell happened?"

"I don't know. One second, he was asking me a question, and the next he just snapped. Something's got him majorly worried. He caught me off guard. I guess the tour's over." I looked at Jesse. "Where'd Sonny go?"

"Said he had to leave." Jesse walked with me toward the door. "Convenient timing." He gave me a look. "Sorry I left you alone. Grim called."

"Not your fault, Jesse." It wasn't; it was mine. I should have been smarter. "Everything okay with Grim?"

"Just business as usual." I could see the lie written on his face, but I didn't push.

"He was pissed you didn't join him last night."

"When's Grim not pissed off?"

"It's the perks of his job." He went to his defense, and I had to admire that. Jesse and Grim were obviously close.

We walked to the car, and I let my shoulders relax when he shut the door. It felt safe there.

"Can I ask you something?" I asked once we hit the main road.

"Sure." He sent a quick text then looked up at me.

"When did you start working for Grim?"

"Um," his squinted as he thought, "it's going on nine years now."

"How'd you meet?"

"Long story short, I was working security for a high-powered client. I saw they were into some pretty shady shit. They made a bad deal, and when they went to pull a fast one, I turned the tables and went to bat for the other guy."

"Grim?" He smiled, and his eyes widened and seemed to glow. Jesse and Grim only smiled like that when shit got crazy. I figured their dark sides had connected that day.

"I was hired on the spot." He laughed.

I chuckled. "I'm sorry I missed that. Sounds like it would've been a good show."

"It was." He looked out the window and thought for second. "Can I ask you something?"

"Only seems fair."

"You seem incredibly resilient, given all that's happened to you. But I have to know, are you really okay?" My smile faded, and I knew the truth showed on my face. I had just exposed how scared I really was.

"Sometimes I am." My voice was barely a whisper.

"That's fair." He nodded then went back to his phone. When we arrived at the hotel, I looked around.

"Jesse? Where'd they take Sasha?"

"They just kicked him off the premises. I'll fill Grim in now."

So, he's still out there. Great.

<hr>

"I don't know, Min." I pulled out my suitcase and slammed the trunk. Morgan grabbed it before it hit the ground. "I'm a shit magnet these days. You sure I should come?"

"You hang out with a biker gang." She slipped her arm through mine. "We're always in shit. And why are you questioning me? You know I'm always right." She laughed and sounded so carefree I envied her. "Besides, Morgan could use the company on the drive, and Tess has been dying to hang out with you."

"I miss her, too." I couldn't help but smile as she tugged me along.

"After the last few weeks, you need a break," she grinned, "and not the kind where you fly out to see your mom in some dusty museum. I love the woman, but you need to let loose, live a little. You need a few drinks so you can relax and open up that lunch box of yours. You know, offer up a snack to someone."

"Yeah," I snorted, "booze and sex does sound like the perfect recipe."

"Great. That's settled, then." She steered me to Morgan's van. It looked to be loaded with everything from suitcases, to ammo, to high-end liquor. It wasn't the first time I'd been invited to Trigger's annual party in the desert. It was held about an hour and a half outside Vegas in some remote place. Every member of Devil's Reach and their friends were invited from all over. They brought their women and, in some cases, even their kids.

"I can't believe you've never come to one of these." Minnie shook her head at me.

I shrugged. "I guess I was just too focused on work." I'd been so focused on getting clients for the hotel that I'd forgotten how to live. I realized I needed to change that, especially now that I was waist deep and up Shit Creek.

"Now," she stepped back to take in my outfit, "though you don't have a man to keep in check, you'll be up against a trailer park full of hoes. So," she pulled out a little black bag, and I smirked at the logo, "I brought you a little welcome to the fun gift." I peeked inside.

"Oh, Minnie, you shouldn't have." Morgan grabbed the bag from me and looked inside.

"What the fuck is this?" He pulled out the small scrap of fabric. "That won't even cover one tit, Kenna."

"That's the point," Minnie huffed at him and tossed it back in the bag when Trigger gave a whistle for us to get a move on. "Change when we get there." She blew me a kiss and hopped on the back of Brick's bike.

"I got room over here, Kenna!" Rail called as a blonde in high black boots and a short leather skirt climbed awkwardly on behind him. "Still room right here." He patted the front of his seat, and I laughed and got in the front of the van with Morgan.

He went quiet, and we listened to music for the first thirty minutes until whatever bothered him got the better of him. He stabbed the volume button and cut the music off. I waited. He sucked on a joint then handed it to me.

"Smooth." I let the smoke out and enjoyed the hit that rushed through my body. "Strong, too."

"It's called Better Days." He stroked his beard and let out a huff.

"Okay, what's eating your ass?"

"I'm worried about ya. You're holding on to some shit. You got jumped in a parking lot, and again at Grim's hotel." *Two times at Secrets,* but I didn't correct him. "I don't know, maybe you should take up that offer that Hong guy offered you."

"How did you know about the offer?"

"I hear stuff. As much as it would kill me to see you go, I don't like seein' you get hurt."

"I love that you care about me, Morgan," I

squeezed his hand on the steering wheel, "but I'm not gonna let someone like Sasha Landry or Sonny Conti drive me out of my job. Jerks are everywhere and aren't you forgetting about the biggest jerk I deal with every single day?" I sighed as the drugs took hold. "My father's made my life hell since I was fifteen. I've hung on this long. I can deal with these guys, too."

"You act tough, sweetheart, but you don't know who's really pulling your strings. Sasha and Sonny are assholes, but they're probably low on the food chain. I don't want anything happenin' to you."

"I'll live. I always do." I looked over at him. "Can this be a free pass weekend? No drama." I paused. "Well, other than the sheer entertainment Rail brings to every party. I just need some time with the spotlight off me."

"Yeah," he smirked, "just for this weekend."

"Good." I reached back, opened the cooler, and pulled out two chilled energy drinks. I opened one and gave it to him then sat back and looked out the window. We were on a side road, driving straight toward some smoke in the distance.

"Party's already started." Morgan chin-pointed at the smoke.

"Can I ask you something?"

"Shoot."

"When did Grim join the DR? And why haven't I run into him with you guys before?"

"Mmm," he nodded like he was remembering it, "Grim met Trigger and Elio after Trigger took over the Lost Lives tournament in LA. It's an underground fighting competition. The best of the best go there to compete. Grim made a name for himself there. He could finish a guy off in under five seconds. They nicknamed him the Vegas Reaper."

"Damn." I could only imagine how fitting that name was.

"Elio tested him to see if he'd take a fall. Grim's got integrity, wouldn't cheat. Trigger started mentoring him, and three years later he asked Grim to join the club. He and Trig and Elio are good friends, and now it's more a partnership."

"What do you mean?"

"The three of them have slowly been takin' over Vegas." He paused as if to choose his words carefully. "They're a force to be reckoned with, to say the least." He grinned proudly. "So, the fact that shit is happening means something pretty fucking huge is coming or is already here. Either way, it's gonna be ugly." I nodded. That was a road I didn't want to even think about.

"I've worked with Jim for a while now. If they're all so close, I still can't figure out why I never heard his son was in the DR."

"We kept his membership low-key while he was away in Mexico. He got pulled into some shit down there. He had to disassociate with us as he got deeper in with some drug lord."

"Castillo?"

"Yeah." He studied me for a moment, probably shocked I knew the name. "He even did some dealings with the Stripe Backs, but he always made sure Trigger knew exactly what was goin' on."

"He's loyal."

"Very." He nodded. "He always kept that he was part of our club quiet. We don't exactly fit the mold for his business. Not that it's ever stopped Grim from making sure we feel comfortable at the hotel. There's always been two sides to Grim, the high-powered busi-nessman who makes million-dollar deals over break-fast, and the man who would snap your neck if you so much as looked at him the wrong way. He's my favorite." He chuckled darkly then shrugged. "Min-nie's been good at keeping you out of shit that's associ-ated with us, but you coming to this party will suck you in deeper. You sure you're ready for that?"

"I think I'm more afraid of the shit I'm bringing to you," I answered honestly.

"In that case," he nodded toward the windshield, "welcome to the party, Kenna."

Holy shit…

Nestled up against a mountain that horseshoed around a massive area was one huge-ass party. Trailers, tents, trucks, and bikes were littered everywhere. At least two hundred people partied like it was spring break. Fire pits burned beside tables, barbecues glowed, even blown-up pools and misting machines could be seen. I couldn't begin to fathom organizing a party like this out in the middle of the desert.

Minnie banged on the door before we even came to a full stop then nearly hauled my arm off as she pulled me from the van. Morgan parked by a line of trailers that looked like they came straight out of a showroom.

"Let's get you changed before anyone sees you in jeans." I laughed as she pushed me through the door and shoved the bag into my hand. "Strip." I didn't waste any time and slipped into the tiny black dress. It was a skimpy bra on the top and an extremely short skirt for the bottoms. "Eight years ago, Tess convinced Trigger to clear the area of rocks and whatnot because we were killing ourselves in our heels."

"Heels!" She held up a couple pairs of matching heels, and I thought she was nuts. Though I lived in heels, this was the desert, after all.

"Remember, we need to dress to keep the guys' eyes on us. There's a lot of tits and ass out there."

"Min, Brick loves you and only has eyes for you. Why go through all of this when you're practically married?"

"How do you think I've kept his eyes from wandering?" She started to change, but I caught a glimpse of tears. Minnie was a strong woman, but Brick was her kryptonite. Maybe she needed more from this weekend than I realized.

"Remind me again why I'm dressing up?" I turned and glanced over my shoulder at the back of my outfit. "Not that I'm complaining, because I look fucking good in this."

"Yes, you do." She chuckled and pulled her cream dress up over her hips. It crisscrossed in the front and dipped low in the back. Minnie didn't have much for boobs, but she had a killer ass.

"You look good yourself, girl!" I waved a finger over her outfit, and she wiggled for me.

"Okay, Kenna, you need to stand out and give that snatch of yours a chance to clear the cobwebs."

"Well, if you insist." We grabbed a bottle of champagne each and headed out to meet with the others. Tess looked amazing in her booty shorts and tube top, though she'd look good in a brown paper bag. As soon as she spotted us, she headed over.

"And why is this not popped?" She took the bottle from Minnie and pressed her thumbs into the cork, and it popped loudly and sent a spray into the air. We laughed together as we held out our glasses.

By the time the sun set, we all had a good buzz on, and the music was loud but not to the point where we couldn't hear each other. We sat around the fire pit near the trailers with the guys and laughed until we hurt at Rail's antics. He'd had way too much to drink and couldn't do up his pants after taking a leak.

"Brick, Brick, Brick," Rail thrust his crotch in his face, "you need to finish what ya started." A girl who had been trying to get Brick's attention moved over to Rail to help him out.

"Wingman." Minnie winked at me but kept her eye on Brick. She frowned, and I felt it too. He seemed distant from everyone. "Speaking of wingman." She put her hand to her mouth. "Hey, Dillon, come here."

"Yes, yes," Tess hooted, "Dillon would be a good match." Tess grinned at Minnie then at me. "He's from the Texas chapter, and he's the VP. Got no little sperms walkin' around, and he's clean." She pointed to her crotch.

"Hey, Min." He approached. He wore a bandana around his neck and a cowboy hat dipped low on his head. "How's your night going?"

"Fabulous." Minnie pointed at me, and we all stood. "This here's my girl Kenna. She works in Vegas."

"Vegas." His dark eyes moved to mine, and he grinned a boyish grin. "I guess they don't lie when they say Vegas has the prettiest gals."

"Nice to meet you."

"The pleasure's all mine, beautiful." He kissed the back of my hand. "Maybe you and I could talk more and get to know one another."

"Sure." I inwardly sighed, though I played along. I could already see he was way too tame for me. I caught Minnie press her lips together and make an *oh, shit, we may have made a mistake* face at Tess.

"Let me check with some people and I'll hurry right back." He tipped his hat to me, and once he was out of earshot, I looked at the girls and threw up my hands.

"Seriously?" I folded my arms. "Have you and Rail switched your book club nights to Nicholas Sparks?"

"Hey!" Rail peeled the girl off his lips. "You will not speak ill of Nicholas. He's a very talented man."

"You read?" the girl cooed at him.

"I do," Rail gave her a drunken grin, "a lot. But it's got to have angst."

Trigger shook his head at us, and Brick closed his eyes and cursed.

"Anyway," I chuckled, "thanks, but I think I got this. Let me see what I can find myself." I moved around the firepit and went for a little walk. I scoped out the men. A few caught my eye, but as soon as they did, their woman caught wind and they moved in and did something slutty. I knew better and backed off. They'd staked their claim first. It was the rules, after all. I walked around a bit more, but I remembered Trigger's warning not to stray too far. Though this was a DR party, that didn't mean all were members. Tess had warned me as well, and I'd heard stories about her first time there. I wasn't about to tempt fate.

"You're new." A guy's voice made me spin around. "Name's Tristen. I'm a good friend of Trigger's." He wasn't bad looking and had a nice smile. "And Tess's, if that helps my chances to talk to you."

"It does," I smiled. "I'm Kenna." I read his patch. "And you're from North Carolina."

"Mmhmm." His smile made me a little uneasy and I wasn't sure why. "So, *Kenna*," he tested out my name, "where are you from?"

"Originally from Los Angeles, but I work in Vegas."

"Which means Minnie must have invited you?"

"That's right."

"First time here?"

"What gave me away?"

"Well, now," he stroked his face, "pretty little woman like you out here walkin' all alone." He looked around. "I figure you aren't here with a boyfriend unless he's a fool. I know I wouldn't let you out of my sight."

"Oh, yeah?" *Okay, he shows signs of an alpha. I could work with that.*

"Yeah." He stepped closer, and I felt a twinge of hope down below. "Why don't we get you a drink and maybe we could —"

Something heavy pushed against my leg, and my mouth dropped open.

"Leal?" Grim's dog looked up at me then at Tristen and started to growl. "What the hell?"

"And," Tristan put his hands in the air and stepped back, "that's my cue to exit."

"What? Why?"

"Because I know better." He cursed then turned and walked away. I folded my arms as my anger rose. Great. My own personal cock blocker.

"Where is he, Leal?" I huffed. The pup seemed to know exactly what I asked. He looked up at me, then trotted over to a group near a firepit. I followed him and saw Grim. He sat in a chair with a very attractive woman on his lap. His gaze fell on Leal as the dog took his place at his feet. His brother looked directly at me and whined.

"Was that fun for you?" I called over the chatter of the group. Grim's face fell as he looked at my expression. He acted like he wasn't expecting me. The woman instantly wrapped an arm around Grim's neck, staking her claim.

"What the fuck are you doing here?" He shifted the girl over onto the chair next to him. "Give me a minute, Kelly." She made sure she kept one hand on him as he leaned forward as calmly as could be. I wanted to tear a strip off him. The fucking nerve of this man.

"Oh, please," I rolled my eyes, "keep your dog on a leash." Leal huffed, and Grim looked down at him.

"Jesse?" Grim called, and Jesse appeared.

"I had no idea."

"Grim." The Kelly woman leaned into him again as

she pulled his hand onto her thigh. "Why don't we go somewhere, and I'll help you relax?" Her effort to pull his attention off me was pathetic. My temper flared. Little did she know, I could give a rat's ass what they did.

"Go get a drink," he ordered her.

"I still have mine," she argued, but he shot her a look that made her stand.

"No," I flicked my hand at her, "please, sweetheart, he's all yours. Just make sure his dogs stay put." With that, I left and hoped to hell he'd leave me alone for the rest of the weekend.

NINE

GRIM

"The last I heard, she was staying in with Dale. They were gonna cook together or something." Jesse shrugged. "My guess, Minnie caught wind of this morning and convinced her to come."

I hissed through my teeth, beyond pissed I hadn't had a heads up she was here. My mind slipped back to that morning and what Jesse told me happened. I'd deal with Sasha, but Sonny was my real concern. Where there was shit going down, Sonny was close by.

"Want me to keep an eye on her?"

I looked around at all the people I knew. I sure as hell wasn't about to chase after trouble. I gave him a quick nod. "Anything happens, come tell me. Hopefully, she'll manage to go one day without getting herself in trouble."

"Understood." He turned to leave but stopped himself. "Grim, when have you ever known Leal to go off like that? He's usually glued to your leg unless you give him the okay." I looked down at Leal, who seemed completely unfazed by what happened.

"It was odd, I know. I never even saw him go." I shrugged it off and pulled the chick back on my lap when she returned. I needed something to tame my erection.

"Ooooh, someone's ready for some fun." Kelly returned and started to grind on my lap, and I let myself go. determined to enjoy myself.

"Hey." Brick sat down next to me and kicked his feet up. I eyed him and silently let out a long breath through my teeth. He seemed to have the weight of the world on his shoulders. He pursed his lips as he studied the chick on me.

"I need another minute."

"Seriously?"

"Or maybe you should take a walk." I warned her not to push me.

"Whatever." She slid over to the other chair next to her chatty friend, and I gave him my full attention. I caught her pout, but she was smart enough not to say anything more. She kept a protective hand on my knee, but I ignored her.

"Vinni's here."

"Really?" That was news to me. Vinni was Elio's cousin, and I hadn't seen him in a long time.

"He pulled Trigger aside. I'm waiting to hear what's goin' on."

"I am, too." I went quiet as I thought for a moment, and the girl's hand began to slide up my leg. I caught it and pressed it back to my knee. She got the point. I was interested in what Brick had to say.

"How much do you know about Simon?" He studied me.

"Simon Gable?"

"Yeah." I could tell it was a loaded question.

"Not too much, just that Cameron hired him a while back. He's quiet and doesn't get in my way, so that's a plus."

"It is." I could tell Brick needed more, so I searched my memory.

"Dad said he's a bit of loner but is one of the best private investigators in town. He's good at finding shit."

"Good." He rubbed his face.

"Why do you say that?" We never bullshitted each other with small talk; it was always straight to the point.

"Apparently, he did a job with my brother about a decade ago."

"Really?" I knew Brick had a brother who'd disappeared. I figured the guy was probably dead and buried somewhere a long time ago. Happened all the time out in the desert. He'd been looking for him since before I even knew him. I heard from Morgan that he'd only ever had one lead, and it pointed to Mexico. Apparently, it was a dead end. "Does Simon know where he is?"

"He's got someone working on it for me." He looked over. "Do you trust him?"

"I don't trust many people," I shrugged, "but aside from the fact that he works with Cameron, he hasn't given me a reason not to."

"Yeah."

"This fucking with your head?"

"Mm." He sipped his beer. "I finally got Jilly into rehab again, not that it'll fix anything," he rolled his eyes as he talked about his sister, "but at least I know where she is. Thing is, it's given me more time to think." He paused, and a painful expression took over. "I never knew my old man, Mom was a fuckin' waste of time, and Jilly's been basically dead for most of my life. I guess I want to know…" He trailed off.

"I get it," I murmured.

Brick barely talked about his personal life, so the fact he'd shared even that much meant his brother preyed heavy on his mind. "Don't know," he started mid-thought, "I just need this loop," he pointed to his head, "to stop spinnin'. It's fucking up my life." I knew he meant Minnie. She'd hinted enough times that she was concerned about Brick.

"You and your brother have two different moms, right?

"Yeah, my mom was the other woman." He made a disgusted face. "She got knocked up with me when my brother turned seven. Guess she showed up at one of his birthday parties with me in her arms and Jilly in her stomach. Let my brother's mom's family know what Dad was up to when he was away at the club. It got ugly. Jilly was only six when Mom died. That was a fucking nightmare in itself."

"I bet." I knew his past was rough. "At least you got Tess." It was Brick who brought Tess to work at the club's bar years back. They'd been good friends, and she needed a place to go. It was how Trigger met her.

"Tess was the best thing that ever happened to me, next to Min, of course." He gave a half chuckle. "Thing is, it feels like I'm chasing someone who doesn't want to be found, ya know?" And there lay the root of Brick's pain. If his brother was alive, why hadn't he ever come looking for him?

"Would you know him if you saw him? It's been a long time."

"I think I would."

"So, let Simon dig. What's the harm? You won't lose if he comes up empty. If he does find him, you win. If he tries to screw you, snap his neck. It's a win-win, if you ask me."

"You sound like Rail." He chuckled and seemed to let go of the topic and relax. "Have you seen—" Suddenly, Leal stood and gave a low growl and looked off into the crowd.

He turned and looked at me, I gave a tight nod, and he raced off. Leal had been taught to sense when danger was around. It was one of the reasons I often left both of them in my suite. Leal in particular had issues with some of the people I dealt with at the hotel. I told Zhar to stay with me while his brother went off to check out the source of whatever bugged him.

"Second thought, I'll be back." I told Brick and ignored Kelly's protest for me to stay. I whisked off in the direction Leal had gone with Zhar on my heels. I slowed as I lost which way to go, and Zhar took over the hunt and ran ahead.

"What the fuck!" a guy yelled, and I picked up speed.

"No, don't." I heard Kenna's voice. "Stop! They won't hurt you." I ran behind a trailer and saw Kenna holding her hand out palm up to some guy who had a gun aimed at my dogs.

I saw red.

I didn't break stride and drilled my fist into the side of his head. It bounced off a propane tank, and he went down. I whirled around and took in the sight. Kenna's bra strap hung down, and her hair was messy.

"Back," I warned the dogs, who were agitated and ready for a fight.

"Un-fucking-believable." She tossed her hands in the air.

Was she nuts? Back here with some random guy? The stories the girls must have shared with her about these parties should've been enough to scare her off.

"First, they want to rip my throat out, now they want to protect me? From what?" She ran her hands through her hair as she eyed the dogs. "So, what? Now I can't even have sex!" she yelled and looked furious enough to rip my eyes out.

I wanted to laugh, but my head spun to the point of pain, so I reached out and shoved her against the side of the trailer. She shoved me back, and I grabbed her hands and pressed my body into hers.

"Did you let him kiss your neck?" I breathed her in and felt my mind slowly untangle my murderous thoughts. "Did he scrape his teeth down your skin?" I latched on to her neck and swirled my tongue around before I sucked and scraped the way that I knew she loved.

"No," she confessed in a moment of weakness. *Good.* "Where's Kelly?" She tried to use her body to thrust me off again, but I took one of her hands and pressed it to my painful erection. Immediately, she wrapped her hand roughly around me the best she could through my jeans and squeezed hard. It was just what I needed, and I unleashed my dark side. All I could think about was getting a taste of her.

I grabbed her by the hips and lifted her on the storage trailer. She kicked off her thong and thrust herself toward me, and I pulled her close, so her knees hit my shoulders, then spread them wide.

I could feel the heat from her as I leaned forward and licked the seam of her arousal. The moment her taste hit my tongue and traveled to my brain, I turned into an animal that had just gotten the first taste of a kill. Everything in me turned hard before I dove deeper inside her, wanting it all.

"Holy shit!" she cried. Her fingers raked through my hair. My brain turned off as I lost control and fed on her. She bucked and wiggled and screamed as I held her. There was no escape for either of us. The more she screamed, the more I wanted. She wrapped her legs around my head, and the spikes of her heels clawed at my back. The sound of the strained leather only fed my addiction.

"Grim, I can't take it!" she screamed, and I turned savage. "Yes! More!" she screamed again as she ground her sex into my mouth. This chick chased after her own death with me.

Things started to push through my mind, Leal leaving my side without permission earlier, Kenna being back here with some asshole, Sasha's hands on her.

Stop! I pushed the intrusion away and drove all my focus back on her. But I was losing it.

I placed both hands on the top of her ass and lifted her off the trailer and sucked hard on her bud, making her fall apart in mid-air. I took every last thing I could from her then pushed her higher and savored the moment. I let her weight fall back against the side of the trailer and put my hands around her throat, then I tore them away and ripped my mouth off her with a frustrated growl. I whirled around and placed her down on the trailer bed.

I needed space. I felt caged and wild. I wanted more but knew it wouldn't happen now. Her taste lingered on me, and I closed my eyes to control myself. I heaved in a breath and clenched my fists to try to gain some control.

She was lain out flat, her chest heaving as her fingertips dragged up and down her thighs like she still rode out her orgasm.

"Fuck." My stomach coiled and my erection beat painfully to my heartbeat. I'd done that before, many times, but this was the first time I had a hard time stopping. I almost feared for her life.

"Anyone see Grim?" A voice that sounded like Vinni's traveled across the trailers.

"We should go." I eyed her.

"I'm good right here." She rolled her head to see me, and her eyes looked relaxed and content. I envied her that look.

"I'm not leaving you alone." I reached up and pulled her down to the ground. She pressed her hands against my arms to stabilize herself.

"My panties?" She held out her hand like it was back to business as usual. I ran my gaze down her gorgeous body and snagged her thong. I gave her a look and tucked it in my pocket.

"Fine." She brushed by but couldn't hide the fact she had shaky legs. We walked to where the others were gathered around the firepit. Vinni was there in conversation with Brick.

"Vinni, what brings you to the party tonight?"

"I wanted to thank you. Well, Elio does, too, but he wanted to personally ensure Tieri got back to Italy."

"Understood." I knew that feeling. There were some things you just needed to do yourself. I eyed Kenna. She had made her way over to Rail, who laughed at something Trigger said.

"Which brings me to this." Vinni turned to address the group. "Once Elio gets what he needs from Tieri and Rosa, we're going to hold a party to celebrate an end to a very long chapter. It will be in Italy, so I hope you can come." He looked at Trigger as he said it, and Trig held up his beer with a nod.

"Fuck, yeah," Rail called, and the rest of the group shouted their excitement. We all knew the story of what happened back in Italy with the Capri family, and this celebration was overdue.

"Count me in." I nodded politely. "Wouldn't miss it for the world."

"Happy to hear it." He raised the phone in his hand to eye the screen, and I caught the incoming caller. "Excuse me." He stepped away. "Hey, Wyatt." I caught his happy expression. I spotted an empty chair next to Kenna and sat in it.

"By the way," Minnie held up a half bottle of champagne and grinned over at me, "Kenna's here."

"Thanks a lot, Min." I glared at her. I reached down and patted Zhar who had bumped my hand for attention. Leal was still on edge but listened when I told him to sit. I scratched his ear, and he leaned into me. I knew they both wished they'd been able to draw blood back there. I felt their pain; we all needed a good de-stressor.

"Any word on the son-of-a-bitch who keeps callin' 'er?" Trigger looked over at Kenna, who laughed with Rail again, then his eyes were back on me.

"She hasn't mentioned it."

"She's nearly naked." Tess chuckled as she leaned

over Trigger's lap. "Where would she put a phone? Besides, she told me she needed a night. Can't we give her that?"

"Yeah." Trigger sipped his drink, and she smirked at him like there was some inside joke going on.

"Oh, fuck, Min," she hissed across the group, "this should be good." I turned to see what they referred to.

"Trigger," I lifted my whiskey glass to my lips, "please tell me he's not DR."

"I didn't patch him in." There were only a handful of times I'd seen Trigger truly smile, and this was one of them. I kicked my leg up to rest my ankle on my knee and stroked Zhar's head as I watched.

"Oh, come on," Kenna muttered as she turned her body toward me. "You're dead, Tess," she hissed.

"I'm sorry." She giggled. "That's Dillon. We introduced him to Kenna earlier." Tess filled me in. "Grim, help her out." I looked down at Leal, who yawned.

"Don't you have something to do?" I said to the pup, but he only offered me a disinterested huff. "I get it." I chuckled. I did notice he hadn't taken his eyes off Kenna, though. *Interesting.*

"Keep moving, man." I waved Dillon off as he looked at Kenna. He pulled in his chin and looked a bit confused but knew better than to approach.

"Kenna," Minnie took her attention, "I wanted to ask you about Yen Hong and that new clothing line he's thinking of bringing to the US." I sat back and tuned out their conversation.

It didn't take long for a few more guys to spot Kenna and start to migrate over like the cockroaches they were. It was the rules of the party. If you didn't have a chick on your lap or a man to give them a death stare when they looked at you, you were fair game. And Kenna's scent was in the air, blowing in their direction.

"Ah, shit," Tess grunted. "Oz is here. He's got a habit of being hands on, and most of the hang-around chicks at the club steer clear." She turned to Trigger. "Babe, maybe you should put the word out she's taken."

"We got eyes on 'im." Trigger attempted to ease her nerves. Leal got to his feet.

Good boy.

I'd never claimed a girl while I was at this party. I wanted the freedom to do whoever I wanted when the urge took me. An alien thought came to me that I did feel some sort of protective vibe when it came to Kenna. I tried to shake it off. Most likely, it was just that the worst of the worst of the DR and their friends were sniffing around her. She wasn't like one of the women who often came to these things. She was different. Or maybe it was just where I'd had my mouth a few minutes back.

I tapped the armrest of the chair as I thought of all

the ways I could kill the lookie-loos. They'd scattered when Oz appeared, but I knew they weren't far.

"Hey, boss," Jesse said quietly. I leaned a little toward him. "I hear Sonny's been asking where Kenna is."

"I see." I cleared my throat and wished I also could get a night off from all the shit going on.

"Leo told him that she was having dinner with your mother." Then he chuckled. "By the way, it was your mom's idea for him to say that."

"Good." I nodded. I was pleased Mom thought of that. She and Kenna were close enough that it was believable. I was still pissed that Sonny hadn't given up; the guy was relentless. I breathed through the anger that boiled inside me. Why was he targeting her? To get to me? Because she hadn't been involved until just recently. What had changed?

"I hate to add this, but there's more." Jesse cleared his throat, and I knew I wasn't going to like this one either. "Leo said something made Cameron lose his shit. Worse than normal. He pulled Sonny into his office, and when he left, he ordered his men to move out. Something not right there."

"Fuckin' isn't." Trigger had been listening and spoke up. "Meet in my trailer in ten." We nodded in agreement.

"What a fucking shit storm," I hissed under my breath to Trigger as Jesse stepped back. "I knew that was going to be crazy, but things are fucking spiraling."

"Ah, Grim." Tess nodded over my shoulder, and I saw Oz about to approach. Leal instantly stood in front of Kenna with a warning to back off.

I clamped my hand down on Kenna's thigh and made a circle of eye contact with those around to make it known she was taken. I was still pent up from earlier, and I had no desire to deal with a bunch of assholes.

"I didn't know you belonged to the reaper." Oz addressed Kenna directly and avoided eye contact with me. "You like the heavy, dark shit?"

"You've no idea." Kenna ran her hand up my arm.

"What trailer's yours?" Oz never went down easy.

"Mine," I answered sharply, and his gaze cut over to me.

"I see." He didn't back away, and I knew he pushed the line with me because of the guys who watched. Oz had an ego that often needed to be brought into check.

"I'm glad you do." I lifted an eyebrow and tilted my head at him, and he raised his hands but looked at Kenna.

"If you change your mind, I like dark 'n dirty, too." He leered at her then turned and walked off. I glared at the others who hovered, and they finally got the hint. Kenna was off limits; it wasn't going to happen.

"Come with me." I pulled Kenna to her feet and walked her over to the picnic table in front of Trigger's trailer. Once we were away from the others, I stood in front of her. "I have a meeting in there. Stay here until I'm finished."

"Excuse me!" She folded her arms, and her eyes shot flames. "I appreciate your help getting rid of Oz, but I'm—"

"Going to stay the fuck right here," I interrupted. "Kenna, just do as you're told."

"Champagne, anyone?" Minnie plunked herself down at the table, and Tess joined her. "Don't even bother arguing, Kenna. Girl, moments like this, it's best we just stay here. Ask Tess."

"It's true. The moment the guys aren't here, shit starts."

"Fine." Kenna sighed and sat next to Tess.

"Let's go." Trigger hiked himself up the step into the trailer.

"Boys." I made a hand motion, and both dogs sat near the girls. I did a quick scan of the area then joined the others inside.

Trigger, Brick, Rail, Morgan, and Jesse all waited as I came in. Triggers huge tailer was simple but high end. These parties rarely slowed, but I knew the guys and their women would often settle in here late at night to hang out.

"Jesse." Trigger looked at him to share what he knew.

"I'm waiting on something else, but this just came

through from Gavin." Jesse connected his phone to Trigger's big eighty-inch TV, and we watched the footage from the security cameras. "Something pissed Cameron off tonight, which brought Sonny to his office." We watched as Sonny arrived with three of my security team. They made sure he went into Cameron's office then settled to wait in the hall.

"Doing their job," I added, pleased my team did as they were trained to do. Jesse nodded.

"They were in there for maybe four minutes," Jesse narrated. We saw the door fly open, and Sonny looking fit to kill. "Then Sonny left. He seemed even more upset than Cameron was." The camera feed switched to the elevator where Sonny made a call asking for someone to ping Matt's cell.

"So, he *did* find out about Matt's death tonight." Jesse looked at me, and I knew we were in for something wild when we got back to Vegas. Matt and Sonny had been close for years. "Okay," I let my mind go, "if Sonny found out about his business partner being dead, that would explain Sonny's behavior but not Cameron's. Something's not adding up."

Brick addressed the whole room. "Maybe Cameron had Matt on retainer. That would explain why he'd be upset he lost another client."

"Matt has a lawyer, Peterson and Lowell," I answered. "They're in Chicago."

"Oh, shit," Jesse pulled our focus to him again,

"look what I just got. This is the last time we can find any video footage on Matt Myers." He switched the TV to an outside feed, and Brick instantly tuned in. We watched as Matt and two other men walked inside Minnie's club.

"Fuck me." Brick hurried to the door and pushed it open. "Minnie, get in here."

TEN

KENNA

"Yikes, that doesn't sound good." I turned to Tess as we watched Minnie disappear inside the trailer. Tess had a puzzled look on her face. "What?"

"Something's going on." I stood when she did. "I'll text Rail and see if I can get a feel for what's happening." She moved a few steps away, and I looked over my shoulder. *Fuck it.*

I hurried over and quietly opened the trailer door. The guys stood in front of a giant TV watching a video. I froze when I saw the man on the screen.

"No, Minnie!" I covered my mouth as everyone turned to stare at me in the open doorway. "How could you!"

"I didn't," she shook her head, "I swear, Kenna. I would never."

"Then how?" I pointed at the screen.

"I don't know. Honestly." I should have known she'd never tell my secrets. I'd just panicked. The stone wall inside me started to crumble as I realized what I'd done.

"You know who that is?" The shock on Grim's face made it ten times worse.

"Something really big is going on, Kenna." Minnie moved closer to me. "No more secrets."

"You're one of us, Kenna," Trigger said from the far corner, "inner circle. Means no fuckin' secrets."

"It's not like that." I looked at the floor and tried to pull up some courage from deep inside. "I wasn't trying to keep it from you, I was trying to *help* you."

"Meaning?" Grim studied me from where he stood. I took a deep breath and fought to think straight. "From the beginning," he added.

I nodded; it was time. I dropped heavily into a chair and began.

"Since I was about fifteen, my father began to have a magnitude of men over. I can't remember a time when the house was ever empty. I was told one of his clients came with a team and that's who they were. I was eighteen when Sasha Landry arrived with a few others." I shifted uncomfortably.

"Don't stop now." Grim waved at me, and I looked up briefly, his gold eyes burning into me.

"Over the years, I'd hear things. Anything important was done in Dad's office. Everything else was just mindless chatter in the background. But there were a few rare times, when they'd forget I was home and hold a meeting with the door open. The day before I met you," I looked at Grim, "I got a call from Mom. She needed something scanned from dad's office. I got home and did what I needed to, and just as I was finishing up, I heard someone come into the house. I slipped out of the office and hid behind a door across the hall. I never liked being in the house alone with any of them."

"Speed the story along." Grim was clearly impatient with me.

"I'm trying," I snapped back, not needing his assholiness.

"That guy, Matt," I pointed to the screen, "and another guy stopped outside dad's office. They were discussing Matt's alibi and how it had to be perfect before he testified in court. That he had to stick to the script so everyone else's matched up. Matt," I pointed to the screen again, "promised he was ready and that's when the other guy held up some photos." I paused; I remembered that awful moment all too well. "Well, I knew I had to do something. So," I took a deep breath, and Minnie cleared her throat.

"That's where I come in." Minnie tried to help me out. "I got a call from Kenna saying this Matt guy was going to be at my strip club that night, and that when he arrived, she wanted me to call her. When he came in with a few other guys, I made the call. Ten minutes later, she arrived."

"Why didn't I know about this?" Brick hissed under his breath.

"You were in LA," she reminded him.

"I'd thought everything through. I planned it down to the last minute." I picked up the story. Minnie didn't know this part. I wanted her to know as little as possible. "I did some digging of my own and found out Matt had been cheating on his long-term girlfriend, who has a pretty powerful father. I also found out he had a whole other family, a wife and kids in Wisconsin. That was going to be my bargaining chip."

"Get to the point of all this, Kenna." Grim stood and moved toward me.

"Grim," Trigger warned, and I gave him a 'thank you' look as Grim backed off.

"I need to tell this my way, Grim. You said from the beginning." I took a breath. "So, I arrived at Minnie's, and like always, got patted down for a weapon at the door. Once Nate cleared me, I headed through the back way to one of the lap dance rooms. That's where Minnie told me he was. She said his two buddies were in other rooms down the hall. I used a key card and got in. No one saw me." I rubbed my forehead and let that night's memory flood through me. "I didn't know," I swallowed back the rush of words that wanted to come out but couldn't, "I just…" I licked my lips as I tried to find the words.

A can cracked open, and everyone looked over at Rail. He started to sip loudly then looked around as if to ask what was up.

"Keep going," Rail encouraged me, and I caught Brick's smirk.

"Okay." I closed my eyes and dug deep to find the set of balls I needed. I had to get this out in the open so I could breathe again. "The moment he saw me, he had the wrong idea about why I was there. He made a move for me, but I was ready and held up the proof about his other family, and that's when things turned. I told him I knew about what he'd been told to do, and that if he testified, I'd out him. I said if he wanted to keep the life he had, he'd need to figure out a reason not to do it. But then," I swallowed, and the rest of my words came out in a rush, "he grabbed me and threw me on the floor, then he was on top of me. I kicked and screamed and then there was a gun and somehow it went off. Then Minnie came running in. I never had a gun. Nate checked. I was cleared!"

"Fuck me." Grim slammed his fist into the table.

"The fuck, Minnie?" Trigger growled and looked at her. "How'd he get a gun in the club?"

"I don't know, but if he wanted to bad enough, you know you find a way, Trig." Minnie's voice was as high as I'd ever heard it. I tried not to think of the mouse as she began to explain her part of what happened next.

"Anyway, I heard a bang, and I grabbed the closest bouncers, and we rushed in the room. Kenna's hands were bloody, and some of her dress was wet, but she had on black so that concealed most of it." She eyeballed me, and I waved her on. "I told her I'd handle it and that she needed to get out of there. When she left, we cleaned up, and the guys disposed of the body the way we always do, and that was that."

"That shouldn't have happened," Grim hissed at Trigger, who nodded. "Do you have any idea how bad this is, Kenna?" Before I could answer, something hit him, and he stood straight. "That guy at Secrets, the one I killed, was he one of Matt's guys? He must've followed you there."

"Yes." I knew better than to withhold anything else. "We bumped shoulders on my way out. He must have followed me to your hotel."

"And were those the same guys who were poking around Minnie's club that night we were all there?" Jesse asked.

"Yeah, that was the third guy. I'm guessing they don't know it was me, because we looked right at one another, and he didn't seem to make a connection. I think they were just sniffing around."

Grim cut me off. "But you don't know for sure."

"Well, no, I guess I just figured they'd kill me when they had the opportunity."

"Truth, Kenna, killing you is the least of your worries with guys like that," Grim snarled.

"Hold on, what about the dancer in the room? Did she recognize you?" Morgan asked.

"I don't think she even saw me. I didn't see her. She was gone the moment the door opened."

"They're taught the door opens once and that's for the client to go in," Minnie explained. "Any time after that, they get the fuck out of there."

"I wanna talk to her." Trigger rubbed his chin.

"Me too," Minnie huffed, "but she bolted that night. It's not uncommon with these girls. She's probably worried it was her pimp. Tracy's skittish, and her pimp is a nasty S.O.B." Trigger gave her a hard look. "But I'll keep tryin' to find her."

"Kenna," Grim positively vibrated with anger when I looked at him again, "what, exactly, was Matt Myers asked to testify about?"

I licked my lips and knew the shit was about to hit the fan. "The Riverside Massacre."

"Wasn't that, like, four months ago?" Brick thought out loud. "Yeah, where that factory hired retired vets, and the owner came to open for the morning and they were all found slaughtered. Necks sliced from ear to ear."

"Yeah." I made a face remembering the photos I'd seen.

"That case is still open, yeah?" Morgan asked.

"Yes." I ran a hand through my hair. *Here we go.* "Matt was supposed to testify, along with a few other people, that they saw the Devil's Reach at the scene." The place went silent. "Given who was killed, how they were killed, and your club's priors, it was going to be a slam dunk case." I looked at their faces. I was the only one in the room who moved. "I had to do something. You guys are family, so…I guess it's done. I killed him."

Trigger moved his head slowly to look at me. So much was written on his face that I couldn't figure him out.

"Kenna, do you know who hired them to do this?" Brick cautiously asked.

I opened my mouth but closed it again as tears burned my cheeks, proof I had a theory.

"Okay." Brick nodded, not needing me to say it yet.

"I'm sorry I didn't tell you," I blurted. I felt raw and exposed but also guilty for implying that maybe, just maybe, my father could be behind it. "And I had no idea who he was to Sonny at the time. I guess I didn't dig deep enough, but I'm not sorry for protecting the people I care about."

"You have no idea what you did," Grim growled. "Sonny won't let this go, not until he finds out who killed his business partner. Not to mention the people they're connected to in Chicago."

"It's my mess." I lifted my chin and ignored the weight of all the repercussions that sat heavily on my chest. It wasn't necessarily a new feeling for me. I'd always fought hard to make my father proud despite all the unwanted attention I'd gotten from men he seemed to bring into my life. I don't know why I constantly tried to make him see me for who I was. I always ended up bearing the brunt of his disdain. Now, with this murder and Hanna's warning, I was starting to think this was going to be my new normal. "I'll deal with it, just like I do everything else." I could feel how close I was to the edge. Grim's face was unreadable. I turned and marched out, slamming the door as I left.

"Whooo." I shook the nerves from my arms and swallowed back the lump in my throat. Now everyone knew my secret.

"Hey, Ken," Minnie came out after me, and I closed my eyes, "I hope you know I—"

"I know," I assured her. "I'm sorry for even thinking it." I felt amped up and uncomfortable in my own skin. A far cry from the relaxed jelly state Grim had put me in earlier. "I..." I scrubbed my face. "I feel like I've been screwing up at every turn. Shit, why did I ever think I could blackmail that guy? Look at me,

I'm half his size! I should have realized he'd come at me."

"You weren't thinking. You were protecting the people you cared about." Minnie came closer. "Trigger doesn't do feelings, but I know that meant something to him."

"And Grim? Because he was ready to claw me in two."

"Trigger underreacts, Grim reacts with feeling."

"Grim's just mad it was his mouth in my lunch box thirty minutes ago and not his dick."

"Whoa, what?" Her face lit up, and I wished I hadn't blurted that out loud.

"Hey, bitch, he was mine first, you know." I whirled around to see Grim's woman Kelly with a girl and another guy. They stared me down. "There're rules at this party."

"Did she just call me a bitch?" I made a face at Minnie, feeling something come over me.

"So, why don't you pack up your fake tits and hit the road," the girl sneered. What, were we in *West Side Story?*

"I could see why you'd think they were fake, given that you've got no reference of your own." I took a step toward her. "If you claimed him as yours, why was he behind the trailer earlier with a mouth full of me?" I pointed to my vag. All my common sense sailed away on the hot desert breeze.

"I've never been more turned on," Minnie cackled behind me.

"So, what you're saying is you're a whore?" She took a step toward me, and her two friends fanned out. The guy was short and had a little bit of blond hair left on his head. He grinned like he was ready for what was about to happen. The girl eyed Minnie but thought twice about moving. Instead, she took off her shoes.

"No, what I'm saying, you gangly piss flap, is that he came looking for me for something to eat." I wasn't even thinking; the crap just poured out of my mouth.

"Slap that nipple right off her turkey tit, Kenna!" Minnie called excitedly.

"Fuck you!" Kelly yelled, and I moved into her line of vision.

"Why, Grim doesn't want you?" I retorted, and her face turned beet red. "Why don't you take your gas station gang and move on somewhere you can get some."

"Slut!" She was slow with the slap, so I ducked and shoved her backward. The second she found her footing, she came running for me. I saw red. I'd never been in a fight before, but I was ready, and it felt good to let loose. Once she was close enough, I tried to shove her again, but she was ready for it and grabbed a fistful of my hair, and we both hit the ground. I somehow wiggled on top and yanked the first thing I could.

"What the fuck?" I held up a chunk of her weave and tossed it aside.

"Stupid slut!" Kelly screamed as I held her down and pinned her arms so she couldn't hit me.

"Come on, Kenna, let out your inner demons!" Minnie cheered me on.

"I know who you are!" Kelly's arms broke free, and she flailed and bucked wildly under me. I squeezed my hips as I tried to hold her down. "You're just a whore." I struggled to stay on top. "You're just like the others. Fuck." She laughed like a crazy woman as she flipped me hard on my back. I fought to grab her wrists, but her knees reminded me I wasn't completely healed as pain billowed up in my side. "You couldn't even keep Dale!" My face flinched, and I knew she saw it. How the fuck could she have known that? Who the hell was this chick?

"Think of what you did, Kenna." Minnie's tone changed to a more serious one. "You're ravenous. You need this."

"You couldn't satisfy a fat-assed trucker," Kelly seethed as she pulled my hair. I saw red again and grabbed, punched, tore, and kicked anything I could. I fought like a demon, and it felt good.

She screamed and increased her own attack.

"Oh, baby! It's a clit to tits fight!" I heard Minnie's excited shouts. "I'm watching you two. If you try 'n step in, I'll be callin' Trigger to tap in," she warned someone.

"The fuck!" I heard Grim shout, but it fueled my rage even more, and I landed a good one and felt wet spray. "Get the fuck off." Suddenly, Kelly was thrown backward, and I scrambled after her, but before I could get to her, someone snagged me by the waist.

"What the hell's going on?" Grim held tightly to my arms as I struggled to get back to Kelly.

"Your side piece was startin' shit." Kelly wiped blood from her nose with the back of her hand. "I just came to warn her off. You and me have a night of fun ahead."

"You accused me of being a whore." I flipped my hair out of my face. I was unbelievably wound up. She'd hit low in a few places, and it felt good to physically work it out. Things weren't sitting well in my head.

"Get lost, Kelly," he ordered, and she glowered at me.

"Fine with me. There's plenty of meat around here. I sure as hell don't need to work for it," she fired back. "Fill your boots with the hoe!" And I went for her again.

"Stop!" Grim shouted at me.

"Why?" I shoved his arms back, and he looked fit to kill. "This was all your fault!"

"Come again?" I was getting under his skin, and it felt fucking good.

"You came here with her, yet you fucked around with me. You made me a target with Kelly just like you did with Jenelle. Don't use me as filler when you're bored with the chicks you're with."

"The fuck you say to me?"

"I have enough shit on my plate. I don't need this too." His jaw ticked, and I hoped my words stung. I spun around and headed into Morgan's trailer. He'd put my bags there earlier, so I figured it was where I was staying.

"She's not wrong," I heard Minnie say to him through the window. "That girl came for her because she saw *you* marking Kenna as *yours* in front of Oz."

"Yeah," he muttered, and I was pleased that Minnie had pointed it out as well.

"Kenna's close to losing it, Grim, and I'm not talkin' about a breakdown."

"Done?" His icy tone made even me shiver, and I couldn't even see him.

"I am now," Minnie huffed.

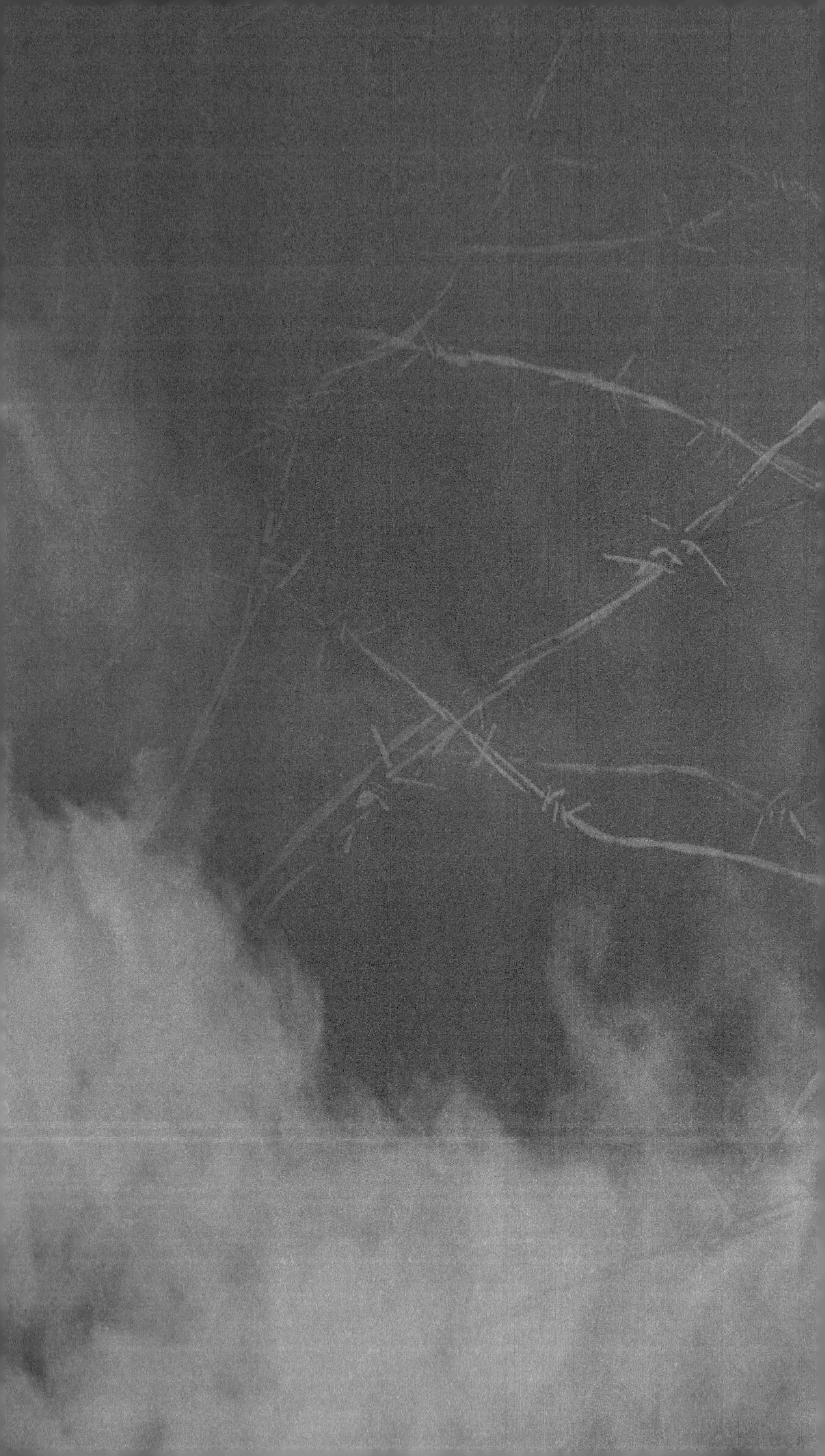

ELEVEN

SIMON

I felt like I was caught in multiple perfect storms, and they were all on course to collide.

Cameron raged over a few more photos with the Devil's Reach in them. They had recently surfaced, and it was more proof that they were there the day Castillo's empire was taken down. Now we just needed to know which one of them actually pulled the trigger.

Sonny continued to fly off the handle as he tried to figure out who killed his business partner.

Jim Gates looked weak, and I knew he struggled now with the return of his cancer. He'd let some things drop as his focus was being pulled from where it should be.

Sasha Landry was going around half-cocked and

avoided me at every turn. I couldn't figure what that was about.

Kenna acted oddly detached from her job at the hotel. She was cool and not as friendly as she'd been. She still hadn't gotten back to me about why I called her.

Then there was me—

"Hey, Simon." Knox strolled in and plunked his ass on the couch, and I slipped on my glasses. "You hear the news?"

"News?" I tried to seem busy as I shifted through some papers.

"Grim's friend Elio caught that Tieri guy. The one who was working with the old bat from the opposite syndicate."

"Rosa, and no, I hadn't heard." *Interesting.* "Where'd they find him?"

"Ready for this?" He kicked his feet up on the table, and I glared at his lack of respect for Cameron's office. "He was working out of Martin Castillo's beach house."

I stilled. What were the odds of that?

"So how did Mr. Capri come to find out this information?"

"My brother." Knox leaned over and fiddled with the wooden chess pieces. "Yup, big brother Grim came to the rescue and caught a win for the Italian mafia."

He laughed a nasty laugh, and I pulled down my glasses and studied him.

"If I didn't know any better, I'd think you held a little hostility toward your brother."

He pulled out a bottle of Jack Daniel's from his jacket pocket and took a swig. Then he began to look at the Mexico photos of the DR at Castillo's place. "I guess when your parents constantly measure your success against someone who's fucking unbeatable," he picked up a photo, "it tends to get old."

"Yes, I guess that would be frustrating. Walking in his shadow, I mean." I watched him empty more amber into his belly and tapped my pen on the desk. I pulled open my drawer and read the label on the prescription medication. "Want something to make you feel better?"

"I'm listening." I opened the bottle and gave him three white tablets.

"It's—" He tossed them back with gulp of Jack. *Okaay.* "If you're looking for Calli, I heard she's at the spa this morning. I think she told her father she'd be back around eleven."

"Fuck," he groaned, "maybe I'll go to the strip joint."

"Why don't you hang around here for a bit? You look like you could use a few minutes of shuteye."

"Sleep's for the weak," he muttered and sounded annoyed, but he didn't move and soon lay back and stared at the ceiling. I wondered how often Knox actually stopped to give his body time to recoup from all the drinking and drugs he took. He sure looked like he needed it.

Suddenly, something hit me, and I jumped up and crossed the room to look at the photo he'd picked up.

"When your parents measure your success to someone who's unbeatable, it tends to grow old…"

I blinked at the jacket and studied the man with his back to the camera. The photos weren't the best. They must have been taken with a shitty cell phone and shared a few times before we got them. I sat down on the edge of the couch where Knox lay.

"If you're going to touch me, can it wait until after I pass out?" he crudely joked, and I dismissed his juvenile behavior.

"Knox," I held the photo up so he could see it, "do you know who that is?"

"Sure," he blinked slowly, "it's Grim."

Huh.

"Why was Grim there?"

"Probably making history by killing the notorious drug lord." As his eyes fluttered closed, I felt the air get sucked out of the room.

"Hey," I hit his arm to jerk him back to me, "do you know if it was Grim who killed Castillo?"

"Yes! Now piss off and leave me be." He rolled his head toward the back of the couch.

I pulled out my phone and texted Cameron. He

could be the one who tells his client Griple why he'll be in prison for life.

> Simon: I found out who killed Martin Castillo. It was Grim Gates.

I looked up from my phone and puffed out some air as I felt the storm inch even closer.

TWELVE

GRIM

I tucked my arm under my head and stared at the stars that littered the sky. The top of the RV was a perfect spot to lie when at these parties. I was social, but I needed alone time to think. I'd left the dogs inside with Jesse, who also needed space to work on figuring out what Sonny was doing. We needed to find someone to take the fall, and preferably someone we could also pin Castillo's murder on. It wasn't a far stretch to have it be one person. Our worlds were interconnected enough. We just needed to get a solid story in place and not talk about it too much. A problem like this usually just took money to make it go away, but that wouldn't work this time.

The tip of my joint glowed orange against the

peppered sky, then it blurred as I let the smoke free. I wished pot would do more for my head. It used to, but it wasn't enough anymore. I needed a woman to settle the chaos up there. The right kind of woman, I thought as I discarded the idea of calling Kelly. She'd pissed me off, anyway. We hadn't come here together, and she needed to remember that. I belonged to no one. Besides, I couldn't imagine her riding behind me on my bike.

Kenna's behavior popped in my head, and I was instantly turned on. She was scrappy and had a wild streak that I liked. Sex with her was what I craved. As much as I hated to admit it, she was right. I'd been using other woman to fill the need when she wasn't around. She drove me to a point where I broke, then I let loose with her.

In the heat of the night, I peeled my shoulders off the cushion and readjusted to a comfier position. It had to be at least a hundred degrees. The queen-sized cushion built into the roof was what sold me on this particular RV. I only wished it had some kind of cooling mechanism. I'd ditched my cut and shirt earlier when I climbed up there in just my jeans. The cool shower I had taken was already a distant memory.

The party was still going strong. Most had migrated over to the main firepit. I could hear the drunken chatter and the beat of the music. The smell of sex, sweat, and booze was thick in the night air.

"Hey." Kenna's voice found me. She had stepped out of Morgan's trailer, and I could see she wore a scrap of white silk and ankle boots. She held a phone to her ear. "Where are you now?" I glanced at my wrist but remembered I was in MC mode. I never wore my watch when I was in this persona. I sat up and pulled out my phone. It was nearly two in the morning. I wondered who the hell she was talking to.

"You're breaking up. You're where?" She ran a hand through her hair, and I swung my legs over the edge and watched her. She opened a cooler and pulled out a bottle of water. She downed about half of it then held the bottle to her forehead, no doubt for the bit of relief it offered. "No, please don't." She shook her head as if the person stood in front of her. "Dad doesn't need to know."

"Whooo!" a guy shouted, and it drew her attention for a moment as he stumbled around with his hand on his fly. She turned her back as the guy wandered off looking for a place to relieve himself.

"Wait. He did what?" She moved the bottle to her neck and down her chest as she grew frustrated. "Of course, Dad took his side." She covered her forehead with her hand and sighed. "It would've been nice if maybe he asked me what happened instead of believing someone who isn't even family." I guessed she referred to the situation with Sasha.

"No, Mom, I'm fine. Grim's security was there."

"Hey," Jesse had climbed up and plunked down next to me, "got a second?"

"Mm," I answered and nodded at Kenna, "just watchin'." Jesse smirked but hid it with his hand as I raised a brow at him. I went back to my joint.

"I was just talking to my guys." Jesse lowered his voice. "Sonny called everyone he knows."

"I figured as much. He loved Matt like a brother." I couldn't believe Kenna was connected to this shit storm.

"Grim," Jesse's tone made me look at him, "Tony Farrell is on his way to Vegas." I frowned as I felt that bomb drop. The Fentanyl Father dared come to my city. *I don't think so.*

"I see."

"Sonny called him. I know you guys have some bad blood."

"That's an understatement."

"True, but maybe we just let him come, poke around, then send him off in a different direction."

"If I don't react to his visit, he'll get more suspicious." I closed my eyes and took a moment to calm my nerves. We were being hit from multiple directions, and we needed to stay level and play our parts well.

"Hey," Jesse pointed, "check it out. He must have got by me when I opened the door."

Leal slowly moved toward Kenna where she sat on the trailer steps.

"Fucking desert," Kenna cursed at her phone, and she shook it. The call must have dropped. When she spotted Leal, her shoulders went back. "You still on duty?" She huffed out an unsure breath as he came a few steps closer. "Well, you'll be happy to know there's no one to cock block, thanks to your boss and his oh-so-fabulous timing." I grinned at her words and wondered what was going through Leal's head.

"Should I go get him?" Jesse eyed me.

"No." I wanted to see what he was up to. He sat a few feet away and simply watched her. His ears twitched as if hyper-tuned to the party.

"You watch me like he does," Kenna huffed and sipped her water, "and just like him, I've no idea what you're thinking." She chuckled. "I bet those handsome ears of yours hear a lot back at the hotel. I bet you could answer some questions for me." She wiped her hand on her hip.

"She's asking for trouble wearing that out there," Jesse mused at me then chuckled to himself when I didn't take his bait. "Well, I'm going to go find me someone to play with." He lifted his beer in a salute. "Night."

"Mm," I answered. I took a last puff then eased myself over to the ladder and slid to the ground without a sound. Leal looked over at me, but I was hidden from him in the darkness.

"What do you see, Leal?" Kenna sounded nervous,

and she slowly pushed off the step. She looked relieved when I stepped into the light. She crossed her arms, and I could see our earlier conversation was still in the front of her mind.

"You think it's smart being out here in that?" I pointed to the scrap of silk that barely covered her ass.

"I could ask you the same thing." She nodded at my bare chest.

"I can handle myself." I smirked at her, and her chin lifted as I stepped in close.

"And as history has proved, so can I. How's Kelly, by the way?

I shrugged. "Haven't seen her."

"I figured she'd be grinding away on your lap right about now."

"Jealous, Kenna?"

"He who claimed me as his in front of the entire party asks me if I'm jealous?" She arched her brow as I ran a finger along her hip and drew the silk higher up her leg. We both looked toward the fire as a shout rang out.

"Those guys are animals." I found her eyes again.

"That from you, Grim?" She huffed as she dragged her fingertips down my chest. I sucked in a deep breath at how intense it felt. "What are you with me?" She tilted her head back, and her hair fell away from my favorite spot.

"A fucking savage." I slammed her body to mine

and hungrily kissed her mouth. She didn't miss a beat and matched my intensity. My hand moved over the curve of her bare ass and under her thong. I could feel the hype building inside me, and I picked her up and carried her into the shadow of the RV. We didn't need an audience. She was mine to devour, and I could barely contain myself.

Bang! A vibration traveled through both of us where our ribs were pressed against each other. She yelped into the kiss, and we both pulled away to look around.

"What the hell was that?" She looked up at me with big eyes. Leal growled, and he raced to my feet.

"Bomb, I think."

Semi-automatics could be heard off in the distance, and I pushed her to the ground.

"Stay low."

"Grim!" Jesse yelled as he threw open the RV door and handed me my handgun plus a shotgun.

More bullets and screams found our ears, and I knew it wasn't our guys.

"Kenna, get inside." I pulled her to her feet and pushed her toward the door. Zhar was on high alert next to me. I stepped in behind her and shoved a gun into her hand. "Point and shoot," I pointed to the clip, "push here, let it fall, add the next. Got it?"

"Wait," she held the gun awkwardly then set it on

the table and whirled around to stare at me, "you can't leave me here!"

"Walls are bulletproof, and you're surrounded by weapons." I open a cabinet to show her more guns. "No one's coming in. Only open the door for the girls, me, or Jesse." Bullets sprayed closer, and I knew I needed to go. I was ready to kill whoever dared to touch the club.

"Gates!" Trigger called from outside, and I looked out and saw him and the guys ready to do battle.

"Don't leave here, Kenna," I grabbed her head and kissed her hard, "that's a Goddamn order!" I pressed my finger into her chest to drive my point home and called my boys to my side.

"What do we know?" I yelled as I came up to the guys.

"Stripe Backs," Trigger snarled, his eyes filled with hate. "Fuckers came down the mountain and attacked the west side."

"Do we know why?"

"Does it fuckin' matter?" Trigger grinned and slapped me on the back.

"Well, let's go break some bones." I grinned back and hefted the shotgun to my shoulder as we spread out. I threw an order to the dogs, and they melted into the shadows.

Brick was next to me and pointed with his head as we drew close to the main fire. The smell of fuel and chemicals hung heavy in the air. A few guys lay nearby, and I could tell by their cuts they were from our New York Chapter. More bodies, mangled from the blast, were close by. We moved forward together and found more bodies, some shot in the head or stabbed to death. Some of them women. It helped fuel our hate for what was to come.

"This way!" one of the guys from a different chapter called out. "Grab your bikes. Some went that way!" Several of his men jumped on their bikes and fired up their engines and tore off across the desert.

Zip! Zip! Bullets flew by my shoulder, and I ducked for cover behind a van where I nearly fell over Rail.

"Howdy, brother!" He grinned at me. "I'm waitin' that fucker out." He pointed to a Stripe Back who'd been shot in the thigh. We watched as he dragged himself across the sand and called out for his buddies to help him. "Guess you almost got caught in the crosshairs." He grinned again apologetically.

"How many?" I saw the top of a guy's head as he peeked out the doorway of one the trailers.

"It's a whole litter." He chuckled. "At least five."

"Five?" I looked around at the chaos that surrounded us, then looked back at the trailer. "How many are there in there?"

"Don't know." He paused as more shots were fired our way. "More than five, though."

Click click click. The shooter was empty. I grinned at

Rail, and we both hopped up and fired. Our bullets tore holes through the tin trailer. We moved forward as Morgan covered us and emptied his semi-automatic into the trailer.

Rail smashed the butt of his gun in a guy's face as we ran by. The sound was deafening. Screams and gunfire seemed to come from everywhere. Rail charged the trailer like Rambo and disappeared inside. I was hard on his heels.

Blood and bodies lay strewn about, but no one fired.

"Anticlimactic." Rail shrugged and ran back outside.

"Jesus." I took a quick look around the area from the doorway before I followed him.

Havoc had been unleashed upon us.

Boom!

We were tossed like toys from the blast of another explosion. I rolled on my back to see a trailer blow up into the sky.

"Fuck!" Rail called out. "That was Tristen's!"

What the hell! These were our brothers, part of my family, and we were being ambushed by these asshole Stripe Backs.

"Grim!" Jesse called, and I hurried over. "There's four over there." He pointed. "Trigger and Brick are on them." He looked over my shoulder. "Morgan just took out three more, but there's a small pack I lost visual on after that blast." He coughed from the smoke around us. "What the fuck are they using to blow the trailers?"

"Something strong." I blinked the sting from my eyes. "Come on!"

We stayed low as we made our way back the way we'd come. A woman's scream tore through the night. I ran toward it and found a Stripe Back trying to get her on his bike. I rammed the guy, and we both toppled over the bike. I rolled and jumped to my feet, ready to fight, but the guy had hit his head and was out. That was a waste. I stomped hard on his chest and felt the satisfying crunch of his ribs.

"You good?" I asked the girl, who nodded then took off running.

"That fucker took out my trailer." I whirled at the sound of Tristen's voice. He held a hand to his bloody head. "Should've seen his face when I shot his buddy in the neck." I saw a gash on his head as he took his hand away. "Go," he waved me off, "I still got one good eye."

I didn't hesitate to get back in the fight. I moved around another trailer, hoping to hell it wasn't going to go off, and spotted a man coming up behind Trigger where he fought with two others.

I steadied my hand, squinted, and drilled two bullets into his skull just as Trigger knocked out one of the men and knifed the other almost at the same time.

He looked at the man behind him then at me. He gave a quick nod.

"Grim!" Kelly shot out from somewhere and slammed into my chest. "Oh, my God, you have to get me out of here!"

Fuck!

"Get her to my trailer," Trigger drawled.

"No, no, no!" She started to flip out, so I slammed my hand down on her mouth so as not to draw attention to us.

"Shut up!" I growled in her ear, and she nodded, her eyes wild.

"Please, Grim," she clawed at my arm, "please don't leave me!"

"Fuck!" I hissed and pulled her next to me.

"They had me then dumped me," she hiccupped, "just because I don't have long—" I pressed a hand over her mouth again to shut her up.

"Grim!" Morgan pointed in the direction of our trailers. He held up three fingers indicating three Stripe Backs were headed that way.

"Come on! Stay behind me." I urged Kelly to follow, and we raced across the open area. She tripped over a dead body, and I caught her before she fell. As we got close to Trigger's trailer, I saw Minnie's head peek up from behind a cooler. When she saw it was me, she covered her mouth. "What the hell are you doing out of the trailer?" Was she insane? "Get in!" I opened the door and pushed Kelly inside. Minnie grabbed my arm, and I looked at her.

"I heard something."

"Not now, Min!" I lifted her off her feet and tossed her inside with Kelly. "Lock it," I yelled. I whirled around and saw Brick, Rail, and Morgan running toward me.

Someone grabbed me from behind and pulled me between the two trailers. I twisted in his hold and saw the end of an assault rifle pointing at my face. I quickly grabbed the barrel and forced it under my arm, so it pointed down at the ground as he pressed the trigger. Bullets kicked up the sand around us, and I snapped my elbow into his face and yanked the weapon from his hand. I let it fall as I snapped his wrist. His scream was cut short by the heel of my boot as it crushed his cheekbone.

"You good?" Brick stopped short when he saw the guy on the ground. "Shit!"

"Just one got away." Rail sucked on a cig that hung from his lips. His lungs wheezed for clean air as he held his gun and pointed.

"Call it in to the others." I looked where he pointed and ran toward my trailer.

Boom!

I was thrown off my feet, and my ears roared. I hit the ground hard and fought the black spots that threatened my vison. Fire licked at my skin as Brick and

Morgan grabbed my arms and pulled me back. It registered that my trailer just went up in flames.

Kenna!

"No!" I pushed the guys off and stumbled to get my balance. I blinked a few times and finally got the ringing in my head to stop. I raced toward the fire, but the flames had already engulfed it. A grip of steel closed around my upper arm.

"Grim, stop." Trigger's growl cut through my brain.

"Grim?" Minnie was suddenly in front of me with a wild expression as she tried to get me to focus on her. "Was Kenna in there?" At my nod, she burst into tears and reached out as Tess crashed into her and they hugged.

"There's nothin' left," Trigger said quietly. "Fuck me." He grabbed Tess and pulled her close.

"Fuck!" I screamed.

"Come here." Kelly put her arms around me and started to sob as she tried to comfort me.

The sound of my dogs barking brought me out of it. I pushed her hands away and ran toward their call. Their barks grew loud as I ran through the dark. I held out my phone light so I didn't trip and almost stepped on a dead guy. I tried to slow down as caution rang in my head. I could imagine a gun pointed at me but ignored it as I continued to run toward the boys.

"Leal," I called as I saw him. He and his brother stood in front of a pickup truck. It wasn't one of ours.

"What is it?" I asked quietly with my weapon out as I slowly moved around the front of the vehicle. The light from my phone spread out in front of me. It suddenly lit up a man. Blood ran from what was left of his face; he was half in and half out of the driver's seat. I heard a sound next to him and flipped the light up. I nearly pulled the trigger in reaction.

"Kenna?" My chest loosened a few notches as relief spread over me.

"Grim?" she cried, but she didn't move. She kept her eyes locked forward, stiff as a statue. "Is he dead?" Her voice was odd, and it sent a chill up my back.

"Yes." I looked around at the pickup truck, wondering what I was missing. I could hear the guys as they arrived behind me.

"Are you sure he's dead?" she repeated.

"I can see inside his brain, so, yeah, he's dead." I pulled the body out and let him slump to the ground.

"No! Don't do that!" She squeezed her eyes shut and tears leaked out. "Grim, go!"

"What?"

"Please," she sobbed. "He said my seat's rigged."

I froze at her words then felt a strange calmness come over me. I tucked my gun away and turned to Trigger.

"Fuck." Trigger held up a hand as he began to circle the truck.

"Just stay still." I fought to think clearly. "I'm not

going anywhere," I assured her as Trigger carefully opened her door and leaned down to look under her seat. "Tell me what happened. Why did you leave the trailer?"

"I did what you said. I heard them at the door." She licked her lips, and I could see her try to pull herself together. "I didn't open it, but they pried it open and came rushing in. I shot one of them in the leg." She sounded pleased at that.

"What did they say?"

"They were looking for you," she sniffed, "and me." That made me look at her hard.

"Okay." I coached her on as Trig and the guys had a confab. I hoped they'd come up with something. I saw Morgan turn toward the truck.

"They brought explosives inside the trailer." Her voice went higher as Morgan reached in and brushed her leg.

"It's okay, hun," he patted her again, "I just need to see what I'm working with here."

"Keep going," I prompted her to keep her focus on me and swallowed back the bile that threatened to choke me. My anger boiled as I forced myself to stay where I was and talk to her.

"Ah, I told them you were in the restroom and when they went that way I jumped up, shot the one who stayed with me in the stomach, and tore off this way."

"Nice." I tried to smile, but it made my face hurt. "Then what?"

"I didn't get too far 'cause someone grabbed me and threw me on the ground." She paused. "He tried to, um…" She squeezed her eyes shut and scrunched up her face, and I felt a level of rage I hadn't felt before pour over me. "But I rammed my heel into his testicles, ending that idea."

"I do love your heels," I growled and slowly pushed that fear out of my head.

She kept going. "He made me get in the truck, said all kinds of things no woman wants to hear, then told me if I tried to run, my seat would blow up. Jesus, Grim, Morgan, please get the guys out of here. Go!" I could see she was starting to lose it.

"You think I'd miss this?" Morgan popped up and grinned at her. "We live for this shit, darlin'." He kissed her cheek and dropped back down beside her.

I urged her to keep talking. "You left out the best part. How'd you kill him?"

"I didn't."

That made me look at her.

"Someone else did."

"Who?"

"Don't know." She shook her head. "Suddenly someone was shooting at us, and he got hit in the head."

"You good, Kenna?" Brick asked from behind me.

"I'm sitting on a bomb, so I've been better." She tried to sound strong.

Morgan was suddenly next to me. "Fuckin' mess," he whispered. "Want a look?"

"I'm just going to move around the truck now. Okay, Kenna, give me a sec." I tried to sound reassuring.

"I'm not going anywhere." Her voice shook as she tried to joke.

The guys stepped back as I looked under her seat at what Morgan pointed out. I ran the tip of my finger where he indicated and felt a wire, then slid it down to where it was attached to the explosive. *Fuck.*

"Got a knife?" I asked over my shoulder.

"No, please, Grim. Just go," Kenna pleaded.

"When have I ever taken an order from you?" I wiggled the knife along one of the panels. If I could just free the pressure sensor from the source, I could disarm it. "Like Morgan said, we live for this shit." I gave her a reassuring grin as Trigger handed me his knife.

"At least move the boys back," she whispered, and I went still. I realized she could see Leal and Zhar in front of the truck. They both stood still and silently stared at us. I used Spanish and ordered the boys away then got back to work.

"Trigger?"

"They're gone," he drawled.

Good.

"He'll get you out safe." Trigger tried his best to comfort her as I gently worked the panel free. "Mexico taught him some." I chuckled and thought how true that was.

"Castillo's men loved blowing shit up," I added as I moved to a better angle. "It kept their hands clean." I caught Trigger's eye, then when he nodded, I flipped the panel free and cut the wire. "Coward's way of offering souls to the reaper, if you ask me." I let out a breath and held up the wire. "Time to go."

"I'm good here." She locked her muscles.

"No." I hooked my arms around her and lifted her straight up.

"Grim!" She buried her face in my neck. In that second with her in my arms, Trigger and I leapt away from the truck. *Nothing.*

"See," I breathed as I placed her on her feet. "Everything's—"

Boom! The truck became a fireball. Kenna screamed as I angled her away from the blast.

"Whoo! Nice tuck-n-roll, Trig," Rail cheered. "That was intense!"

"Jesus." Morgan checked his limbs then hooted as he patted around and felt his dick was still in place.

My grip around Kenna loosened as she pulled back to look around. Her hands shook when she ran them through her hair. The light from the flames flickered across her tear-streaked face while the shadows around us danced.

"It's okay," I breathed.

"Yeah." Her voice broke as the guys all gathered around us.

"Shit, what's with these guys and explosives?" Brick shouted, and we all looked at the fires around us. The stink of gasoline and smoke made our eyes run. "What the fuck was that all about?"

"Stripe Backs trying to make a fuckin' statement. Better be the last of 'em," Trigger grunted, rubbing sand from his Mohawk. "You good?" he asked Kenna.

"Yeah," she repeated, her expression stunned.

"Let's go." Trigger turned, and we all hurried back toward the burning trailers. Trig's famous party spot looked like a war zone. The guys immediately went to check their bikes. Trigger's face was like stone, but I saw his look of relief that they were okay. They all went to inspect the damage to their respective trailers and gear.

"Hey, Grim," Brick lit a joint as he approached, "we caught one." I looked over at him.

"Where?" I snapped my knuckles, feeling my skin heat.

"By Morgan's trailer."

I glanced over at Kenna and saw she was in conversation with Morgan.

"Hey," I made her look over, "you think you can ID someone?" She nodded.

We hurried over to where Tristan and Oz stood next to Morgan's trailer. The guy had his legs and arms bound. I pointed him out to Kenna.

"Do you recognize him?"

She stepped around me and didn't hesitate. "He was the one in charge, when they came in the trailer."

"Is he the one who touched you?" I rubbed my thumb over my fingers, feeding the rage inside me. "Kenna."

"He never got to do much." Her lips twitched and she held her head high. I saw her touch her chest, and my gaze dropped to her breasts that were outlined in white silk. The idea of anyone putting their hands on her made me itch to break something.

I slowly turned and faced the son of bitch who had just had his fate sealed with me.

"Rail, gimme your cig." He didn't hesitate and held it out. I bent over the man and pulled his head back, then held the tip above the man's eye. "Why?"

"Fuck you," he spat, and I pushed the cigarette into his pupil and relished his screams. He screamed and bucked while I let it eat away his vision. "Shit, shit, shit!" I pulled it out and let him drop. Leal and Zhar materialized from somewhere and approached. Both bared their teeth and growled.

"Why?" I repeated as he groaned and shook his

head in pain. I untied his arms and grabbed one, then with a practiced jerk, popped it out of the socket and snapped his forearm in one movement.

He screamed in agony.

"Why?" I tried again as I studied him. The guys stood by and watched. They knew this was my kill. "Fine." I snapped his other wrist, and he writhed in pain. His bound legs thumped against the ground.

"Breath through it," I advised as I jerked the first arm again.

"All right, all right!" His face was blood red and sweat rolled down his cheeks. "We came for you!" He heaved then looked over my shoulder. "And for her."

I hid my emotions well, but something shifted inside.

"You got one good eye, so you better get explaining," I warned.

"Once Big D's son took over the Santa Monica chapter, shit went sideways." He gasped in pain then hurried on when he saw my arm move. "He…he might want peace with your fuckin' club," he directed his comment at Trigger, "but the rest of us don't. Us original guys want nothin' to do with you, or you, fuckin' rich boy." He spat dangerously close to my feet, and I kicked at his broken wrist and was rewarded with a scream. "All right, all right," he huffed and licked spit from the edges of his mouth. His blackened eye made him look like a madman. "We know about Caleb's meeting with you all. He's weak as shit. Won't last a fuckin' month. We ain't like him. We want Vegas. We'll start our own division, an' we got the money comin' in to make that happen."

That caught my interest.

"We're gonna take over!" Spit flew as he yelled.

"You can fuckin' try." Trigger stood with his arms folded and looked at him like the piece of shit he was.

"We already have," he sneered. "Your rich buddy's hotel was just the start of what's to come. When you don't have a pres to answer to, you can make deals with whoever you want. We got ourselves a deal, and it's a good one." He lifted his head to glare at me; his bravado was pathetic.

"Making deals like that will punch your ticket to an early grave," I advised him, but he shook my comment off and turned his attention to Kenna.

"That's where you come in, bitch." I fought not to kick him again. We needed the info he was spewing, and he wasn't long for this world.

"What do I have to do with this?" She stepped forward but I held out an arm to make her stay where she was.

"That's right," he chuckled, "listen to your boyfriend, darlin'. He made the mistake of calling you *his* at Caleb's meeting. Seems the reaper does have a weakness."

"Well, lucky for us, you won't be around long

enough to report anything to your crew." I licked my lips and waited for the moment I could end his life.

"I ain't afraid to meet my maker. Shit, I've scored lots of points with him." He spat again and gave a pain-filled laugh. "It's not me you need to worry about." He aimed a one-eyed leer at Kenna. "Watch out, pretty lady. When you surround yourself with dark shit, evil has a way of finding you."

I quickly closed the gap between us and drilled my fist as hard as I could into his chin. Blood sprayed as his jaw cracked from the blow and he slammed into the ground. Tristan pulled him upright again, and I grabbed a fistful of his hair and drilled my knee into what was left of his face. I punched him furiously over and over. I could feel the bones shatter under my fists.

"You don't need to see this." Tess urged Kenna inside Morgan's trailer.

I didn't stop, even after they left. I couldn't feel my fists. It wasn't until Trigger pulled me off and he and Rail dragged me toward the trailer that I snapped back to reality.

"Hey," Trigger got in my face and held me hard against the siding, "there's nothing left."

"We need to send them a message." I heaved for air.

"Leave somethin' to send." He pointed with his chin toward the mangled body. "It's time to stop takin' the hits." Trigger's intense gaze made me listen; he never spoke more than he needed to. "Time you made a decision."

"What?" I needed to think.

"You know what," his eyes burned through me, and I could see he meant Kenna, "and make it fast." He pushed off and looked at Brick. "You and Morgan round up the prospects. This shit better be cleaned up by mornin'." He tore open the door to his trailer. "Where the fuck's Kenna?"

"Morgan's trailer." Minnie's voice was low and cautious.

THIRTEEN

KENNA

"Tess." Trigger acknowledged me as he suddenly yanked open the trailer door. His massive body blocked the view from outside. "Need a minute with Kenna."

"You want me to stay?" Tess held his troubled gaze. I knew she'd asked more for me than for him. Trigger stepped aside, and she knew it was her cue to leave. He pulled her close and roughly kissed her lips as she passed him. I envied their relationship, he loved her unconditionally, and their love was raw and deep. Passionate. They expressed everything through touch. I gulped as Trigger jammed his body in between the bench seat and the table. He put his hands against the table and pushed back against the leather seat to get more room. His tiny wife had been comfortable there just moments before.

"It's time we talked." His green eyes bore into mine as I fought the urge to run. I'd never had a one-on-one with Trigger other than asking him for the favor for my father. Morgan had been with me then for support, and I wished he was now. To say the man was intense was an understatement. I wished I hadn't changed for bed. My silky, black nightdress barely covered my ass, and my hair was still wet from the shower I'd taken. But here we were.

"You good?" I nodded, and he stroked his chin. He seemed to take a moment to find the right words. The smell of weed and leather filled my nose, and it instantly made me think of Grim.

"Trig." Brick tossed open the door but stopped short when he spotted us. "The prospects are here cleaning shit up. Should be good by daylight."

"What are prospects?" a chick asked someone outside the window.

Rail filled her in. "The guys who want to join the club, they need to prove themselves first. They do all the shit work so we don't have to." I blocked them out and focused on the others.

"Good," Trigger grunted over his shoulder, and to my surprise, Brick slid into a seat by the door and pulled out his phone. It interested me that Trigger didn't tell him to leave, but I was glad he didn't.

I suddenly felt a little more comfortable and sat a little straighter.

"Why?" he asked as his eyes found mine again. I felt like I'd missed part of his conversation. My brows pinched, and I knew he referred to the murder I'd committed.

"Because." I paused and thought twice about my words. Now was the time to be as truthful as I could, so I pushed my defenses away and let my mouth run. "Because you guys are more like family than my own. Because I think some of what's going on involves my father, and I think I might have been witness to more things than I realized over the years."

"Such as?"

"I don't know, but I don't think my killing Matt Myers made me a target. I think I was a target long before. I just didn't realize it." I rubbed my hand over my neck as the tension built inside me. Something gnawed at my subconscious like I was on to something. I just wasn't sure what it was. "Maybe a part of me thinks I did it because I'm trying to make up for what's to come."

"The fuck that be?"

"That's what I'm trying to find out." I let out the breath I held. "For the record, I never set out to put Minnie in danger. I'd never do that." I shot Brick a look, and he nodded. "I never meant to kill Matt either. I was just looking for information. I know what I did was stupid, but," I looked Trigger dead in the eyes, "I won't promise it won't happen again. I'm loyal to a fault."

The skin around his eyes creased as he penetrated my mind, and if a look could squeeze the air from your lungs, Trigger's would do it. I didn't back down because it was the one thing I was sure of. Loyalty to the ones you loved. It was what I lived by.

I nearly jumped when his heavy rings hit the table, he leaned back, and one hand threaded through his shoulder-length Mohawk.

"I'd never patch in a chick," Trigger said, "but if I did, I'd start with you." My eyes widened, as that was the last thing I thought he'd ever say. I caught Brick's reaction, and his head shot up and his mouth dropped open.

"I—"

"I don't agree with what you did at Minnie's," he interrupted me, and I knew now wasn't the time to speak, "but I sure as shit appreciate you lookin' out for us." I gave a tight nod. "You're a part of this family now, whether you want to be or not." He knew I did. "Somethin' to know, if you're gonna approach a situation like that, chances are it's gonna go south. You need to know who you're approaching, who they're tied to, and when it comes down to you or them, you better be ready to pull that fuckin' trigger."

"I can do that."

"Killing's the easy part." He didn't seem to like my answer. "It's after that's shit. Constantly lookin' over your shoulder, not trustin' anyone. Betrayal from ones you thought you could trust." His mask slipped for a second, and I could see the scars that were hidden from view. "And when you're alone and the silence fills your head, that's when it starts to change you." He pointed to his head.

"I understand," I whispered. I knew what it did to your mind already. It was almost the worst part.

"You're deep in this, Kenna."

"I can handle it."

"Can you?"

The door swung open, and I almost jumped up as Grim came in covered in blood. He nodded at Brick and pulled off his t-shirt, and as he balled it up in his hands, he seemed to notice us. His expression went from pissed off to confused then became unreadable. He took in my wet hair and black nightdress, while I let my eyes roam his rock-hard chest and stomach. A fleeting thought that I couldn't wait for the day I could truly take in his artwork made me instantly heat.

"The body's on its way to Cali." He directed that to Trigger then tossed his shirt in the sink. "I need a shower." He disappeared into the bathroom.

"If I can handle him," I head-pointed toward the bathroom then met Trigger's intense eyes again, "I can handle everything else."

"Fuckin' see, won't we?" He waited for a beat then pushed himself up from the table and left without another word.

"Not even a game plan for when we get back to the city?" I looked at Brick. "I'm glad I'm friends with his wife, because he's difficult to read."

"Most I've heard him talk in a long time." Brick huffed. "I hope you know what you're getting into."

"Meaning?" I used one of Trigger's famous one-word answers.

"Meaning," Brick grabbed us beers from the fridge and eased into Trigger's vacated seat, "I've been right here with Tess years ago." He twisted off the top and handed me the bottle. "Warned her a man like Trigger was easy to fall for but not easy to be in love with." He eyed me over the top of the bottle.

"Look, I'm not going to play the game where I pretend I have no idea what you're talking about. I've been through enough tonight, and not to exhaust myself further, but I will say this. I'm not looking for love. I'm not looking to date. I'm just looking for a man who meets my needs in bed. He," I pointed my bottle at the bedroom door, "does that for me. End of story."

"See, that's the problem." He chuckled. "It always happens when you're not trying."

"Isn't that for pregnancy?"

"Fuck if I know," he cringed, "but what I do know is Grim Gates has traveled the world partying with the hottest women you can imagine. He lived in Mexico for a decade with a gorgeous woman." My head jolted at that. "Yeah," he nodded, "didn't know that one, did ya?"

He gave me a minute to digest that one, but I didn't comment.

"Then he came back here and had his pick of women ready to fall on their knees for him. Jenelle somehow seemed to get a hold on him, claws in tight, anyway." He seemed to think about that one and screwed up his mouth. "He keeps her at arm's length, but I see he hasn't completely kicked her to the curb, at least not yet." He nodded then looked at me. "Somehow, you seem to have all his attention."

"We've just got the same taste in sex," I assured him with a shrug.

"Yeah," he smirked around his bottle, "that's what it is."

"Look," I closed my eyes and felt his words swim around my head, "even if the unthinkable was to happen, what's so bad about Grim?"

"From a good friend standpoint, nothing. He's fucking awesome. He's Trigger's prodigy, for fuck's sake. I've never seen Trig or Elio Capri, for that matter, take someone in the way they did Grim. Especially when he didn't have any family history with them."

I shrugged again.

"Friendship and work-ship are vastly different than

a relationship." He tapped his bottle against the table in thought. "Grim might've had a better upbringing than Trigger, but he's got a dark side like Trig. Don't know where it comes from. He's got a one-track mind sometimes, and if you're not on the receiving end of it, you're invisible to him. Can you handle being something to him one day and nothing the next?"

"I don't plan to be any part of it." Except for the sex. I liked the sex.

"Fine," he shook his head, "yeah, sure. Just remember Tess didn't listen to me either."

"Tess and Trigger worked out," I reminded him.

"They're the exception to the rule." He stood, frustrated. "I like you, Kenna. You're smart, hot, and have so much going for you. I just don't want to see you get hurt. Hear me on this."

"Sure." I stood and leaned my hip into the counter.

"Just be careful. Trigger nearly broke Tess, and I wouldn't want that to happen to you too."

"Okay, I hear ya."

I watched him leave and sagged into the counter, feeling the weight of the night seep into me. Movement from the prospects as they cleaned outside had me wishing I was alone in my house away from everything so I could fold inward. My phone lit up on the counter, and I tipped it up to see who it was.

Cameron: Where are you?

I flipped the phone over and dropped my head into my hands on the counter. I had no strength to deal with him right now. It vibrated again.

> Cameron: Why is your location
> turned off?

"Seriously?" I was an adult and hardly needed my father to know my every move.

A warm hand slid up my spine, over my shoulder, then settled around my neck. Instantly, my frustration with my father melted away as my body jolted awake at his touch.

"Interesting choice of clothing for a meet with Trigger," he hissed as he pulled my back flush with his chest.

"I was heading to bed when he came in." His tone instantly got my back up. "Which is where I'm heading now." I tried to pull away, but his grip tightened.

"It's been a shit night," his tongue licked down the shell of my ear, "and the only thing I want right now is your body under mine." Moments later, the heat from his erection burned against my leg. He spun me around and put me on the counter. He grabbed my thigh and hooked my leg on his hip as he lined up and pushed himself to the root inside me.

"Jesus, Grim!" I cried. I hadn't been ready for that; it wasn't like he was small. His lips were on my neck in his favorite spot, sucking away as he flexed his hips with another deep thrust.

"You wanna fight me, sweetheart?" He chuckled in between sucking. "We both know we get off on that."

"You're such an asshole." I shoved his shoulders, but he didn't break rhythm. Grim was a beast, and there was little to nothing I could do when he wanted me. Not that I'd ever stop him. This was where I wanted to be, too, and I couldn't help but thrust right back.

"I want more." He yanked my top down and buried his face in my breasts. I flopped my head back with how good it felt. Everything inside me burned in a ball of excitement. He increased his pace, and our breathing became louder as we both chased what we needed. "I could tear you in two with how much deeper I want to be," he grunted as he lifted my leg high to get a better angle.

"Ah!" I cried, which only fueled him more. Suddenly, the door opened behind him, and a stunned Kelly stared at us. Grim didn't notice, so I grabbed his bare ass, knowing it was a perfect view for her, and gave it a squeeze as a dirty smirk raced across my lips.

"Such a slut." She flipped me the finger as she backed out and slammed the door behind her.

Grim's lips skimmed my neck up to my lips where he devoured my mouth. His hand moved down my back and around my hips, then he lifted me in the air with such force that the second he slammed back into me I came with a throaty scream. He came right after me, nearly taking the wind from my lungs he squeezed me so hard. My hair hung over my face and whipped around. He looked up at me once he shook the climax off and he set me down on the counter again. He reached up and moved my hair back off my face. It was an intimate move, and we both felt the moment then pushed past it.

"I should shower." I tried to slip off the counter, but he blocked me.

"No," he took my hand and pulled me to the bedroom, "get some sleep."

I didn't have the mind space to argue, so I climbed under the covers and felt him join me. His front hit my back, and he slid himself back inside me from behind.

"I'm still wound," he muttered, "and the only way I can sleep next to you is in you." His hand cupped my boob, and I heard his breathing slow. I didn't complain. It felt nice, and I was too exhausted to think how odd it was that he was holding me while he slept. I knew the awkwardness would be there when we woke, but until then, I'd enjoy the feeling. Just as I drifted off, I remembered Brick's warning.

The next morning, I sipped my coffee and avoided Minnie's stare from across the table. We had been shaken awake around noon and told we needed to get a move on before the trucks arrived. There was still a lot of cleanup to do.

Kelly was in fine form as she tried everything in her power to get Grim's attention. For some reason, it bothered me. *What the hell did Brick do to me?* I shifted with discomfort and wished he'd kept his thoughts to himself. I watched Kelly out the window as she sashayed around the guys.

"What?" I finally gave in to Minnie's face. She wasn't giving up as she tried to read my mind.

"You seem different. Are you okay about, you know, all that happened last night?"

I hadn't given last night all that much thought.

"I'm just processing." I sipped the warm brew.

"Did something happen between you and Grim?"

"What?" I looked back over at her. "No."

"Fuckin' bitch." We both looked up as we heard Kelly call after Grim as he approached our trailer.

"So, my girl left, and I don't have a way home. Any chance I can get a ride with you, Grim?" She followed him inside. He grabbed my bag from the seat next to me and tossed it outside by the step.

"The trash truck arrives any minute now, Kelly." Minnie smirked at her. "I'd bet you'd feel more comfortable riding back with them rather than on Grim's bike."

"Touche," I muttered.

"You know, Minnie, your girl's a skank." Kelly put a hand on her waist, and I rolled my eyes.

"My bike's already gone," Grim said. "My guy drove it back before sunup. Jesse and I are driving the RV back since we're a few men down. None of us want to risk the roads today." He huffed as he shut a drawer then locked it. "If you need a ride, there's room."

"The fuck," Minnie's face dropped with disgust, "Grim."

"There's plenty of room." I stood and dumped the rest of my coffee in the small sink. I'd lost my taste for it. "I'm heading back with Morgan in the van."

"When was this decision made?" Grim glared at me.

"I came with Morgan, and I'll leave with Morgan. Anyway, I'm not about to be the third wheel on the way back." I glanced at Kelly then tossed my cup in the trash.

"You're such an idiot, Gates," I heard Minnie scoff as I headed out the door.

I grabbed my bag from where Grim had tossed it and headed over to Morgan.

He eyed me. "You look pissed."

"You ready to go?"

"Yeah."

"Good, because I'm over the desert right now."

As soon as we were inside the city limits, I felt my phone vibrate with a message.

> Unknown: It's time to pay up. By 10pm I expect something useful.

"Shit." I tossed it on the dash and covered my eyes. "Why do I always feel like a pawn? When do I get to be in control of something?"

"Who we talking about?"

"Men, Morgan, all the men in my life, and especially the faceless one that has a grip on me."

"I feel like this is a Minnie conversation."

"It's not." I sighed. "That asshole who attacked me in the garage is demanding something on the guys." I gave him a quick glance. "It's fine. It's not like we didn't know it was coming."

"Doesn't make it any easier."

"Nope." I closed my eyes and tried to sort out how to play this one.

I made a quick exit from the van when Morgan dropped me off, but he parked and joined me as the service elevator opened.

"If he's texting you, it means he's watching you again."

"Thanks." I appreciated him being with me. We stepped inside, and I used the black and silver keycard to bypass all the floors.

"That's fancy."

"Perks of the job," I fibbed, not wanting to get into Grim right now. I could only imagine Kelly's hands all over Grim on the ride home. I shook the irritating thought away, annoyed I even felt a ping of jealousy in the first place.

"Hungry?" I tried to get my mind on something else.

"I could go for a steak."

"I'll call room service once we get inside and have a couple sent up."

We made it up to my floor without seeing anyone, thankfully. I never see my neighbors, so the coast was clear as I unlocked the door. We slipped inside, and I instantly locked the door and looked around. My suite suddenly seemed so big and cold.

"Someone's here." Morgan put a finger to his lips then pressed me into the wall as he pulled his weapon. Suddenly, I saw someone in black pants and a black hoodie step out from the wall. The person's face was hidden by fabric.

Flashbacks of the garage flickered through my brain as panic bubbled up inside me.

"Stay back," Morgan growled as I grabbed a decorative umbrella from its holder and held it up with the sharp end pointed toward the shadowy figure.

"I'm doing what you asked." I shouted and eyed the panic button Jim Gates had installed in the place when I moved in. "You told me I had until ten o'clock!"

"Kenna, it's me," a familiar voice said. She pulled the hood down, and I felt the air rush from my lungs as I let out the breath.

"Hanna?" She nodded, and I dropped the umbrella, but Morgan still held his gun on her. "It's okay. She's a friend," I assured him, and he slowly lowered it. I raced across the marble floor and took her in my arms as she broke into tears. "How did you...?" I stopped the thought and went with a different question. "Where have you been?" I noticed Morgan was on the phone.

"Running." She sniffed as I pulled her over to the couch. I noticed Morgan hung back with the phone to his ear. "Kenna, we need to talk, and I really don't know if I should be here right now."

"Morgan's here. We're safe," I assured her, but she was wide-eyed as she stared at the reaper holding a skull on his back.

"He's one of the motorcycle friends you talked about?"

"Yeah." I sat down by her feet. "Hanna, how did you get in here?"

"Zara let me in." I looked at her, confused. Zara might be my dad's secretary and a friend, but she certainly didn't have a key to my suite. "She told Leo she left some files here and needed them, and since you were away," she shrugged, "Leo trusts her and came here with her. She flirted with him and kept him busy so I could slip in."

"Smart." I tried not to show how much that bothered me. Leo could do no wrong in my eyes, but having it be that easy to get inside my place made me feel less and less comfortable. Again, no control even over my own suite.

"Kenna," Morgan pulled the phone away from his mouth, "Grim wants you to take this up to his place."

"Tell Grim it's happening now. He can wait." Morgan lifted an eyebrow.

"Did you hear that?" He squinted as he spoke into his phone again. No doubt Grim was fired up after what Morgan would have just told him. "Kenna, he—"

"I don't care what he wants," I snapped. I felt bad at letting my anger go at Morgan. "This doesn't involve him." I made an apologetic face at Morgan.

"Copy that." He spun on his heel and muttered something to Grim.

"You're here now, and by the looks of it, you're not staying long, so please tell me what you know. Why did Sasha attack me the other morning to find out what I know?"

"He did what?" She looked panicked.

"Look, a lot of shit's going on, Hanna, and to be honest, I don't even know where to start, but I really need to know what you know."

"Yeah, okay." She took a deep breath just as the door swung open and hit the wall with a boom. Hanna squeaked and dove to the floor.

"Get up and get moving," Grim ordered. He reached for Hanna's arm and pulled her to her feet. She screamed in fear.

Rage burned through me.

I jumped up and grabbed Hanna's other arm and pulled her behind me. Then I got in his face.

"Are you insane?" I yelled.

"You're making me insane." He snarled at me and tried to use his massive body to intimidate as he towered over me. "Both of you, upstairs, now."

"No." I knew his temper was about to blow, but I'd be damned if I'd let him dictate what I could and couldn't do. This man had such nerve. We stood there and stared at each other in equal fury.

"This shit has to stop, Kenna." He licked his lips. "You're being irresponsible, bringing trouble to the hotel." I knew he was just looking for excuses.

"Fine. I'll leave and take Hanna with me. That way we won't draw any trouble here. But on my terms, dammit."

"No, you need to stay where I can keep an eye on you." He hesitated. "And whatever this is all about." He whirled a finger to include Hanna.

"Fuck you! Make up your mind, Grim. You just said you want me to take my 'trouble' out of the hotel." An expression flashed quickly over his face, but I couldn't read it. He positively vibrated.

"Ah, if I may, Grim, ah, that's actually a good idea." Morgan took a cautious step forward, and Grim looked at him.

I felt the corners of my mouth turn upward slightly, and my brow lifted as I took the win. I knew enough not to test my limits with Grim, though, so I stepped back and nodded.

"I know a place that's just off the strip. Not many would go there." Something passed between him and Grim, and after a moment, Grim's mouth twisted then he nodded. "I could take Hanna down first, wait a few minutes then you two come out after." He spoke quietly to Grim for a moment as I turned to Hanna.

"Hanna, are you okay?" I asked my poor friend. She looked like she was in shock. The poor girl had no idea what was happening. "We're going to go somewhere safe, okay? Then we can talk. You go with Morgan. He'll keep you safe, then we'll meet up there."

"Yeah, okay," she slowly nodded and zipped up her hoodie, "just don't be long. Promise?"

"I won't. I promise." I patted her arm. My stomach tightened as I looked at Morgan, who gave me the thumbs up and a look of assurance. Once they were gone, I glared at Grim then turned on my heel and headed for the bedroom.

"Where are you going?" he called after me.

"To get dressed." I slammed the door just as he had earlier.

I wiggled into a silver dress, heels, and worked a boatload of dry shampoo into my hair. Thankfully, it had dried in waves, and with the help of some hair-spray, it had a messy look. I needed to look like I was about to work a shift. I threaded some sparkly earrings on, and a few bracelets. A squirt of perfume, and I was ready to go in under eight minutes. Impressed with myself, I opened the door and found Grim pacing the hallway.

"Christ, Kenna," he grunted but his eyes told me he was thinking all the wrong thoughts, "don't you own sneakers?" He followed me out of the suite.

"Think about it, Grim. If I show up in sneakers and a hoodie, everyone would know something was up." I stabbed the button, and we descended toward the lobby.

"For the record, I'm against this idea. What did Hanna say?"

"We never got time for her to say anything before you burst through the door and scared her to death," I muttered and gained a glare from him as the elevator doors opened.

"That mouth of yours is trouble." His hand landed on my back as he steered me through the lobby. "Shore will meet us at the back exit," he said quietly just as Jayden intercepted us.

"Mr. Gates, I need a quick word with you, if you don't mind." He avoided eye contact with me.

"Not now, Jayden." Grim moved around him.

"Sir, it's important."

Grim's lip curled as he spun around and then seemed to remember we needed to play this out. "What is it, Jayden?"

"Mr. Sonny Conti is here, highly intoxicated, and he won't leave. Given that Ms. Lodge," he glanced at me, "just recently signed him as a client, I thought I'd ask how you'd like to handle it."

Shit.

"Remove his ass."

"Grim," I whispered as Jayden cleared his throat, and I saw his glance go to Grim's hand on my hip.

"Wait here." Grim gave me a hard look then hurried away.

"Kid yourself all you want, Kenna. You two have something going," he huffed imperiously.

"Jayden," I stopped him as he went to leave, "we've nothing going on, as you say. We certainly aren't dating —which, by the way, is none of your business if we were. I'm sorry I said I already had a date to the fundraiser, but I've tried countless times to express to you I'm not interested. You simply refuse to hear me."

"I've known you for a very long time, Kenna. Excuse me if I thought there was something more there. I was wrong." He gave me a quick look. "Whatever, it doesn't matter anymore. I met someone the night of the fundraiser, and it's going well."

"I'm glad. Happy to hear that." I looked over his shoulder and couldn't spot Grim. I didn't have time for this. My phone vibrated, and I saw it was Morgan. He wondered where we were. "Damn, Jayden, please tell Grim I simply couldn't wait." I stopped myself. "If you don't mind."

"Yes, of course." He forced a smile. "I'll tell him."

"Thank you." Maybe—just maybe—Jayden and I could be in the same room together and I wouldn't have to cringe at the thought.

I found Shore waiting by the car, and he looked at me oddly.

"Miss Kenna, I understood Mr. Gates was coming?"

"He got pulled away by a client. I couldn't wait. Let's go." I jumped in the back, and Shore quickly pulled out. I appreciated that he got the sense of urgency.

"How much trouble will I be in?" he asked as we stopped at a red light.

"I'll handle him." I sent Morgan a text that I was on my way.

"I'm sure you will." He chuckled.

Shore pulled up to the old Motel Six and didn't unlock the doors right away.

"Miss Kenna, I really don't feel comfortable dropping you off here alone."

"Sadly, this is nothing compared to the last few days, Shore. I'll be fine. Morgan's here."

"Yes, Mr. Gates said he was, Miss, but..." He sighed. "It's room six upstairs." He still looked unsure as he unlocked the doors. "Chocolate," he suddenly said.

"Huh?" I ducked to look back in the car.

"I like these seashell chocolates. They've got creamy centers." I smiled at his attempt to stall and shook my head.

"Consider a big box of them waiting for you in the locker room tomorrow." I gave him a reassuring smile and closed the door. I made my way up the rusty stairs to room six.

Morgan opened the door and looked around for Grim.

"Long story." I moved inside, and he shut the door. I immediately went to Hanna and gave her a hug. Then as she settled on the bed, I pulled up a chair next to her. I looked around and hated that the place looked like it was set to be used as a sting for prostitution. "I'm so sorry this night's been crazy. It seems my whole life is crazy right now, but Hanna, you've got my undivided attention. You really need to tell me what's going on."

"Okay," she tucked her hair behind her ear, "just hear me out before you judge. I'm not proud of what I did with Sasha, but—"

"Hanna, I don't care about Sasha or any of those

guys. I care about you and about what you need to tell me. Please skip to the important parts."

"Well," she hesitated for a second, "after you stopped seeing Sasha, he started paying attention to me." She tugged at the sleeve of her hoodie. "I'm sorry, but I liked him."

"I could not care less. Really." I wanted to scream and get her to move her story along.

"We'd hook up whenever you and I were back from our internship in Morocco. You'd go to visit your family, and…" She obviously wasn't going to pay attention to my plea to leave out her relationship with Sasha. I had no feelings left for him, but there was still a part of me that didn't want to hear it. "He always insisted on seeing me the moment we were back, asked questions, wanted to see pictures. I thought he was the real deal when he moved to Morocco and said he wanted us to be more to each other."

"Wait, he was living with you there?" I tried to push the hurt aside. Hanna knew me, so she knew how much Sasha had screwed with my heart. He'd been the one who took many of my firsts from me, so to hear this news stung. I may feel nothing for him now, but there was a girl code, and she knew she'd failed me.

"Yes." She swallowed hard, and her eyes pleaded for forgiveness. "He arrived a week before you suddenly turned down that big offer in Burj Al Arub and decided to work at Indulge."

"Holy shit, how did I not know this?"

"You had a lot on your plate, and people always pulled you in different directions. Including your father."

"That's true." I remembered how intense that decision had been. My father was insistent I take the job at Indulge, but ultimately, it was Jim Gates who won me over. But still…

"Sasha was so excited to be with me. He seemed happy. We both were. Then when I told him about you leaving for the States, something changed. Like he was upset or something. At the time, I didn't put it together. He started having late night phone calls." She wiped away a tear. "Long story short, he said he couldn't be there full time anymore, and he'd have to split his time with me there and the rest back in LA."

"Okay." I tried to absorb everything she was telling me. I'd known none of this, and it was hard to curb my impatience with her story.

"When he did visit me, he always pumped me for information on you. I didn't think anything of it because I was in love with him." She laughed like she was stupid. "I know. Pathetic, right?"

"I disagree." I smiled warmly at her. After all, I reminded myself, Sasha wasn't worth the pain he caused, and now she had experienced it, too. "You thought he was the real thing. There's no fault there, Han."

"Well, it took some time, but I saw it. I played dirty. I pretended you were coming back to visit me for a while. I wanted to see if he stayed so he could see you."

"And?"

"He did." Her mouth twisted. "I was jealous. I kicked him out, said a lot of things I didn't mean, but I wanted to hurt him. He told me he loved me and tried to say he only asked about you because your father and you weren't talking, and he was worried about you. I made him leave anyway." Her eyes grew teary.

"Well, that was a lie. My father knows my next move before I do." I gave her a look. "You know that firsthand."

"I know." She nodded, but I could see she was still bothered by the whole thing. "But you're gorgeous, Kenna, and it wouldn't be the first time I've lost a guy's attention when you walked into the room." She held up a hand to stop me as I opened my mouth to comment. "But I realized I really was in love with him, so I went to the hotel the next night to apologize. He was staying at the Gordoff." She attempted a smile at me.

"So, William gave you a key?"

"Yeah," she chuckled, "perks of our job, right?"

"Yeah." I eyed Morgan. He had his gun drawn and kept watch through the stained curtains.

"I almost wish he hadn't." She drew my attention

when she looked up at the ceiling. "I let myself in and heard him talking to someone in the bedroom. When I realized he wasn't alone, I kind of sneaked in quiet. The door was partly open, so I peeked in. He was on a video call. He was talking to a man," her gaze shifted to mine, "about you."

"Me?" Something cold washed over me.

"The man was giving Sasha orders to return to Vegas and watch you."

"What?" I shook my head, confused.

"He was packing his bag as he talked to the guy."

"Do you have any idea who this guy was?"

"I can show you a video of him." She pulled out her phone. "Leo has the actual video. I sent it to his office, again thanks to Zara, but he has no idea what's on it. I figured an extra copy was a smart idea in case I went missing." She swallowed hard and licked her lips.

She handed me the phone, and I pressed play.

Boom!

The door was suddenly kicked in, and the phone flew from my hand as I dove for Hanna and dragged her to the floor behind the bed. Two men raced inside. Morgan fired off two shots, but neither man seemed affected. Morgan fell hard as both guys slammed into him. Then a third man entered and swung the butt of his gun at Morgan's head and knocked him out cold.

One of the men suddenly landed on me hard. He choked on blood, and I realized as he struggled to breathe that he'd been clipped in the neck by one of Morgan's bullets. With all my might, I pushed him off me in horror as his friend came to help him. Then I looked up at the third man.

No!

"Why the fuck did you have to show up that day!" Sasha's voice made my lungs seize. He pulled Hanna and me apart and sent me flying across the room.

As I hit the wall, he came for me. I opened my mouth and screamed.

"Hanna. Run!" I barely recognized my own voice, then I dove at Sasha and headbutted him in the gut. He gasped, caught off guard, as she shot out the door. He grabbed me with a murderous expression and backed me up until I hit the wall. My mind frantically tried to find an escape.

He glanced at the two men. One was now obviously dead, the other stood and stared blankly at Sasha. I eyed Morgan, who hadn't moved since he'd fallen.

"Did she tell you?" He turned his eyes back to me as his fingers dug hard into my arms.

"No, you interrupted." I tried hard to keep the panic from my voice.

"I don't believe you."

"I don't really care if you do." I couldn't stop my mouth.

"You haven't changed, have you?" He smirked.

"Still the smart-mouth girl who always pushed back against her father because she couldn't see what was happening right in front of her."

"Feel free to fill me in." He ran a hand down my arm, but I ripped it away.

"For someone who's supposed to be so smart, you really are dumb." He grabbed my arm again then leaned in to smell my hair. "Didn't you ever wonder why one day we suddenly showed up at your house? Why we never left? Why your mother always tried to keep you away but your father always wanted you to hang around so the men could ogle you? Kinda sick, if you ask me."

"You're hurting me." I pretended to wiggle in pain, and he slacked off his grip a bit. I nudged my knee into position and waited for the moment to strike.

"Well, Kenna, I'm going to let you in on a little secret. Daddy fucked up. He made a deal and dragged you into it. I was just supposed to watch over you, but you mistook my interest, and I had a little fun of my own." He chuckled.

"And are you proud of that? Taking advantage of a young girl?"

"A wild chick who wanted to have some fun, proud doesn't begin to describe it."

"You're disgusting."

"That's not what Hanna thinks." He gave me a nasty smirk before he pulled a gun from his waistband

and pressed the barrel against my chest. I hated that I let out a little cry. "Cameron still thinks he can fix things, but I have very little faith in him, especially now Grim Gates is back fucking shit up. His old man's is dying, and he's running around piling up bodies. The man's soulless."

What?

My mind immediately flew back to a few things I'd noticed but hadn't registered until now. *Not Jim!*

"You say he's soulless? You, with a gun to my chest when I've done nothing wrong." I could barely get my words out. The tip of the gun felt like a magnet to my heart. I squeezed my eyes shut for a second to gain some strength. Slowly, I tilted my head up to stare at him dead in the eye. "You broke my heart once without a second thought, so if you're going to kill me, at least have the balls to look me in the eye." It sickened me to know that his was the last face I'd see before I died as he cocked the gun and I blinked back the darkness that wanted to take over.

"Look away," he directed.

"No." I balled my fists.

"I need your family out of the way, Kenna." He almost sounded apologetic. "We're ready to make our move." I refused to even blink as I kept my eyes glued to his. "Dammit, bitch!" he screamed. "Look away!" Suddenly, the gun was kicked from his hand and his head snapped to the side with a terrible crunch. As he fell at my feet in a heap, his eyes were replaced by a set of stone-cold gold ones.

"Huh," squeaked out as I blinked away tears. Grim's face was a study in sheer red-hot anger.

"Shit," Morgan groaned, and Brick was immediately at his side. He helped him to his feet. "Kenna? Hanna?"

"Kenna's okay, man," Brick said as he looked at Grim then at me, and back to Grim again. "I'll get him to a doctor."

Grim nodded, and finally his eyes released me, and he looked around the room.

"Grim?" I whispered and pulled his attention back to me. "I need Hanna's phone."

I started to search. The room was tiny, but it wasn't anywhere I could find. Grim leaned down and checked the guy's pockets but came up empty. "It has to be here." My voice sounded like someone else's.

"It's not." He looked around then out the door as a car motor could be heard. "She must have it. We need to go."

What a nightmare the night had become.

Grim didn't say anything on the drive back to Indulge; he just stared out the window. I didn't remove his hand from my thigh. I noticed Shore wasn't behind the wheel. Grim's main driver Cartwright was the driver this time. I hoped nothing had happened to Shore, but I'd pull at that thread later, as my brain was firing all over the place and I couldn't seem to focus. I allowed Grim to steer me to his penthouse, and once inside, Leo waited by the bar. He and the dogs looked us over.

"Hey, Kenna," Leo wrapped me in a hug, "are you okay?"

"I am." I eyed Grim as he went to pour himself a drink. "Have you heard from Hanna?"

"Zara called and told me what happened, and she's got Hanna tucked away for now. She admitted what she did. I'm sorry I let her trick me."

"It's okay, Leo. I'm just glad Hanna's all right." I blew out a long breath, pleased she was okay. "Did she take her phone?"

"I'm guessing not, because she asked if you had it. And not just that," his tone made my stomach drop even further, "the copy of the video she gave me, it's been messed with."

"What?" Grim took my phone from my hand. I was still too stuck on what Leo said about the video to care. "Oh, no, what do you mean, messed with?

"I'm sorry but it's been tampered with."

"But Hanna doesn't know who Sasha was talking to. She won't be able to ID him." My heart sank. "What time is it?"

"Almost ten." Leo showed me the time on his phone.

"It's been handled," Grim grunted from the couch

as he tossed me my phone. "Like tonight would have been if you'd waited." He glared at me.

"Grim." I sighed as I felt the night's events land heavily on my chest. I glanced at my phone and saw a text exchange with an unknown number. Wait…

"You're going to New Orleans?"

"He is. For work," Leo answered. I looked at Grim and knew he was frustrated I'd ignored his last jab.

"Morgan could have been killed, Kenna. Hanna too, and you—" Grim stopped himself and cursed under his breath. "I've never met a woman I've wanted to kill and fuck at the same time."

"Kenna." Leo's calm voice cut through. I'd heard him use that voice before when Grim was about to lose it. "Tell us everything that happened. Maybe it'll help us find out who messed with the video."

"Yeah, okay." I pulled a blanket from the side of the couch up over my chilled body and tried to remember everything while I secretly realized I felt uneasy that Grim was leaving.

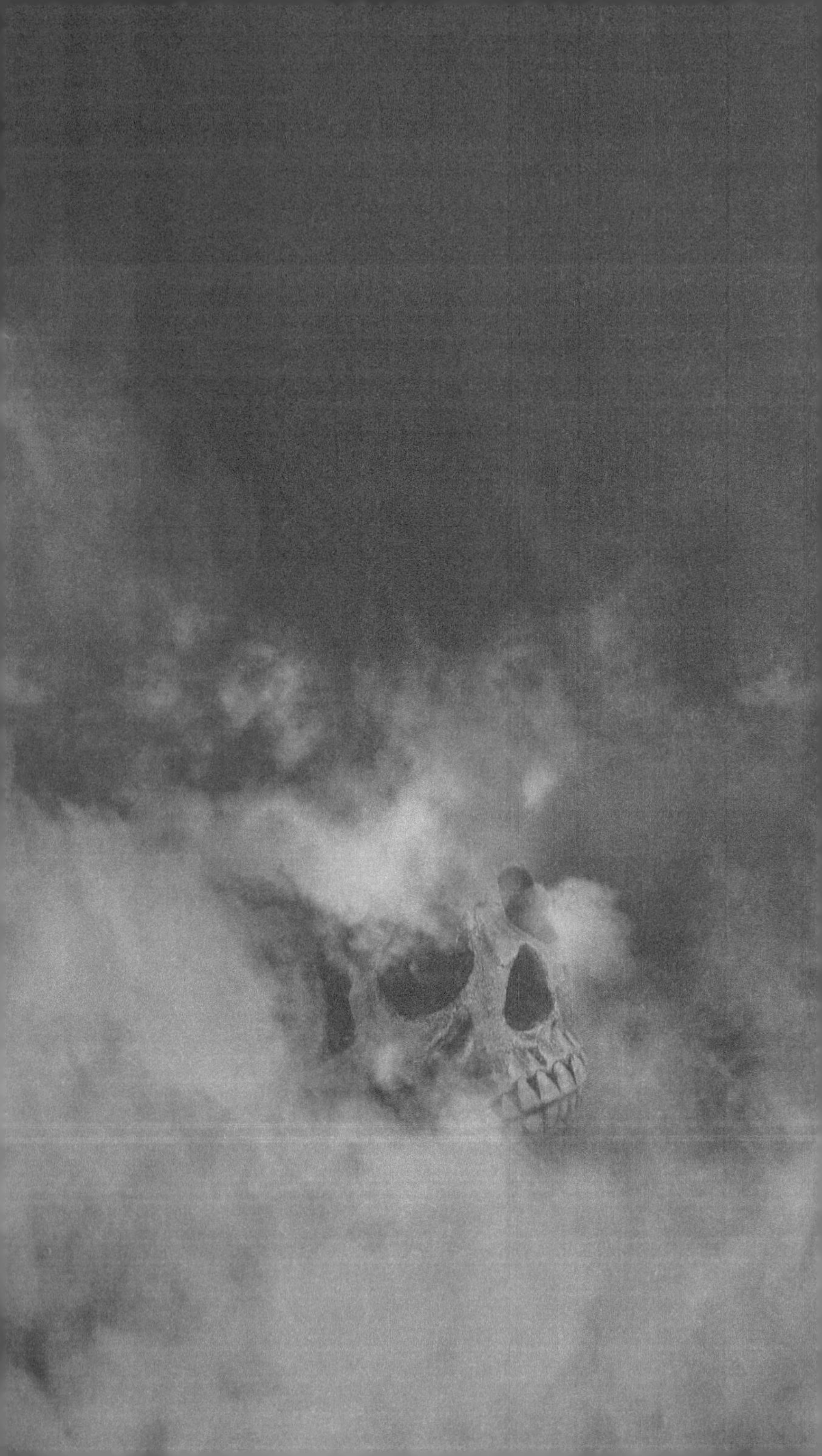

FOURTEEN

GRIM

I studied Dad's expression as Hanna's video played on the laptop. I'd been the one who had tampered with the original in Leo's office. I'd made a copy for myself. I couldn't risk he or Kenna might slip up. Leo meant well but showed his emotions on his face, and Kenna was reckless at the best of times. We needed to make sure our next few moves were played out perfectly. One wrong move, and we could tilt the table.

"I see." Dad closed the laptop and leaned back in thought as I unfrosted the glass. The view out across the hall and over the city came into sharp focus. "I'm not surprised by much anymore, but this certainly was unexpected. Do we know if Cameron was behind that order? Or is Simon working for someone else completely and was told to give Sasha that order?"

"At this point, I've no idea. Simon was the last face I expected to see on there." I shifted in my seat as I thought how many times I'd seen him watching Kenna. He obviously didn't think I'd noticed. "There's a part of me that thinks Sonny could be behind it." I wanted him to be the one. I could picture myself breaking every bone in that ugly body.

"He face-planted into his Lamborghini and dented the hood last night." Dad tried to hide how much that entertained him. "Your mother gifted me that video clip this morning." He chuckled darkly. "For some reason, I don't think Sonny was behind this one, son. He was overheard talking to Tony Farrell about Matt's sister and how she needs money for her son's medical bills. I think Sonny just went off the deep end last night."

"Maybe." I rubbed my lips in thought.

"I have to say," Dad turned the laptop, so it pointed away from the hallway windows, "this part makes me wonder if he was actually looking out for Kenna as opposed to anything malicious." He pressed play, and Simon's voice could be heard.

"I need you to watch over her. He's unpredictable right now, and I can't have her walking around with-out..." The rest was muffled.

Dad turned the video off. "I don't know Simon well enough to say he's good or not."

"I guess time will tell."

"Do what you must to get that answer. We don't need anything happening to her."

"Agreed." I could think of a few inventive ways to get Simon to talk, but I pushed the delightful thoughts away for now. "Do we have any idea when the great Fentanyl Father will be arriving in town?"

"I believe he arrives this morning."

My fingers curled into fists at the idea of him being here when I'm not.

"Convenient timing."

"Indeed." Dad suddenly pulled out a handkerchief from his breast pocket and dabbed his forehead, and I instantly jumped up and got him some water. "Thanks." He let out a tired cough. I sat back down next to him as the door opened.

"I'm fine, son," Dad reassured me, and I shot a glare at the person who dared interrupt us, but it quickly faded as I saw Kenna. She had her face turned as she spoke over her shoulder.

"I need to draw the line here, Dad." She seemed exasperated as she walked into the office. "I have no interest in going to dinner with him tonight." She jumped when she saw us sitting at the conference table. "Oh, my goodness," she checked the time on her phone, "I'm sorry, Mr.

Gates. I thought we'd be way early. Please excuse the intrusion." She looked embarrassed. "Did I have the time wrong? I thought this room would be free."

"No apologies needed." Dad gave her a warm smile as he wiped his mouth. "Grim and I just needed to go over our notes from our morning meeting." He handed me a file and stood. "Let's get these off to them before tonight, son."

"Sure, Dad." He seemed slower in his movements than normal, and it didn't go unnoticed by Cameron. *Fucking parasite.*

"Let me help you." Cameron held it open, and I heard him offer to help walk Dad to his office. Once they left, Kenna glanced at me.

"I was going to get the table set up for Mr. Ines. Would it be best if I come back?"

"Morey Ines?"

"Yes," she answered with a questioning look. I couldn't help but think what a snake Cameron was for bringing him here. "He called my cell and asked if he could meet with me. Something about a client." *That's unexpected.* "Is it a bad time, Grim? Should I come back?"

"No," I waved at her, "I'm almost done." I let my mind run for a moment. "Does your father know Morey Ines is the client you're seeing today?"

"No. Dad's on a rampage with a more important client right now." She finger-quoted then cleared her throat as the door opened behind us. "Okay." She set the pile of note pads and files she'd brought on the table. "Let's see," she muttered to herself.

"Kenna." Cameron's voice was annoyed.

"You have my answer, Cameron." She kept her head focused on her task.

"Well, this time I'm going to override you." He made my blood boil. "His son likes you and wants to take you to drinks at Alibi. I need this client happy, McKenna. You'll do this."

"I said no." She closed her eyes and took a deep breath. "I've lost count, dammit."

"He'll meet you in the lobby at seven."

"He'll be waiting for a long time, then." She didn't miss a beat.

"McKen—"

"Dad," she snapped as she hit her hands on the table, "his son is aggressive and arrogant and has zero influence over his father's decisions. You've done this before. You both pawn the jerk off on me so you can think straight. The guy's a pervert and can't keep his hands to himself. And, thanks to you and this new client you've dumped on my lap at the final hour, who I now have to fit in between this guy who at least had the decency to book a meeting, and the football wives." She sucked in a breath. "I don't have the time or the friggin' patience to deal with that perv." Her words came out in an exasperated tirade. She positively breathed fire. *I like it.*

"You will," Cameron shouted. It made her jump, and I hit my limit.

"Enough!" I growled sharply and slammed my fist into the table. "The answer is no, Cameron. She's your fucking daughter, so show some respect."

"If I wanted you involved, son, I'd—"

"Don't fucking call me son, you—"

"I'll do it," Kenna interrupted. I could tell by the way she rubbed her forehead she didn't have the energy to fight him or hear the two of us get into it. "Seven in the lobby. Fine."

I jammed my teeth together and looked down. I scribbled something I remembered about the morning meeting and waited for Cameron to gloat while I counted to ten.

"See, if you fought me less, Kenna, wouldn't—"

"Kenna can't attend tonight because she won't be here." *Scored.*

"I won't?" She looked at me, confused.

"No, you're needed in New Orleans."

She studied me for a beat then turned to her father with a shrug. "Then I guess you'll just have to find someone else to entertain the pervert."

"Need I remind you, Kenna, that you work for me, too." He glared at her and refused to look at me. "You've taken quite a lot of time off lately."

"She works for me," I continued to take my notes, which I knew would irritate him further, "and my decision is final."

He made some kind of noise then left.

"Thanks for the excuse." She looked exhausted. Her father took a lot out of her.

"Not an excuse." I signed my name at the bottom of the paper. "We leave tonight. Be in the lobby by six."

"Wait, no, Grim, I can't go." She'd been placing pens in front of the pads at each seat, "I've got this lawyer coming in, and Cameron's client coming in shortly, I have the wives of the Raiders team coming in tonight, then the team checks in tomorrow for their summer night pool party."

"You're not the only hostess here, Kenna."

I felt her study me, but I gave her nothing.

"No, Grim." She set the box of pens down and moved to the water tray and started to set out crystal water glasses. As she did, her skirt rose, and I saw her garter belt. I licked my lips and tried to stifle a moan, and she gave me a slit-eyed glance. "If you need a side chick on the trip, Kelly's most likely listening outside the door right now."

"You insult me, Kenna. I wasn't referring to a side piece." I lifted an unimpressed brow.

"Well," she leaned over and rolled a pen across the table toward me, "I'm needed here."

I leaned back, not pleased that she'd tried to brush me off.

"Funny how you think you have a choice in the matter." She paused and took a deep breath, and I instantly regretted my words. I sounded like her father. "Kenna, you've proven several times that you can win over very difficult potential clients. You're smart, witty, and can handle yourself. Even with perverts." I chuckled and was rewarded with a twitch of her lips. "I'm not saying you'll need that for Chef Trahan, but having you there would really help with his friends. They heavily influence his decisions."

"Oh, so, what you're saying is you need me?"

"Kenna…" I swallowed back my normal snarl. "Yes, I do." I noticed my coffee mug was empty, so I headed over to the cart for a refill while I felt my way through this new territory.

"Or is it that you don't want me here alone when the pervert arrives, or the football team, or the…" She gave me a sexy smirk, and I felt my pants tighten.

"I won't lie, that's one of the perks to you coming."

"Grim." She rolled her eyes.

"Kenna," I set my coffee down and tried to fight my natural need to dominate, "you're great at what you do, and I think you'd be a huge asset to this trip. I'd like you to come."

She leaned against the table and studied me as if she considered my words.

"All right." A small smile spread across her sexy lips, and I found myself moving toward her.

"Smart move." I grabbed her ass and pulled her tight body to mine. "Pack more of these, too." I tugged on her garter belt.

"Ms. Lodge?" My brother Knox stood in the doorway. He looked hungover, and sleep deprived, also pissed. "*Lawyer* Morey Ines is here for his meeting." He spoke in a tone that let us know he was displeased he'd had to escort him there.

"Thank you, Knox." She turned back to business mode. "If you don't mind, Mr. Gates." She tilted her head at me.

I smirked when she called me that, and she flashed me a scowl and pointed at the door with her head.

A balding, slightly overweight guy in a cheap suit entered. He looked frazzled as he mopped the sweat from his forehead then held out a hand.

"Thanks for seeing me." He dropped the hand, which I ignored. "Oh, you must be the famous Grim Gates." He swallowed noticeably and glanced at his watch, as if he needed something to do.

"Mr. Ines." I inclined my head. "I understand you're looking to sign on with Mr. Tame?"

"Ah, no," he looked confused, "I just wanted to ask a few questions about your hotel for a new client who's coming into town." He tugged at the sleeve of his jacket and looked away. He was lying. *Interesting.*

"I see." I let it go. I didn't have time to dig too deep, and given the man's mannerisms, I figured Kenna could easily handle him alone. He glanced at Kenna, who leaned over the table, quickly finishing up the last few things. I eyed the man hard and saw sweat break out on his face again as he took his eyes off her legs.

"Have a good meeting." I almost bumped into Knox where he leaned on the wall just outside the door. He followed me down the hall.

"Grim, we need to talk."

"What?"

"Did you really kill Martin Castillo?" That stopped me dead in my tracks. I whirled around. Where in the hell had he heard that name? "Shit, man." He tripped over his own feet and had to right himself. "People are talking."

"What people?"

"People." He shrugged. "I heard rumors and wondered if it's true."

"It's not," I snapped.

"Given your reaction, I'm thinking maybe you—"

"Hey," I slapped the side of his head, "get your shit together, Knox, wake the fuck up, and see what the hell's happening around you."

"What do ya mean? Shit!" He ducked like I swung at him again. "Why are you always so fuckin' angry?"

"Because I'm watching my brother piss away his life listening to rumors while everyone around him is working their ass off!" I glared at him. He looked like he was about to say something but changed his mind. He cursed then spun around and headed toward the elevator.

"Check in with Dad today," I called after him, then I headed toward Leo's office, knocked twice on his door, and popped my head inside.

"Good time?"

"Yeah." He put his phone down as I came into the room. "You look pissed."

"Oh, just dealing with Knox's bullshit."

"He's young." He smiled. "Ease up on him a little, will ya?" I shook my head and tried to put Knox out of my mind. I sat heavily in a chair and propped an ankle over one knee as I attempted to tamp down my anger.

"Look, Leo, I want to talk about Mexico." His face instantly showed worry. "It's okay. I know things didn't run as smoothly as you'd have liked, and I know there's a lot of shit going on here too. You did your best to take over for me, and the two trips you made there to close the accounts was enough. I left a lot of things unfinished, and it wasn't fair you had to clean it all up when I came home." He looked relieved. "Look, how about you come with me and Kenna to New Orleans this week?"

"Yeah?" His face lit up.

"Yeah, I think we both need this."

"Okay." He nodded as his smile widened. "Kenna's coming?"

"Yeah. I'm trying to sign Chef Trahan for Secrets. I really want him, and I'm told he relies heavily on his friends' opinions. Kenna's good with people. Better than me lately." I rubbed my head. "I think she'll be an asset for this deal, and I could use your help too."

He nodded. "I agree, Kenna's good. I'm looking forward to spending time with her too. She's cool people."

"Good. It's all set, then. We leave tonight at six." I smacked him on the back.

"Evening, folks." The captain's southern drawl flowed over the intercom of my private jet. "We should have smooth sailing all the way to New Orleans. Our flight will be three hours and ten minutes, so please sit back and enjoy the sunset." We heard a click as he shut off his mic.

"Your drink, sir." The flight attendant batted her pretty lashes at me, and I moved back so she could put the whiskey down in front of me.

"Miss?" She addressed Kenna, who smiled and took the white wine I'd ordered for her. She thanked the young woman and turned to Leo.

"You look like you're ready for this." She grinned

and clicked glasses with him. He was already a couple drinks ahead of us. "I guess it'll be a little vacation for you?"

"Yeah, I really needed a break. It'll be fun." He grinned as he held up his glass to me.

As the two of them chatted I looked over at Jesse, and he flashed four fingers at me. I nodded my agreement. If he felt four rather than five of our security team had what it took to be on this trip, I wouldn't disagree.

Jesse leaned forward and kept his voice just loud enough for me to hear. "I want to swap out the young one when we land. I've already made the call."

"Good." I nodded and always appreciated that Jesse didn't accept anything but the best when it came to our security. I sat back and enjoyed my drink as I listened to Kenna and my little brother chat. It was nice to see Leo relax.

"Well, let's get down to business." Kenna reached for her bag. "Here you are." She handed me a file then passed one to Leo. Jesse looked surprised as she reached over and gave him one as well.

"And what are these?" I had flipped the folder open to a few photos and picked up one of a man with a tattoo gun in his hand.

"These," she leaned back, "are Chef Trahan's friends. Well, the ones who have something in common with each of you, anyway." She was all business. "Leo,

Doug loves snowboarding and has a place in Mammoth. He also has a love for all things hiking." She held up a photo. "You will work your love for this stuff into conversation. You hook, reel, and land. The key here, guys, is to let them do the talking. You just get it started." She looked at each of us. "People will think the conversation is going swimmingly when they're the ones talking. You'd be surprised how much people will tell you."

"I can do that." Leo started to read his file as Kenna looked at me, "Grim, Peter is mad about tattoos. He's a fabulous artist and has done many celebrities, so naturally he'll be drawn to you. However, when I dug deeper, I found Peter's true passion is bourbon. Just like you, he too is a fan of Old Rip Van Winkle."

"What?" I held my hand up. "How on Earth do you know about that?"

"I know a lot of things, Grim. It would be wise for you to remember that." She arched a brow, and Leo chuckled quietly. "Where was I? Oh, yes. So, keep that information and turn it into an asset. I've checked, and your hotel has a bottle waiting." She looked at Jesse.

"Don't think you're getting out of this." She smiled. "I know you have a job to do, but you also see all, and with that, I particularly want you to watch Brent." She held up a picture, and he nodded at his folder. "He's the slippery one of the bunch. He's been arrested a few times, nothing major, but he's a wild card. If any of them was going to try something, it'd be Brent."

I caught Leo's eye, and I knew we shared the same thought; this was one of the reasons Kenna was on this trip. Though we were well prepared for the business end of things, she'd taken it that much farther.

"To me, these are the three friends who have the most input in Chef Trahan's life. They've known each other since college."

"What about you?" I challenged and was pleased when she pulled out a stack of files of her own.

"I have everyone you do, as well as Trahan, his mother, and his girlfriend of three weeks." She rolled her eyes. "Girls see dollar signs *and* great food."

"Impressive."

"Thanks." She sipped her wine. "I think if we know who we're targeting and are able to roll with whatever they throw at us, we'll have a good chance of signing him." She looked at her phone and her face lit up.

"What?" I was curious what made her smile that way.

"Dale's giving me culinary terms to use at dinner." I felt Leo's gaze on me as I watched her text him back.

"You two dated, right?" Leo asked lightly.

"We did." She continued to text.

"For how long?"

"Not overly long." She shrugged.

"Who ended it?" She looked at him and lowered her phone. "Call me interested."

"Why?"

"I guess I'm just trying to understand why he gave you up." He sent her one of his charming smiles. "You have a lot to offer, Kenna."

"So, there *is* flattery in your DNA. Good to know." She tossed me a look, which I found rather amusing. "Let's just say he wasn't interested in being faithful."

"Ouch."

"Yeah," her face showed how deeply that hurt her, "but it worked out for the best."

"How?" Leo pushed, and I sat back and watched my brother dig into her personal life. I wondered just how far she'd let him. We were interrupted briefly as the attendant handed out more drinks.

"I thought I wanted what he had to offer, but it turned out I really didn't." She took a sip.

"What do you want?"

"I have no fucking idea." She laughed and lifted her glass for a toast. "To having no idea what the hell we want, and to keep ourselves open to new things." The way her eyes slid over to mine made me wonder what went through her mind at that moment.

We spent the rest of the flight in light conversation. I wanted to ask about her meeting with Ines but decided it could wait.

We drove to the Four Seasons and checked into our

suites. I excused myself, as I had some work to finish before I could relax for the night. Jesse followed me up.

"I made the switch, Grim. I like this guy better." Jesse leaned against a desk in my large suite. He seemed comfortable with his decision to swap out one of the men from the security detail. "We're going to do a few laps around the building to give them the lay of the place."

"Sounds good." I waited for him to leave then ditched my jacket and tie and set up my computer to work. A few times I eyed the door. Kenna's suite was just across the hall, and I was curious to know what she was up to. I angled my chair to face the opposite wall and finished off what was needed of me.

I rubbed my tired eyes and undid the first few buttons of my dress shirt. It was nearly midnight, but I was restless. The thought of Kenna being so close nearly drove me mad, so I grabbed my wallet and keycard and headed down to the bar.

"Scotch, neat, top shelf." I pointed to the bottle of Glenlivet.

"Are you having a nice evening, Mr. Gates?" The staff had been instructed to be aware when I was in town and my likes and dislikes. Perks of owning your own hotels.

"Yes." I took the glass and downed the amber liquid then slid it over to him for another.

"Your brother arrived just a bit ago." He nodded

toward the other end of the room. "I must say he has extremely good taste in women."

"Oh?" I turned to look. Leo sat with a gorgeous woman. His laugh reached me and made me smile. Good for him. "Who is she?"

"Paige Marie from Long Island. She's in pharmaceutical sales and does very well."

"Married?"

"No."

"Travels alone?"

"Sometimes, but she sometimes she brings her sister."

"Good." I nodded and turned back and picked up my drink as I decided to give them some space. I threaded through a crowd of men who looked to be a part of a bachelor party and up to the fifth floor. I remembered the pool had a nice sitting area, and there'd be no children up at this hour. It should offer a quiet place to let my mind breathe.

It was empty as I hoped, and the breeze felt good and helped to keep the heat down. I found a dark corner and sat on a lounger that overlooked the crescent-moon shaped pool. Beyond that was a spectacular view of the Mississippi River. I took a deep breath and relaxed. Modern torches flickered shadows across the closed bar area, and light music kept the sound of the traffic away.

Kenna's voice found me. "Hey." I looked around as

she glided into view. Her hair was swept up into a messy bun to keep it out of the water. "Are you following me?"

"No."

Her white string bikini glowed in the pool lights. It was so transparent I could see her nipples through the fabric when she came up to the side.

"Cameron's been blowing up my phone." She made a face. "I needed a break."

"I can imagine." He was always up her ass. He probably even knew she was in the pool.

She looked up at the sky. "Leo made a friend."

"I saw."

"Good for him." She moved until the water was just under her chin then came up again, and the way the water glided down over her skin made my body react. "It's nice to see him relaxed."

"It is." I studied the curve of her breasts, but when she went quiet, I met her eyes. "What?"

"Morgan filled me in a little about how you joined the Devil's Reach." *Did he, now?* "So, which persona do you like better, motorcycle Grim or business Grim?"

"Depends on the situation." I shrugged and couldn't think of a time when I'd ever spoken openly about both sides of myself.

"Explain," she urged, and my natural reaction was to shut her down. I didn't like anyone digging into my life, but for some reason, I was trying to find the right explanation.

"I started fighting when I was young. Seems I pack a deadly punch. I carry a weapon but prefer my hands. The Devil's Reach allows me to handle business without fear I'll tarnish the family name." I sipped my drink. "So, in that respect, I enjoy wearing the leather, but I also enjoy the business world and I like to stay on top. I want to be the best at everything. I'm power hungry and dominate all things in my life." I held her gaze for a beat longer, driving my point home.

"Wow. Do tell," she scoffed.

"Don't ask if you don't want to know." I shrugged and took another sip.

"I do want to know." She moved closer to the edge of the pool near my lounger and looked up at me.

"You've been my greatest challenge, actually." I raised my glass at her as I thought about why she asked me that question. "Which do you prefer, me in a cut or me in a suit?"

"Hm," her eyes lit up with amusement, "wouldn't you like to know?"

"Yes, I would."

She changed topics. "Are you feeling positive about landing Chef Trahan?"

"I have a few concerns, but we're as ready as we can be. Thanks to you." I added that last bit without thought and surprised myself. She pushed back to tread water as though absorbing my comment, then came closer to rest her chin on her hands. "I mean that." I really did. "That you dug into his friends and got all that info on them. It was impressive."

"I hope you didn't mind me including Jesse, but he is head of your security."

"Jesse does background checks on anyone I deal with. It's part of his job. The fact you gave him a heads up on the Brent guy, that impressed him as well as me."

"I'm glad I could help, then." She smiled then turned and began to swim back across the pool.

Something my mother said a while back repeated in my head. *"People underestimate a gorgeous face, son. Kenna is constantly having to prove herself worthy of being in a man's world. If people would just set aside their own ego and see what she has to offer, the sky would be the limit. Your father sees that, and it would be wise if you did too."*

"How was your meeting with Morey Ines?"

"I'm still trying to figure it out."

"What do you mean?"

"Morey booked the appointment because he wanted to show a client around the hotel, but every time I brought that up, he redirected the conversation."

"To what?" That piqued my interest.

"To me. He seemed to want to know about me."

"I see. Didn't that send any red flags?"

"Of course." She rolled her eyes. "It wasn't like he was digging so much as he seemed to be fact checking. Like on something he heard."

"Which was?"

"I'm not sure. We were interrupted by Cameron. He wanted to try again to get me to skip out on this trip so I could entertain the perv."

"I don't know how you do it." I pushed back the flair of anger. Cameron hadn't won, and she was here with us.

"It's challenging," she let out a long breath, "but he's my dad."

I grunted then felt my phone vibrate. It was Leo.

> Leo: Find Kenna and meet me at the
> bar. I have someone I want you to
> meet.

I waited until Kenna returned then held out a hand. "Leo has requested our presence at the bar. He wants us to meet his friend, I imagine." She took my hand, and I lifted her out of the water. The strings on her skimpy bikini top strained under the weight of her breasts. Without thinking, I rubbed the pad of my thumb over a perky nipple. At her look, I fought back everything inside and handed her a towel.

"I'll go change and meet you there." She grinned and stepped around me as I let out a breath. I had to force myself to hold back my constant response to her body. I'd paid her a compliment earlier, and she didn't need it followed up with a sexual response. She didn't deserve that, especially from me. I signaled Jesse to have one of the guys go with her up to her suite, then headed to the bar.

"Grim!" Leo's wide smile told me he was well into the bottle of gin that sat next to his glass. His ear-to-ear grin made me laugh. "Come join us, brother." He made the introductions as I took a seat at his table. I spotted the bachelor party fellow from earlier. They were in full swing on the opposite side of the bar. Charlie brought me a fresh drink.

I ordered a glass for Kenna. "Glass of Bryant Cabernet Sauvignon as well, please."

"You found her?" Leo looked at his phone. "Her phone was turned off."

"Cameron," was all I said, and he let it go. I tried my best to seem interested in Paige. She seemed very nice, but my thoughts drifted to Kenna in her bathing suit.

"Ah, there she is," Leo literally bounced in his seat, "looking mighty fine in her little black dress." I frowned as one of the men from the bachelor party whistled.

"Wrong party, girl!" he hooted, and she waved with a smile as I pulled out the chair next to me. As she slipped onto it, she offered her hand to Paige, and Leo introduced them.

"Sorry for taking so long. I had to change, then the client I met with this morning emailed."

"Morey Ines?" I had to ask.

"No." Leo held up a hand. "No work talk. Please, guys, my head needs a break."

"Yes, and fair enough." Kenna leaned over, and the smell of her perfume made my head swim. "I'll fill you in tomorrow."

"Kenna," Paige pulled her attention, "Leo tells me you're a super host for Indulge. What's it like working for these two?"

"Tell the truth." Leo broke out in laughter. "Whatever's said tonight won't be held against you later. I promise."

"I never agreed to that," I chimed in, and Kenna laughed with Leo.

"Okay, just give me a little insight into these two." Paige rephrased the sentence.

Kenna pointed to Leo. "He's the sweet one."

"Aww." Paige grinned at him.

"You can always count on Leo to be the first to give you a hug and make sure all's okay. He's the teddy bear of the family. Don't get me wrong, he's a shark at what he does, but he's got a fluffy center."

"I do wear my heart on my sleeve." Leo winked at

her. I had to agree my brother could be a softie. He genuinely liked people, and it showed. It was one of the reasons I felt the need to protect him so much.

"And Grim?" Paige looked at me.

"Where to begin with Mr. Gates?" Kenna grinned at me, and I watched as she thought. "Intense, temperamental, unpredictable, bossy as hell," Leo went to say something, but she held up a hand, "but with all of that, he's wildly smart, always puts his family before himself, and would kill for you."

"Sounds like you have a couple of great bosses." Paige smiled around the table. "What about you, Kenna? If you entertain clients, you must get hit on a lot." My God, this woman just dove right in.

"Yes," Kenna nodded, "it's all part of the job."

"Does your boyfriend ever get jealous?"

"I don't know. Do you, Grim?" Leo grinned at me before he laughed into his glass, and I pulled the bottle out of his reach.

"Grim? Oh, he's not my boyfriend," Kenna assured her as Leo snorted.

"Oh, really." She ignored Leo. "Does that mean I can introduce you to my friend? He's right over there." Paige waved toward the bachelor party, and I cleared my throat as Leo laughed harder.

"Enjoying yourself?" I glared at him.

"I'm just proving a point."

"Which is?"

"You have feelings for her." He scooped up a handful of peanuts from a dish.

"My goodness, someone's letting loose tonight." Kenna leaned back in her seat. I slit my eyes at her as I saw something flicker across her face. "You know, Leo, I think I might join you in this carefree mood."

"Ohh," Leo leaned across the table, "what does McKenna Lodge have going on in her pretty little head?"

Kenna reached out and slid a water glass to the middle of the table then slid mine over as well. Then she scooped up the bottle of gin and poured us each a double then topped up Leo's. Paige pushed her own glass over.

"We don't have to be up and moving until two in the afternoon, right, boss?"

"Right," I agreed. I couldn't help but enjoy how much I liked her nickname for me.

"Then let's have a little fun."

A bottle and a half later, and we were way past tipsy, maybe even drunk. I wasn't sure. I usually only drank that way when I was with Trigger and Elio. It wasn't easy for me to let go. I needed control, but I trusted that Jesse and the team had things in order. There weren't many people left, just a few stragglers from the party across the way.

Why not?

"Wait," Kenna tried to catch her breath from laughing, "you didn't skinny dip!"

"I did," Leo covered his face as he continued with his story. "Mom was mortified, but that was just because her client's son decided to snorkel."

"How old was he?" Paige was enjoying herself.

"Fifteen." Leo looked over at me, and I reined in my own laughter. "You think that's funny, why don't we share some of Grim's stories?"

"I have none." I glanced at Jesse, who looked away. He knew better.

"I beg to differ."

"If there were, any witnesses have been well paid for their silence," I assured them.

"I wasn't paid off that time in Singapore. You know, when you were found buck naked asleep in that rickshaw."

Kenna's eyes went wide. "What?"

"Or the time you sang karaoke in France."

"You sing?" Kenna covered her mouth. "That's it, Charlie, we need a mic!"

"He's really good too." Leo kept talking.

"Many have disappeared for a lot less." I laughed at how true that was. "Don't make me do something you'll regret, little brother," I joked as I enjoyed the banter.

"All right," Paige stood then held on to the table,

"this took a dark turn." She eyed me, and Kenna laughed harder.

"You have no idea, Paige. But dark is what makes him so delicious." Kenna leered at me.

"Gotta love when the truth shows itself." Leo laughed as he grabbed his jacket. I chose to ignore him.

"I think it's time we all got to bed." I stood and helped Kenna to her feet. "I'm calling it."

"Yes, bed sounds like a good idea." Kenna stepped back quickly, then took my arm. "Oh, there's the gin." She gave me a playful look as she wobbled. "He was hiding there for a second."

"Tends to do that." We all moved toward the elevator.

"Good night." Leo wrapped his arm around Paige as we arrived at our floor. They disappeared into his room.

I looked down to find Kenna watching me.

"What?"

"It's nice to see you smile."

"I smile."

"No, you smirk because you're usually thinking dirty thoughts." She chuckled, and I grinned at her comment. "See, right there. I like your smile." She pulled out her keycard, but I took it from her and led her toward my door. "Oh, oh, there it is. Now you're thinking a dirty thought."

"Whenever you're around, I'm always thinking

dirty thoughts." I tapped the card to the door, and it opened.

"What are you thinking right now?" she purred as we walked inside.

"You sure you want to know?"

"I really do."

I removed my shirt and in two strides was in front of her, then I whirled her around in my arms and bent her over the couch. I was pleasantly surprised to see she wore a garter belt.

"You listened."

"Trust me, I shocked myself on that one, too." She giggled and moved out of my reach when I tried to grab her. "Maybe there was a part of me that was curious what you'd do if I listened."

"Good things happen when you listen." I took a step forward, and she backed up and licked her lips slowly.

"Actually," she reached back and unzipped her dress and let it fall, "great things happen when I don't."

"Fuck…" I drew out the word as I took in her black and red lace bra, matching panties, and garter belt. With those black heels and her expression, she looked hot enough to scald me as she ran a hand through her hair.

"I thought you'd appreciate the colors, since they do seem to be your favorite." She gave me a hungry look as I removed my belt and wrapped it around my hands. I snapped it hard, and she jerked. "That made me so wet."

"Come here," I ordered, and she shot me a wicked expression as she moved toward me. Once she was close enough, I grabbed her head with one hand and slammed her mouth to mine. As I directed the kiss, she undid my pants and pulled down my boxers. I fell heavily into her hands. She moaned as she gave me a pump. I walked us back to the couch and ripped away just long enough to pull her onto my lap as I sat. She straddled my thighs as I undid her bra and slid my fingers under the garter. Her silky skin sent shock-waves through my gut. Her hair drove me wild as it skimmed my chest.

All the while, we kissed like it was our first. I pulled aside her panties and slid my hungry erection inside with a hiss. "You *are* wet." I muttered against her lips as I let myself lose control in my addiction to her body.

"I've been this way since this morning," she confessed.

"You should have told me." I kissed down her neck. "I'd gladly have helped."

"If I told you how many times I needed—" She stopped abruptly and stood. I caught my breath as I slid out. "I should go."

"The fuck you should!" I jumped up and grabbed

her around the waist. I bent her over the desk and regained my place. I held her tight and thrust a few times to ensure she was back under my control. "Don't ever do that." I slapped her ass hard.

"Grim, I shouldn't," she tried to protest, but it was followed with a moan.

"Don't ever try to keep this," I patted between her legs, "from me, Kenna." I fought not to punish her. "I can't promise my actions." I pumped against her, and she gripped the side of the desk to brace herself.

"Grim!" she screamed, and I took her hard.

Both my hands slid up her sides to her shoulders, and I pushed her down to meet each of my powerful thrusts. I could barely see straight as I built to a blissful pace.

"More!" Her words barely made it through my wild mind. My hand went around her neck, and I pulled her backward. Her back bowed. "Yes!" She grabbed my wrists and held on tight. I looked up and saw a mirror reflecting our crazed expressions. It was a dark, intimate moment, and though I wanted to look away, I couldn't. The moment she came, I felt her body shudder and squeeze around me. I let go with her, and we both shot off. I slammed her body to mine as she clawed at my arms, and I bit down where her neck met her shoulder. It felt like a year's worth of pent-up energy just let go inside me. Finally, our breathing slowed, and her body relaxed against mine.

My phone rang on the table behind me.

"You should take that." She scooped up her dress and bra from the floor and disappeared into the bathroom.

"Grim," I answered sharply.

"It's Trigger. Got a moment?"

I turned to see Kenna leave the suite. "Yeah."

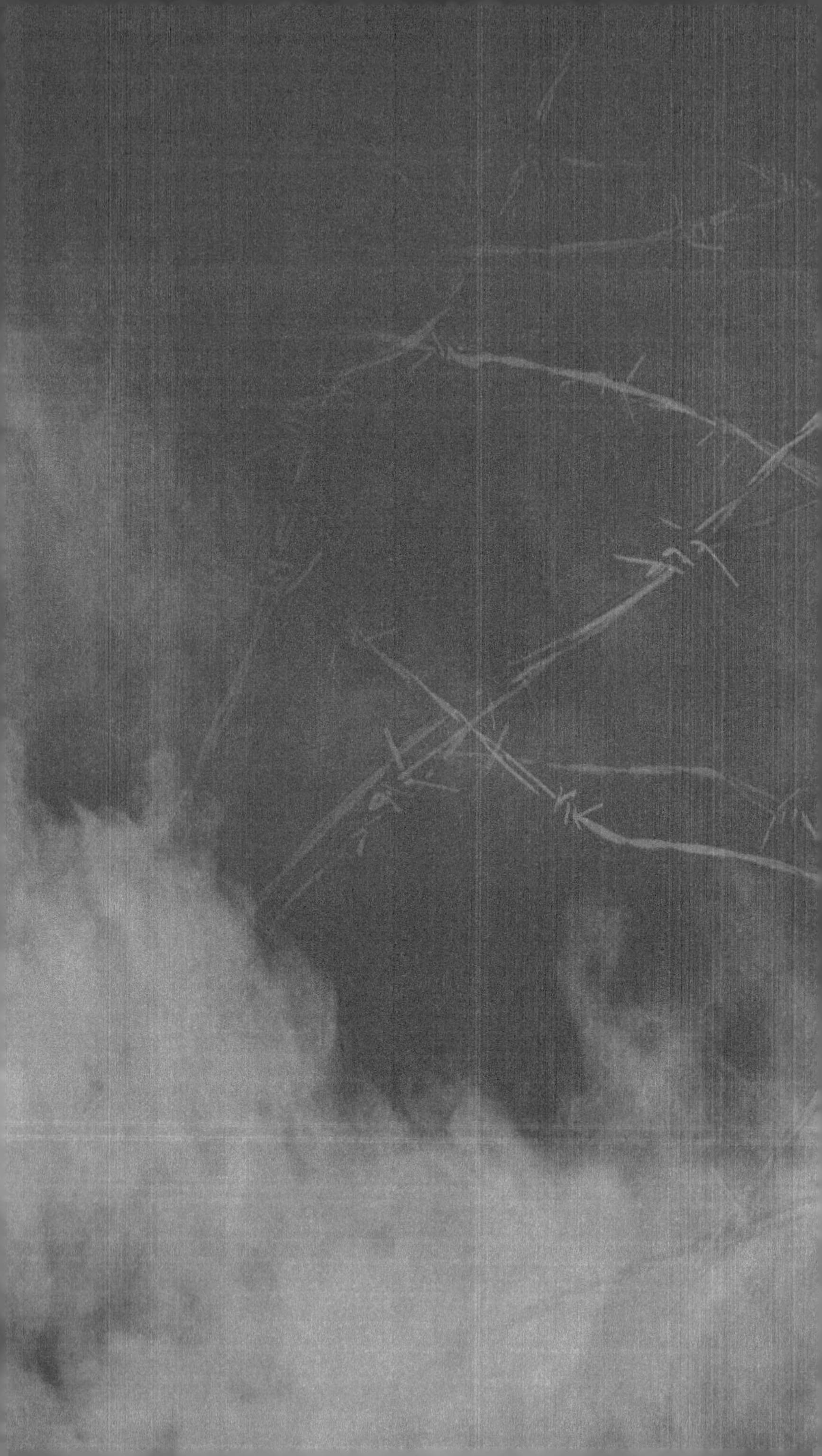

FIFTEEN

"Can I offer you some more tea?" The waitress smiled at me as I sat and soaked up the ambience.

"Please." I flashed her a friendly smile and leaned back as she poured the specialty tea into my rose blossom cup. I enjoyed the fancier side of life, and Mary's Teahouse located off the Strip was a particular favorite of mine. It was a nice place to be while I patiently waited for Kurt to arrive.

"The Queen's Square is my favorite, too." She pointed to my yet untouched sweet that was nestled in a deep velvet wrapper and placed on a doily.

"It's been mine since I was a little boy." I spun the

doily around to admire it. "I often wait for my second cup before I'm ready to indulge."

"A man with restraint." She grinned playfully. "Well, don't let me interrupt. Enjoy."

"Thank you." I noticed Kurt coming up behind her and looked away to give her the hint to leave. Normally, I'd continue to chat with her if I was alone, but I needed to know what Kurt had been up to.

"Anything for you, sir?" she asked as he appeared next to the table.

"Bud Light?"

I closed my eyes with a silent curse. "He's fine, thank you," I assured her with a grimace, and she gave me a small wink. I waited until she was out of sight before I made a show of checking the time on my phone. Kurt didn't look impressed as he looked around.

"I know I haven't spent much time in Vegas for the past few years, but seriously, a tea house, and with flower walls." He turned his nose up at the whimsical flowers that divided each table. I thought they provided a pretty, intimate setting.

"There is nothing wrong with enjoying the finer things in life." I sipped my tea. "Besides, it's the last place anyone would think to eavesdrop."

"That, we can agree on."

I dismissed his comment and jumped into why I invited him to join me here. "Have you found out anything about that phone number that's harassing Kenna?"

"Not really." He leaned back. "The number's a dead end. It belongs to a burner. What did Johnny find out?"

"He tapped Kenna's phone, thankfully after she had Leo Gates do a sweep. We found one message after she got back from the desert and had that mishap with the Stripe Backs." I gave him a look, and he shrugged.

"I had nothing to do with that."

"You sure about that?"

"I'm focused on what I need to do, and attacking an entire motorcycle club on their turf isn't on my to-do list."

I believed him. "Good. Anyway, this time we'll be ready, and when he texts her, we should be able to ping wherever it's coming from." I skipped over the details; Kurt knew more about spyware technology than I did.

He nodded. "That's good. Besides, whoever it is only seems to be driving her into Grim's arms. So, the faster—"

"It's all for show." I cut him off and shook my head. There was no way those two would be able to co-exist in the world of love. Kenna was much too smart for that, and it was obvious they could barely be civil to each other at work.

"When will you see the world without your blinders on?" He rolled his eyes and dropped his elbows heavily on the table; the silverware clanked loudly. "And if it isn't?" He eyed me hard, and I thought about the possibility of the two of them truly together. "Mmph," he snorted, "you've got one Tame girl. Maybe focus on keeping that one in check and leave Kenna for Cameron to deal with."

"If," I drew out the word, "the unthinkable did happen, I'm not sure how Cameron would handle it. Grim's done so much damage already, and that would no doubt push him over the edge."

"And whose fault would that be?"

"I know, but I don't want to see Kenna caught in the crossfire."

"Look," he rubbed his face, clearly not enjoying the conversation, "if Kenna is fucking around with Grim, that's on her. She's a grown-ass woman. Surely, Cameron can see what I do."

"Cameron can barely see past his own nose, and as time goes on, he's becoming more preoccupied with you-know-who's condition."

"Well, I get that. We don't need a repeat—" He lowered his voice when the waitress whisked by.

I finished his thought for him. "No, we don't."

"Seriously, though, Kenna and Grim might be enemies, but there's sexual tension anytime they're in the same room." He rubbed his head in frustration. "They always win, don't they?"

"Winning isn't determined by your sexual partner,

but by who is the last one standing after the war's over," I gleefully reminded him.

"Do you ever forget anything I say?"

I smiled warmly. "What's the fun in that?"

"Smartass." He looked pissed as he turned up his nose at the napkin ring and flipped it over. "So, why did Ines have that meeting with Kenna the other day?"

"No clue." I removed my glasses and used a fresh linen napkin to clean the lenses. "I was wrong about him. He's not as weak as I thought."

"Say the word, and he's gone."

"Sadly, I think he needs to be a side character in this little play for a while longer. If he went missing, they'd notice."

"Perhaps, but if he IDs you and shares why you approached him, that's an entirely different shit storm coming our way."

"Agreed," I pushed my glasses back into place, "which is why when Kenna gets back, I'll need to see how she is with me."

"And if she's different?"

I knew better than to answer that question. "We'll cross that bridge when we need to."

"I'm sure we will." He checked his phone, and his face twisted, then he turned it around to show me a photo. "Need any more proof?"

I studied the photo of Kenna in a tiny white swimsuit standing in front of Grim. His hand seemed to caress her breast. "A photo is a mere snapshot of time."

"Your IQ is much higher than that, Simon. Wake up and smell that fucking fake flowers!"

"Fine." I pushed my glasses higher up my nose. "That just means we need to work harder and keep Cameron off their radar."

"Or you could warn her that daddy dearest will flip his shit if he finds out."

"That's not a bad idea. She does seem to want to keep the peace between the two of them."

"And now you know why." Kurt stabbed my sweet with a fork and ripped off the corner of it. The red syrup oozed out like an untimely death...I was suddenly tossed into a memory.

He swung the gun away from the Stripe Back where he lay next to his bike and pointed it at me. "You're such a waste." His voice dripped in disappointment.

I lost it. I screamed and lunged at him. I drove the axe into his chest as hard as I could. He jolted, and his eyes went wide as he slumped to the ground. I was pulled down with him because of my death grip on the handle.

"Maybe not," slipped from his lips as the light behind his eyes went out. Blood oozed around the blade and pooled by my knees. I shimmied back and jumped to my feet as my head rushed to catch up to what I'd just done.

"Oh, my God!" I looked down at my hands and saw the blood on them. I wiped them desperately on my pants as I

tried to stop the shakes. Then the sound of a Harley drew my attention. I knew I needed to get out of there. I pulled the axe out of his chest and dragged him next to the dead Stripe Back. Then I drew on my knowledge from childhood. I'd witnessed the worst of the worst, and made quick work framing the Stripe Back for the murder. I slipped away with a quick look over my shoulder. Justice had a fucked-up way of evening itself out.

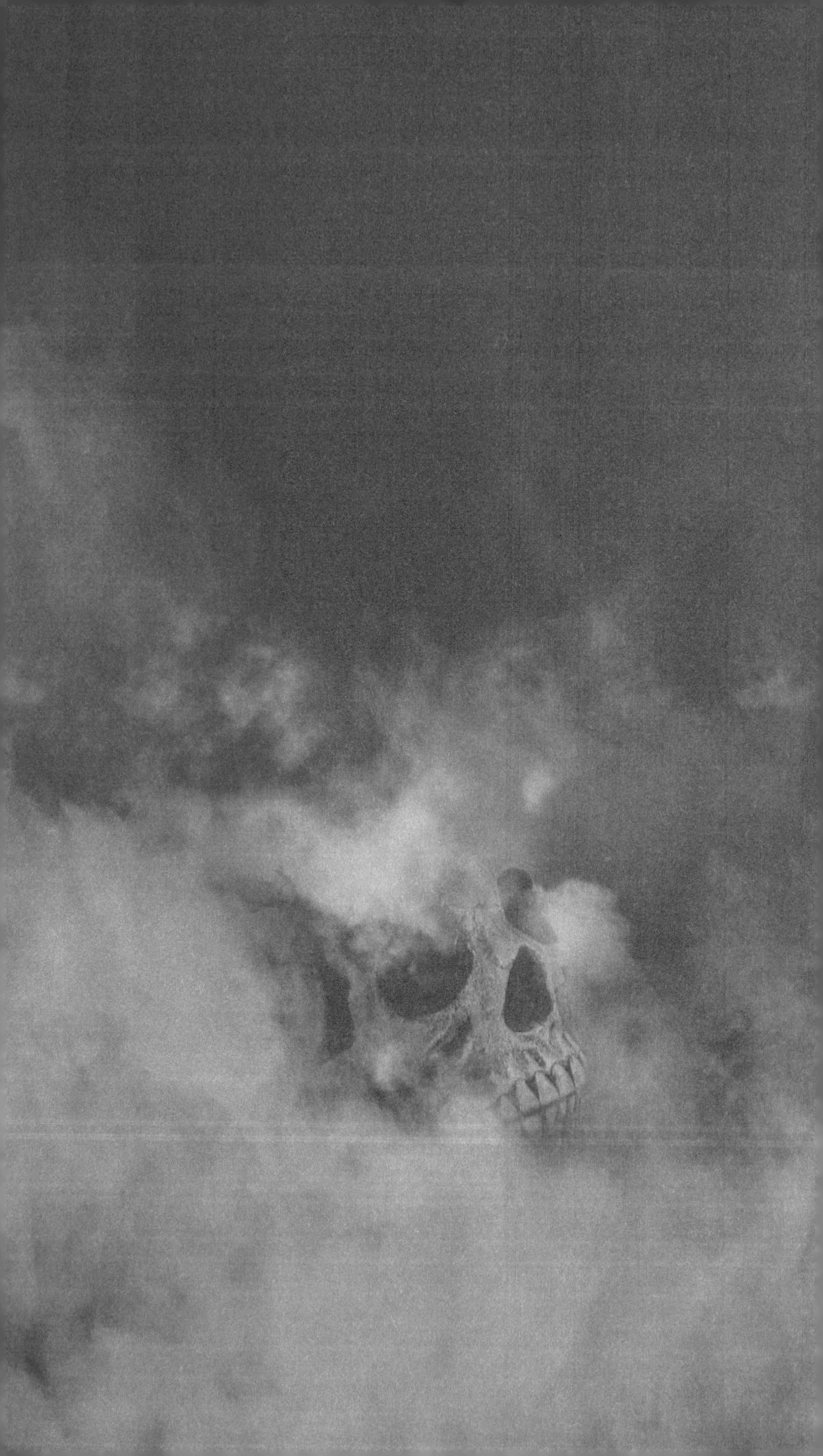

SIXTEEN

GRIM

"Leo's hurting this morning." Jesse chuckled as we rode the elevator down to the lobby bar. We had planned to meet there before we left for dinner at the Restaurant August. Chef Trahan was working, and the plan was to do a test run before our official meeting the next night.

"Gin'll do that when you drink it the way we all did last night. I'm glad my headache finally went." I grimaced at Jesse, and he laughed again. "Any word from Kenna?"

"Just that she went for a swim this morning."

"So, she's alive," I muttered, annoyed that she'd avoided my calls. I'd wanted to ask if she'd heard anything from Simon or Hanna. Little did she know my father was curious about that, too.

He took a call as we stepped out, and I scanned the place for Leo. I spotted Kenna leaning against the bar in a midnight blue dress. The front crisscrossed and was gathered at the hip. A long slit down the length of it showed her bare leg.

"Christ," I growled at the instant reaction my body had to hers. Her hair was curled and swept up on one side. When she saw us, she turned to Charlie, the bartender, with a smile and waved goodbye. I didn't blame Charlie for the way he studied her as she walked toward us. Kenna drew several looks from the bar as she moved. Her sparkly purse matched the pin in her hair. She was something to watch.

"Wow," Jesse mouthed as he ended the call, and I had to agree she looked beautiful. I'd never cared to notice the little details of a woman's attire in the past, but with Kenna, I found myself paying attention to the small things.

"Gentlemen," she addressed us, "you both look very nice." She slid her gaze down my front, and I felt my pants instantly strain against the zipper. Lust was a bitch when Kenna was near.

"So do you." Jesse nodded politely as he put his phone in his breast pocket. "Blue looks good on you."

"Thank you." She eyed my scowl.

"You didn't answer your phone." I jumped into business; I needed a distraction. Didn't this woman own cotton? The silky fabric hugged her curves, and I struggled to fight my desire to slide my hand inside that slit in her skirt.

"I was busy." I noticed Jesse stepped away.

"When I call, you pick up."

"What crawled up your ass today," she snapped and ignored my bullshit.

"You," slipped from my mouth, and I closed my eyes to calm myself. The morning call with my father hadn't gone as well as I'd hoped, and I used the frustration of it on her.

"I did nothing but enjoy some delicious hot sex with you." She stepped up close, and her perfume sent my head into a tailspin as it clawed its way into my senses. "You know you liked it as much as I did," she drawled. "So, if you insist on behaving like an asshole this evening, let me know now. I'm more than ready to take you on." She raised her chin and begged me to challenge her.

"Ready?" Jesse closed in and looked at the two of us.

"We need to talk about Morey," I muttered.

"Sure, sweetheart." She flashed me a grin. "After dinner?"

"Yes." I glanced at Jesse and saw he had a shit-eating grin on his face.

"I have a feeling tonight is going to be really fun." Jesse grinned again.

"Fuck off."

I heard him chuckle as we headed outside.

I stepped back so Kenna could slide into the stretch limo. Leo and Paige were waiting inside, and the smile on my brother's face when I joined them was proof he'd enjoyed the rest of the night with Paige. It was a just short car ride to the restaurant. We were seated quickly, and our drinks were served just as we got settled.

I knew my secretary had called ahead to make sure they took care of us. I also made sure she didn't let them know exactly who was dining. News would travel fast to Chef Trahan that I was eating there the night before our meeting. It was one of the busiest nights for any restaurant, and I wanted to see how the food compared. The fact that Vegas never sleeps is true, so perfection could never slip, especially at the busy times.

We took our time to order and made sure we picked dishes that would appeal to Secrets' demographic. The menu was impressive, and a few things stuck out to me that I might incorporate in my own restaurant.

I noticed Kenna frown as she glanced at her phone before she tucked it away.

"Is someone sweet blowing up your phone?" Paige wiggled her eyebrows.

"Just my friend, Minnie." She reached for her wine and took a big sip.

"Yikes, problems in friendship land?" Paige lifted her glass as she dug a little too much for my liking.

"No," Kenna chuckled, but I knew something bothered her, "someone was asking for me at my friend's work. I guess he wasn't pleased I wasn't around."

"Can't be anyone too important if they think you work at Minnie's." Leo chuckled.

"What kind of work is Minnie into?" Paige looked over the top of her glass.

"She owns a nightclub," I answered before Leo said much more.

"A Vegas nightclub?" she cooed. "Sounds fun."

"I didn't recognize the person's name." Kenna shrugged. "I'm sure it's just a mix-up." She turned the wine bottle around to display the label. "Have you tried this before, Paige? It's got a nice, full body."

"No, I haven't, but it's good. I just have to use the restroom then I'll enjoy some more."

"Okay." Kenna sounded pleased with that, as I knew it was one of her favorites. Leo helped Paige out of her chair and escorted her to the restroom.

"What was the name?" I asked when Kenna leaned back in her chair and the others were out of earshot.

"Tony Farrell?" Her brows pinched when my face turned to stone. I pulled out my phone and saw two missed calls from Minnie and a text warning that *Fentanyl Tony* was poking around. *Son of a bitch.*

"Let me guess, that was really a message for you?" Kenna studied my face.

"Seems I've missed her calls." I tucked my phone away.

"Who is he, anyway?" I barely heard her as my mind spun like a magnet in different directions. Could he suspect that Kenna was behind Matt's death? If so, how? Or did Sonny drop her name to him just to fuck with me? "It's fine if you don't want to say. I'll just call Morgan."

"He's part of Sonny's crew in Chicago. They call him the Fentanyl Father. He's been trying to take over drug distribution in Vegas for years."

"Wait," her chest heaved, "could that mean…?"

"It means nothing right now," I assured her as I watched for the others to return.

"Did you know he was coming?"

"I suspected it, yes, but I couldn't move this meeting." I caught sight of Leo. They were on their way back.

"Is that why you invited me along?" Kenna suddenly sounded pissed. I saw Paige hold up a finger to Leo as she greeted a friend by the window.

"It certainly helped." I ignored her as I watched Leo glance over his shoulder at me. He pointed toward the door. Who did he see?

"So, it wasn't because I was good at my job that you asked me to come?"

Fuck me. A flash of rage burned through my body as I caught sight of him. How in the hell was Sonny Conti here?

"You son of a bitch," she hissed quietly, "and to think I fell for that. I appreciate your attempt to protect me, but next time, don't pay me a compliment unless you honestly mean it."

What? I quickly backtracked what she'd said. *Shit.* She looked away, so I wrapped my arm around her chair and moved in close, so she'd be forced to hear and see me.

"Look at me, Kenna." I slid my hand over her bare leg under the table and her angry eyes met mine, "I never lied to you. You're great at what you do, and I see it. You really stepped up the game for this interview, but," she held my gaze, "I couldn't leave you alone in the city with everything that's going on, let alone Tony fucking Farrell." I squeezed my napkin in a ball and dropped it on the table. "Look, I know you've had a life full of shitty men, but don't ever clump me in with them." I kept Sonny in the corner of my eye as he spoke to one of his friends.

"All right," Kenna whispered, and I watched her throat contract and fought the urge to kiss—my lips touched hers before I knew what happened. It was reckless and flirted with a line I never intended to cross in public. I pushed between her lips and swiped across her tongue, giving in for a moment. It took everything for me to pull away.

"You see who's here?" Leo made a pissed-off face as the two of them took their seats, oblivious to our moment.

"Yeah, I saw." I sat back but kept my hand on Kenna's thigh as the snake slithered his way toward us.

"Well, would you look at this?" Sonny clapped his hands with fake joy, and Kenna's leg tightened under my hold. Sonny could play his games all he wanted, but I'd caught his face before he put on his fake smile. Something weighed heavily on him, and I could only guess it was Matt Myers' death. The grooves of his face were deep, and there were dark circles under his eyes. "What are the odds I'd run into you, Grim, all the way here in New Orleans?"

"I'm sure the odds were all in your favor." My words came out like smooth molasses, but my 9mm was burning a hole in my back.

"Mmmm, Kenna, you're looking all kinds of good in that dress." He licked his lips and leered at her. "I'd ask if you're having a good time, but given that I just saw Grim's tongue down your throat, I'd say the night is lookin' good."

"I called it," Paige whispered, but Leo shook his head for her to stay quiet.

"You're really workin' your way up the family ladder, Kenna, but I guess it's in your job description to cater to everyone's needs." He winked at her, and when he looked at Leo, she tried to move my hand off her leg. I wouldn't budge.

"Don't you have some other girl to roofie?" Kenna took a sip of her wine. "Or will no one touch you since you faceplanted in your Lamborghini?" She took another sip as he stared at her in surprise. "I'm thinking you hurt more than just your face but also whatever the hell you call that toothpick that pokes between your legs." My eyebrow went up at her words, but I quickly recovered. Leo used his napkin to hide his smirk, and I shot him a look to warn him not to feed the fire.

"Well, well, well, our beautiful little lady has a nasty side." Sonny inclined his head at her and put his fingers to his mouth.

"Excuse me," the hostess appeared and addressed Sonny, "your table is ready, Mr. Conti."

"This has been really interesting." Sonny smiled. "I'm sure this won't be the only time we'll run into each other this trip." I wondered just how long he'd been following us. We watched as he went with the hostess. He took a seat along with two other men at the table. It wasn't lost on me he made sure to sit facing us.

"Should we leave?" Leo asked.

"No." Kenna plucked a strawberry off her plate like nothing fazed her.

"I have no idea what that was all about, but can we

rewind about how you two kissed?" Paige tried to lighten the mood. She was obviously clueless to the people she dined with and had no idea a trigger-happy murderer had been inches from her just a moment ago. When I thought about all of us, I almost smiled and wondered what people would think if they really knew who they were surrounded with.

"Mr. Gates?" The waiter interrupted my thoughts as he held a tray. "I was asked to give you this." I slid the little silver container from the tray, and along with it a piece of cardstock that had been folded in half.

"Thank you." He whisked away, and I unfolded the card as I thumbed the top of the container open.

I had a few left over. I figured you could put them to good use tonight. – Sonny

Three white roofie pills stared up at me.

He's dead.

I snapped it closed as Leo grabbed the note.

"Fucking psycho." Leo looked over at me. Paige, still oblivious, drew his attention with more questions as I tossed my napkin on the plate. I was ready to drill my fist into his eye socket.

"Grim," Kenna slid her hand over my lap and leaned close to my ear as I stared at Sonny. "Think about it."

I tuned in to her breath on my skin. I needed an anchor to keep from ripping his throat out in the middle of restaurant.

"He knows what he's doing. He's not here by accident. He's got nothing to lose and I don't see he has anything to gain; he's just an asshole. But you've got a deal to make tomorrow, and it's important to you. He'd love nothing more than to mess it up." She discreetly massaged the erection that had suddenly made itself known. It had zero fucks about Sonny.

"He saw us kiss, which probably sent his own ego over the edge." Her tone deepened, and I was glad the place was busy. "Let him wish my hand was on him instead of you." My grip tightened on her leg as she rubbed harder. "Don't let him win."

"Leo," I pulled myself together and called across the table, "let's order another bottle." I pointed to the wine and wrapped my arm around the back of Kenna's chair.

"All right, let's do this." Leo grinned and signaled for the waiter. We could all play this game.

***

"Is it always so exciting and mysterious with you brothers?" Paige's voice was full of fun as she put her arm through Leo's. They walked in front of us down the sidewalk. The humid air was full of music and people partying. Jesse hadn't liked the idea of walking, but I noticed he didn't say no to her. Another man under her spell.

"It's the world of money and power," Kenna answered her. "It brings out the good, the bad, and the ugly."

"So, who was that guy?" Paige started to dig again, and Kenna changed the topic.

"Hey, everyone," she clapped her hands and looked up at me with a big smile, "I heard about this band. It's close by, and I'd love to go hear them play."

"What kind of music? who's playing?" Leo walked backward and looked interested.

"Cajun Cat. They're a mix of it all jazz, blues, swamp." She smiled brightly. "Swamp just so happens to be one of my favorite kinds of music. They're a local band, playing in a pub."

She tried hard to get us on board, but I wasn't feeling it. My mind was still stuck back at the restaurant as I imagined my hands snapping Sonny's bones.

"I don't know." I wanted them all back at the hotel.

"Come on, music's rooted deep in the people here. Besides, if you truly want to bring New Orleans to Vegas, we need to experience New Orleans while were in it!" She scrunched up her nose when she saw she hadn't won me over yet. "Jesse," she called over her shoulder then hung back as she worked her magic to convince him.

"So, are we doing this?" Leo asked as he looked at me.

"Yes, I suppose. It's fun watching her plead her case," I joked darkly.

"You are all kinds of messed up, Grim." Paige glanced at me.

I shrugged. "Better you discover it now."

"Jesse's on board." Kenna joined me again with her hands on her hips.

"Of course, he is." I snagged her around the waist and hurried her along.

Voodoo's Basement turned out to be a small pub just three blocks down from the restaurant. I appreciated the short walk and one entrance into the place. If Sonny still followed, he'd be spotted quickly. It wasn't overly busy, and the band had been on break and were just getting started again. We snagged a table in the back corner while Jesse spread out the guys. The low lighting and the chill vibe of the locals in the place helped calm my need to spill blood.

"This band," Kenna started in as we settled, "does covers and mixes in their own music."

As the music started, I leaned back and took a breath. The lead singer lit up from ear to ear as he licked his lips then let out one hell of a sound. He started out with Eddie Lang's *Troubles, Troubles*. After that, they played three songs I didn't know, and I was captivated. They were a four-person band. Three men and one woman. They each pulled their weight with the instruments and their energy never faded. After a while of enjoying the music, I found myself watching Kenna watch the crowd. Just when my curiosity got to me, the music faded and the man at the mic said they needed another short break.

"I'm impressed." Leo turned his chair back around toward the table.

"I loved the fourth song," Paige chimed in. "The growl in his voice gave me goosebumps."

The lead singer approached our table. "Kenna Lodge?"

"Yes, that's me." Kenna stood and shook his hand. "Please sit."

"Thank you." He waved over the woman. Leo gave me a surprised look but went with it. Clearly, Kenna had been expecting them to come over, though a little heads up would have been nice.

"Leon and Kate, this is Grim and Leo Gates, and this is Leo's date, Paige."

"Nice to meet you all." Leon smiled warmly. "What did you think?"

"Goosebumps on the fourth song." Paige spoke up first, no shocker there. Her sales background showed her need to talk first.

"I'm so happy to hear that," Kate thanked her. "What about you, Grim?"

"I really liked it." I nodded. "Your voices complement each other, but what I liked most were your strong instrumentals. Do you like playing the classics as much as your own stuff?"

"Very much so," Leon said. "We're here to play music for everyone, not just those who know our songs. We play to honor those who paved the road for us to stand in front of that mic."

Good answer.

Kenna took over the conversation then. She asked how they started as a band and how often and where they traveled for gigs. She was good at asking the right kind of questions that led to interesting answers. By the time they left to play their next set, she knew something about each of their families, their favorite kinds of foods, and I was sure even if they had a pet.

"You know," Paige leaned over the table, "if you ever wanted to leave Vegas, you'd be amazing at sales."

That wasn't going to happen.

"Thanks." Kenna sipped her water. "I love my job, and I suppose you could say sales plays a part in it, actually, but there's so much more."

"I agree," I found myself saying out loud, which drew her attention to me. I saw her eyes light up at my words.

The music started, and we all went quiet.

"*Summertime* by Louis Armstrong," Kenna breathed and put a hand to her chest. "This is one of my favorites."

"Dance with me, Leo." Paige pulled Leo out of his seat, and I heard him laugh as they moved to the dance floor. A few other people swayed to the rich, slow music. The lighting was low, and the dance floor looked dark and seedy. I rather enjoyed the vibe.

It wasn't often I felt comfortable in public, but given how small the place was, and that it had few if any windows, and the fact that my brother had my back, I figured what's one dance? Besides, it gave me a reason to touch Kenna.

I stood and reached out to her. She looked surprised then studied me for a second before she slid her hand into mine and joined me on the dance floor. I pulled her into me. She kept a little space between us, so I honored it. We were, after all, in public, had a stage-five stalker on our heels, and we weren't a couple.

I slid my hands around her hips and let them settle low on her back.

"When did you contact them?" I glanced at the band.

"This morning," she whispered for only me to hear. "Their manager got back to me right away, and we met for coffee."

"Is that why you didn't take my call?"

"Part of the reason, yes."

"And the other?"

"Your texts had a tone to them I didn't appreciate." She raised an eyebrow. "I'm kidding." She smirked. "I was working out the contract with Knox, which is like trying to get a bunch of chickens to all look one way at the same time." I chuckled at her example; it was spot on. "I have a really good feeling about these guys, Grim. I think they offer more than just music. I think they bring heart and soul to the stage."

"Okay, I agree." I found myself trusting Kenna's gut and felt confident in the deal. "I'll get Knox to complete the contract."

"No need." She grinned and leaned her head to one side. "He did come through for me, and I already got it to their manager in time for her to go over it with them. It just comes down to you. If you offer it to them, you've got the Cajun Cat at your restaurant for four days a week."

I shook my head and studied her excited expression. "My mother was right about you."

"What did she say?"

"That you're not only beautiful but a force to be reckoned with."

"Your mother is a very wise woman." She laughed lightly.

"So are you." I slowly pulled her in closer, and she allowed it. I pressed my cheek to the top of her head, and our bodies swayed to the slow beat. I moved my hands over her silky back and breathed in her scent to lock it in the memory. Every breath I took awoke parts of me I kept tightly locked away from others. I wasn't an easy man to be with, nor did I care to be with a woman for any length of time. I wasn't a jealous man, but as time unfolded, I found myself staking my claim over her. I relaxed and let myself sink into the moment.

As quickly as I let my walls down, I felt them built right back up. What was I thinking? I needed to keep a layer of protection. I never wanted to allow myself to be vulnerable to anyone, let alone a woman. I needed…

As if she sensed a change in me, Kenna looked up and something flickered across her face as we tried to read each other's thoughts. Then she stretched up and I leaned down, and our lips touched gently. The lust and urgency we typically felt, the need to tear one another apart, seemed to take a step back and let another emotion take the spotlight. We'd kissed like that only once before, and it had scared the shit out of me. But I couldn't stop; I had lost control of my brain.

Her hand moved into my hair, and every nerve ending tingled with electricity. I pressed her closer to me as we held the kiss and the tempo. It was a heady experience.

It wasn't until I tuned back in to the song that I noticed the band had extended it a few extra chords for us. Kate gave me a smile as the last note of the sax played out slowly. I pulled back from Kenna and looked down at her.

"Grim," Kenna whispered, her eyes were glossy, "I think I might…"

"Grim." Jesse cut her off and was suddenly at my side in my ear. I gave a nod and waved to Leo to get ready to go.

"Go offer them the contract." I released Kenna and gave her a little push toward the band.

"Okay." She hesitated for a moment and seemed to gather herself, then hurried off to speak to them.

"What's going on, Jesse?"

"Jason lost sight of Sonny. I think it's best we head back."

"Yeah, okay." I quickly joined Kenna and expressed to the band that I was pleased it wasn't going to be the last time we would hear their music and that I'd be waiting on the contract. I handed them my business card and whisked Kenna away.

SEVENTEEN

KENNA

Minnie: Did you tell Grim that Tony
was asking about you?

Kenna: Yeah, we're back at the
hotel now.

I glanced at Grim where he was speaking to Jesse and his team. We'd all decided to meet in Grim's suite. I knew he wasn't happy Paige had come along, but she was Leo's guest, after all. She seemed to be more focused on how nice his view was, and his mini bar and the Sonny thing didn't appear to faze her.

Kenna: What can you tell me
about him?

My phone buzzed and I saw she'd decided to call instead of texting me. I understood. The less that was typed out, the better.

"Tony is a wicked son of a bitch," she said when the call connected.

"Aren't they all?" I sighed and thought how it was just one more name to add to the list. "He's connected to Sonny, right?"

"He is. He's part of the crime family in Chicago. He, Sonny, and Matt go way back. It would make sense that he's here." She hesitated and added, "But not that he was asking about you."

"It's more about Grim, I think, given the way Sonny was at dinner. My thoughts are Sonny's ego's hurt, and he's enjoying screwing with Grim."

"That's my guess, too. Sonny would have had you in a body bag by now if he knew the truth." She stopped herself. "Sorry, girl, I just mean I think he'd make a move if he knew."

I caught Grim's gaze and realized he'd been watching me.

"How's the trip going? Getting your fill of Grim?" She tried to lighten the mood.

"That and then some."

"What does that mean?"

"It means," I turned away, "I don't know."

"Shit, hang on," she sputtered on the other end of the phone. "Is this an 'I don't know, and I need some

Minnie and champagne talk,' or an 'I don't know, and I need some molly and a bottle of vodka talk'? With Minnie, of course," she added.

"Both, maybe." I shrugged like she could see me. I wouldn't turn down a little ecstasy right now.

"Start from the beginning."

"That's a bit tricky."

"You're not alone?"

"That's right."

"That's what master bedrooms and balconies are for."

"All right, hang on."

I really needed some Minnie time, so I snagged Grim's coat off the chair and disappeared out onto the balcony. The cool night air felt good, and his scent engulfed me as I wrapped it around myself. My body tingled as it hit my brain.

"All right, where to begin?"

She helped me start. "What's throwing you off? Is he being extra pricky?"

"No, I think he's actually starting to see why his dad hired me. What I'm capable of. He gave me like three compliments since this trip started."

"God, he's such a dick," she deadpanned, dripping with sarcasm.

"See, that's the thing. Grim and I run on the fact that we can't stand one another, but now he's showing me this side of him that I-I..." I couldn't bring myself to say what I felt.

"Is the sex still good?"

"If possible, it's better."

"So, the sex is like a porno, but you're getting a better version of Grim?"

"Yes."

"Kenna, I know we are two seriously jacked up individuals, but isn't that a good thing?"

"Yeah, I mean, I guess." I rubbed my head as I was flooded with conflicting emotions.

"What am I not getting, babe?"

"I'm starting to care," I blurted and covered my mouth like I couldn't believe what I'd just admitted. She went quiet. "I don't want to. I'm not ready to care about someone like that again, and fuck knows Grim doesn't feel the same way." I just let my mouth run. "I'm scared, I'm losing control, and right now I need to be stronger than ever with everything that's going on in my life. Like tonight at dinner, Sonny Conti showed up! That's insane and so fucking scary that I would've run if Grim hadn't been there. My brain just shifts into this place where-where—"

"Where?"

"Where I used to go when those men first arrived at our house. It's like this shutdown thing I do to protect myself, only now I'm an adult doing reckless things that get me deeper and deeper into trouble."

"Kenna, take a breath, hun."

"Then there's Grim. We had this moment on the dance floor tonight where he kissed me and it was like all that panic and grit that lines the inside of me, it just dissipated." My fingers went to my lips. "I don't like all that romance shit, but when Grim held me and we kissed, I felt so…free."

"Damn, girl," Minnie hissed, "sounds to me like you're falling in—"

"I will shoot off your vagina and wear it as a bow if you even think of uttering the L word."

"My vajayjay *would* make an excellent head piece," she cooed in agreement. "So, do you want the Disney answer or the bare snatch, I mean facts?"

"Bare snatch." I hated to be coddled.

"You're a badass chick who's handled herself like a biker's bitch for years." Minnie's tone was serious, and I appreciated the pep talk. "I don't need to list the shit you've got in your life; you know all that. I will point out this, though. You've been dealt a shitty love life. You were played with by fucking Sasha when you were barely out of a training bra, God don't rest his fucking soul." She snickered and took a deep breath. "Then you're cheated on by two men, Raymond, who's a complete tit, then Dale, and I know you still care for him. We all love Dale, but personally, I wouldn't toss him a wrinkled old foreskin to pull him out of the water to save his life." I chuckled. "So that brings us to

Grim Gates, a ruthless, dominating, alpha male, who's used to having everyone do what he says. And, girlfriend, you don't fit that mold."

"Nope."

"But he's also a great friend to all of us and has a big heart behind all that ink. Who knows? Maybe he's letting you in because he likes you too."

"Christ, I feel like I'm in high school." I dropped my head. "Why can't things get clearer as we get older?"

"Because we like the darker side of sex, and that shit doesn't come with clear windows. It's all tinted stuff."

"Yeah." I felt something in Grim's breast pocket and found a joint. Trigger and Grim seemed to have an endless supply of the stuff. *What the hell?* I lit the tip and sucked in the sweet drug and let it swim around in my head. "Thanks, Min. I needed this."

"Tits and ass."

"'Til under the grass." I chuckled and ended the call. "Shit." I huffed a cloud of smoke out as I tried to shed everything we talked about.

A pair of tattooed hands slid over the railing on both sides of me, and I turned to meet a set of gold eyes. I wondered how long he had been listening. Hopefully, not long.

He eyed his jacket, then the joint between my fingers.

"Everything okay?"

"Something like that." I had trouble looking him in the eyes. "What about you?"

"Something like that." He used my own words as he took my hand and pressed his warm lips to my fingers to take a hit off the joint. It was purely sexual; he'd done it before. He seemed to like finding ways to touch me.

"Did everyone leave?"

"Everyone but Jesse." Of course, Jesse never seemed to be far from Grim.

"I guess I should go, too." I handed him the joint and walked back inside. I took off his jacket, but when I went to place it on the back of the chair, he put his hands on my shoulders.

"You started to say something on the dance floor before Jesse came over."

"I..." I felt my confidence dip. "I don't remember."

"That doesn't seem like you, to forget something."

"First time for everything." I shrugged away and handed him his jacket.

"Why do I feel like you're lying to me?"

"Because you're not getting your way." I stepped back. "I think it was just something to do with the band."

"See, you're lying." He followed me to the door then slid his hand around my neck and tipped my head back, so I looked up at him. "Your mouth lies, but your eyes tell me something's bothering you."

"Sonny showing up tonight rattled me." His face softened, and he nodded like he understood. "Sometimes it gets to be a lot," I confessed, and he rubbed his thumb over my bottom lip. "Goodnight, Grim."

He leaned down and gently kissed me in that soft way we'd shared earlier. "You know where I am." His expression confused me. Then he stepped back. "Goodnight, Kenna."

***

This was the make-or-break dinner. I chose to wear red to empower myself and because I read Chef Trahan's mother loved that color. I needed to pull out the big guns, and I came prepared. I shopped all afternoon with Paige, and we beat the guys to the restaurant.

"This place looks swanky." Paige looked around as we were seated at a gorgeous table. "I've never been here before. Call me crazy, but why aren't we eating at the August? Isn't that where Chef Trahan works?"

"Yes, but he's not going to discuss an offer to work as a chef in someone else's place while sitting in his current place of employment. That just wouldn't happen and would be very unprofessional."

"That's true." She admired my dress. "You look amazing."

"Thank you." I caught my reflection in a mirror. My deep red dress dipped low in the front and low in the back. It was classy but sexy with some beadwork on the bust. I wore my usual 'going out' hair that fell in long, soft curls. I'd made sure my makeup was more dramatic to fit the feel for the place.

My chest tightened for a second when I saw Jason, the security guard Grim had sent with us, suddenly look toward the door. I thought he'd spotted Sonny. I followed his line of sight, and to my relief, it was Leo and Grim. Paige and I stood to greet them, and I had to smile when I saw they were dressed almost like twins. Fine tailored suits, with similar gray ties over light-colored shirts. Even their slicked back hair was the same. If Grim wasn't tattooed and more muscular, you'd have to do a double take at who was who. They both looked sexy, and more than one head turned as they made their way toward us. We both stood to greet them.

"Evening." Grim leaned in and kissed my neck. "If that dress was designed to attract my attention, it's working." He dragged his gaze up my body, and I smirked. I enjoyed the heat from his hand on my lower back as he helped me into my chair.

"You look hot yourself. You both do." I nodded toward Leo. He waited until I was seated then settled in next to me. "Chef Trahan should arrive any moment now with his guests."

"So, did we plan this?" Paige waved her hand from Leo to Grim to indicate their outfits. I swallowed back any more last-minute comments about the dinner as Grim caught my eye. I could see his patience with her was growing thin.

"Great minds, I suppose," Grim replied. "In fairness, my brother and I both love Brioni." He pulled at the lapel. "I brought him up right." He smiled at his brother; Leo grinned back at him. He adored Grim maybe more than he did their father, and that was saying something.

"Ha! We just both have good taste. You had nothing to do with it." Leo laughed, and the rest joined in. As we laughed, Grim looked at me in a way that brought a small blush to my face. A warm prickle of something went through my chest.

Jesse stood a few feet away and caught our attention. He signaled our company had arrived.

"Is everyone ready?" I asked as I shifted my head back to work mode.

"It's like you're going into battle." Paige giggled, and I shot her a look that now wasn't the time to play around. This was important to all of us, especially Grim.

Chef Trahan arrived with four men, as well as his latest girlfriend, who clung to his arm. I had done some research on her and knew she was merely the latest in a string of women for him. She'd have very little influence on any decision he'd make. However, the fourth man was a mystery. I was caught off guard for a moment. I quickly searched my memory for his face on social media, but he didn't seem familiar. I caught myself and readjusted my mind quickly; this was where I shined. I would just have to work extra hard to figure him out.

"Mr. Gates, it's a pleasure to meet you." Chef Trahan shook Grim's hand as he stood. "This is my girlfriend, Fleur."

"Mr. Gates, I see the rumors are true," she breathed in her deep southern accent. She flipped her long, dark hair and batted her lashes at Grim. The way she blocked my view with her shoulder told me she was a pro. "You do take the breath away at first glance," she drawled. Yup, didn't take a lot to figure the girl could sniff out money a mile away.

Note number one, Grim can be a distraction for Fleur.

"Need to keep the ladies on their toes." Grim winked, and I thought Fleur just got pregnant. I grinned at my thought, and Grim glanced at me. "Fleur, this is Kenna Lodge. She's a host at my hotel."

"A host?" She turned to look me up and down. "As in at a little restaurant host?"

Okay, I see your game. Act all innocent, but rude enough to keep the attention on you. I was fine with that; I'd been up against a lot worse than this little money hungry girl.

"No," I chuckled politely, "I work closely with the high rollers in the casino and make sure everyone's stay is as pleasant as can be."

"So why on Earth are you here?" She made an overly dramatic face at her friends. "We're not high rollers."

"She's here," Grim stepped in, "because Kenna will ensure Chef Trahan gets whatever he needs, should he decide to accept our offer."

"Seems like that's something you all would do." She turned away from me and eyed Grim.

"Now, now, Fleur. Don't you go worrying about Miss Kenna here. She's all right." Chef Trahan patted her hand and urged her into a chair next to him.

Isn't she pleasant.

Introductions were made as the others found their way to their chairs. Conrad Leopold was our mystery guest, and the moment the waiters swooped in to take our drink orders, I took the opportunity to do a quick Google search.

Trahan and Grim talked quietly, and I heard him thank Grim for the opportunity. The two men seemed to hit it off.

"Kenna, how did you enjoy the food last night?" Trahan asked me once the drinks arrived. Seems the staff must have told him we had dined there.

"It was lovely." I sipped my wine and took a moment to think. "As someone who hasn't spent much time here, I appreciated the descriptions on the menu." He nodded. "The presentation of each dish was wonderful, but the flavors," I put my fingers to my lips, "simply delicious. The way the sauce complimented the scallops was divine, and there was just the right amount of heat from the rice and sweet from the peppers. It was like a symphony to my palate."

"Could you say that in a Yelp review?" Peter joked, and the table chuckled.

"Already submitted." I was one step ahead of them. It was one thing to tell them what I thought, but it was another to back it up.

"Seriously?" Brent pulled out his phone, and I glanced at Leo, who grinned ear to ear. "Well, shit, she did it."

"Brent," Trahan scowled at his choice of words, but he smiled at his friend all the same.

"I sure as shit did." That granted me a belly laugh from Trahan and an approving look from his buddy, Brent. Okay, I was making a little progress.

"Thank you, Kenna. That's quite a compliment." Trahan patted his chest.

"It was quite the experience." I tipped my glass at him.

On cue, Leo set his still open phone on the table. It displayed the home screen of him on Mammoth Mountain. Of course, Doug, who was conveniently next to him, glanced down at the screen.

"Is that Mammoth?"

"It is. Ever been?"

"Yes," Doug's eyes widened with excitement, "I have a cabin up there."

And off they went.

Grim's hand slid over my leg and gave it a quick squeeze. I was pleased he was happy.

"Grim, I do have to ask." Trahan cleared his throat. "I heard a rumor that your hotel's been targeted by the Cartel. Is that something I need to be concerned about? I understand there was a fire, and your hotel was set back a few weeks from its grand opening."

"No need to worry about rumors, Trahan. You don't get to where I am today without pissing off a few people along the way, mind you." Grim was cool as could be. "Rumors have a way of gaining drama as they spread. What's more entertaining, that there was a backlog in the delivery of a product, or that the Mexican Cartel sent men to delay my hotel opening?"

God, he was good.

"So, it wasn't the Cartel?" Brent questioned.

"Depends on how exciting a story you want." Grim winked.

I loved it. He wasn't confirming or denying the truth.

"Could we have a bottle of Old Rip Van Winkle after dinner, please?" Grim ordered as a waiter leaned in. Peter tuned right in.

"It's his favorite." I rolled my eyes like Grim ordered that expensive bottle all the time.

"I should've known you'd be a bourbon fan." Peter rolled up his sleeve and showed off an impressive ink drawing of a decanter. "This is my own brand. I developed it two years ago."

"You got a card? I'm working with my salesmen next week, and I'd like to give it a try." Grim put the offered card in his wallet. I'd already sent that information to Grim before the trip, and it was in the works to get a few cases.

"I know you'll like it." He sounded confident. "Any of that ink from Mexico?"

Two hooks were now set. Moving on.

Brent and Conrad were quiet and talked among themselves. They drew Trahan in whenever they could. The girlfriend was obviously not a fan of mine and had refused to make eye contact through the meal. I didn't want to make a mistake and underestimate her.

I could try to win her over, or focus on Brent and Conrad, or I could just focus on Trahan, but something told me Fleur had more of a hold on Trahan than I'd given her credit for.

I nodded at Jesse to make a play at Brent. I found out that Brent had a love of martial arts. I'd given Jesse a watch I'd borrowed from our bartender, Charlie. He had been in a tournament once. It was a weaker play, but I needed to separate Conrad and Brent in order to gain access to Conrad.

Jesse, who had stayed a few feet away through the dinner, but always in earshot of our conversation, moved in and pretended to whisper something to Leo. He made sure to flash the watch where Brent would catch it.

"Nice watch." Brent eyed it briefly, but it gave me a chance to get Conrad's attention. I had nothing, so it had to be just me.

"Have you lived here your whole life?" I asked as I stabbed a tomato with my fork.

"Nope, born and raised in a military family. Moved around more times than I can remember. You?"

"Grew up in Los Angeles, later moved to Las Vegas."

"Do you like it, the fast-paced city life?"

"I do. I'm someone who goes in forty directions at once, and I couldn't imagine anything else."

"Sounds intense. Must not leave much room for dating."

"It doesn't," I sipped my wine "but I'm fine with that. I really love what I do, and that alone is fulfilling."

"Until it isn't." He shrugged.

"And when that day comes, I'll cross that bridge." I noticed that Fleur had turned away slightly to talk with Paige. I figured she didn't see her as a threat.

The rest of the dinner flowed nicely. I kept Conrad in conversation and pulled in the others when I could. My goal was to show them who we were to lower their defenses. The more I could find things in common, the more they'd feel comfortable.

By the time our dessert arrived, Trahan looked relaxed and there was lots of chatter around the table.

Over the bourbon and after-dinner drinks, Trahan finally turned to Grim and sat back to do business.

"I've looked over your contract, Mr. Gates," he addressed Grim. "I appreciate your meeting my requests and the opportunity does sound like once in a lifetime."

"So, what's holding you back?" Grim kept his eyes on Trahan.

"I'll admit Vegas makes me nervous. My life is here in the south. The thought of such a huge change makes me apprehensive, but I have to admit it's also very appealing. Appealing enough to accept."

"What!" Fleur shouted before Grim could react. "I didn't think you were serious about this, let alone ready to sign, Tratra! How could you do this to me?" Fleur's eyes positively radiated fury. "What am I supposed to do?"

"Now, Fleur, calm down," Chef Trahan begged as Fleur sprang up and knocked over her wine glass.

"You're a bastard. You're all bastards!"

"It'll be all right, Fleur." Leo stood and tried to calm her. "I'm sure you and Chef Trahan will work this out."

"Work it out!" She slapped Leo's hand away and got in his face. "You and your brother think you can come out here and take him away, just like that." She snapped her fingers. "Well, I beg your pardon. No one asked me if I wanted to move. You'll regret this, all of you." She practically ran from the restaurant, and we all went silent. I caught Peter's shrug at Brent like, *oh well.* Clearly, she hadn't been part of the plan to come along.

"Well, wasn't that just something!" Paige went to say more, but Leo put a hand on her arm to stop any further comment.

"I apologize for the theatrics, ladies and gentlemen." Chef Trahan held up his hands. "Southern belles are known for...livin' and lovin' hard. I'll smooth things out with the little lady shortly."

"Well, I for one, am very pleased you're going to join us, Chef." Grim held up his glass, and we all drank.

"We'll do our best to make you feel at home, Chef," Leo added.

"Thanks to Kenna, I'm partway there."

"What do you mean?" Grim looked at me, confused.

"You signed Cajun Cat last night, right?"

"Yes."

"Well, Kate's my cousin. You didn't know that?"

"No," Grim looked at Leo then at me in shock, "I had no idea."

"Well, thanks for giving them a chance. It means the world to me, and it also made this decision a lot easier." He pulled out his contract and signed the last two pages with a flourish.

Grim grinned at me and shook his head like he couldn't believe it.

The cork flew in the air, and champagne bubbled over the top as Charlie poured us a glass each.

"Congratulations!" Leo called as we clicked our glasses together. We had all returned to the hotel and decided to continue to celebrate at the bar.

"Shit, sorry, man." A fellow jostled Grim's arm as he tried to get the bartender's attention. I recognized him from the bachelor party the previous night. "I haven't got my sea legs"

"That's all right." Grim moved back slightly. The fellow reeked of beer. Then he spotted me.

"Wowza."

"How about we get a table?" I asked as Grim wrapped an arm around my shoulders. I rather liked this new side of Grim. I felt wanted and protected.

"Yes." Paige hobbled over to the closest empty

table. "These new shoes felt great in the store." That her feet killed her was obvious, poor girl.

"They are beautiful," I complimented. "What we girls do to look great."

"Yeah, but ouch." She laughed and kicked them off. The guys relaxed as well. They loosened their ties and laid their jackets over a spare chair.

"It certainly was a successful night." Grim reached for his glass.

"I have to ask." Leo turned in his seat to see me better. "How could you not tell us who Cajun Cat was?"

I sighed, feeling really good inside for the first time in a long time. "I wanted you guys to like them for them, not because of how they could help sweeten the deal. At the end of the day, everything's done in the best interest of the hotel, right? Cajun Cat are good, authentic New Orleans talent. They deserved to be chosen for how well they played."

"Pfff." Grim grinned. "You're a smart girl, Kenna. No one could fault you on your research."

"Remember that the next time you come at me, Mr. Gates." I smirked, but it quickly faded when a gorgeous woman walked up to our table. The way she rested her hand on her slight bump, it was obvious to me she was pregnant.

"Grim?" His name from her lips made me go still.

"Talya?" He was suddenly on high alert. "What the hell are you doing here?"

"Could we talk?" She looked around at all of us. "Alone."

Everything inside of me went cold. Suddenly, Leo looked at Jesse, who broke out in a nervous chuckle. Jesse never broke character.

"Oh, shit."

"Ahh," Leo joined him in his internal freak out, "Kenna, this is Talya, Grim's, ahh, friend from Mexico. They lived together for some time."

"Leo." Grim cut his rambling words, which sent a jolt through me.

All the air shot from my lungs as words Brick said in the desert found their way back to me. *He lived in Mexico for a decade with a gorgeous woman.*

"Grim." Her tone was all business now, as I sat unmoving and watched his colorless face.

"Well, all right, then," Leo playfully pushed to his feet, "but I'm taking the gin." He snagged the bottle. "You comin', Paige?"

"It's your last night. Sure, count me in." She snagged her shoes and walked in her bare feet after him. She waved and called a goodbye to me as I hopped up and gathered my purse.

"Jesse, make sure Kenna gets to her room," Grim ordered with a quick glance at me.

"I think I can manage, thank you." I forced at smile

to Talya. "Have a nice night."

"*Gracias.*" She looked away.

Once inside the elevator, Jesse's fingers tapped against his leg like he was freaking out inside.

I took pity on him. "Don't worry, Jesse. I won't dig for answers." The door opened as we reached my floor, and I pulled out my keycard and stopped him from following. "Jason's wondering what's up. You should go explain things to him. Something tells me he needs you more than I do."

He stepped back inside, but as the doors started to close, he stopped them.

"I honestly have no idea what's happening right now," his worry was evident, "but for what it's worth, I've always been on team Kenna."

"Thanks, Jesse."

He stood and held the elevator doors open until I went inside my suite. I heard the clank as they closed. How the night had changed. I moved like a zombie to the couch and dropped my purse at my feet. I leaned over and pulled out my phone and dialed my person. I needed her more than anything, in the state I was in.

"Is this episode two of *Kenna and Grim's One Snatch to Live*?" Minnie chuckled, and I forced all emotion from my voice.

"Min, who is this Talya girl from Mexico?"

"Whaa…?" There was a second of silence. "Shit, okay. Ummm. She's the chick he lived with for like ten years when he was there. There's a story there, but I don't know the details. I think there might have even been a third person involved in it all. Anyway, there was something at some point, but I don't think it was for too long. I should really dig more." She'd begun to ramble, which made me panic. I heard a door close on her end. "Okay," she took a breath, "why do you ask?"

"Because she just showed up here, looking for Grim. Oh, and plot twist, she's pregnant." Silence. "Minnie?"

"Fuck."

EIGHTEEN

GRIM

"I'm sorry to interrupt your evening, Grim." Talya stared across the table at me. I hadn't seen her since I moved back from Mexico. "But we do need to talk."

"So you've said."

"Breathe, Grim."

"Not until you tell me how you found me here."

"I have my ways, Grim." At my expression, she made a face. "Oh, for God's sake, I phoned Jim."

"Forgive me, but you're the last person on Earth I thought would show up here like that." I nodded at her belly.

"Relax," she rolled her eyes, "it's not yours."

"Clearly." I waved at her to take a seat. "We'd have

to had sex for it to be mine." Talya had been in love with someone else, but her parents would never have allowed it. When I arrived in Mexico years back, they wanted us to hook up. They were determined she'd marry a man with wealth. Over time, we'd become good friends, and we made a deal to pretend to date to keep her parents happy. It worked for me because it allowed me to develop a relationship with her family. They were big in the local drug trade.

"We'd have made gorgeous babies." She shrugged.

"Perhaps in another lifetime." I was fond of Talya but had no interest in being pulled into her world.

"I could use a new lifetime." She caught a tear with the back of her finger. "Look, Grim, things aren't good right now. As you know, my parents planned to move their business farther into Rosarito. Things took a bad turn when you left Mexico."

"So I heard."

"After Castillo died, it became a war. Any chance your army friends want a round two?"

"They weren't friends of mine," I explained, "just acquaintances." Trigger had let Talya know about the plan to take out Castillo. He knew she held no loyalty to her parents, but she was loyal to her people. He didn't want to risk her being in the line of fire when the hit on Castillo and his crew went down. Though she was ruthless in her own right, and not someone you'd want to bring to a family dinner, she had a heart.

"Regardless," she handed me a piece of paper, "your 'acquaintances' may want to check this out the next time they use their satellites, nanny cams, or whatever they use now to know when and where we'll be." If she only knew just how closely they all were being watched. "It's time for my generation to step in and take the helm."

"I can pass it along." I tucked the paper in my pocket.

"Grim, Papa got a call from a man a few days after you left," she said in Spanish as some people walked by. We both knew what it could mean if anyone overheard us. The cartels' reach was wider than anyone could imagine.

"From who?"

"I don't know," she leaned forward, "but this man also has a problem with you. He offered a way for Papa to cause you great hardship."

"Which was?"

"Your hotel." She watched my face as that sank in. "The man said there were people looking for work, and they would be more than happy to do the job. I guess they are messing about with your workers."

"I see." I tried to curb my temper. "Well, that's already been dealt with, so…"

"Grim," she squinted at me, "open your eyes. The word is out that you're the mark. Vegas is the prize, and that pretty young thing upstairs, she's just as connected to all of this as you are because of your family and your mutual biker friends. Someone wants to control Vegas and is determined to take you and everyone you love down. You're tangled in a web, Grim, and the spider is heading your way."

"Why me? Us?"

"Because you control the drugs, you have the most wealth, you've teamed up with the bikers and the Italian mafia, and you're a powerful man many want to see fall. Then they will swarm in and take the spoils."

She studied me as I digested her words.

"What's your father's next move?"

"That, I'm not sure," she tapped her fingers as she thought, "but whoever it was that called him sounded like he was going to see this through to the end."

"Did he have an accent?"

"To me or to you?" She smirked. "He sounded like you."

Fuck, that narrows it down.

"Grim, on a whole other subject." She suddenly looked unsure. "Do you know where Eric is?" She rubbed her belly.

"Is Eric the father?"

She paused as though she wanted to control her emotions then nodded.

Oh, fuck.

"It's the only reason I'm keeping it," she admitted. My chest tightened. I felt grief. This would not go well for either of them. "Do you know where he is?" she asked again.

"No," I lied, and I knew she caught it. She nodded a few times as she processed why I would lie. *Fuck.* I didn't like the position I was in. "Talya, did Eric ever say anything to you? Anything to explain where he went?"

"No. But I know Eric loved me."

"He does," I corrected. I didn't know the real Eric, but I knew the day I saw him with all his Blackstone army friends that he loved her.

"Something tells me that he won't be coming back anytime soon."

"Not in the way you'd think." I should shut my mouth. I'd already crossed a line.

"Okay." She took a deep breath.

"What do your parents think?"

"They don't know." More tears fell. "I left when I started to show." She rubbed her belly again, clearly in love with the part that was Eric. "Their only daughter pregnant by a man who worked for Castillo?" She forced a dark laugh. "I just need some time to figure this out."

"If I ever could find Eric," I cleared my throat, "would you like me to pass along anything?"

"No." She shut me down flat. "I need to think. Maybe sometime. I'll let you know." She stood, and I joined her. She hesitated for a moment then leaned over and hugged me. "Be careful. There is a lot of darkness around you right now, and I'm scared you can't see it all."

"Thanks, Talya. You know I care for you. Look after yourself and…" I nodded at her belly.

"Yes. But, Grim," she pulled back and stared up at me with such concern that I almost reached out for her, "please keep my baby a secret until you hear from me. I've already put a target on my back talking to you, let alone having Eric's baby."

"I will." I intended to keep that promise; my loyalty was with Talya, not Eric.

"I'm going to my cousin's place in Mexico City." She pulled out an envelope with Eric's name written on it and handed it to me. "*Por favor*, when you hear from me, get this to him."

"Okay."

"We never spoke, and I was never here." She turned on her heel and left without a backward glance.

I caught Jesse's worried expression as he approached me. "Well, that was unexpected."

"Her father Jerry was behind my hotel shit," I grunted and pulled my jacket off the chair and shoved my arm in the sleeve. It was too tight. Leo must have my jacket. "The fucker still made a play after all I'd done for him over there." We moved through the bar and into the already open elevator. Two women giggled at us, and from the smell of them they'd been out at the bars. I hit our floor number and glanced at Jesse. "I think it's time we sent him a message."

"I think so."

"We've been warned countless times about," a giggle from behind us reminded me we weren't alone, "how we're a mark. I think it's time we send them all a message."

"Light some shit up?" Jesse's eyes twinkled. "I'll make some calls."

"Good," I huffed, and my mind spun with the night's events. The doors opened, and the tipsy chicks stumbled out. They waved as the doors shut.

"And she's pregnant?" Jesse whispered, no doubt terrified it was mine.

"She is." I eyed him when I felt he'd held his breath long enough. "Eric Noah's the father."

"Oh, thank fuck!" His hand hit his chest, and I turned to look at him. "Sorry, boss, but you've got something much better going on with Kenna."

I had to agree but then felt my walls shoot up. "She's fun, but that's where it ends."

"Sure, boss." He chuckled as we headed down the hall. I stopped at Leo's door and went to knock but stopped myself. I heard something crash and chuckled to myself. This was our last night of vacation, Leo and Paige could use the fun.

"Leo's got a good thing going." Jesse smirked.

"Yeah, and so do I. Which room?" I asked Jason as he joined us.

"She's in yours." His face was unreadable.

Excellent.

"Call you later." Jesse waved as I slipped into the suite. I heard Jesse's door close next to mine.

The room was dark and, to my surprise, rain beat at the windows. I tossed my jacket on the bench and saw Kenna on the couch. She watched the rain as it poured down the massive windows. We rarely got to enjoy that in Vegas. Her dress hung over the dining room chair, and she was in one of my dress shirts. So, she hadn't gone to her own room yet. *Interesting.*

"Hey," I called softly. I wasn't sure if she had heard me come in.

"Oh," she swiped her cheeks quickly with her hand as she stood, "I, ah, I wanted you to know that both contracts are submitted. Your father's beyond happy with your progress, and he can't wait to celebrate when we get back." Typical Kenna, dove right into business.

"Good." I tossed my phone and keycard on the tall bar top. "Nice shirt." I eyed her nipples as they poked through the fine Italian fabric.

"I needed to change but didn't want to risk missing you before you went to bed." She came close and joined me at the bar. She leaned over and rested her arms on the marble slab. I enjoyed the way my shirt exposed the bottom of her ass. "Grim," she swallowed, "I think maybe we should end the physical part of us."

I felt a flash of anger at the thought. "Is that so?"

"Yes," she tried to sound confident, "though these last few days have been great, I think maybe we should end it now. While things are good. I mean, so many things are coming at us. We need to focus on that. You know, Secrets and Chef Trahan and everything." She was all over the place. "Besides, you've got some other things to worry about now."

"Such as?"

"Grim."

"Kenna?"

"Don't be an asshole." She sighed loudly, and I stepped closer. "If the baby is yours, I don't want to get in that way of that."

"It's not mine," I purred and slipped my hand under the shirt to feel the back of her smooth thigh. I was happy she wasn't wearing any panties.

"Are you sure about that?"

"Quite." I tugged her against me.

"Not to point out the obvious, but since we've been having sex, you haven't worn a condom. I told you I took protection and we both know we're clean, but was she? Protected, I mean. How can you be so sure?"

"First," I swatted her ass hard enough to make her head stop spinning with nonsense, "you're the only woman I haven't used a condom with in a very long time. And second," I sat her up on the bar and moved between her legs, "Talya and I never had sex. She's in love with the guy who got her pregnant."

"Really?" She bit her bottom lip, and I leaned in and kissed her neck.

"Really." I drew in her skin to mark my spot. Everything inside of me hardened, and my head went light with her taste. I quickly undid the few buttons that blocked her bare skin from me.

"Grim, why don't you wear a condom with me?"

"I want to feel all of you." I knew she'd said something, but I didn't hear her, I had a one-track mind—to be in this woman. I grabbed her breast and caught her nipple with my lips as I used my free hand to ditch my pants. Her fingers tangled in my hair and pulled as she gave in to me. There was no need to prime her first. She was ready, and her body shimmered in what little light there was in the room. I lifted her hips and brought her forward and cried out as I pushed into her.

I wrapped her legs around me and carried her to the pool table where I laid her flat out in front of me. "Lose the shirt." I helped rid her of it. I lifted her legs straight up and wrapped an arm around them, giving me a different feel. I moved in and out a few times and felt a wild thrill rush through me. Her breasts bounced and her lips parted as I got as deep as I could. She was wild as she moved against me. I saw her need was as strong as mine.

"And if I was to get pregnant?" Her words barely registered as I felt my eyes roll back in my head. I swore her body sucked me in tighter at each thrust.

"I'm not going to stop fucking you, if that's what you're wondering." I was so captivated in that moment I could hardly form a word. Her face twisted and a sheen of sweat broke out over her forehead with her efforts. All I knew was I needed even more. I let go of her legs, reached back for a pillow, and pushed it under her lower back. She moaned and bucked as I went even deeper inside her. She had to reach back and hold on. I went wild at the sight of her then flipped her over to take her from behind. She clawed the felt and cried but took everything I gave her.

"Fuck, woman," I palmed her ass and increased my attack on her, "you drive me to madness."

Her sounds of delight as she finally let go drew me to a headspace I'd never achieved before, and every-thing inside me tightened then exploded in white hot light. It was pure bliss and serenity rolled into one. I wrapped my arms around her waist for an anchor as I tried to hold on to the best feeling of my life.

When I could see straight and my lungs returned to normal, I peeled off Kenna and helped her to stand, then I took her chin in my hand and looked into her exhausted eyes. Then I scooped her up and carried her to the bedroom and laid her down on the bed. I crawled in next to her and slipped back inside.

"Just when I didn't think it could get any better," she murmured in a dreamy voice, "you go and do that." She reached back and patted my hip.

"Remember that when you're talking shit about ending our physical relationship." I drew her closer to me and locked her in place with an arm. I took a deep breath and filled my lungs with the scent of her shampoo. I was totally relaxed as I relished the moment of us being alone and me back inside her.

Her breathing evened out, and just when I thought she'd fallen asleep, she whispered, "It's all fun and games until one of us finds someone to fall in love with."

I stilled at her words; my insides twisted with a sudden insane jealousy. I tried to brush away the foreign feeling that invaded my body, but it didn't work.

Shit.

Kenna had woken before me, and I was pissed to find myself in an empty bed. I quickly showered, changed, and packed my suitcase after I stomped through the suite and realized she was gone. I cursed when I read the note that I found on the bar top. I'd had other plans for her.

Meet you downstairs. - Kenna

I swiped the keycard off the table and headed downstairs where she and Jesse sat with the other two security guys as they enjoyed their coffee.

"Coffee, black with a dash of sugar." Kenna handed me a cup as I joined them.

"Thanks."

She questioned my mood. "How could you possibly be grumpy, this early in the morning?"

"I wasn't finished with you yet." I didn't care who listened at that point. Jesse snorted into his mug but wisely didn't comment.

"There's always tonight." She lifted a brow.

"Nice to see you listened."

"Well," she leaned in, "you put up a good fight."

"I do love a good fight with you." I hooked her waist and smashed my lips to hers.

"Grim," she whispered when I let her go, "careful. People might get the wrong impression." "What? That we're fucking?" I chuckled but as I said it, something pinged in my chest, and I had to look away from her.

"Anyway," she brushed off my comment as she looked around, "where're Leo and Paige? She said she'd be down for coffee before we all left for the airport."

"They're probably going at it again," I huffed and glanced at my watch. I shook my head as I remembered he'd taken a bottle of champagne to his room.

"Let's go get him, Jesse." I waved for him to follow while the other two guys stayed with Kenna.

"I'm glad we're heading back," I admitted. "I'm ready for a few bouts in the ring once we're settled."

"I would've thought you'd have worked out a few kinks on this trip." Jesse grinned, and I swatted him on the back.

"I'm still a little amped up." I laughed. "I could've gone another round before coffee." I shot him a grin, feeling pleased with all the fuckery I had gotten this trip.

"Leo!" I knocked on his door. "Get your ass up. You're late!"

"I take it you smoothed things over with Kenna, then?" Jesse matched my grin as he sipped his coffee.

"When have you ever questioned my sex life?" I waited for Leo to drag his ass to the door.

"Never, but this isn't just about sex, my friend." He laughed, knowing he was getting under my skin. "I'm thinkin' it's more than that."

"Well, thanks for the heads up." I banged on the door again. "Come on, man." I pulled out his spare keycard and held it up to the screen.

"You can deflect all you want, boss," Jesse started in again as I pushed the door open, "but I've never seen you care about anyone the way you do about Kenna."

A sudden surge of adrenaline tore through me,

even as the blood from my head plummeted to my feet.

Instantly, we both pulled our weapons, and I stood frozen as Jesse swept through the suite. I locked eyes with my brother. But Leo's stare was lifeless.

"Clear." Jesse's voice sounded miles away.

"No." My arm fell as my weapon suddenly became too heavy to hold. I dropped to my knees near my brother and tried to make sense of what I was seeing.

"What the fuck?" Jesse was at my side.

Leo lay on the floor in the center of what looked like the middle of a compass, legs in positions that were inhuman. He looked like he'd been stripped bare and draped in white linen. A bundle of sage smoked beside him, and animal bones and bowls of chicken feet and hair defined the circle. A knife protruded from his chest.

"What the fuck?" Jesse repeated in disbelief.

The blade was buried in the center of my brother's heart.

"It's like some kind of crazy voodoo ritual," Jesse whispered.

My brother was an offering to the gods; my brother was a sacrifice.

My body slowly shut down. Inside my brain, I felt the doors slam shut one by one. Pain flooded my head. Then I felt myself harden as I knelt and studied my little brother. There was no time to mourn.

"Oh, God!" Kenna's cry registered with me as she came into the room, "Grim?" She covered her mouth as she stepped into my line of vision. I could barely look at her; I was rooted in space. "Leo." She swallowed back a sob as Jesse went to her. "Who could do this? Why?"

"Jesse," I ordered. He turned her away, but she pushed past him and made a strange sound. I tilted my head and studied her as she bent over to look more closely at Leo.

"Don't touch anything!" Jesse grabbed her arm.

"Wait," she blurted but pulled her hand back. She seemed to focus on Jesse's arm. "Oh, my God." Kenna's horrified expression made me wonder what she saw that I didn't. I looked at the scribble of lines without emotion.

"What?" Jesse glanced at me then back at her.

"I think I know that symbol," she whispered and pulled out her phone to snap the morbid photo.

Anger rushed through my blood and filled the emptiness that had taken hold inside me. The possibility she could possibly know anything about what had happened in this God forsaken hellhole burned.

"How could you know anything?" My voice boomed through the room, and she jumped.

"I," she stumbled as tears flowed down her cheeks, "I might be wrong, but—"

"Jesse, get her the fuck out of here. Get her to the airport. Send her home." I couldn't breathe.

"Grim," Jesse said softly, and I glared at him and warned him to tread carefully, not to say anything other than *yes, boss.* "What about the situation back home? Should she go back alone?"

Fuck.

"Give her two men." I turned my back to them.

"Go with Jason, Kenna." I heard her crying softly as Jesse spoke to Jason, then he came back inside.

"Grim," Jesse's voice made me focus for a moment. He put a hand on my shoulder. "Paige." I turned and looked where he pointed toward the window. She lay naked, half-buried in a pile of clothes on the floor. I spotted my jacket next to her.

Jesse was on the phone then. As he made a few calls, I tried hard to pull myself together. I needed to take action; I knew things needed to be done.

Something stuck out from the breast pocket, and I forced myself up off the floor and walked toward it. I removed a handkerchief from my pocket and picked it up. The *Hanged Man* tarot card. *What the hell?* A memory from the night before rushed back. The man who bumped into me at the bar. I flipped it over and saw a signature on the back as Jesse came to my side.

"Leo took my jacket last night. My God, this was meant for me, not him."

NINETEEN

KENNA

Jesse handed my bags to a flight crewman then put a hand on my shoulder and turned me toward him. "Kenna." He leaned in close, so I'd look at him.

My mind was hazy as I tried to focus on him. I wasn't new to processing death, but Leo's terrible murder was a whole different story.

"I need you to buy me two days. Your silence will help. Can you do that?"

"Yeah." I nodded numbly.

"Watch everyone, Kenna. We don't know what we're dealing with yet, but I'll have my best two guys, Jason and Lorenzo, keep a close eye on you." He pointed behind me, but I didn't look. "They'll always be there, but pretend they don't exist, don't make contact unless you have to. You may not always see them, but they'll be there. I promise. Just try to go on as normal."

My brain fought to catch up. "Wait, what about Jim and Laurel?" I instantly felt a whole new wave of pain as I thought about his parents and what they must be going through.

"They're already on the way here with Knox."

"Oh, my God, Knox," I gasped, shocked I hadn't considered him in this entire event.

"It's all been handled, Kenna. Now I just need to make sure you can do your part."

"I can." Tears leaked.

"You think you can figure out that strange symbol?"

"Yes, I didn't forget." I tried to pull myself together.

He smiled warmly, and I was in awe of how well he handled the situation. I now truly understood why Grim hired him.

"I'm worried about Grim," I couldn't help but confess.

"Me too." He opened his mouth then paused like he second-guessed his words. "For what it's worth, you're the only one I've ever seen who even got close to the real him." Then his hand left my shoulder so fast I jumped. He read a text.

"Jesse," I whispered and pulled his attention back to me, "I feel like you're telling me he's done with me."

"He's in a dark place, Kenna. The darkest I've ever seen him. I'm not sure where things will go from here. I gotta go." He turned away then stopped himself. "Two days," he reminded me. "I'll be in touch. You can do this."

Right. I climbed the steps and didn't remember a single thing after I hit the cool leather seat.

"Ma'am," a woman shook my arm and drew me out of a dead sleep, "we've landed, and your ride is here."

"Oh," I rubbed my sore neck, "thank you."

"Of course." She offered me her hand to help me up then held out my purse. "Have a good rest of your day." The concern showed on her face. I tried for a smile but didn't offer her a comment.

The moment I deboarded, Minnie raced into my arms and squeezed me hard.

"Jesse called Trigger, told us everything. I just can't believe it."

I broke as she walked me over to her car. Brick and Morgan stood next to it, and both looked at us in sympathy, but didn't say anything. I buried my face in my best friend's shoulder and sobbed my heart out as we drove.

"Let it all out," Minnie rocked me, her own voice

full of tears. "We're going back to my place, and you can talk then."

Once we were there and I had a chance to splash water on my swollen face, I pulled myself together and joined my friends. I did my best to fill them in on what I knew. It was the hardest night I'd ever had.

Trigger rubbed his face after I finished talking but showed no emotion. I knew these men had been through their own pain over the years and had a lot of practice on masking their feelings. "Jesse said something about how you might have recognized that odd drawing on Leo's arm."

"Yes, I think so."

"From where?"

Minnie threaded her hand through mine and tried her best to comfort me. I loved her for it. Tess sat on my other side. I appreciated the buffer she presented between me and her husband. Trigger was big and scary, and in that moment, his anger made him even more so.

"The night that, I—" I choked on my words and tried again. "The night of the Matt Myers mishap," I choose my words carefully, "I was followed to Secrets by one of his men, the one Grim dealt with. When he lifted his arm, I saw a tattoo on the inside of it, up here." I pointed to the spot high above my bicep. "I only picked up on it because Sasha had one kind of like it. Well, like one part of it is the same, anyway. The other part is kinda different." I tried to picture it in my head. "I don't know," I sighed and felt stupid. "Maybe it's some kind of club thing, or maybe it's from a movie like *Fight Club,* with my luck lately." I huffed.

"It's okay, Ken," Tess said. "It's a start, right?" She looked at Trigger.

"She's right." Trigger nodded. "Show me what part you remember they both had."

I used my finger and drew in edit mode on my phone to outline what I remembered.

"It was sort of like this. It's the part I remember on the guy and on Sasha." I held the sketch out to Trigger, and he sent the marked photo to his phone.

"Minnie," I sniffed, "when your guys dumped that piece of shit Myers, anyone catch any tattoos?"

"There was one that was mentioned but not like that. I'll ask again." She pulled out her phone and started to text.

Brick finally spoke up from the back of the room. "How's Grim? I mean, all things considered."

"Scary dark." I shook my head slowly and closed my eyes. "How ugly is this going to get?"

Everyone went quiet.

I stayed away from people as much as I could. I made up what I hoped was a good story for why I probably seemed off. Yen Hong sat across the table and kindly chatted about his latest venture. He filled in the silence as he sensed I needed to be still. I sat, overwhelmed with grief. Leo had been a good friend, and during our trip he'd had so much fun. His lifeless body that spoke of torture and cruelty played out in my head over and over. His beautiful soul robbed for some godforsaken reason. I tried not to think how the aftermath was nearly as chilling.

"I'm sorry, Kenna." Yen pulled my attention, and I tried to recall his last few words. "I'm sorry for whatever is bothering you so." He gave me a sad smile. "I know what you told me, but I sense it goes much deeper than that."

"It's…" I was too tired for words.

"It's okay," he leaned forward and rested his warm hand on mine for comfort, "I won't pry, but know I am here if you need anything or even if you just need a good cry. It worries me to see your eyes so dim."

"Thank you, Yen. I may take you up on that when I can."

"I hope you do." He stood. "And not to seem insensitive, but I have a meeting in ten."

"No, please go. I'm terribly sorry. I'll be fine." I smiled and watched him leave. I had to pull myself together. I had clients to deal with who were not as understanding and needed more from me. Then once again I felt the panic grow. I needed to get out of there.

I found my way to the rooftop bar, a place that had brought me such happiness just a short time before. I liked it there; not many people were able to pass security to enjoy the area. It kept it private, and I felt secure. I briefly wondered where Jesse's two guys were and glanced around. I didn't spot them.

"Another," I held up my glass, now drained of wine, as the bartender came close. "Please," I quickly added with what I hoped was a warm smile. The staff were like family, and I'd never be rude.

"Heads up, hun." He looked over my shoulder as he poured. I couldn't bear to know who was next to make my day worse.

"Please just go away," I whispered.

"I just wanted to check in on you." My father peered down at my glass of wine and ordered the same for himself.

"You noticed?" I told my filter to fuck off for the night, and so she happily left the building.

"I suppose I deserved that comment from time to time." I wrinkled my nose at him and put my glass to my lips. His voice seemed a little lighter, not his normal tone, one phone call away from a stroke. "Do you know why I'm so hard on you?"

"Please, Dad, I can't do this conversation right now." I batted back a dam of emotion. "I know it's because you see something in me that reminds you of you, and that's why you treat me like a bag of shit."

"Bag of shit?" He pulled in his chin as if hurt.

"First words that came to mind."

"I see." He nodded as he thought. "Well, you might be partially right."

"Not partially." I took a large sip of wine.

"McKenna, I'm hard on you because you can take it."

"Can I?" I stared up at him. "Because I've taken a lot up to now. As a matter of fact, Dad, I'm about ready to burst with all I've taken."

"Why is that?"

"Because—" I stopped myself and realized what I had been about to blurt. "Because I've hit my limit." I pivoted. "I lost a big client contract yesterday."

He studied my face, and his own softened. "It's not the first contract you've ever lost. It'll be okay."

"No, it's not." I wiped a tear away. "When has it ever been okay?"

"McKenna, you're human, and so am I. I'm not perfect. You know I've lost a big client before, and it nearly cost me everything."

It may not have cost him everything, but it sure as hell took years off my own life, and apparently it still was.

"Do you remember, Simba?"

"What?" His change in subject lost me.

"Simba. That albino rabbit you got when you were eight. It had big, red eyes."

"Of course I remember, Dad. I begged you for a bunny for years."

"Right, and when I heard the neighbors had a litter of babies that time, I made sure I got one for you. It was for your eighth birthday. You named him Simba." I was honestly shocked he'd even remembered that. "You forced that little bunny into dresses and bows and even got him to sit like a dog." He chuckled lightly. "I still have no idea how you did it."

"Poor thing."

"Not poor thing, because you loved him, and he knew that, and that's why he tolerated you."

"What's the point of this memory, Dad?" I didn't trust this sudden tenderness.

"My point, my sweet girl..." He raised a hand to show his intention and tenderly wiped a tear away. Who was this man? "I'm hard on you because I love you, just like you were hard on Simba because you loved him. I know I don't stop long enough to listen most days, and my temper can be an easy four." He chuckled at his number, and I let myself soften a bit. "But for what it's worth, I'm proud of the woman you've become. I knew you were destined to do great things. It was one of the reasons I wanted you here, so I could see your success grow. I didn't want to miss that."

"Really?" I wished this moment, one I'd dreamed about for half my life, wasn't laced with the agony of the past few days. Maybe there was a reason for the timing. If there was ever a time I needed something to remind me that my father still loved me, it was now. I was sure the man he once was lived on inside, even though he hurt me repeatedly. My mother had stayed married to him for a reason. She must see this side of him. She knew it was there.

"Really." He pulled me in for a hug and kissed the top of my head. "Now, are we done with the drinking?"

"I think I should get to bed."

"I agree." He pulled away and smiled from ear to ear like he was proud he'd been able to have that moment with me. "You look so much like your mother." He tucked my hair behind my shoulder. "Strong and full of life. Ah..." He stopped himself like he remembered something. "I'm off to help your mother with some things in Reno, so I'll be leaving here shortly, but remember tomorrow is a new day filled with new possibilities, my dear."

"I love you, Dad."

"I love you more."

I reached for my purse then gave him a hug. "Thank you, Dad." I turned my tired body away and headed for my suite. As I stepped through the door, I felt a small smile tug at my lips. I forgot sometimes how much I yearned to be cared for, but more importantly, loved. I knew I was surrounded by family, but a father's love was something special, and the unexpected affection from him was just what I needed.

The next day was spent on the golf course with Salazar. He filled me in on how he'd made things right with Mr. Hong. Though I was pleased to hear it, I wasn't quite sure Yen was as forgiving as Salazar was playing it off. But nonetheless, he was making an effort, and the two seemed to be cordial. It was all good.

It was day three since I'd gotten back, and a day on the golf course was a good way to clear my head. My thoughts went back to earlier in the morning. I'd had a message that there was an all-hands-on-deck upper management meeting on the twentieth floor from Jim Gates. I hadn't even known he'd come back. I had not heard a word from Grim, but I hadn't heard from Jesse either.

When I arrived, my stomach bottomed out as I took in who all was there. The entire Gates family sat at one end of the long table, and whispers from the staff about what was going on made a dull roar in my ears. Grim's expression was cold and lifeless as I slipped into my chair and hoped he'd look over. I didn't expect much from him after all that had happened, but I'd expected him to at least register me. I caught Jesse's gaze from across the room, and his expression held such sadness, it was almost like he was apologizing for Grim's behavior. Knox leaned over and whispered something to Grim, but he shook his head like he couldn't deal with whatever it was that Knox said. Grim looked over at his mother, and she nodded and gave Jim's arm a pat. Jim stood and addressed the situation in New Orleans.

Jim's emotion would have cracked even the most heartless, and I was shocked he was able to take point on the meeting, but I knew a man in his position had to ensure that every person in the room knew just how important it was that we controlled the narrative of the story. His family had to show they were still and would always be in control, no matter what was thrown at them. After his brief explanation of what had happened, he made it clear that everyone was to take a "we know nothing concrete yet" stance. You could have heard a pin drop in the room as Jim reached for his wife's arm. He gave me a quick glance before they walked out, leaving the room in heartbreak.

"Hey, Kenna." Jayden leaned toward me while the others in the room began to whisper together as they filed out. "Where's your father? This was all-hands-on deck meeting."

"LA," I whispered as I reached for my purse, "helping mom out."

"Oh." He nodded. My father's lack of presence at such a meeting would have surprised most everyone. "Seriously," he touched my arm, "are you okay? I know you and Leo were close."

"I'm really not sure what I am right now." He stood when I did. "But thanks." I was pleased we had reached a point in our working relationship where we could have such a conversation.

"You know where to find me." He patted my shoulder, and we stepped back as the Gates brothers went to exit. I tried to speak to Grim, but he brushed by me with Jesse hard on his heels. A few minutes later, I got a text.

> Jesse: Heading to LA, sorry for the lack of response from both of us.

"You know what's strange?" Salazar pulled my thoughts back to him and away from this morning's meeting. I got myself in check.

"What?" I sipped my lime water and watched him swing.

"The hotel seems off. I know the whole family are away, but there's something in the air."

"It's not often they're able to go away together. I'm sure it's nothing." I shrugged. Who was I to tell him they were back. I certainly wasn't going to get into any conversation about it at this point. He'd know soon enough. "I agree that when the owners are away, their seconds in command, so to speak, tighten things up. It wouldn't be good to have something go wrong on their watch."

"No, it's a darker vibe than that." He nailed the

feeling perfectly. "Doesn't help that Sonny Conti seems to be here full time now. I don't like the man."

"Agreed."

"What's his story, anyway?"

"New money, thinks he's God's gift to women, as you saw firsthand." I raised a brow, and he gave me an eye roll. "He loves to make Grim's life hell at every turn."

"And yet he's a client here."

"It's a long story."

"Care to share it?" He swung his club again, and I found myself reaching for my sweater. The temperature had dipped, or maybe the mention of Sonny just brought on an internal chill. I wished I knew if he'd had anything to do with Leo's death. It couldn't have been a coincidence he'd been around when it happened.

"I would rather swallow a box of tacks than discuss that man."

"Understood." He chuckled and focused on his game.

I knew my main clients couldn't miss my change in mood, and I was pleased they only fished lightly for information. Most had enough problems of their own in the lives they led. They gave up when I didn't bite, but it wouldn't go on much longer. The word would be out. I still hadn't heard anything from Grim. Only the text from Jesse that they were leaving for LA.

The evening was early when Salazar excused himself to go to his suite. I was sure it had everything to do with the drinks he'd shared with friends on the green. I was pleased because the knot in my stomach had come to the point of pain.

I had a bad feeling something was about to go down. Jesse's reassurance that his trusted security would watch things carefully wasn't cutting it anymore. A prickly sensation went up my back. I checked the time on my phone; it was seven on the dot. I spotted Jason watching me from the front desk of the lobby. *Fuck it.* I didn't care what Jesse said about not talking to them. I went over and stared at him straight in the eye.

"Hey, Jason," I stopped in front of him, and he stood straight and looked uncomfortable with my presence, "have you heard anything from Jesse or Grim?"

"No." I assumed he was lying, but it still felt good to ask.

"If you do?"

"I'll let you know."

"Thanks."

"Holy shit, McKenna Tame, as I live and breathe." A man approached with a huge smile, and Jason took that as a cue to quickly move to the other side of the lobby.

"Hi, Benny. What are you doing here?" Benny was an old friend from high school. We'd kept in touch, and in the past had enjoyed the odd night of fun just hanging out. Nothing had ever come of it. He looked great, very handsome in a new suit.

"I'm in town for the week on business. I heard you were working here…" He trailed off. "Are you okay?"

"It's been a really bad week." I huffed out a breath.

"Come to dinner with me tomorrow night. If anything, I'll make you laugh."

"I'd like that, but—" I stopped myself. "You know what? I think that's just what I need."

"Great. Here's my card. You know this place best. Pick a spot and time and text me the details."

"I will." I pushed a smile through then headed toward the elevator.

"Hi, McKenna," a familiar voice called, and I turned to see Darcy, Grim's dog walker, going through the lobby. She waved as she approached.

Leal made a squeak as he strained toward me. "Whoa." Darcy tried to pull him back.

"It's okay." I reached out and let him sniff my hand, then I slowly moved to rub the top of his gnarly head. He stilled a moment then pressed against my hand and allowed me to do it.

"Um," she cleared her throat, "that's not a good idea."

"It's okay." I gave him another little pat. His brother didn't move toward me, but I gave him a warm smile and a soft *how are ya, boy.* "We're at the growing acquaintance status, I think."

She grinned and raised her brows. "They barely let me touch them other than to put on their leads."

"They've seen me at my worst," I confessed. "I think that counted for something."

"Maybe. They don't give me any trouble, though. Do ya, fellas?" She smiled at them. "They're good pups, just not overly friendly with people."

"Huh! They are Grim's, after all," I said with dry humor.

"Have a good walk, boys." I used Grim's name for them, which I always thought was sweet, but that feeling was quickly replaced with a growing nausea that things might never go back to normal between all of us.

"See ya when I see ya," Darcy called.

I waved as they left and caught sight of Simon in conversation with a man. He looked over and smiled and began to walk toward me.

"I hope you still have all your fingers. You couldn't pay me enough to pat those dogs."

"They're pretty sweet once you get to know them."

"I'll take your word on that." He inched his glasses farther up his nose. "So, where is everyone? It's been very quiet around here."

My phone buzzed in my purse, and I fished around for it.

> Jesse: In LA, chasing a possible lead.
> Hope to be back by the day after
> tomorrow. Sorry about today. He's
> hard to get through to right now. I'll
> be in touch.

"Sorry, Simon," I indicated my phone, "I have to go."

"Oh, of course." He stepped back. "Well, it's nice to have you back."

I barely heard him as I typed my reply.

> Kenna: Understood. If you can just let
> him know I'm thinking of him.

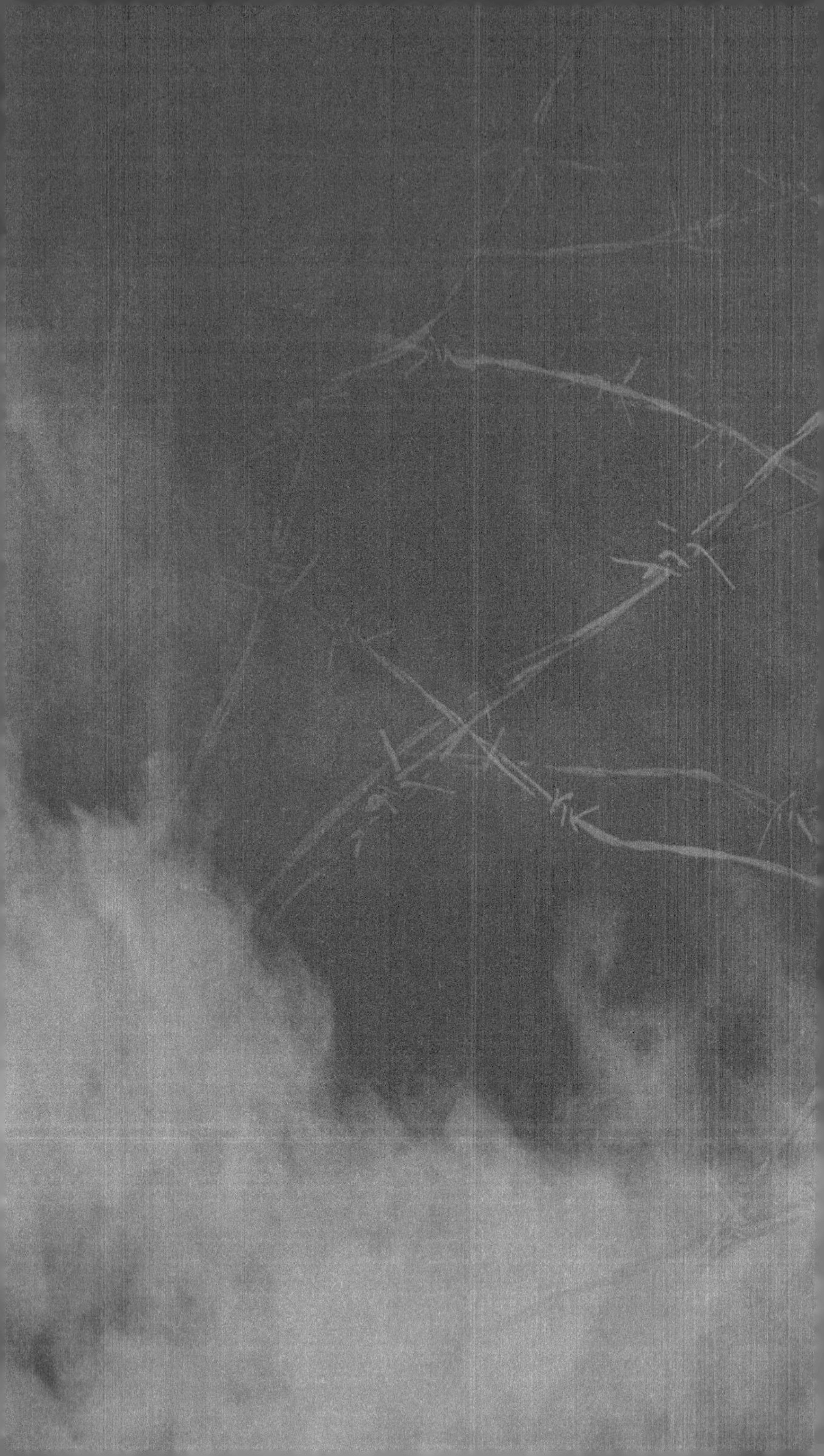

TWENTY

SIMON

I hated this place. Always had. It was well-known as a spot for dirty deals to go down, and the fact that I sat across from this man with his little weasel eyes made me swallow hard and hate it even more. I felt slimy and was glad there was a table between us.

There was just something about him that didn't sit right inside me whenever he was near, which I was glad wasn't often.

"What do you say? Join us. We're all family here." I felt like he was trying to sell me on joining a cult. Maybe the bar was just a front. My imagination began to go wild at the thought. I glanced around nervously.

"Why me?" I desperately tried to focus on anything but those cold eyes.

"Why not?"

"Seriously, I'm a nobody. I haven't even held a gun before." Sure, that wasn't entirely true, but I was the last person who would ever put on a leather cut and take orders to kill someone. After all, my nickname growing up was Harry Potter. I always had my nose in a book; my imagination always ran high as I lived through each one. I was totally out of my comfort level in a urine-soaked bar, and one I would probably have to clean.

"You're smart. You can learn."

"No." I cut him off. "Sorry, but no. I'm not interested at all. I'm not sure where this is coming from, but it's a hard pass. It will never happen."

"Simon," my name shot off his tongue like venom, and a quick flash of his real self poked through, "I don't need to explain myself, nor do people say no to me." His dark eyes glittered, but what sent a shiver through me was his tone. I didn't know why, but it gave me the much-needed push to find my backbone. I had a voice and a choice.

"I know people don't say no to you, Allen, but there's a first time for everything." I stood and held up my hands when two of his men pointed their weapons at me.

"You've been warned, boy." Allen licked his bottom lip, clearly trying to hold his temper down. "What comes next is on you."

"Understood."

I blinked a few times to get rid of that memory. That one conversation had changed my entire life, and I had to live with the consequences. I shuddered and forced my body to relax as I spotted Kenna. She looked lovely as she greeted someone who had come into the restaurant.

"There you are." Kurt sat down next to me. "I lost you after you spoke to Kenna in the lobby." I shrugged as he reached out and snagged my beer and downed more than half of it in one deep swallow. He didn't often show his face, but lately he'd become more comfortable. I didn't mind so much. I didn't have too many friends, and Kurt was easy to sit with.

"Did you get me anything to take to Brick?" I needed something to show I had looked into his brother's whereabouts. I'd promised Trigger, and I got the feeling he was only a step behind me in that situation. The last thing I needed was him or Brick breathing down my neck, pissed I hadn't given them anything.

"I'm working on it." He bumped some ketchup on my plate, and I frowned at the sudden red invasion down the side of my baked potato.

"I take it by your calm demeanor you haven't heard yet." He spoke in such a precise way that it caught my attention even as I watched Kenna across the way fiddle with her necklace. She often did that when she wasn't comfortable with a situation.

"Hear what?"

"Rumor has it Leo Gates was murdered during their trip to New Orleans."

"What?" I turned my head so fast that my neck popped. "I haven't heard a thing. Cameron hasn't reached out."

"My guess, Cameron doesn't know."

"Are you sure?

"Of course, I'm sure." He sounded annoyed.

"Do you have proof? I can't believe it."

"I'm working on it."

"Shit. Who else knows?"

"No clue, but I've got my contacts." He puffed up. "Not many know, because you clearly haven't gotten wind of it yet." He looked so pleased he knew before me I wanted to smack him.

"Damn." I covered my face. I'd been so preoccupied with other stuff I hadn't paid enough attention to what was going on at the hotel. "I need to tell Cameron. What, exactly, do you know?"

"Well, apparently, there was an upper management meeting held this morning. I heard they pretty much made it known that Leo was the one who was killed at their hotel. I'm not sure what more proof you need."

"How did I not know about this meeting? I wonder whether Cameron was there." I rubbed my head, confused. I really was way out of the loop.

"Don't know." Kurt shrugged and shook his head.

"Shit, if he wasn't there…" I licked my lips as my mind went off in different directions.

"Yeah, good luck with that." Kurt shrugged again. I

knew Cameron was going to flip out if he wasn't there for that meeting. He hated to miss anything.

Kurt opened his phone, but quickly put it back down. "Just deal with the boss. Nothing else's come in. I'll tell you when I know more. What about her?" He pointed his chin at Kenna. "Maybe she knows something."

"Maybe?" I shrugged. I sure as hell wasn't going to tell him I'd been watching her more closely lately.

"You two are supposed to be friends. Go feel her out."

"Later." I waved him off as a text came in on his phone. "She's talking to someone right now."

"Interrupt her. It's pretty big news." He made a wry face when I didn't reply and then tapped his screen. A moment later, he head-pointed at Jayden, who'd rushed over to Kenna.

"Something's up for sure," I whispered and felt lost on what was going on around me.

"The Gateses have been targeted again, and not in the way you think." Kurt held up his phone.

TWENTY-ONE

KENNA

"You know, you're just as gorgeous as you were in high school." Benny tapped his wine glass to mine. "Now, is this the part where you're going to tell me you're getting married or something?"

"No, marriage isn't in my cards," I sidestepped his flattery, "but I'm not exactly single either." Or was I? I didn't really know the answer to that. What I did know was my head didn't have room for anything more. "What about you?"

"I was dating," he sipped his wine, "but she's in Kentucky and my heart's in the west, so things just fizzled out. She's great, and we still talk, but she's moved on, and I need to as well."

"How very mature of you." I was pleased to hear Benny was still the same.

"You really are a knockout." He shook his head and smiled in a way that showed he was happy to be with me. It was a good feeling. "You know, I've never told you this, but the few times I mustered up the courage to ask you out, your dad's men always seemed to get in the way."

"What do you mean?" I knew the guys were always around, but they never seemed interested in the few male friends I'd had. My girlfriends, maybe, but that was typical.

"I called them the gatekeepers."

"Gatekeepers?" I chuckled. "They were annoying to me, but I didn't think they paid much attention to any of my guy friends. Did they?"

"A few made their presence known."

"Let me guess. Sasha?"

He laughed and made a face like I nailed the nail on the head. "Let's just say there was a time he made sure I knew you two were something."

"I'm sorry, Benny. I didn't know that."

"It wasn't your problem. You were gorgeous." He shrugged. "I'm sure there were plenty of guys who had their eye on you. Sasha was just marking his territory. I'd have done the same."

I looked away as the memory of the way his body had slumped to the ground after Grim killed him suddenly flashed before my eyes. "Well, he isn't around anymore." I didn't elaborate further.

"He wasn't the worst of them, actually." He pursed his lips in a way that caught my interest. "And from what I can see, nothing's changed much."

"What's that mean?"

"It means I'm still being watched by one of the same sleazeballs from all those years ago." He nodded over my head, and I turned to see Sonny watching me from a few tables away.

Wait. What?

"No, Benny, that's Sonny Conti. He's from Chicago."

"Trust me, I'm very aware of who Sonny Conti is."

"But I only just met him this past year. I signed him as a client." Something prickled at the back of my neck, and I tried to sort out the confusion.

"You might not have known him, but he sure knew who you were. He and your father go way back. I'll never forget the time I bumped into them at a bourbon club in Venice. I was with my father, and Sonny made a point of making sure I knew I wasn't welcome in your world."

"Sonny Conti?" I repeated. I wasn't getting it. "He's known my father for years? Told you to back off from me? Back when we were in high school?" This didn't make any sense.

"Yes."

"And you're a hundred percent certain that the Sonny you're talking about is the same man five tables over by the window?"

"Yes."

"But that's impossible." I couldn't grasp the idea. I never remembered ever seeing Sonny at my home or with my father.

"Excuse me." Jayden was suddenly at my side. He cleared his throat in that irritating way he often did when he wasn't pleased about something. "Kenna, a word, please."

"Um, Jayden, I have the night, off and obviously I'm busy with someone." He didn't even glance at Benny.

"Trust me, you want to hear this."

"Jayden, my head is—"

"Kenna." His expression was serious.

"All right." I looked back at Benny. "I'm sorry, but can you excuse me a moment?"

"Of course." He eyed Jayden who stood, obviously agitated, by our table.

"Kenna," he whispered as I got close. "Someone's targeted Grim's dogs." I turned to look at him straight on. "Darcy took them out tonight for their walk and she didn't come back. There's footage of someone jumping her out front in the parking lot. Leal got away, but Darcy and Zhar were taken."

"What?" My head spun.

"Trigger's right outside." He leaned in. "Kenna, I don't know if Leal made it."

"Benny," I whirled around, "I have to deal with something important. We're going to have to do a raincheck."

"Can I help?" He stood, but I grabbed my purse and hurried away without looking over my shoulder. I heard his voice behind me. "I'll call you."

I tried to focus on my steps as I wound through the busy restaurant, not wanting to draw attention to myself. Jayden was hot on my heels as we hit the parking lot, but slowed to a halt as we approached Trigger.

"Leal's hurt. He went that way." Trigger pointed down the strip. "Minnie and Tess are already walking the alleyways, but I want you to look too. Leal likes you. He might respond to your voice."

"Yeah, okay." I turned to look at Jayden and saw Benny fast approaching. "Can you intercept?"

"Fuck." Trigger looked like he wanted to say more but thankfully didn't.

"Where the fuck are Grim's guys?" He seemed to remember that not everything was right in our world either.

"Trigger," I shook my head, "I got this." I had to assume Jesse's security team was somewhere nearby, but I didn't have time to think.

"Yeah." He understood now wasn't the time to pussy hold me.

He answered his phone. "What? Good. Kenna, we've got eyes on the van that took the girl and Zhar." He fired up his bike, and people all around looked over. "Call me if you find him." He roared off while I ran in the opposite direction.

I knew the girls would look in every place possible. They knew this town backward and sideways. In a flash of inspiration, I suddenly knew if Leal was hurt, he'd head to Secrets. It was quieter there and a place he often went with Grim.

I headed for the same entrance I had that night when on the run after killing Matt. I moved quickly through what was left of the construction and pushed on the door the security kept unlocked for their rounds and slipped inside. I paused to listen and turned my phone flashlight on and began to shine it around. The light bounced over the marble flooring. A chill went up my spine as I thought of one of the boys being hurt. It would surely push Grim over the edge, if he hadn't gone over already. Why would someone do this? My mind went to poor Darcy, and I had to push it all back.

"Leal," I called quietly. "Leal, are you here, boy?"

Nothing.

I made my way through each room, then at the elevator I spotted a smear on the floor. I bent down. It looked like a wet footprint, small and not from a human. I touched it and shone my light on my finger. Blood.

"Leal?" I tried to use a calm voice so as not to scare him. "I'm here, sweetheart. Leal?"

When I turned the corner into a little alcove, I heard a faint whimper. His eyes lit up in my flashlight. He let out a low growl, and I could see him lift one of his legs.

"Oh, no, poor boy, are you hurt?" I slowly approached and tried to assess the situation; he was scared, and there was a dark stain on his thigh. "Oh, sweet boy, what happened to you?" I quickly tapped Grim's number on my phone, but I was sent to voicemail.

Shit.

"Grim," I whispered after the beep, "I'm sure you've heard and you're on your way already. I've found Leal at Secrets. He's..." I paused as the poor pup whimpered at me for help. "I'll get him home."

I quickly called Trigger and filled him in. As I waited for our ride, I moved closer to Leal and talked to him quietly. I held out my hand, and he licked it. His poor body shook.

"I won't leave you," I promised. "I've got you."

It was Jason who came for us. He hesitated when Leal snarled at him as he got close.

"Hang on." I took the blanket he carried and carefully covered Leal's head with it. I talked softly to him while Jason gathered him up. "Be gentle. He's hurt." I hurried with them outside and into the car.

"Have you heard anything about Zhar or Darcy?"

"Trigger didn't tell me anything except to come get you and take you to the vet hospital. Sorry." He didn't look happy. "I'm sorry I didn't see you leave," he said, white-faced. "Last I saw, you were having dinner with that guy, and I went to grab a coffee. Shit, Jesse's gonna have my hide."

"Don't worry about that right now. Let's just get him to the vet." I didn't have time to feel sorry for the guy.

Leal whined unhappily during the short ride back, and I internally cursed at every red light. It only took about five minutes, but the poor pup had me emotionally strung out by the time the vet met us at the big double doors. I wasn't surprised that Grim would have an on-call doctor and an assistant waiting to step in.

"Kenna, is he okay?" Jim came up to me as they whisked Leal inside.

"I think so." I tried to sound in control. "What about the others?"

"Trigger's still on it but that's all I know." He pinched the bridge of his nose. "Grim just told me what happened and asked if I'd meet you here." I could see he was a step away from breaking down. "I'm sure it'll all be okay."

"It will be," I assured him as his tired gaze went to

the doors Leal had been taken through. "Why don't you go back to the hotel and get some sleep? I'll stay with Leal. You can check in at any point, and I promise I'll answer you."

"No, I should—"

"With all due respect, Jim," I lowered my voice, "you've been through the wringer. No one would think anything of it if you went to get some rest. If we're going to get through all this, we need you well." I hoped I didn't cross a line by referring to how ill he seemed. I softened and played one last card. "You should go be with Laurel. No mother should be alone right now, given…"

"Yes," he cleared his throat, "perhaps I should." He unexpectedly pulled me into a hug. "Thank you, Kenna."

"Of course." I watched him as he left. He looked much older, suddenly, and my heart went out to him as his driver opened the door and he disappeared inside.

I pressed my hands into the wall and took a breath to steady myself. *Breathe, Kenna. In and out.* I slowly gained control and took in my surroundings. The place had little photos of animals on the walls and shelves of toys and treats. I sat in one of the chairs by the wall and closed my eyes while my mind spun with all that had happened.

Christ, what was the next blow to come? Who would go after Darcy and the boys? What the hell did

Benny mean that my father knew Sonny all these years? Had Sonny been watching me, too? Was he behind the attack at the hotel? Could he have anything to do with all this? Holy shit, Grim was going to lose it. It was way too much.

"Hey," Jason said behind me. "He's stable. The doc got the bullet out. They're just stitching him up now. Then they'll be bringing him back to the hotel. If you want to go now, we can meet them there later."

"No, thanks, Jason." I got up and turned toward the doors. There was no way Leal was going to be alone tonight.

"Mr. Gates should be home soon."

"And until then, I'll be with Leal."

"Understood." I caught his nervous nod in the reflection of the glass doors and took pity on him. "Don't worry, Jason. I'll put in a good word for you with Jesse."

"In here." I directed the vet and his assistant into Grim's penthouse. An unconscious Leal was hooked up to an IV and looked comfortable on whatever medication they had given him.

"This way, please," I rushed ahead and opened Grim's bedroom door, "on the bed."

"You sure?" Jason asked as he helped lift the pup off the gurney.

"Yes." I waited for the doctor to finish up.

"I'll come back in the morning." The doctor explained, "He should sleep through the night, but try to keep him calm and stress free if he wakes. If anything changes, here's my number. Call me." He handed me a card. "Please tell Mr. Gates…"

"I'll be sure to tell him how well you've looked after Leal," I cut him off and waved for him to leave. "Jason, you need to leave too."

"I can't. I have orders."

"And now you have some from me." I raised my chin. "Leal hates people in his space. It stresses him out. I'm sure not having his brother here will prey on his mind too. I understand your position, but—"

"I'm not leaving you alone." He looked uneasy. "They'll behead me."

"Fine," I nodded, exhausted, "but you can't be in this room, then."

"Okay," he raised his hands, "I'll be right out there." He pointed over his shoulder, and I nodded. He'd get no more argument from me. When he left, I took a deep breath and stepped toward the bed, only to have my heel wobble on something. I looked down at a bright orange bra that had wedged under my shoe. I kicked it aside, and it landed next to a pair of matching panties.

"Nice, Grim." I grimaced and sank onto the mattress. I kicked off my heels as the hurt that he'd had a naked woman up here since he'd come back, when I'd been so worried, burned in my throat. I got my emotions in check and tried to focus on the bigger picture.

Leal let out a little squeak, and I turned to find him eyeing me from where he lay.

"It's okay, I'm here." I inched up the bed and lay beside him. I was close but extremely careful not to touch him. He might be high on strong medication, but the boys had been trained to kill first and ask questions later, and who knew what affect the meds would have on his mind. He blew his lips out and whimpered, but he didn't growl. I figured I'd just speak to him, so he knew he wasn't alone.

"Everything's going to be all right, Leal," I whispered. "I promise you I won't let anyone hurt you. Zhar will be home soon."

I repeated my chant over and over not just to calm him but for me as well. I felt my eyes grow heavy and gave in to the dark abyss.

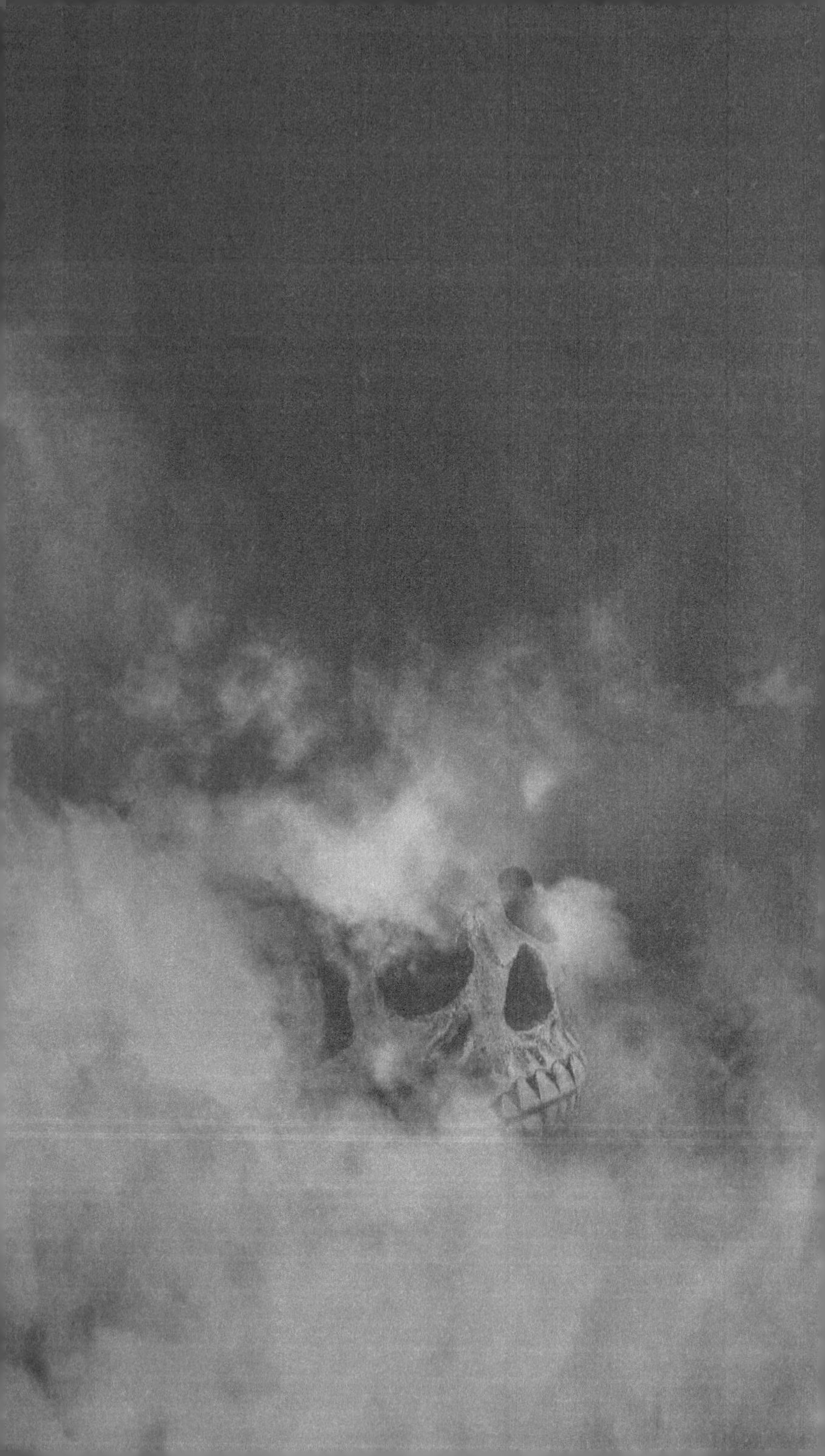

TWENTY-TWO

GRIM

"**F**ound him," Trigger grunted from the other end of the phone. "He's in with your vet. Seems fine."

"And Darcy?"

"Shot to the head. Brick made a few calls. The local PD's looking after her. It'll be taken care of."

I slowly turned the car into the parking lot as I tried to deal with what he said. Darcy didn't deserve that.

"I'm here now. I'll be in touch."

Cartwright opened the car door, and Jesse and I hurried up to my suite. Jason quickly jumped to his feet as we entered.

"Evening, sir."

"Where is he?"

"They're in the bedroom."

They? I didn't miss a beat and pushed by him into the room. I wondered who the hell was in there with Leal. When those legs came into view, I knew exactly who it was. I swallowed back my anger when I saw them. Her arm was draped over Leal's shoulder, and they were both fast asleep. When I whispered to him, he lifted his head for a moment and whimpered. Relief flooded through me as I realized he was okay. I stroked him between the ears and spoke to him quietly.

I reached out to stroke her arm then pulled it back sharply.

"Kenna." Her eyes fluttered open, then she quickly sat up and blinked to focus in the dim light.

"Oh, I didn't know when to expect you."

"Well, I'm here now."

"So you are." She slipped on her shoes as I took off my jacket and tossed it on the chair. I sat heavily next to it and sighed deeply. I was exhausted.

"On your way out, tell Jason he can go."

"After all this, you're being an ass?" she snapped.

"Did you expect anything different?" I shot back.

"You're welcome." She dripped with sarcasm as she flicked a pair of orange panties toward me with the toe of her shoe.

"Fuck," I muttered under my breath.

She went back to the bed and leaned over Leal to whisper in his ear, then she headed for the door.

"He's all yours," she huffed as Jesse came into the room.

"Are you sure you want to watch this again?" Jesse hesitated briefly then handed me the laptop when I flicked my fingers at him.

He set a drink next to me as I pressed play. The hotel surveillance video came up on the screen. I watched the man who had 'marked' me enter the hotel. He watched me for a few minutes then made his move. I saw him bump into me and slip the tarot card into my jacket pocket. He left seconds later with his phone to his ear.

"Any word on the plates of that car?" I turned to Jesse, who watched from the bed where he'd settled next to Leal.

"Nothing yet." His voice was low so as not to disturb the dog.

I turned back to the video and continued to watch. Paige's mouth never stopped as she and Leo waited for the elevator. As she talked, I watched my brother pat himself down and pull out the tarot card. He flipped it over then shrugged and put it back in the pocket. He continued to pat himself down until he located his keycard. It was in his back pants pocket. As the doors opened, Leo stumbled, and Paige grabbed his arm and they laughed together. I watched again as the two men got into the elevator with them.

"I just don't get it. What kind of hit man fucks up

their mark that badly? I'm all tatted up, but my brother doesn't have a single tattoo."

"Remember, these guys go off very little detail. They get a text, a dollar amount and first come first served on the kill. They saw him pull out the card and figured he had to be the mark. It's not the first time, and it won't be the last."

I downed the rest of my drink in one angry swallow and pulled back my arm to throw the glass at the wall but stopped short as Jesse suddenly stood.

"They're here." He went to the door and opened it. Brick came inside with Zhar and removed his leash. Zhar padded directly toward me, and I gave him an ear rub.

"Hi, buddy. I'm so glad you're okay." He sensed Leal and went over to the bed and jumped up and settled next to his brother. I saw their feet touch, then Leal whimpered and pulled his paw away.

"The vet's going to call you tomorrow, but he's fine." Brick leaned against the wall. "Sorry about Darcy."

"The family's been contacted. Laurel's already sent flowers," Jesse said to Brick. "They'll let us know when the funeral's going to be."

"Trig wants to meet down below tomorrow. Between Leo and now this, things are so fucked up right now." Brick shook his head as he spoke. I saw him glance at Jesse when I didn't comment. I didn't trust my voice at that moment. Brick turned to the door. "See ya then."

I turned back to the video once Brick left and rewatched the part where the two men followed Leo and Paige down the hall and, as they stumbled to unlock the door, they were shoved into the room. I fast forwarded the video to where I could have saved my brother but chose Kenna.

"You couldn't have known, Grim." Jesse's voice was quiet.

I slammed the laptop shut and muttered that I needed sleep.

My eyes popped a moment before my alarm went off. Sleep had found me, but it had come with a cost. I relived that video over and over in my dreams. Every version was different, but they all ended the same. Leo was murdered, and I'd chosen sex over saving him. Zhar was tucked against my side; he stretched with a yawn and wagged his stub when his eyes met mine. They were never allowed on the bed, so I knew he was eating it up.

I turned to my other side and saw Leal was watching me. He whimpered, and I knew he was due for some more pain medicine. I hopped up and fed it to him through his IV and stroked his back as it pushed through his system.

"You did good, boy," I whispered when he tried to lift his head, "and I promise I'll catch this fucker and drill him into the ground." He nuzzled my hand. "I'll even save you a bite," I promised. "You get some sleep." His eyes slowly closed, and I was thankful he wouldn't feel any pain for a few hours.

I glanced at the orange panties on the floor and grabbed my phone to text my brother.

> Grim: Knox, if you want to entertain women, do it at your place.

I showered, dressed, and headed out to the kitchen where I found Trigger and Brick slumped on my couch, and, by the looks of it, they'd spent the night. When they spotted me, Trigger sat up and snapped his neck.

"They were two hired men." Trigger jumped into business as I poured some coffee. "One of 'em took a look at me and shot himself." He shrugged. "The other's being held downstairs." A surge of excitement went through me. It didn't last, but I was thankful for the shot of adrenaline.

"Good." I handed him a steamy cup of coffee as Brick blinked around the room and saw we were both awake.

"How's Leal?" Brick rolled his shoulders and unfolded from the couch.

"Good, thanks to you guys." I eased into the chair. I noticed Zhar stayed glued to me.

Trigger leaned his arms on his thighs. "Things are

fucked up, but going after your dogs seems real personal."

"I know." My phone rang, and I saw it was my father. He needed to see me.

"What do you want me to do with the fucker downstairs?" Trigger asked.

"Let him sweat it out. I've got a meeting with Dad, but I want a piece of him."

"I hear ya." Trigger stood as Jesse came in.

Jesse held up his phone. "I got the footage from that night, with Darcy and the dogs."

"And?"

"They ran into Kenna before they left."

"Push it through to the TV."

He pressed play, and I relived another video I knew would haunt me.

***

"Okay, Trigger's good for four p.m.," Jesse informed me as we walked down the hall. Zhar led the way as we approached Dad's office for a meeting. I glanced in the direction of Cameron's office and wondered if he'd heard the news about Leo yet. God fucking forbid he'd play nice for a few days.

"I'll call the guys and make sure everyone's there." Jesse looked at his phone as a text message came in. "Ridder and Lawson better find something out on

Darcy. The guys have been extra fucking quiet lately." Jesse's frustration with our spies showed. I got it; everything seemed off lately. "Speaking of which, there's Lawson now." He tapped his phone and started to text him back.

"Good." I felt the loss of Leal covering my left, and it didn't sit well with me. Nothing sat well with me lately. The darkness that had rooted deep in my chest slowly smothered all parts of me. I felt hollow and cold inside. I felt I deserved it. I didn't have the right to feel any other way after how I'd let my brother down. I flinched at the memory that continued to haunt me. I watched it over and over on that video. I saw myself turn and head to my own room to indulge my own needs instead of checking on Leo.

"I've got to go," Jesse called as he headed down the hall. "I've got to talk to Kenna."

I didn't ask why. I just opened the door to Dad's office and was surprised to see my mother and Knox in conversation.

Instantly, I was on edge. I didn't have the energy for him right now.

"Take a seat, son." Dad set a coffee next to me as Zhar plopped down next to my feet.

Mom spoke first. "Before we start, Grim, how is Leal?"

"Fine."

"Kenna was smart to figure out he'd go to Secrets. It's where Leal would go to look for you."

"Yeah."

"Have you spoken to her since you've been back? How's she holding up?"

"Dad, are we going to start this meeting?" I ignored Mom's probing.

"She seemed fine at her date last night." Knox snickered. Just for once, I wished he'd grow up.

"With who?" Mom homed in on Knox.

I squeezed my eyes shut and tuned out their mindless chatter. I had no patience to deal with it.

"I know we have a lot to deal with right now," Dad cut them off, "but we've had a win, and I want to share it. I got news from Deborah, and we won the bid for the property across from the Encore."

"That's wonderful news." Mom smiled, but her exhaustion showed through.

"It's a positive thing," I muttered, attempting to make an effort, but my pain took over. "I wonder what shit storm will follow that purchase?"

"I know things are bleak right now, son, but the world doesn't stop because we hurt. Leo would have loved this." Mom's voice held a warning.

I reached down and stroked Zhar's ear. "Leo wanted a lot of things, and one of them was not to be six feet under."

"Oh, too soon," Knox breathed.

I pushed my palms against the table and glared at my brother. "You weren't there, like always." I felt my temper rise to a dangerous point. "You've no idea what it was like," I snarled. "You only know what cheap perfume and the inside of an empty bottle is like."

"Boys," Mom pleaded, "we don't need this right—"

"If I'd been there," Knox interrupted loudly, "I would've made sure our security walked with them to their room. After all, we're the Gates family."

I lunged at him and knocked over my chair. Zhar jumped up as my fist met Knox's cheek. Before I could get in another swing, Dad grabbed my arm.

"Enough!" he bellowed. "Knox, get out, go get some ice. I'll deal with you later." Dad turned to me. "Grim, sit down. We need to talk."

I rubbed my hand and fed off the pain that pulsed through my knuckles. Dad went over to the bar and rattled about as I settled back in my chair and glanced in the direction the little shit went.

He handed me a scotch. "Grim, how are things going with Secrets?"

I eyed the glass; it was, after all, only mid-morning. "Good. We're on time for the opening."

"Excellent." Dad hesitated. "Son, I need to tell you something, and you won't be happy with me." That pulled my entire attention. "When I went to visit you in Mexico, I led you to believe my cancer was back, but it's not."

I glanced at him in shock, and then at Mom. She nodded at Dad to continue.

Relief was quickly replaced by confusion as I looked from Dad to Mom. I thought about all the times I'd seen him act sick. *What the hell?* My anger flared.

"Before you blow, listen to me, please." Dad held up a hand. "Your mother and I suspect several people who are embedded in our lives are trying to undermine us. There've been several things that I know have been off. Your mother and I came up with a plan. I needed to seem vulnerable and hoped that would make them bold enough to show themselves. I began to realize if I wanted it to look real, you'd have to come home. I needed you here. I needed the whole family around me, to present a united front, if you will. It worked."

That was a lot to unpack. I had been certain Dad was sick; he'd played his part well. My mind went over some of the times I'd been concerned about him. Certain people had been around. Then my brother pushed through my thoughts, and I remembered our conversation on the plane.

"Leo suspected there was something going on. Did he know the truth?"

"He never said anything to me." Dad screwed up his face. "We'd planned to tell you both what was going on when you got back from New Orleans. I'm just so sorry I never got to tell him I wasn't ill."

Jesus. I couldn't believe he went to the grave not knowing. My stomach burned.

"Tell me it's Cameron!" My fingers curled into fists, needing a reason to kill that conniving bastard.

Dad's expression said it all, and I jumped to my feet, but he raised a hand. "Stop! I'm not sure about Cameron. I'm really not. Every time I think it's him, something happens that makes me question it. We have to tread carefully here, Grim. Until we have absolute confirmation, we can't show our hand." Dad tugged his tie in frustration.

"So, it could be him." I wasn't giving up easily. I hated that man.

"We're sure some of the men he works with are involved. Trouble is we're not positive he's behind it," Mom added cautiously.

"He might be smart, but I know he's really an idiot." Dad got up and ran a hand through his hair. "I can't believe all that's been happening. He was a good friend once. He did a lot for me when I needed it. I wonder if it was ever real." He suddenly really did look frail, and my hatred for whoever was behind all this almost boiled over.

"Jim, I know it's been eating at you, but now we're going to get to the bottom of this once and for all. Maybe he's just being played and doesn't know anything." Mom sent him a sympathetic look. "Now, I want you both to listen." Her tone made us both look over. "The Gates family won't be beaten. No one will bring us to our knees. We've worked long and hard to create a life for our family here." Her face was set and her voice strong. "We know this seems to be some sort of long con, it's been going on for a while now, and the only way we can win this is by waiting it out."

"Okay." I nodded. I understood that much. "Tell me the names of who you suspect so far."

"All right." Dad nodded and sat up straight. He placed a hand over my mother's. "I think it's time we tell him everything."

TWENTY-THREE

KENNA

"How ya holdin' up, baby girl?" Rail turned his chair around and hung his arms off the back of it as Minnie took a seat next to me. I know they were concerned about my state of mind after Leo's murder and everything else that was going on. It didn't help that I probably looked like shit after being up for more than half the night looking for Leal.

"I'm still here, so I'm better than some." I closed the lid to my barely eaten pasta salad and pushed it aside. Rail snatched it up, flicked the lid back off, and dove in.

"You should really eat." Minnie scrunched her nose up at him. "Did you eat breakfast?"

"Yeah." I'd had a banana around five.

"I'm worried about you." She stroked a hand down my arm.

"I'm not the one to be worried about. I just feel bad for Jim and Laurel. They must be beside themselves."

"You see Knox today?" Rail mumbled around his fork.

"No, why?"

"Guess he pissed Grim off in a meeting this morning and was rewarded with a fist to the face."

"What?" Minnie and I looked at one another.

He scraped the bottom of the plastic bowl so as not to miss anything. "Yeah, it's not like he didn't deserve it. The kid's a punk."

"He has his moments," I agreed, "but what made Grim do it?"

"Don't know." He slurped a noodle, and Minnie snagged the bowl away from him. "Hey!"

"You sound like a damn porno," she snapped and closed her eyes like she was trying to get her head back on track. "Okay, clearly, Grim is really on edge. Kenna, that's your cue."

"My cue?" I laughed sarcastically. "Oh, hell no." I tossed my phone in my purse. "I opened myself up to that man, and he slammed the door shut in my face. Trust me, I'm the last person who can help Grim Gates."

"He's grieving." Minnie tried to smooth the situation over.

"I know." I sighed. It was hard to describe how much the conversation bothered me.

"You know," Rail chewed on the end of the fork, "we men suck at feelings, and often lash at the ones we love because we can. You need to remember we don't mean it. We just need time to process what's going on inside." Minnie and I both stared at him as his words sank in.

"That's…" Minnie stumbled with a complex expression. "That's actually true. Wow, Rail, that was well said."

"I seek to please." He leaned back to stretch like he loved the moment. "I went to a Dr. Phil seminar last week, and I've got three dates just from spewing that guy shit to the ladies."

"There it is." Minnie rolled her eyes. "Anyway," she drew out the word, "I've been meaning to ask, have you had any more texts from that guy who attacked you?"

"No. It's odd, really. I haven't heard anything in days." I snagged my phone from my purse and went to his last text message.

"Don't you find that a bit strange?" Minnie tilted her head at me.

"Yeah, a bit." It actually was a bit odd, now that I thought of it. I hadn't gone there in my head lately because of everything else that had happened.

"Give it here." Rail held out his hand, and I reluctantly passed my phone to him.

"No more selfies," I warned, and he smirked. He was so naughty.

"This should get his attention." He clicked the screen and a moment later handed me back my phone. My eyes bugged out at his message supposedly from me.

> Kenna: Grim's brother died, and I have photos from his death. Do you want them?

"Rail," I felt like I was betraying the Gates family, "what if he says yes?"

"Then we send fakes." He held up his phone. "I have a whole fuckin' album dedicated to murders on here."

"Why would you have that?"

"I get bored?" He thought. "And I like to get creative. But if that number's still active and he's monitoring it, he'll take the bait."

"And if not?" Minnie asked before I could.

"Then maybe he got caught? Or," he wiggled his eyebrows in delight, "someone ended that little nightmare for you."

"Jesus." I stared at the text. It somehow felt like a betrayal to the Gates family. It burned a hole in my stomach.

Minnie suddenly sat up straight, and it put me on high alert. "Kenna, close that text." Her voice was urgent. Just as I did, she called out, "Grim!"

I felt a hot prickle shoot up my back as he spotted us. He whispered something to Jesse before they came over. Zhar walked slightly ahead of him and sat near me as soon as they stopped.

"I haven't seen you since you've been back." Minnie gave Grim a hug. Jesse seemed to have his total attention on his phone. Maybe he used it to avoid looking at me. "I'm so sorry to hear about Leal. How is he?"

"He's fine," he assured her and instantly dropped his hand to pat Zhar. My heart squeezed for him in that moment. I knew how much he loved his boys. The two of them had even grown on me.

"I'm so glad to hear that," Minnie breathed then dropped the topic as she read his vibe. "How's Knox's face?" She sounded honestly sympathetic.

"Fine." His tone was low and raspy but sharp. He obviously didn't want to stop and talk. Something caught his eye, and he and Jesse tuned in to Jayden as he whisked by with someone I didn't recognize.

A strange, cold vibe fell over them, and I felt goosebumps run along my arms as I watched them watch him. Grim's shoulders were stiff, and his hand twitched at his sides. It was obvious to me he wanted to pull his gun from behind his jacket.

Suddenly, my phone buzzed on the table, and Minnie, Rail, and I all turned to stare at it. I tried to snatch it up a little too quickly and sent it flying. It landed at Grim's feet. He leaned down to pick it up and, without a care, read the message. His expression instantly hardened, and my stomach twisted into a knot as he handed it to me and I read the text.

Damn.

> Benny: How about we re-do our date?
> We have so much to catch up on.

I slowly relaxed; it wasn't my unknown caller. I let out a sigh of relief. I looked at Rail and gave a little head shake to let him know it was okay, but when I looked at Grim, his jaw ticked, and his cold eyes drilled into mine as if he tried to penetrate my thoughts.

"I'm late for a meeting," he grunted when I didn't react. He looked at Minnie. "I'll see you tonight."

"Okay," she squeezed his arm, "I'm here whenever you need me."

I watched them leave then closed my eyes in relief as I covered my mouth with my hand.

"I think I felt my soul slide out of my ass when he read your message." Minnie sank into her seat. "Who was it, anyway?"

"Just an old friend. We had dinner last night, but it got interrupted when the dogs went missing."

"Shit, I can't imagine. Poor Darcy. I really liked her." Minnie frowned. "Who's this guy?"

"Just a friend. I told him I was seeing someone just to put him off. He gets it."

"I see." She studied me for a beat. "You should bring him tonight."

"Tonight?" Had I missed something?

"Trigger called his buddy Elio, and he and his cousins arrive tonight from Italy. We're having drinks on the rooftop."

"Oh." I hadn't heard anything about that. "I think we'll just stick with dinner."

"He's game for tonight." Rail held up my phone, and my eyes popped when I read his text message asking Benny to join us.

"Rail!" I snatched my phone back, already trying to find a way out of it. "Seriously?"

"Now you have to go or we'll drill him ourselves."

Minnie cursed then laughed and leaned toward me. "Just come."

"I don't have a choice now, do I?"

"Nope." Rail gave me a shit-eating grin as I spotted a new hire with my to-go order. "Wear something slutty, you know, for me." He ducked as I swatted him.

"Here you are," she beamed at me and turned the cup around to read my name scribbled on the side, "Kenna. A double black and an extra-large cinnamon-raisin muffin." She set my order in front of me.

I thanked her and tipped her well as Minnie eyed my order. She knew me well enough to know I wouldn't touch a raisin if it was the last food on Earth.

She nudged the bag when I stood. "What's with the shriveled-up balls treat?"

"It's called progress." I didn't want to get into it right now. "And it takes two to make that happen, so this is that."

"Oh," Minnie caught on right away, but I did notice she gave a concerned looked to Rail. *Odd*. "See you tonight." She smiled warmly.

I scooped up the bag, blew her a kiss, and she looked smug and clocked Rail in the head as I left.

It felt strange to come to the twentieth floor and not make a point to avoid my father's office. It always represented the gates of hell to me yet, there I was with his favorite treat and a coffee, voluntarily dropping by for a surprise.

"Knock-knock." I pushed the door open. "Cam—" I stopped myself. "Dad?" His office was empty. I crossed the large room that looked out over part of the Strip and set his coffee and treat on his desk. My phone rang, and I saw it was Hanna. Oh, my God! I quickly answered it, happy she called me.

"Hanna?"

"Hi." She sounded better. "I just wanted to let you know I'm settled back in LA with my parents."

"I'm so pleased to hear that." I really was. "How

are you dealing with everything, you know, with the whole Sasha death thing?"

"Um," she sighed, "I'm getting there. I've decided to see someone for it." My stomach sank, and she quickly filled the silence. "It's okay. I've learned my lesson, Kenna." She lightly laughed. "They'll get a watered-down version of what happened."

"Okay." I instantly thought of Grim snapping his neck and knew some people could handle that side of life and others couldn't. Though she hadn't actually seen Sasha die, she knew he'd been killed and how. "Well, in that case, I'm glad you're getting help. I'm sorry things went down the way they did." Something suddenly hit me. "Hanna, can I ask you something?"

"Sure."

"Remember Sasha's tattoo, the one that was on the inside of his bicep?" She cleared her throat, and I could tell a little ping of jealousy still rested below the surface.

"Yeah, what about it?"

"Did he ever tell you what that was for?"

"It was just some high school football thing he got with his team." Well, that was lie, because I had seen Sasha play football with the guys in the back yard, and that man had zero skills even in touch football. He'd sure never been on any team.

"Oh, okay." I let the topic go.

"Why would you ask me about that?"

I sat in my father's soft leather office chair and leaned into his desk as I quickly thought of something to say. "I just saw it on someone else recently and thought it was strange they would both have it, so I wondered if it had meaning somehow. Anyway," I changed topics, "you're home, you're getting help, so when do I get to see you next?"

"Not until you come here." Her tone softened. "I think I've had my fill of Vegas for a while."

"Then the moment I can get away, I'll come visit."

"I'd like that." She started talking about her new job when I swiveled in the chair and knocked my knee on the inside of the desk. *Ouch!* A strange clink sound caught my attention. I hit the side again, a bit softer, and I heard it again, but this time the bottom drawer popped open from the impact. I leaned down close to see it. *What the hell?*

"Hanna, hold on a sec." I pulled the phone away from my head. A faint smell found my nose, and I reached down and snagged a twist of hair that stuck out from an envelope and held it up in the light to study it. *Ew.* Something strange passed through me, and I looked down at the drawer again. I eyed the padded envelope that lay there, then I looked around the office with a guilty feeling. I pushed past it. My nerves on edge, I carefully lifted it out and peeked inside. Two shiny cufflinks lay in the bottom. I carefully turned it over and saw it was addressed to my father but there was no return address. What was really strange was the stamp and postmark read New Orleans.

"Hanna?" I put my phone back to my ear. "I'm sorry, but I have to go."

"Oh, okay. Hope to see you soon."

I clicked off without another word and quickly shut the drawer, tucked the envelope in my purse, and moved around the desk.

I screwed up my face as I studied the treat I'd brought for my father. The happiness I'd felt so briefly was now replaced with confusion and uncertainty. I picked up the bag and the coffee and spun on my heel to toss both treats into the trash by his door. As I hurried down the hallway, I met Laurel coming out of the conference room.

"Mrs. Gates," I smiled, "have you seen Jesse?"

"Good morning, dear," she greeted me warmly, but I noticed her eyes were puffy, and her reactions were slow. She touched her head like it hurt as she thought. "I believe he's in a meeting downstairs."

"Downstairs?" I drew out the word trying to think where that would be. She pointed toward the elevator, and we walked together. "Mrs. Gates, when was the last time you got any sleep? You look exhausted."

"I'm not really sure. Let's see, when did you all leave for New Orleans?" She brushed a tear away, and my heart broke. "The world works in strange ways, doesn't it?" She sniffed.

"It certainly can work in the worst ways." I put a hand on her back and gave her a little pat. I'm so sorry, Mrs. Gates, about Leo." Then my father's face pushed through my thoughts, and it suddenly felt like I held a secret in my purse. I needed it out of my possession. God, I hoped there was an explanation for it. As the elevator doors parted, she stepped inside and pulled out her black and gold keycard. I carefully stepped in beside her and watched as she moved like a robot to tap the card to the keypad. Then she pressed the lobby and floor fifteen at the same time. My memory went back to when I'd seen Jesse do that after that terrible night when Grim's car was all shot up on the way back from the desert. *Interesting.*

Laurel stepped out then held the doors from closing. "Leo thought very highly of you, you know." Her eyes glossed over. "You're a brightness in an otherwise very bleak time."

"That's a really nice thing to hear." I felt a lump form in my throat. "Thank you, Mrs. Gates. He was a lovely man."

"Laurel," she said tenderly. "You need to start calling me Laurel. We're closer than that." I wanted to sob for so many reasons, but her kindness toward me at such a difficult time squeezed my heart until it hurt.

"I will," I paused and tested out her name, "Laurel."

"Better." She stepped back and dropped her hand. "I have some calls to make." She turned as the doors slid shut, and I felt some tears spill over. As I descended toward the unknown, I shifted my head back to what I needed to do.

I watched as the numbers on the screen went from the lobby to the parking lot, to the basement, then continued to drop. My heart pounded as it slowed to a stop, then I waited for a beat and peeked out, looking both ways before I stepped out onto a shiny marble floor. I expected to hear my heels echo off the walls, but everything seemed strangely muted. The hallway was long, but with a wall at one end there was only one way to go, and it was toward two massive steel doors that stood partially open.

"And what about you, Ridder?" Grim's voice slowed my pace as I grew close.

"Sonny's been hanging tight with Trident Melvern, Jr. at the Mac since he's been back. Other than that, he's been keeping a low profile. I'm still waiting on confirmation about exactly where he went that night in New Orleans."

"Alibi or not, Sonny knows something!" Grim boomed as I stepped up to the door and peeked through.

"I agree." A man who I assumed was Ridder nodded.

Grim sat in a black velvet chair that looked like something from his penthouse. He wore all black and sat ridgid as he barked orders to the others. Suddenly, Zhar, who lay at Grim's feet, looked right at me. Jesse seemed to catch this motion and looked down at him.

"Trigger, Talya wanted me to give you this." He slid something across the table. "Locations and dates to pass along to your Blackstone friends."

Trigger nodded and tucked it away. "And the retaliation on her parents?"

"I've got people there ready to make a move, but we're waiting to see—"

I jumped when Jesse's face suddenly appeared in front of me. He slowly opened the door just enough to slip himself out into the hallway with me.

His face was white as he looked around. "How – how did you get down here? You can't be here."

"Yet here I am," I whispered as I lifted my purse and pulled out the envelope. "I'm bringing this to you, not Grim, just you. Don't let him fly off the handle until we know what it's—" I didn't even want to say the words out loud. "Just," I felt panicked, "find out who these belong to."

He waited for me to give it to him, but I hesitated. "All right, Kenna, I can do that."

"I found this about twenty minutes ago. It was in

the bottom drawer of my father's desk. I don't know why it was there, but," I struggled for the right words, "here." I handed it to him, and he glanced inside and looked puzzled.

"Okay," he was all business, "thank you for bringing this to me. I'll look into it."

"No, Grim," I eyed him, "not until we know anything. I'm nervous of what he might do."

Jesse closed his eyes then nodded. "I don't like the idea of holding anything back from him, but I'll do it this one time."

"Thank you. I need to go." I turned and hurried back down the hall.

"Kenna?" I heard Grim's voice behind me. "What the fuck is she doing here, Jesse?" He sounded furious, and I kept walking. I assumed Jesse slipped away. "Kenna, stop walking."

I didn't, at least not until I reached the elevator and stabbed the button several times. It finally opened, and I flew inside. The thing wouldn't budge. *Damn.*

"Really, Gavin?"

I glared at the camera and heard him say, "Sorry, boss's order."

"I told you to stop," Grim boomed. His voice bounced around the inside of the steel box. I crossed my arms ready for a fight. "What the fuck are you doing down here?"

"I needed to see Jesse."

"What? Why?"

"I had a number he asked for." I lied, then jabbed the button to close the door. I knew it wouldn't shut, but it would piss him off that I'd done it.

"How do you know about this place?" He glared. "Did you follow me?"

"Wow," I laughed, "do you really think I'd bother to follow you? You really have a God complex, don't you?" I held his gaze, and he broke eye contact. "If you must know, your mother actually helped me, Grim, and she told me where to find Jesse."

"She would never." He shook his head.

I pressed my lips together. "She did."

He squinted in confusion then straightened his back. "I see."

"I'm glad you see." I gave him a defiant look. "So, can I go now?"

"Gavin," he said into his phone, and the buttons immediately lit up. I didn't waste a second as I hit the button for the tenth floor.

"You need to be very careful, *sweetheart*." His voice was cold. "You've overstepped where you don't belong. You might overhear things down here that aren't meant for you."

"And if I did?" I challenged. "What are you going to do? Hurt me? Snap my neck? Toss me in the desert?" I was like stone, and that was how I needed to be. Grim and I had obviously lost whatever we had in New

Orleans, and as much as that hurt, I couldn't let him see it. "I'm not afraid of you, Grim."

He stepped forward and backed me up to the wall then towered over me the way I loved. I swallowed hard.

"It means you don't belong in my world." His hand slid up my body, over my breast, and stopped at my throat. His thumb stroked my collarbone. He studied me as if he were in a trance. I hated that I breathed deeply to draw his scent into my head. I missed him, and I hated that I did. "If you heard the wrong thing," he brushed his lips over my jaw gently, as if savoring the moment himself, "I can't be responsible for any of my actions anymore."

"So, you'd hurt me." The pain that coursed down my throat straight to my heart was far worse than anything I'd ever felt from a man. I needed to be careful. I accepted his warning, not sure exactly why, but I knew I had to accept the writing on the wall. We weren't meant to be.

His hand quickly retracted as though the heat burned his fingers. The honey gaze he had in his eyes dissolved, and a stone-cold expression replaced it. He pulled back as though to rein himself in. He turned his back as the doors closed.

"Christ." I leaned my heated body back against the cool wall as I shot upward toward the living. I felt like I just had a moment with the Reaper.

• • •

Later that day, I had a request from an old client. He was in town and had a few hours free and wanted me to join him at the poker table. After only an hour, he met some friends, and I was only too happy when they decided to join him. A happy client always made the job easier, and it also meant it gave me more time to prepare for the evening ahead. I wanted to look my best. I knew there'd be some new faces at the rooftop bar, and if I didn't look my best, Minnie would be all over me, concerned as to why I didn't. I was so tired of everyone asking me if I was all right. The Gates family should have been everyone's focus. Not me.

I arrived on the top floor and was hit with a wave of heat. I checked myself once more as I went by a mirror. My light pink dress was like a second skin, but the temperature made it feel even tighter. The girls were front and center, and my dress hit high on my thighs. Minnie knew I always felt confident in this color, so I made sure to rock it with a metallic heel. My dark hair was long and wavy, and my makeup light.

I suddenly wondered if my stalker was going to be there. I looked around quickly and bit my bottom lip. I reassured myself with the fact that he hadn't taken Rail's bait on that text message. I couldn't figure out why he had gone silent. Maybe he'd given up on the texts and just watched me in person. I squeezed my eyes shut and pushed the thought away. I stopped and sprayed on a little perfume, took a deep breath, and headed toward the others.

"*Sei molto bella.* You must be Kenna." A man, who was obviously Italian with that gorgeous accent, stepped in front of me as I approached the others. He grinned then playfully kissed my hand. "But if not, may I buy you a drink?"

"Oh, no, brother," another Italian I knew as Vinni interrupted. "This is Kenna." He draped an arm around the other man's shoulders.

"Hello, Vinni." I smiled to show I remembered him. I chuckled as I thought of him here with Trigger and his guys. He always avoided Trigger at all costs. It was no secret he was terrified of him.

"*Scusa,* I figured it was too good to be true." He winked and offered a hand. "I'm Niccola, Vinni's brother."

Ah, yes, the famous Capri brothers and cousins to Elio Capri, the Mafia Don of Italy.

"Older brother," Vinni corrected him.

"Older, yes, but also wiser and much more experienced." They playfully bantered while he held my hand as though it was a delicate treasure.

"It's a pleasure to meet you, Niccola." I smiled when he kissed my hand. You had to hand it to the Italians, they knew how to charm a lady—unless you were on their hit list, of course. I chuckled to myself.

"Trust me, Kenna, the pleasure is all mine." He flashed another big, white smile while he threw a glance at the others.

"Is it working?" Niccola asked as Vinni looked over at the others.

"Yes."

"Is what working?" I was curious to know what he meant.

Niccola offered an arm, and I took it. "We're just testing out the waters to ascertain how far our dark but dear friend has gone."

"Which dear friend? Because, no offense, but there are a lot of people here." I ran through my mind all those I knew who would be there for drinks. All the main members of the Devil's Reach, and their significant others. Grim and Jesse, of course, and I knew Elio would be there. I assumed he was the tall, handsome one with his back to me. I wasn't sure how many of his Mafia syndicate traveled with him besides these two, his cousins.

"The one who is watching you with such intensity." Vinnie laughed. "I do think he would put a bullet into anyone who looks at you the wrong way. It could be fun."

"You've got it all wrong." I smiled at him and enjoyed his spunk. "We may have had something once, but not anymore."

"Really?" Vinni raised a brow. "Because we have all

evening to be proven wrong."

Kill me now, an Italian Rail.

Vinni conveniently made sure I sat right next to Grim, then he wedged his way between Minnie and Rail so I had to shimmy even closer to Grim. Rail eyed me thoughtfully, and I waited for him to say something. For once, he only cocked an eyebrow and grinned at me.

I was so pleased to be their source of entertainment.

Niccola introduced his cousin. "Kenna, this is Elio Capri."

He sat across from me in a gorgeous Italian suit. His dark eyes found mine as a smile broke out behind his finger that rubbed across his lips.

"Nice to meet you." His sexy accent gave me goosebumps, or maybe it was because Grim's hand moved to his thigh, and it brushed by my bare skin.

"You as well." I smiled politely. He carried a level of dominance that almost made me shiver. He wore a large black ring, and it flashed in the lights that hung above us as he ran a hand through his thick black hair. Elio was an attractive man but, much like Trigger, he didn't seem to pay attention to the other women around us.

"I see you wore pink." Minnie admired my dress. "And your heels are fab." She studied my face. "Nice try, though." She drew out the words thoughtfully, and I knew she saw right through me.

I was trying to be okay, I wanted to be okay, but truth was I wasn't. I'd been through a lot and now, with Grim shutting down on me, I felt vulnerable. I wished I'd never let him in.

"However," she eased up, "I do approve of your girls being out." She pointed to my cleavage with a laugh. "I'll always approve of that."

"Thanks," I nodded at her and noticed Rail's face suddenly morph into an evil smile.

He rubbed his hands together. "It's showtime!"

Oh, shit.

"Hey, Kenna," Benny held up a beer, "I found you."

I swore my entire body broke out in a sweat. "Hey, you did." I pushed to my feet and stepped forward to give him a hug. "Sorry about the other night," I whispered as I pulled away. "Things had gotten a little crazy."

"Sounds like it, and no problem. I'm just pleased I get to spend more time with you." He looked around at the others. "Hi, I'm Ben, or Benny to some." He winked at me.

Rail, of course, took the lead and did some quick introductions, but when he got to Grim, I noticed he made sure to mention that he was my boss and one of the owners of the hotel.

"I'm looking forward to giving your new hotel a try when it opens." Benny was good at being polite, but I could tell the guys made him nervous. After all, biker guys and well-dressed men who reeked of mafia weren't exactly inviting company.

"Come sit." Tess politely stood, being the sweetheart she was, and moved to sit next to Morgan so Benny could sit. The vacated seat was next to Trigger. Benny looked sick as he took in the size of and look of him.

"Your seat's still open." Rail gave me a gentle push back toward Grim, and I eased back into my spot. Grim didn't move as I sat. I smiled warmly at Benny, trying to ease his concern for the present company.

"So, Benny," to my surprise, Brick piped up, "how long have you known Kenna?"

"Let's see, now." He rubbed his chin and looked at me as he thought. "Since junior year of high school. Right?"

"Yes," I nodded, "you'd just made the baseball team, and I was on my way to volleyball practice."

"Good memory." He beamed, clearly pleased that event had stayed with me.

Brick peeled the label on the side of his beer. "You ever dated?" I shot Minnie a look for help, but she pretended to sip her drink. *Thanks, Min.*

"Lord knows, I tried to get her attention." Benny laughed. "She was a force to be reckoned with."

Rail snorted. "Nothing's changed."

"Well, in all fairness, she was always surrounded by boys at school, *and* at home." He looked at me and tilted his head. The conversation we'd had the other night came screaming back to me. I started to panic. "And I see nothing has changed and that piece of trash is still hanging around."

Oh, no.

"What piece of trash?" Grim grunted, and I felt my head go light. I swung my gaze to Jesse with a look of pure terror. I hadn't shared those particular details with them yet.

"Sonny Conti, that rich guy from Chicago." Benny missed my expression that begged him to shut the hell up. "Not that he spent much time there."

"Wait," Grim looked at me, and I felt a blush creep up my throat, "Sonny Conti used to hang around Kenna?"

"Hang around, no." Benny took a swig of his beer. "But he was tight with her father."

Grim's gaze burned a hole in the side of my face. "Well, that's news to me."

"As it was to me," I chipped back, "when Benny told me."

"I saw him last night, when we were having dinner." Benny kept going. "Still hovering in the background. Seems not much has changed."

Trigger leaned forward and stared at me than at Benny. "Cameron's known Sonny since you two were in high school?"

"Maybe longer, I'm not sure, but since high school for sure."

"Elaborate." Trigger gave a quick look at Grim.

Benny finally tuned in to the vibe and chugged most of his beer, buying a moment. I, on the other hand, felt sick and wished I could dissolve into thin air.

"One night, I was at a work dinner with my father, and I saw Cameron was there too with someone else. I was building up the courage to ask Kenna to the winter ball and thought it would be nice to ask her father's permission." He looked a bit sheepish. "I mean they were a rather intimidating crowd." He looked at me, but it was a bit late to warn him off now. "Anyway, I approached him, and it seemed to go smoothly, but then Cameron took a call and left me without a clear answer." I could practically hear Trigger's frustration with all the useless details Benny shared. Between that and Grim's scowl, my nerves were shot. "I had come that far, you know, so I wasn't going to give up. The guy with him made me loosen my tie. If you know what I mean. He looked to be around my age." Benny swallowed and looked at me but got nothing. "He was a little rough around the edges." He looked around and seemed to realize who he was with and quickly looked down at his hands and blurted the rest. "Turned out his name was Sonny Conti. He flexed his muscle, and by that, I mean a handgun and shared some colorful words about me staying away from Kenna."

"Where was this dinner?" Grim asked.

"Ah, some bourbon club in Venice."

"Go on." Trigger stroked his chin.

"Senior year, I ran into him again." Benny's expression begged me to help. "Remember when we met at the park for pictures for homecoming, and there was a coffee shop across the street?"

"Yes," I couldn't help but answer. I was on the edge of my seat. I remembered that day well. "But Sonny never once showed his face there, Benny. I'm sure I would have remembered. I *think* I would have."

"He was there. He was with some guys, and they were talking to your father."

"Oh, my God," something hit me, "I remember Dad took off, saying something about needing to find a computer." I searched my brain to pull more of the memory forward. "And he was meeting Sonny?"

"Yeah, the creep saw me with you and thought we were going together. He got all up in my face and threatened me that he knew where I lived and that he'd fuck with my sister if I continued to go out with you."

"Why?" My words failed me. "Why didn't you ever tell me?"

"Kenna," his voice softened, "your father was enough for you to deal with on a good day. The last thing you needed was to be upset during homecoming."

"Well, it was kind of you, but I'm so sorry you had to carry that."

He shrugged. "I survived. I'm only sorry I wasn't strong enough to ignore him. I was young." He shrugged. "But I'm glad we were able to keep in touch anyway." He smiled. "We've had a couple of fun times since. I hope I haven't said anything wrong here." He looked around at Grim and Trigger. Neither of them said anything. "Well," he turned to me, "I'm happy to see you again, looking," his eyes widened, "unbelievable. I'm sorry that Sonny Conti's still hanging around."

"There's a lot that doesn't make sense right now," I admitted, and Minnie leaned into me to give me some quiet love.

"I know you said you're not exactly on the market, but I'm here with you now, and the night's still young." He smiled and took a sip of his beer.

Vinni and Rail both leaned forward and gave me shit-eating grins. I rolled my eyes and reached over and took a long drink of Minnie's martini.

"So, what do you all do?" Benny asked the group once the silence got to be too much.

Rail stood, pulling up his pants. "Come on, Benny, let's get you another drink."

"Rail," I warned.

"Um, sure." Benny downed the rest of his beer then got up and began to walk toward the bar. I jumped up and grabbed Rail's arm.

"Rail, if you mess with him, I swear I'll burn your body and hide the ashes where even God himself can't find them."

"Darlin', I sold them to the Devil years ago." His face lit up with a happy grin. "Now, let me get to know our new friend."

"Be nice," Tess stuck a finger out, "and don't start trouble."

"I'm just welcoming Kenna's man-friend to the group." He clapped his hands. "You all should take notes from me."

"We sure are learning a lot tonight," Grim grunted as he swirled the ice around his glass.

I drained the rest of Minnie's drink, and Tess slid hers over in my direction. I mouthed a *thank you.*

"And just when were you going to all share this with me?"

I used my lips to slide the olive off the toothpick as I glared at Grim. "Right around the time you stop acting like an asshole."

Elio cleared his throat and laughed as he glanced at Niccola.

"Now do you understand why we love Sienna?" Niccola said with a grin at Elio. I was too fired up to care much about what he meant, or who Sienna was.

"Grim, I only found out from Benny right before I heard about Leal." I tried to control my temper. I hated that I felt the need to explain myself to him. The thought that he'd ever think I'd hold something like that back from him was insulting.

"Was your phone broken?" he snapped.

"Was yours?" I couldn't believe him. "I barely had time to register it myself when I had to leave *my* date at the table," I used all the wrong words, but I wanted him to be as pissed as I was, "to look for *your* dog. You're welcome, by the way."

"Oh, my friend," Elio shook his head and he studied Grim, "I'm so glad I came, if only to see you get a taste of such fire." Elio twisted his wedding band, clearly unfazed by our fighting. "Reminds me of my beautiful wife. Also," he glanced over at Tess, "reminds me of someone else I know." Tess glanced at Trigger and shoved his shoulder playfully.

"Yeah." Tess chuckled as Grim and I glared at one another. "Grim's met his match as well."

"That he has." I stood and snagged my purse off the table. "Please excuse me, everyone, but I need something stronger." I left before I said something I couldn't take back.

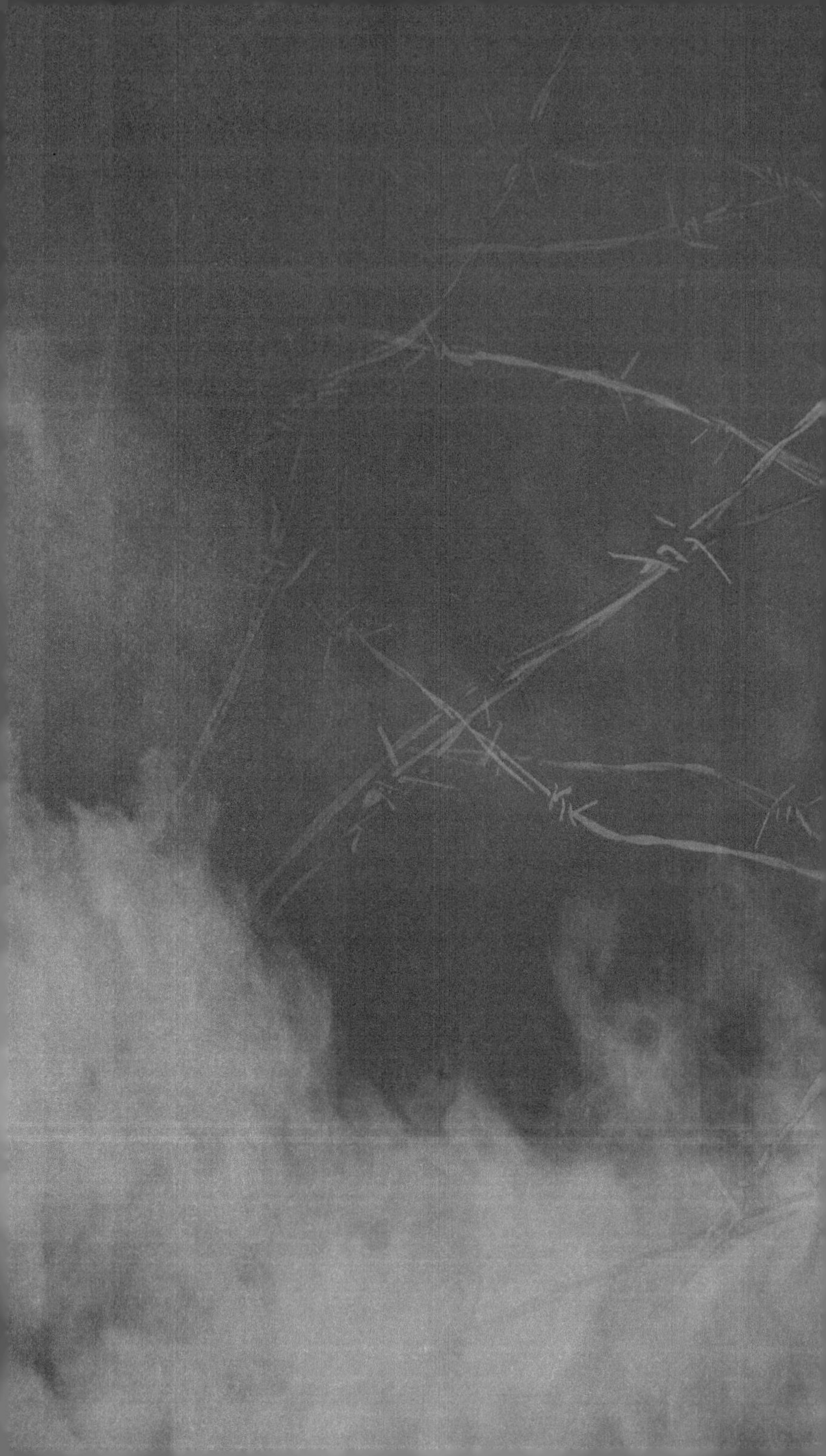

TWENTY-FOUR

SIMON

I was warned he'd retaliate, but after a few years of silence, I thought I was in the clear. Who was I to them, anyway? I was just a man trying to live a simple life. I had no reason and definitely no desire to be a part of their club, yet there I was in my own home with a dead body on my kitchen floor and the FBI with their guns pointed at me.

"Hands up, turn around, and walk backward to the sound of my voice," the agent ordered, and I complied out of sheer fear.

I was read my rights and walked outside for all my neighbors to see. I couldn't believe what was happening. I was the quiet man who lived in the little house at the end of the lane. I took pride in my property, took pleasure when someone would stop and chat when I went out to mow the *grass on a Sunday afternoon. I enjoyed my simple, quiet life. Now I would be the talk of the town, and I blushed at the thought. Then I saw him. He sat on his bike under my big shade tree at the side with an expression that burned itself into my memory.*

"When do I get to call my lawyer?" I asked as I was handcuffed.

The agent turned me around and gave me a hard look of distaste. I thought for a moment he contemplated not answering me. "When I say so."

"Understood," I whispered and reassured myself that in a few days I'd be back home laughing it off with the neighbors about how big a mistake it all was. This just wasn't me. I wasn't a killer of some innocent person.

"You made your choice," Allen called as the agent stopped to unlock his car. "See ya on the outside."

"Get lost." The FBI agent flicked his hand, and Allen turned over his bike's engine, and I could hear his laugh as he sped down the street. I was suddenly left with a boatload of fear that I just might not be able to walk free from this.

"Duck." The agent pushed my head down, and I awkwardly shimmied into the back seat. "Get comfortable because you got a long road ahead of you." He slammed the door, and I swallowed down the panic that tore at my chest.

What the hell just happened?

After that, my memory blurred on the details. I remembered my lawyer warned me not to react and to sit quietly even when so-called eyewitnesses were called and lied about me. I had no family to support me, no friends appeared in the courtroom, the media didn't care about my plea that I was being framed. I was just another criminal, a man who supposedly got into a fight with my "drug dealer" and killed him. I suddenly had zero control over my life, and it was going down the drain faster than I could take my next breath.

Allen thought of everything. I'd been served up on a silver platter for the FBI. Slam dunk.

"What did he say?"

I looked at my lawyer in disbelief as he tugged at his cheap tie and looked relieved rather than disappointed. "The judge, what did he say?" I repeated as I felt my soul leave my body.

"He said fifteen to twenty, but out in ten if you behave." I blinked at him and tried to register the length of time that had just been robbed from my life.

"Stand." The officer pulled me to my feet and yanked me away. When I turned to glance one more time at my lawyer, I saw him use a rag to dry his forehead and knew the truth. Fucking Allen was everywhere. I had ten years to retaliate.

"What a fucking nightmare." Cameron burst through his office door and jolted me from my past. I quickly got my head on straight and stood up, rubbing my dry contacts. It had been a while since I'd let my head go back to such a dark place. "What do we know?"

"Not much." I wished I had more to offer him, but the truth was the Gateses had the details of Leo's death under lock and key. "Grim had the whole floor of their suites sealed down at the hotel even before the police arrived. Everyone who entered Leo's room had to be vetted. No one else could get near the place."

"Can't Kurt pull some strings? Talk to the staff. Someone must know something."

"He's digging, but not much luck. No one's saying anything. I've got a couple calls in to people to see what they know. I'm just waiting for some call backs."

Truth was, I had Kurt building a package for Brick on the whole brother search thing once he told me he hadn't been able to find out a thing on Leo's murder. I had to give Brick something soon or he and Trigger would be after my hide.

"Damn!" Cameron tossed his phone on the desk. "Did you send Jim and Laurel the flowers?"

"Yes, the very next day," I assured him. "I made sure they knew you were thinking of them and that you were trying to get a flight out asap."

"Good." He pulled his chair out and huffed as he sat.

I hesitated to share this next piece of news; he was already walking a fine line.

"By the way," I took my glasses off and cleaned the lenses with the side of my shirt, "Mr. Griple called again." I shifted my weight from foot to foot as I watched Cameron's face fall. For years we've worked on keeping Griple out of prison, but his trial wasn't going to wait. No matter how much money he and Cameron tossed at people, he still faced a life sentence for a hit back in Carson City. This was bad—really bad.

"Fuck," he closed his eyes, "why of all people did that tattooed shithead have to kill my fall guy?"

"Martin Castillo had a lot of enemies, Cameron. If it wasn't Grim, it would've been someone else. It was a matter of time. We all knew he'd be taken out at some point."

"Are you siding with him now?" He peered over his reading glasses at me, his face red. "You know what it means if Griple goes to jail."

"I know," I didn't need a reminder; it had been the elephant in the room since practically the day we met, "but avoiding his calls will mean he'll send more sharks." I paused. "Speaking of which, where the hell is Sasha?"

"Fuck if I know." Cameron shrugged. "You ask Kenna?"

"No." My mind went to how she'd looked when I saw her on her way to the rooftop bar.

"Calli's back." He shifted some papers around, and I knew he was pleased I was off the Griple topic. "She was looking for you this morning. Something about a case number." He waved his hand at me. "Make sure you find out what she wants."

"Of course." I could use a good night of stress release.

"Oh, yes, I need you to get rid of that envelope I was sent. I want it out of here." He leaned down and opened his desk drawer. "What the hell?" I moved close as I saw him freeze. He shuffled some things around. "I put it in here, but it's gone."

"You sure?" I moved around the desk.

"Yes, I'm sure it's gone," he snapped. "It was here, and now it isn't."

"Maybe you moved it?"

"I'm not senile, Simon. I know when I move something!" He leaned back in his chair and pinched the bridge of his nose. "I need to think." I knew what that meant, and I rushed to get out of there. As I passed by the trash on my way to the door, I noticed a cup of coffee sitting on the top. It had a bit of coffee dripping from the lid. *Odd.* I looked over my shoulder at Cameron, who still had his eyes closed, and gently touched the cup with my finger. It was full. I turned the cup around and saw Kenna's name written on the side of it.

"Did Kenna come by to see you today?"

"No. Why are you still here?" He sounded annoyed.

Oh, shit. I charged toward the rooftop to find Kenna.

TWENTY-FIVE

GRIM

The noise in the bar faded in and out as I thought about Leo and how I was never going to see him again. Death was a normal thing in my world, but if I was honest with myself, I thought if any one of us was ever going to go, it would have been Knox because of his reckless behavior. It was why I'd hired an extra security team to watch over him—not that he knew. He was young and stupid, but I'd give up my life for him in a heartbeat. I was the oldest. It was my job to protect them, and I felt sick that I was still alive and Leo wasn't.

"I know that look." Elio sat down next to me. I couldn't believe he'd come all this way to support me in the loss of my brother. I knew he had a lot to deal with back in Italy. "I can't imagine losing one of them." He nodded to his cousins Niccola and Vinni, who were like his brothers. "I can't imagine how you must feel, but I do understand loss. I lost Sienna, perhaps not in death, but twice in my life I had to face that terrible feeling that I'd never see her again." He sat back and studied those around us, then pointed in Kenna's direction with a question.

"She's just a distraction."

"Perhaps no longer." He shrugged and nodded toward Benny. He had his hand on her hip as she moved aside for someone to order at the bar. A tiny part of me clawed out from behind the curtain in my head and begged me to rip his hold off her. I squeezed the glass in my hand then put it down before I cracked it.

"All right, I'm here now as a friend. Tell me what you need me to do." I knew he referred to Leo. "All my resources are at your service."

I licked my lips and knew if I was going to catch whoever killed my brother, I'd need to go loud.

"Get the word out I'll give a million US for anyone who can tell me who did it and two if they bring him to me alive."

"Done."

"But," I ripped my eyes from Kenna, "I want proof."

"Of course." We both sat in silence. I knew Elio had

a network of people who could get the word out quicky and effectively, not just here in the USA but across multiple countries. Transnational organized crime had no limits. My family were well known, and there were no borders or rules that would stop someone who wanted to hurt us.

Elio tapped his temple. "Be careful in here." He lowered his voice. "Trigger spent most of his life lost inside his head, thanks to his father. Allen was truly a cruel man. I'd hate to lose another of my friends in that darkness. Remember, it was only the love of his woman that pulled him back from that awful place." He glanced at Tess, who seemed to realize she was being talked about and looked over and smiled. "Leo wouldn't want you to go full Grim Reaper." He paused. "Well, perhaps a little." He grinned to lighten the mood.

I appreciated that he cared. He was a lot more vocal than Trigger. I thought about our friendship over the years. I was a mix of the two of them, and maybe it was why the three of us hit it off so well. We not only meshed in the business world but also in our love of the ring.

"Just so it's said," I needed him to know, "I appreciate you coming, given what you're dealing with at home." I knew he'd finally captured Rosa and Tieri, enemies of his family he'd been hunting for years. "I'm glad you got those two. I'm sure they're on ice until you get back." He had to be itching to get at them for all they'd put him through. There was a side to that, though, that appealed to me, so probably to him as well. Let them sweat over what was to come.

"This is where I need to be. It's what friends are for, Grim. You'd do the same. Besides," he chuckled, "I believe my Sienna is enjoying her time with them." He gave a sinister grin. "I need to let her have her fun. She suffered considerably at their hands."

"Well, in that case, I'm happy for her." I felt the corners of my mouth tug at the dark thought of his wife having some fun with those who had tried to destroy her life.

"I heard you have someone on ice yourself," Elio mused, "one of the men who was involved with hurting Leal and Zhar?"

I nodded. "He'll be our dessert after our evening drinks."

"I'm looking forward to it. Any ideas in mind?"

"No clear plan, but you know how I love the snap of bones. It's been too long, and I'm savoring the moment. I want it to be something we'll all enjoy. Their pain is just what I need at the moment. Lots of pain."

"Trigger and I, of all people, understand that need." He nodded and looked up as

Niccola called out and held up a phone. "*Mi scusi.*" He slipped back into Italian as he stepped away.

"Well," Minnie draped her arm along the back of

the couch Elio had just vacated, "you want the good news or the bad news?"

I cursed inside and waited for her to tell me.

"Your bother just arrived with Calli hanging on his arm."

Great. Her sister's here. I spotted them. Knox had his back to us as he chatted to someone. I hadn't spoken to him since I'd punched him at the meeting.

"And the good?"

"I lied about that. It's worse. You're about to have a visitor. She'll be here in about five seconds."

"Who?" I wasn't ready to deal with anyone else. It had been a bad enough day.

"Your skin tag of an ex." *Shit. Jenelle.* "You want me to kick the vagina flap out or run interference for ya? Oops, too late."

I stilled as Jenelle's hands slid over my shoulders before she leaned down to kiss my cheek.

"Oh, baby, I just heard about Leo. It's just terrible." I closed my eyes and controlled my temper. "What can I do?" She moved around the couch and sat on my lap then wrapped her arms around my neck.

"Getting off his lap would be a start," Minnie muttered, and Jenelle threw her a dirty look.

"Jenelle," I pushed her hips away from me, "off."

She pouted and swiveled to sit next to me, obviously not registering my tone. *Shit, woman, read the room.*

"Grim," she ran a hand over my leg, and I rubbed my head as I tried to think, "why don't we go to your place and get a drink? I know I can make you feel better if you let me try."

I pushed to my feet and whirled around.

"Jenelle, I need you to back off." I stalked away from her. I caught Minnie's grin and knew she and Tess would be only too happy to help. I stopped at my usual corner of the bar, and the bartender immediately came over. I pointed to the Lagavulin, and he nodded. I needed something different, and the strong, peaty taste of that single malt seemed perfect for my mood. "Three fingers." He didn't miss beat and filled the glass with a good three ounces then tapped in a little extra. Thank god someone was able to read a room.

"Anything else? Mr. Gates?"

"No." He'd know to put it on my tab, as usual, but I tossed an extra twenty down. He thanked me and was smart enough not to linger. I sipped my drink and let my head have a moment. I forced out the noise and tried to push back the anger that had consumed me since Leo's death. I allowed myself a few moments to look around. Fucking Jenelle had the most impeccable timing. She'd always seemed so blind to how I felt. She couldn't take a hint when it smacked in her the face. I watched as Minnie and Tess seemed to have her pinned at the table. I turned away and scanned the crowd.

What the fuck was he doing here? Simon watched Kenna from a spot near the door. My mind went back to my conversation with Dad. I didn't trust him. He sure as hell wasn't welcome up here in my space. Anyone connected to Cameron Tame was my enemy. Well, I guessed I made a few exceptions. I glanced over at Kenna. My eyes then went to her sister, and I closed my eyes briefly as I fought the pain yet again. My anger burned hotter than ever. The whole damn Tame family was nothing but trouble. Look where it got Leo. I took another swig of the strong scotch and tried to calm myself before I did anything I'd regret.

Knox's voice found me. "Hey." I ground my teeth; I wasn't ready to deal with him. I wanted to be alone. "Grim?"

I refused to look at him and hoped he'd get the hint. I just took another drink and stared into the glass.

"Look, I know things were said the other night, and I know things haven't been great since you got back from Mexico, but are we good?"

I ignored him and watched as Simon moved closer to Kenna, and I felt my temper rise, if that was even possible. I felt my brother's eyes on me, and he sighed and turned to look in the same direction I did.

My head went back to the video Hanna had taken and wondered what the rest of the conversation had been between Simon and Sasha that day. As far as I was concerned, he was just another predator in the grass until proven otherwise, and I didn't like the fact that he seemed to have his sights on Kenna. An unexpected wave of what felt like jealousy took over, and I tried to stomp back the need to protect. I'd never shared that it was Simon on the video talking to Sasha with anyone but Dad.

"Grim, will you just listen? I know you think I'll never measure up to Leo, but I want to try. I hope you'll give me a chance."

"This isn't the time, Knox," I warned.

"Look, I just wanted to say things are getting more serious with Calli, and I was thinking that maybe she and I could be something more. I know now isn't the time, but I could use some brotherly—" I held up a hand to him as Simon went to the bar and a moment later threw back a shot while glaring at Benny, who had put his hand on Kenna's shoulder. They both laughed at something. He seemed to make a decision and pushed his glasses up his nose and took a step in their direction.

Fuck that.

"We'll talk later." I brushed by Knox and blocked Simon's approach. With my back to him, I hooked Kenna around the waist and pulled her away from Benny. "We need to talk."

"Hello to you, too."

I ignored her tone. "You need to leave."

"Excuse me?" She laughed. She pulled in her chin

and stared up at me. "Who do you think you are?" I knew she was appalled at my behavior, but I didn't care.

"Kenna, just come." My hand flexed on her hip, and she allowed me to draw her away from the bar a few steps. The heat from her body hit me in a wave, and I drew in her scent. *Shit.* I felt an intense need to throw her down, and I shook myself. "Let's not forget you're being watched and—"

"So, what? I should go back to my suite and hide when I have a motorcycle club, the Italian mafia, and the Vegas Reaper," she pressed a finger into my chest, "two feet away from me? She studied my face. "Something tells me I'm safer here than in my lonely suite." Her gaze flickered for a hair of second, and I found myself wondering how she was doing with everything. I had enough sense to know she'd been shaken by all that had happened but just as quickly reined it in. "I don't think I'm being watched anymore. I haven't had any texts since the desert. Besides, Rail tried to bait him, but nothing happened."

"That's news to me."

"Everything okay?" Benny came up to us. His eyes dropped to my hand that was still on her hip.

"No." I glared at him.

"Yes," Kenna smiled warmly at him, "we just need a moment."

"Kenna," I warned, "you need to leave."

She glared at me, and I pulled her in closer to me as I saw Calli's face and knew she had just spotted Kenna. *Fuck!* Just my luck. Two hardheaded sisters about to go at it.

"Maybe I'm the one who should leave." Benny read the situation, or maybe he noticed Kenna didn't pull away.

"That would be a good idea," I agreed.

"Grim, seriously?" Kenna put a hand on her hip.

"I gave you an order," I reminded her. Her cheeks flushed as she swallowed back her comment. She turned to address Benny.

"I'm sorry for his rudeness and the fact that he thinks he can order me around." She cut her eyes back to me for a moment. "He's delusional at times and just needs to be put in his place. If you could excuse us, I'll be back in a moment." She grabbed my hand and pulled me to follow, but her sister stepped in our path.

"Oh, look what's at the bar." Calli snickered. "I thought you said we hadn't ordered any adult entertainment tonight, babe," she tossed over her shoulder to Knox, who wouldn't make eye contact with me.

"Really, Calli, now?" Kenna rolled her eyes and looked at Knox. "You could do so much better, Knox."

"Enough." I couldn't take their arguing. I pressed my hands against Kenna's waist and steered her away from them to the far corner where it was slightly quieter.

"When I give you an order, I expect you to follow it," I said through clenched teeth.

She whirled around and stuck a finger in my face. "When are you going to get it through your thick skull that I don't take orders from you?" she yelled, and I saw Benny make a hasty retreat toward the exit.

"I need you to listen, for Christ's sake." I gritted my teeth and tried to restrain myself from choking her. "We're leaving. We have someone to deal with." I allowed myself a moment of satisfaction at the thought of inflicting great pain on that waste of space downstairs. It would give me just what I needed, if only for a while. "I want you to go back to my suite and wait for me there."

"I've got a friend here. I can't ditch Benny two nights in a row."

"He just left." I raised an eyebrow. "Unlike some people, he can take a hint."

Her shoulders sagged as she shook her head in defeat. "Damn you, Grim, your hints are far from subtle. You use your big scary—" she paused and moved her hand around "—ness, to lead people to believe I'm yours. When I'm not. Why do you do that?" She stared right at me, and I threw my wall up so her words couldn't affect me. "You need to learn to back off and stop playing mind games with everyone."

I rubbed my chin and took a moment as I eyed Simon, who watched us from the bar.

So, I played dirty. I didn't care.

"Look, Kenna, I'd like you to go to my place, because as much as I can't believe it, you worked your way past Leal's defenses, and I think it would do him some good to see you. He was shot, after all, and is still healing."

Her face softened, and I knew I had her. It wasn't a complete lie; I'd never seen anyone get as close to Leal as she had.

She lowered her head and took a deep breath. "What about Zhar? How will he handle me being there?"

"He'll follow his brother's lead," I reassured her. "He'll warm up if Leal does."

"Fine," she looked away, "for Leal."

"For Leal." I hid that I was pleased I won. "Jesse will take you down."

"I think I can manage."

I opened my mouth to protest but shut it again. I needed to pick my battles. "Fine." I walked her to the elevator to ensure Simon had no opportunity to approach her.

"Grim," she turned as she stepped inside, "I…" Then she shook her head. "Actually, never mind." She dropped her hands as the doors closed.

"Ready to spill some blood?" Brick asked from behind me. "I know I am."

"Yeah." I immediately shifted my brain to what I needed to do. I heard the others come up behind us.

"We're all here," Jesse let me know.

"All right, and Jesse?"

"Yeah, boss." He moved to stand in front of me.

"Simon's at the bar."

Jesse nodded. "I'll get Jason to watch him." He made a call as we headed downstairs.

My friends all leaned against the wall as they waited in anticipation to see what kind of entertainment I'd bring them. I was known to be a tad theatrical with my kills. After all, with Trigger and Elio's reputation for their own inventive styles, I had to keep up. I smiled at the memory of a few momentous pieces. I could have used the mine, but dropping someone into that dark abyss and simply hearing them scream for help just didn't seem ruthless enough. No, I needed more.

"Who hired you?" I directed my question to the piece of shit who stood tied to a heavy cinder block by one of his legs. His face was badly beaten, and he cradled one of his arms I'd had a bit of fun with as my introduction to the event. As much as I wanted to beat him until his last breath, I needed to feed my internal hunger for revenge for my boys and Darcy. Not to mention my company deserved something a little different, and who was I to deny them that? Something a little extra, particularly for Leal.

The man boldly chuckled, and I mentally rolled my eyes. They always had a set of balls until they saw what I would bring to the table.

I studied my watch and for half a moment wondered what Kenna was up to in my place. Her scent had worn off my bedding from when she'd lain with Leal, and I secretly hoped she'd lie down with him again so it would return. The scent of that woman did wonders for my head.

"Jesse." I flicked my hand, and he turned on the water. It gushed from the side of the wall and pooled at the man's feet, thanks to the slope in the floor.

"I'll take a drowning any day." He looked unimpressed, and I just smiled and let him think drowning was all he'd have to endure.

I looked around at my friends. Trigger watched, expressionless, while Elio whispered something to Niccola with a smile. Rail shifted his weight from one foot to the other as he ran his mouth to Brick about all the possibilities I might come up with. I could feel the anticipation build. Unlike the battered fool before me, they knew me well.

"One Gates down, four to go." The man snickered and drew my attention back to him. My eyes clouded as a loud, ear-piercing ring filled my head.

"Jesse," I called again. My voice was laced with a

menacing darkness, and the mood in the room changed as I slowly let the reaper in.

A door slid open, and a sixteen-hundred-pound Nile crocodile wove his way into the room. He looked exceptionally pissed off and swung his head left then right as it looked around for its next meal. His handler and team provided a safe barrier for me and the others.

The croc suddenly set his unblinking reptilian stare on the bloody man who stood in three feet of water.

"Fuck me," Rail said gleefully. "It's like Christmas and a Sunday picnic all rolled into one."

"How could you know?" The man's suddenly terrified expression latched on to mine. There was obviously something I wasn't getting, and it made me wonder. "That's impossible!"

I kept my expression unfazed as I tried to read his mind. I glanced at Jesse and caught the same interest in his face as he gave me a quick glance.

"I'll ask you one more time." I kept my tone even. "Who hired you to go after my dogs?"

He eyed the croc as it sank under the water and licked his lips, then he looked at me as if weighing his options.

"Ah…" The handler looked unsure. I knew he wondered if he should step in and stop the kill. "It's a matter of seconds now, Mr. Gates."

I opened my arms as if to say *you have seconds left to live.*

"It's poetic, really," his battered face nodded, "to be killed by one of our own." The croc lunged and snapped his jaws around his hips and rolled with him under the water. The huge jaws tore his body apart as he violently shook him like a toy. The water turned red as he slammed his body hard and his torso was severed from his legs.

A sense of unease dampened my enjoyment as I watched the man being ripped limb from limb by those incredible jaws. What had he meant?

"Jesse."

"On it, boss."

I knew Jesse would already be on the new information, and as he left, Elio and Trigger approached.

"Fucking first." Trigger flipped his long forelock back with a swipe of his hand.

"Impressive," Elio agreed. We all watched as the croc finished up. His handler waved his men off to let the reptilian beast finish his meal.

"Shall we meet later to discuss this rather interesting new information?" Elio looked at me then at Trigger.

"Give me a little time," I needed time to process, "then I'd appreciate the help."

Instead of bringing me a little peace, I felt wound up and worse off than before. I didn't look back as I left and headed for my place. By sunup, there wouldn't be a trace of what had taken place with the croc. The man who had hurt my boys and killed Darcy had been erased from this Earth, and the croc would go back to his tank until his special skills were needed again. I should feel a lot better, but the words he'd spoken with such acceptance replayed in my head.

I burst through the doors of my suite to find the living room empty. She better not have fucking left! The bedroom was empty, but Leal lay resting on his bed with Zhar not far from him. They both looked up at me but stayed where they were. I could smell her perfume and knew she'd been there.

"Where is she, boy?" I gave Leal's head a pat. He yawned and let his head flop back down. Zhar's ears perked up and twitched to let me know he wanted attention, too.

"You're back." She stepped out of the bathroom, and I made a show to drop my gaze slowly down her front. She was still in her pink dress, and it showed off her breasts perfectly. "How was your meeting?" She made a nod toward my battered hand. "Successful?"

I ditched my jacket and undid the first few buttons on my dress shirt.

"Yes, but not rewarding." I watched her slowly make her way to the door. "Where are you going?"

She patted Zhar's head. Clearly, they'd made some progress while I was gone. Then she leaned down and patted Leal after he let out a pathetic whimper. "I'm going home."

"No."

"Yes." She didn't miss a beat and slipped out into the hallway. I followed her.

"Kenna."

"Grim."

This wasn't the day to mess with me, and my temper heated again. I reached out, grabbed her waist, and pushed her against the wall.

"Grim!" I slammed my lips to hers and devoured her mouth. She began to protest, but she gave in, and I felt her response when I pulled her hips into me. I showed her just how much I needed her.

"My head's so fucked up," I confessed when I let her catch her breath. "It's like the darkness is consuming me and I need a way to release it."

"Who did those orange panties belong to?"

"Kelly." I saw her face twist with disgust. "I didn't sleep with her. She came with Knox's side chick, stripped down, but nothing happened. I kicked her out." I paused. "I swear."

She stared at me intensely for a moment then pushed me back with both hands until I met the opposite wall, and she kissed me hard then pulled away from me. As I watched, she reached over her shoulder and gracefully unzipped her dress and slowly peeled it off her body. It dropped at her feet, and she stepped out of it.

"I promised myself," she said quietly, "that I would

help you get through this tragedy in any way I could. If this is what you need…"

She turned toward my bedroom in her lacy panties, and the sight of her cheeks as they glowed in the red under-light made my breath hitch. I let my head fall back against the wall as guilt took over my thoughts and reminded me why I'd kept my distance from her in the first place.

Lust won out, and before I knew what I was doing, my belt was undone, and my painful erection found relief. She lay face down over the edge of my bed, her gorgeous ass on display. She had kept her heels on and had flung her bra over my pillow. I slid my hand over her bare ass and fought to rein myself in a bit, but her smooth skin drew my head into a trance. I didn't check to see if she was ready. I knew Kenna was always ready when I was near. History had proven that. I lined up and plunged all the way in. A shiver shot across my skin as she pushed back with a moan. "Fuckkkk." I grabbed her hips and slammed back in, then out, then in again. I leaned down and licked her spine then morphed it into a kiss at the nape of her neck. I forgot how much I needed to be inside this woman that I couldn't help but taste her.

I got on my knees above her and pressed her hard into the bed as I pumped against her. The sounds she made drove me mad, and the need to feed filled my head. She fisted the sheets and held on as I stabilized myself then thrust so hard it made her scream. I lost track of time as I fed, but I couldn't seem to get deep enough, or fast enough. I just built and built, but release wouldn't come. I heard her voice but not the words. Her fists pounded against the mattress, and it finally got through to me that she was having trouble breathing from that angle.

I flipped her over as concern filled me, but only for a split second as I saw the expression in her eyes, and as her legs wrapped around me, I knew she had the same desperate need. Her face and breasts were slick with sweat, and it came to me as I took what I wanted that she was the most beautiful thing I'd ever seen. My urge to break her, to have her submit to me became all-consuming, but at the same time I knew I fed off her hate.

"More." She pushed herself frantically against me. I knew I was one step away from losing all sense of her safety. "Give me more," she screamed and took my hand and wrapped it around her throat. "Lose yourself with me."

Her words got through to me, in spite of my wild thoughts, I quickly pulled back from her and put my hands to my head as a sharp pain drilled behind my eyes.

"Grim?" she whispered. "What's wrong?"

I dropped my hands and glared at her as though she wasn't the person who could bring me release in this fucked up world. "What's wrong?" I repeated and felt my temper rush to the surface as Leo's lifeless body flashed in front of me. "What's wrong is I can't believe I chose you over saving my brother!"

"What the hell did you just say to me?" She pushed herself upright and covered her breasts with an arm.

"I heard something crash!" I snapped. "Fuck knows what was happening in that moment when I stood there, right outside his room, but all I could think about was getting to you."

"Okay," she stood almost in slow motion, as if she thought I'd break, "but Grim, Leo wasn't killed because you chose me. He was killed because people were after you."

"He was killed," I corrected her, "because he took my jacket. They marked me at the bar, he took my jacket, flashed the mark around in the lobby to Paige and everyone else. He probably wondered what it was. Then they followed him all the way up to his room and killed him. It should have been me dead in that room. Butchered like some animal." I could feel the sob deep in my chest and swallowed hard.

Her face paled and her eyes watered. "Oh, Grim. I had no idea." She cleared her throat. "Why didn't you tell me?"

"Why do I need to tell you anything?" Hurt filled my chest and dug its painful claws into my flesh with the realization that I would never see my brother again and it was my fault.

"You were only there because I needed to win over a client." I hated that she was crying. Why should she be the one crying? "And," I wanted her to hurt as much as I did, "I wanted you along to fulfill my tastes in the bedroom. You're good for that."

Her face recoiled in shock as my words sank in. I knew it was the lowest of blows, but misery loved misery.

"Wow." She pushed by me to grab her dress and shoes. "I get that you're hurting, Grim," she sniffed, "but that was low."

"I could go lower," slipped from my lips.

She turned to look over her shoulder as she pulled on my dress shirt. "Oh, yeah?" She wrapped it around her body and came to stand in front of me. Her chin was raised in defiance, and I knew she wanted a fight. If that was what she wanted, I wasn't about to back down. We were too far into this now. "Let's hear what you have to say."

I let the gates of hell open inside my head and let the dam that I'd been holding back since Leo's death flow out without a care.

"You've got a pretty face and big tits. It's why your father uses you to win over his clients. It's what my father sees too, and why I keep you around. I—"

Crack! She slapped me across the face, and a deep

thrill vibrated through me. A slow menacing smirk spread across my lips. I felt alive.

"That's right. You might think it's your brains, Kenna, but even your sister can see who you really are."

Tears streamed down her white face, and part of me screamed to repair the damage I'd just done, but I couldn't. I was too far gone and just wanted to ease the terrible guilt I felt. I ignored every warning inside me as I lashed out blindly. I wanted to tear her apart the way the croc had ripped up that piece of shit who had hurt my dogs. I wanted her to feel the pain I felt.

"Congratulations," she managed to say, though her voice was raspy and barely above a whisper, "you've just managed to hurt me worse than anyone in this world."

I thought she'd say more. I thought she'd fight, but she just stepped around me, opened the door, and disappeared down the hall. I stood there a moment then pulled on my pants and sank into the couch.

Zhar pushed his nose under my hand and rested his head on my thigh. Then Leal whimpered and got up. He hobbled to the open door and looked at the direction she'd taken and whined. He awkwardly sat and waited as if she was going to come back.

"She's gone, Leal. She's not coming back."

TWENTY-SIX

KENNA

"What did he do now?" Minnie folded her arms and leaned against the wall of my suite as I slipped into a neon blue bikini. I was about to meet Yen Hong for a pool party he'd set up to entertain one of his younger clients. The guy was in town until tomorrow, so I couldn't put him off. My job spanned many areas, and if Yen Hong wanted me to wear a glittery g-string and dance around the pool, I'd do it. The harsh sting of Grim's words the night before were far from forgotten, but I'd managed to pull in my hurt and try to understand what had happened.

"He's in pain." I hated that I was smart enough to see what was really going on with him. Being an adult sucked sometimes. I reassured myself that he'd acted like a hurt child who needed to strike out. In reality, I just wanted to say fuck it and go back to our daily fights. I hadn't realized I'd missed our regular faceoffs. He was fun to mess with.

She nodded. "So, what did he do this time?"

I held a cover up in front of me in the mirror. "Said some very nasty things."

"You seem really calm for a woman who's had nasty things said to them by the reaper himself."

"Calm isn't a word I would use for how I'm feeling right now." I decided against the black coverup for a white one.

"Okay," she studied me in the mirror, "on a scale from Jim Gates to daddy-dearest, how badly did he hurt you?"

"Oh," I chuckled darkly, "we're way past daddy-dearest."

Minnie moved so she could see my face more clearly in the glass. "Are you okay?"

"Let's just say I looked over Yen's offer to work for him in Hong Kong again."

Her face fell, and she turned me around by my shoulders. "Ken, no. This is where you belong."

"I know," I assured her, "and I know he's hurting and that he lashed at me because I saw him at his most vulnerable, but he did some damage I'm not sure I even want fixed."

"Fucking Jeezelle." She snickered, and I followed her out of the closet.

"What does that delusional twit have to do with anything?"

"She showed up last night, tried to get him to take her back to his place. He tossed her to us, but I knew just having her show up would screw with his head. So, between her wide-open legs and Leo, I'm sure he's a mess."

"He blames himself for Leo's murder."

"How?" She looked confused.

"I guess he almost went to see his brother that night, but then changed his mind and came to me instead."

"Holy shit. That's terrible." Minnie put her hand to her chest.

"Yeah, and then last night, after Grim's nasty payback, I left his place in nothing but his shirt, and got caught by Jesse in the elevator on my way back to my room." I closed my eyes, embarrassed Jesse had seen me that way.

"Men," she huffed. "Maybe Grim and Brick need to spend some time together since he's in a dick mood right now too."

"What now?" I felt bad I hadn't asked about her and Brick lately.

"Same shit." She curled up on the couch. "He acts like he wants more, then he pulls away. Something's going on with him and Trigger. Brick seems happy for a bit then disappears on some job and returns in a shit mood." She covers her eyes. "Like, pick a mood and fucking stick with it."

"I'm sorry, Min."

"So am I, for you."

"See," I laughed, and it came out like a snort, "this is why turning lesbian looks so damn appealing as we get older."

"Amen."

The lobby was in full swing with a bus load of tourists all chattering about their day at the Hoover Dam.

I checked the time and saw Yen had written to say his friend was still in the casino and he'd be a little late for our meeting.

"Great. Spend your money." I chuckled to myself. Suddenly, someone clipped my shoulder hard and sent me into a tailspin. I put my hand on a pillar to steady myself. Once I caught my breath, I looked around and saw her. I couldn't miss that face full of freckles, and my stomach dropped.

I saw Grim across the lobby; he watched and began to walk my way. He must have caught my encounter.

The woman pushed her stringy hair out of her face,

and I was instantly thrust back to that night in the parking garage.

"I see the bruises have healed." She looked me up and down, and images of my attack flashed before me.

"Don't think he's not still watching you." She laughed like she was high on something.

"What?" I felt the air get sucked from my lungs.

"He saw you at the bar with your new boyfriend. He better watch himself or he'll be next."

"Holy shit!" He really was still watching me.

"Trust me, bitch, there's nothing holy about this guy."

Grim appeared then and waved at someone. Seconds later, security made their move. One grabbed her arms, and the others blocked the view so the tourists wouldn't see.

"Get her in the back," Grim ordered and looked back at me. "What the hell was that all about? Are you okay?"

"Not even close."

"Come with me," Grim ordered, and I stopped short and looked at him. "I'll need you there when we question her." His voice was a lot more civil.

"All right," I agreed.

A short while later, we gathered in Grim's office. The woman managed to keep up her cocky attitude.

"You know I recognize you from Dirty Demons."

She snapped her pink gum like she was twelve and thought she was cool.

I cut her off. "Tell me about the man you're working with." The last thing I needed was Grim finding out I danced at Minnie's club.

"Don't know." She kicked her hooker heels up on the table, but Grim knocked them down, nearly making her fall out of her chair.

"Talk or choke on my fist," he threatened, and she rolled her eyes. Clearly, she'd dealt with aggressive men before. Men like Grim wouldn't necessarily scare her much. I needed another tactic.

"I'll give you a hundred if you tell me who he is." I pulled a bill out, and Grim scowled at me, but the chick grabbed it and held it up to the light to check if it was fake then pushed it into her skimpy cleavage.

"Like I said, I don't know. I only danced at Minnie's for a few months when I started to see this guy hanging around the place." I texted Minnie and filled her in and asked her to come to the hotel. She might be able to help.

"What did he look like?" I cut my eyes at Grim to let me continue without any interruptions.

"Tall, slim, kinda has a Brad Pitt thing going on, but looks like Liam Neeson in some lights." I closed my eyes and envisioned all the ways I could make her talk. Christ, now I was getting dark. "He always wanted a lap dance but not much more. He seemed to just want to talk more than anything."

"About?" Grim cut in.

"Her." She pointed at me. I looked at her then at Grim, and I saw the vein in his jaw tick. I shrugged to show I had no idea. Who the hell was that man?

"If the money wasn't so good, I'd be jealous, but a girl's gotta eat."

"What did he want to know about me?" I felt sick at the idea of someone watching me for such a long time.

"I don't know, this and that. He smelled like horses."

Maybe a kick to the throat would do this chick some good.

I was relieved when I heard a knock at the door. One of the guys opened it and Minnie burst in. She looked fit to kill.

"Tracy! You fuckin' little bitch." Minnie grabbed her by the hair. "You tell these people what you know, or I'll—"

"Minnie, let's talk a minute." Grim pointed with his chin at me, and the three of us stepped out.

"She'd better be a fine-ass dancer, Min, because there are no lights on upstairs." I pointed to my head.

"She's got a dragon tat that wraps around from her muff to her ass biscuit." She shrugged. "Men seem to love it." Then she seemed to remember our conversation and cut her eyes from Grim and back to me. She raised her brow, and I shook my head. I didn't want her to say anything, especially with the situation at hand. Now wasn't the time for her to take on Grim's attitude. "Right, well, give me ten minutes with the bitch and I'll get her talking." Minnie stroked my arm then went inside. That left Grim and me alone in the hallway.

"Kenna," he started.

"No." I held up a hand. "It's too early to go another round with you, Grim. Especially when you leave me to find my own release at the end of it all." I knew that would give him something to think about.

My phone rang, and he glared at Benny's name on the screen. I smirked at the idea of Grim's mind going crazy as he thought I went to see Benny last night and not to my own room with my showerhead.

"Hey, Benny," I turned my back to Grim, "I'm really sorry, but I'm with a client right now. Can I call you back in a little bit?"

"Sure." He didn't sound sure. "Hey, look, I'm really sorry for leaving you like that last night, but I got the feeling if I hadn't, I'd have been escorted out by Grim's men."

"Please don't be." I chose my words carefully. "Last night was really fun, and I'm looking forward to seeing you later."

"As friends, though, right?" I found it humorous that he was clearing the air. "Because I don't want to get into the middle of something. I like my head where it is." I laughed, and he did too.

"Right." I loved Benny, but as a longtime friend, and it had been fun to catch up.

"So, see you tonight?"

"Yes, I'll see you later. I'm looking forward to it." I hung up and turned to find Grim's hands curled into fists and his jaw locked in place. Two could play the asshole card.

"This is what I know." Jesse rushed toward us down the hallway and broke the silence. "I tracked her on the cameras. She was approached by a blacked-out Toyota Camry. She had a conversation with someone, but I couldn't see their face. She got in the back seat of the car and was driven straight here to the hotel. She was dropped off at the curb, then the car disappeared into traffic. The plates were fake."

"According to her pimp, he hadn't seen her in months. She owes him money, so we could use that."

"All right." Grim pulled him aside and spoke quietly as I leaned against the wall and wondered how dirty Minnie would go to get information.

My phone buzzed in my hand.

> Salazar: Heading back into the city for an unexpected week. Bringing some friends. I wanted to give you a heads up that they might want to sign on as clients to Secrets. I'll be in touch.

Finally, some good news.

> Kenna: Great, thanks for that. I'll be
> ready.

"One phone call to her pimp and the bitch sang like a canary." Minnie came out, and Grim hurried back over.

"Well?" He jumped right in.

"She's running from her pimp and was laying low, given that she showed her face when that guy attacked you, Kenna."

"Okay." I wanted her to keep going.

"Since she's not turning tricks or working for me, she needed money. I guess delivering information on you was more appealing than standing on the corner. I guess this guy wasn't a regular." She paused. "I already texted Tess to look at the tapes. I'm pretty sure he used a fake ID and cash, but that's not unusual. He asked questions about you, Kenna. That's how she knew about who Hanna was. He was the one who knew her, she didn't. He just gave her a script to use."

"What?" My head fought to catch up.

"Could Hanna be a part of this?" Grim snapped at me.

I cut him a look. "Don't even."

"Grim," Minnie stepped in, "my guess is he found the information and made her use it to convince Kenna." She sighed when her phone rang and threw me a look. She was afraid to leave us alone. I waved at her to pick up, and she shrugged. "What did you find, Tess?"

"You should call Hanna," Grim started once Minnie answered her call. "Find out whatever information you can."

"She's not behind this."

"She was jealous about your past with Sasha," he reminded me, "and was wrapped up with some crazy shit including that video with…" He paused, and I suddenly tuned in to the fact that maybe he'd swiped that phone from the hotel room.

"Finish your sentence." I took a step toward him. "Did you take the phone from the hotel room and see who Sasha was speaking to?"

"I didn't take the phone." He towered over me as I pressed my chest into his. I was sure he could feel my anger vibrate off me.

"Kenna," Minnie's voice broke our moment, "he watched you."

"Huh?" I turned toward Minnie's pale face.

"He had a key." She was being deliberately vague, and it took me a second to follow her words. Then it hit me like a bucket of cold water poured down my back.

"A key to where?" Grim cut in, but it was as if the two of us were in our own little world.

I dropped my head and wondered which time the

sick son of a bitch had watched me dance when I thought I was alone.

"I'm so sorry. I had no idea."

It was such an invasion of privacy it made me feel ill, but as much as it made me feel sick, we could use this. I wasn't about to let that bastard win. Minnie put a hand on my arm.

"No," I shook my head, "we use this."

Minnie looked at Grim, who radiated anger at being out of the loop. "I'm not so sure that's a good idea."

"It is if Brick and Morgan are filled in." I dangled the bait.

"And Grim too," he grunted beside us.

"You know what scares me the most," Minnie slid her hand to her stomach as we both continued to ignore Grim, "is that if I don't go along with this, I know you'll do it by yourself."

"That's right, I will."

"Fine," she nodded as she thought, "if you really want to do this, we need to find something that will appeal to her more than what this guy is offering her. Grim," she turned to him.

"Oh, I am in the room." He snickered.

"Open your wallet because we need cash."

My life was like a whack-a-mole game in paradise. One moment I'm fighting the enemies that want to hurt me, and the next I'm sipping a pina colada in a pool surrounded by three fine-ass Australian men and Yen Hong, who I just adored.

"Can I ask you something?" Yen pulled away from the others when the girls arrived to entertain.

"Mm?" I leaned my head back and let the sun beat down on my face.

"I heard about Grim's brother, Leo. I'm so sorry."

"It was," I kept my eyes closed, "devastating."

Yen swam to sit next to me on the submerged bench by the bar. "Was that why you were so upset the other day?"

"Yeah." I really didn't want to talk about that. I just wanted to be out of my head for a bit and enjoy the pool and my yummy drink.

"You seem to carry a lot on your shoulders sometimes."

"Sometimes."

"Forgive me for overstepping, but just so it's said, my offer for you to work for me in Hong Kong doesn't expire."

"You're too kind, Yen." I used my straw to play with the slice of lime between the ice. "I have a lot going on here, that's true, but right now, I can't even imagine walking away from it, but I'll remember that."

"I'll do you one better." He waved someone over who handed me an envelope. "Open it."

I set my drink down and dried my fingers on a napkin. I tore the envelope open, and inside was a piece of paper with a phone number to his private pilot, a passcode to one of his penthouses in Hong Kong, and the name of a man who would be my private escort whenever I arrived.

"Of course, all the details have been emailed to you, but this was much more dramatic." He smiled shamelessly. "The next time you're having a bad day, or you just need to get away, you've somewhere to go for a change of scenery." He tightened the tie on his teal, barely-there swimsuit. "And who knows, maybe you'll love it enough to stay and work for me."

"You sure know how to be persistent." I gave him a hug. "Thanks, Yen, for showing you want me this badly."

"This is nothing. Just wait until you come and visit. That's when I'll really win you over."

"You know what? I believe you when you say that." I grinned happily.

Yen shifted in his seat. "Grab your phone and snap a picture of this moment." He waited as I tucked the information in my purse and opened my phone. "We'll hang this up the day you sign." He smiled wide and leaned in for the shot.

"It'll be a wonderful memory." I snapped our selfie.

"But first, let me see the picture, because if any wrinkles are showing we're retaking history." I laughed and swiped to show him the picture. At his indrawn breath, I glanced at the phone and realized I'd swiped back too far. He looked at the closeup of the drawing I'd snapped that had been left on Leo's body. My face flushed at how wrong it felt that he saw it.

"Stop at nothing, outlast your enemies, be the fear."

"Yen, what does that mean?"

"It's the saying from the Potens." He pointed to the photo, and I nearly dropped my glass into the pool.

"Potens?" I leaned my arm along the pool's edge. "What's that?"

"Not that, *they*," he corrected. "Back in the late forties, early fifties, the mafia was raging here in the US. In the sixties you had the classics come up from New York. John Gotti, Al Capone, and my personal favorite Salvatore Maranzano. He led the Five Families." He waved his hand as if to say *and on and on*. "Of course, there were others in Chicago, Philadelphia, LA, but in ninety-seven, the FBI put something in place called the RICO Act that brought in harsher punishments, and that helped pull back the crime."

"Okay." I drew out the word.

"Sorry, I'm a history buff on crime." He adjusted his sunglasses. "Good to know what kind of company you're dealing with." He gave me a sly smile, and I chuckled. We both knew great wealth came with a whole different playing field. "All right, while the FBI were trying to stomp out that crime wave, a new organization started to fester in LA. Started by a man named Jimmy Turner. Jimmy had family all over the US and had powerful pull in Mexico, El Salvador, China, places like that. When he saw what was happening here, he took the opportunity to move in and start the Potens."

"Does it stand for anything?"

"Yes, Potens is a Latin word for powerful. From the word *potentate,* which for them referred to the Metriorhynchidae Potens."

"You've lost me again."

"May I?" He chuckled and pointed to my phone, and I handed it to him. "See this here," he drew his finger to outline the rather sloppy drawing of a crocodile, "is actually this." He went to a webpage and pulled up a photo of their logo.

My mind went to the tattoo Sasha and the man who had attacked me at Secrets had. "All members had one on the inside of their arm. Half was the Potens logo, and the other is their own design. It's how you can tell who they are without having to say it. They were very paranoid and extremely secretive. They rose to the top of the crime syndicate here in US because they were patient, still, and played the long game like a lion in the grass."

"What were they after?"

"Control, mostly." He finished off his drink. "They wanted everything. Money, of course, control of the drugs coming in and out of the borders, politicians, businesses, they had a hand in it all."

"Did something happen?"

"Jimmy got greedy, then became sloppy, thought he was untouchable and killed another family that was trying to mess with his business. It was all the FBI needed to take him down, and when they did, it was like the organization just closed its door and fizzled out."

"Why?"

He shrugged like he was frustrated he didn't have the true answer. "I don't know. It's a fascinating story with no real end. I've read more than one article on them. Some say he told them to fade away until he got out. Others speculate that the leaders of each state were rounded up and killed. Either way, Jimmy got life, and the Potens never resurfaced."

"So, they're not around today?"

He poured some suntan lotion on his shoulders and rubbed as he thought. "I've heard rumors, but nothing concrete. I keep my head up because I'd be a target to the Potens these days. I spread my money all over the world and move product through Vegas now, thanks to the Gates' connections." I knew product meant cartel drugs.

"Okay, this drawing," I had to dig further for Leo, "why would someone draw it?"

"It's their signature." He smiled and waved at one of his clients who held up his drink as he enjoyed a lap dance in the water.

"So, a member of the Potens would draw this if they did something bad, like kill someone, and you could tell by their drawing who did it?"

"No," he laughed, now preoccupied with the woman's dance moves, "they'd hire a hitman. You know, they'd tell someone to get the word out, and it would go out to hundreds of hires, and whoever picked up the hit first would draw the Potens symbol, then mail a photo back to get paid."

"And if they were active in today's world, they'd most likely send a text back and forth?"

"I would. Who mails things anymore?"

"Is there any way you could link the photo to the hitman?"

"Not normally. It's more about the Potens getting credit for the murder without getting their hands dirty. They were smart because they stayed under the radar. Patience and brains, that's a missing art nowadays."

I leaned back and let all the information sink in. If I hadn't seen the tattoos myself, I would think the drawing was there to send us on some wild goose chase.

"Why do you have a picture of it, anyway? Are you interested in crime symbols and history yourself?"

"Not really. I just found it in an old book and wondered what it was." I shrugged it off.

"Well, I hope I didn't bore you with too much detail."

"Why not enjoy a little dance yourself?" I noticed he still watched the lap dance. "Do you mind if a slip away a little early?"

"Not in the least." He waved me off as the bartender gave him a refill. I jumped out of the pool and spotted Calli and Knox. She laughed as she replaced the empty drink in his hand with a full one. I hated that she was with him; he deserved someone better.

"Hey," Simon was suddenly in front of me, "have you seen your father since he came back?"

I thought back to what I found in my dad's desk and wondered if Jesse had found out who they belonged to.

"No," I lied. "Is everything okay?"

"Yeah," he pushed up his glasses with one finger, "I just figured, given what happened to Leo, you two would have touched base by now."

"I will," I felt a flicker of pain flash through me, "but I have to find Jim right now."

"Well, don't let me keep you." He smiled kindly. "Have a good day."

"You too."

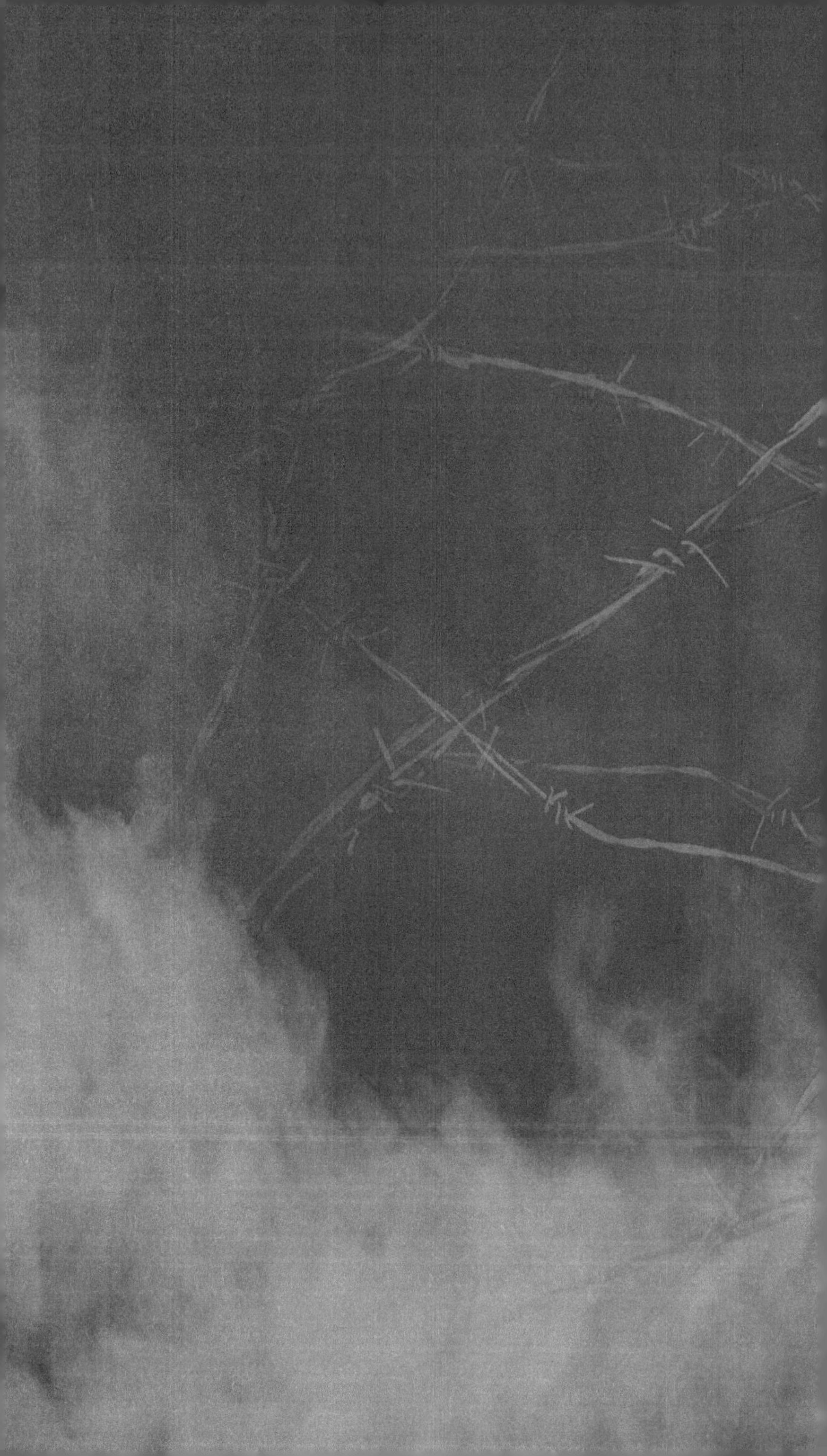

TWENTY-SEVEN

SIMON

California State Prison

"**I**nside." The man pushed me past the steel bars and into a six by six room that smelled like cold concrete and urine. I couldn't believe what had happened. I'd totally underestimated Allen, and because of that, I now shared a cell with a tattooed version of Arnold Schwarzenegger.

"You might want to lose the virgin-in-a-biker-bar look, if you're going to survive this place," the man grunted at me as he did push-ups against the side of the bed. "You get top bunk."

"Yup, okay." I tossed my few things on the ratty

mattress and ran a hand through my short hair. "I'm Simon."

The man stopped his push-ups and eyed me. He was strong and thick, a little taller than me. I was tall and wiry. I knew I wasn't strong physically, but I was mentally, and that would be my weapon.

"Simon?" He repeated my name. "Sure, okay." He smirked, and I pushed my glasses up my nose. "You call me CM."

"CM?"

"Cellmate." His smirk grew wider. "When you're ready, we'll get more personal."

"Fair enough." I jumped when an inmate stopped in front of our cell with a cart of books.

"What fairy tale do you want?" He held up a true crime novel, and CM moved out of the way.

"Umm," I scanned the titles on the spines, "do you have any of the classics?"

"Do I look like I know what a classic is?"

"Sorry." I went back to scanning the titles.

"No, please, take your time." The man's words dripped with sarcasm, and I picked up the pace.

CM reached through the bars and pulled out one called Catch-22. "This one." He waved the man off and handed it to me.

I ran my finger along the ripped spine. "I feel like there's a meaning here."

"We'll see, won't we?" He went back to his workout. I

heard a man from another cell whistle at someone and hoped it wasn't me.

"We got a pretty one, boys." He confirmed my worst fear as his words made the others around us cheer.

I closed my eyes and pushed back the hell that wanted to show itself. Once I had my head in check, I leaned my back onto the cool wall and flipped to page one.

As the years passed, I learned that rage was a tricky thing. It festered inside, clawed at your flesh, and begged to be unleashed in some explosive way. I finally learned I was different from many of the inmates. Rage wasn't for me, not anymore. It was different now; I was different. I had complete control over my emotions. I stored them deep down inside, under a tight lid, with the knowledge that all good things came to those who waited. I had slayed a demon once, and I could outwait the rest.

The warm sun beat down on my face as I leaned against the brick wall in the far back corner of the prison yard. It had been thirty-four days since I stepped foot in this piss hole, and the thought that I had at least another twenty-some years was a hard pill to swallow.

"Hey, pretty eyes," the predator who lived across from our cell called, "I got something for ya." He grabbed his pathetic excuse of manhood and stuck his tongue out like the nasty perv he was.

I loathed this place.

"We got a problem here?" CM moved to my side and shot the man a look. He raised his hands and looked away from me.

"Was just seeing if the boy wanted to play."

Boy? I hadn't been a boy since I was nine years old, and my father took me to a strip joint.

CM raised his arm, and the man nodded and left. His buddies followed.

"Ever consider gaining some weight and fuckin' up your face?" CM chuckled as he took a seat next to me.

I took pride in my slim figure and clear complexion. Though I was on the skinnier side, at least I was healthy and had low cholesterol.

"What did you show him?" I pointed to his arm.

He pushed his finger into the dirt and drew a circle. "I'm part of a club." He looked around. "It's elite and highly private." He drew up his sleeve and lifted his arm to reveal a circle tattoo. It had what looked like a crocodile swirled around the top and looked almost tribal.

"What's the purpose of the club?"

"Power, money, fear." He grinned. "We're taking back something that was once ours."

"What are you, like, the mafia?"

He leaned his head back and looked at the sky. "In a way, yes. I can tell you more, if you're interested in joining."

"No," I shook my head, "I don't want to belong to anything."

"You say that," he continued to draw circles, "but you're marked as jail bait, and I won't always be around to interfere."

"And you think some black ink is going to protect me?"

"No, but they will." He pointed toward the other inmates. "You can't spot them, but there's a lot of us in the group, and we protect our own."

"It was because of a fucking club that I'm even here."

"I know." He nodded, and that caught my attention. I'd never shared who was behind my ruined life.

I pondered the idea, but I'd been badly scarred by Allen and pushed it right out of my head. I belonged to no one.

He got up and dusted off his knees. "Something to think about, anyway." He lit a cigarette and slowly wandered away from me.

"Hey," he looked back at the sound of my voice, "what's the name of the club?"

"Potens."

TWENTY-EIGHT

GRIM

We could have had this meeting on the twentieth floor, but I couldn't run the risk of anyone hearing. If word got out that Elio's men were digging, the fuckers would scatter. Everything had to be hush-hush. I made the unusual decision to hold the meeting at the office in my suite rather than go to the basement. It would be easier for my parents.

"This is the list of hitmen for hire in the New Orleans area." Elio clicked a button on the keyboard, and a list of names, pictures, and locations came up on the screen. "Because we can't assume he wasn't from out of town," he tapped another button, "I cross referenced the list with this one from nearby, and here's what I found."

"Impressive." Dad stepped closer to the screen and rubbed his temples. We could be looking right at Leo's killer, and there was a part of me that figured we should just kill them all, and maybe I would.

"I've still got my men on the ground digging for more." Elio tried to ease the sting of all the photos. "It's just a matter of time before something shows itself."

I glanced at Mom sitting on the leather couch. I reached over from where I perched on the armrest and gave her hand a squeeze.

"And there's zero chance Alina Li could be behind this?" I needed to be sure it wasn't Alina. Since we'd broken up after Singapore, I found out she had ties to Chicago. She had me fooled for a while, and I was glad to be rid of her. She had been ruthless.

"No, *mio amico*," Elio assured me, "Jesse already had me look into her." I gave a nod, relieved I didn't need to deal with anymore crazy exes.

"It's important not to make any moves yet." Elio pointed to two men on the screen. "That being said, these two here are connected to the Fentanyl Father."

"Which means chances are they're connected to Sonny," I grunted, knowing the fucker was keeping his distance from Indulge but remained in Vegas.

"Excuse me." Kenna's voice had us all whirl toward the door. How the hell did she get up here without me knowing? Then it hit me. The fucking keycard was still under my name, so she bypassed the security system that kept everyone else out. "Mr. Gates," she avoided my glare, "my deepest apologies for the interruption, but—"

"It's not a good time, Kenna." I cut her off, but she stepped into the office with her chin held high.

"I'm sure it isn't, but I would never have come up here if I didn't think this was incredibly important and something you need to hear."

Dad turned off the screen and waved her in. "Of course, Kenna."

"Kenna, please come in, dear." Mom smiled.

"Perhaps I should step out," Elio tucked his phone in his breast pocket.

"Actually, Mr. Capri, I think you might need to hear this too."

"Please, Kenna," he inclined his head, "and it's Elio." He took his seat, and I waved her to a chair. I was outnumbered.

"I know this is an extremely sensitive topic, and this comes with my deepest respect, but I think I might know who is behind Leo's killing."

We all sat in silence as she told the story Yen Hong had described of the organization called Potens. She answered every question we threw at her. I glanced at Elio when she mentioned the crocodile. Now I knew why he was shocked.

A few tears trickled down her cheeks as she pushed on, and the longer she spoke, the more I felt shitty for the way I'd treated her. I'd known what I was doing. I'd pushed her away purposely because I knew she cared for me. I hurt, and I wanted her to hurt like me. The only problem was no one could feel the hurt I felt, because Leo was dead, and I knew it was supposed to be me.

"Elio," my father addressed him when Kenna finished, "no rock unturned, no door left unopened."

"I'll pass the information along." Elio looked at me, and I gave a nod that I had nothing to add. "I'll be in touch." He left.

"Thank you, Kenna." Mom's voice caught. "I know that was hard to bring us, but you just gave us a new direction." Dad put a hand on Kenna's shoulder and kissed the top of her head then took Mom's hand and helped her up. He murmured something about going to their suite to be alone.

Once they left and we were alone, Kenna pulled herself together and reached for her purse.

"Kenna."

"No." She held up a hand then turned and headed for the door. I pressed a button on the table to lock it. "Grim."

"Hear me out."

She whirled with fire in her eyes, and I was glad we were in my suite. If she screamed at me, no one could hear. "No. I did that last night. I gave my body, and fuck me, I even gave you a little of my heart, and where did it get me? A whole lot of nastiness, a kick to the gut, and a knife where it hurt the most."

"Yeah, I was prick last night," I admitted.

"Don't do that." She stepped close as angry tears pooled in her eyes. "Just because you acknowledge that you're prick doesn't justify your behavior."

"I wasn't justifying anything. I was agreeing with you that I was a prick."

"Are—" She stuck her finger in my face. "You don't think Leo's death affected me, too?" Her voice went up. "I worked with him for almost a year before you walked into my life. He was the nice one, the one who actually cared what came out of his mouth. Where you—"

"I what?"

"You hurt people. Use their own demons to tear them down to join you in your misery. I would never do that to someone I—" She stopped herself.

"You what?"

"No." She looked away.

"Finish your sentence." I pressed my chest into hers and towered over her in the way she loved. "Kenna."

"Cared about." I could tell those were not the words she wanted to use, but at least she said it.

I threaded my fingers through her hair as my other hand slid up her throat and tilted her chin to look at me. "I do care," I stumbled over my own confession, "about you."

"You have a hell of a way of showing that."

I raised a brow then dipped low to snag her lips. "Let me show you how much I do."

"No." She pushed against my chest, but I grabbed her wrists and spun her around to hold her in my arms. My lips pressed to her ear, and she wiggled to get free.

"The day you walked into the office and sold this hotel to Salazar like a fucking pro turned me on like no other." I moved her hair to kiss her neck. "Then when you shot venom at me over a misunderstanding with your client and me in the spa that day, well, that," I sucked on my favorite spot, "that was the day I knew I was capable of feeling for a woman." Her body relaxed as my words sank in. "I generally hurt the ones I let in. But you," my hand moved down her front but stopped at her stomach, "when you're near, you make the pain go away."

"What are you saying, Grim?"

"I'm saying I'm sorry." I couldn't believe I just uttered those words, but I did.

"I won't tolerate that from you, Grim. I'm better than that."

I kissed her again. "You are." I slowly released her, so she'd know it wasn't purely sexual. She wiped a tear and nodded. Then Leal hobbled out of the bedroom.

"Hey, baby." She brushed by me and knelt to rub his head. He pushed into her with a whimper. Who the hell was this dog? "Do you still hurt?" He complained again, and I rolled my eyes. For someone who hated anyone in his space, he sure didn't have a problem with her.

"Is he eating?" She slit her eyes at me.

"Yes."

"Taking his pills?"

"Yes."

"Getting lots of rest?"

"Why are you questioning me?" I glared at the little shit that was getting more attention than I was.

"Because you're a prick," she smirked over her shoulder, "and I wanted to make sure *Leally* is getting what he needs to get better."

"The fuck you say?"

She chuckled as she stood and gave me a playful look. "You heard me."

"You have three seconds to come over here."

"Nah," she dropped her purse on the bookshelf by the door, "I think I'd rather make you work for this one." She bolted from the room, and I threw a glance at Leal and chased after her.

I peeled my body from hers and tried to catch my breath. We'd gone three rounds, starting in the kitchen, dining room, and ended up in the bedroom. The tight grip around my chest was gone, and for the first time since Leo's death I felt like I could live.

"I've got a meeting." I grabbed her and tugged her to me so I could kiss her once more. "Rest up because I want more later."

"I'll be right here, in the same position." She laughed.

"I'm going to hold you to that. I want you exactly that way." She rolled her eyes and looked sly.

I reached for my phone to check the time and saw my inbox was light. *Good.* I tossed the phone in the sheets and rolled to hug her once more then hopped off the bed. I avoided Zhar, who looked less than impressed he'd been locked in the room with us. I heard my phone alert me there was a text message just as I got to the bathroom door. Kenna fished though the sheets and picked it up. Her face fell, and I realized I'd left it open.

"No," she cried, and I leapt toward the bed to snatch it from her hand. The words on the screen changed everything.

> Jesse: Confirmed it was Cameron who put the hit out on you. He got Leo killed.

Kenna's mouth moved, but I couldn't hear her. My ears were filled with a high-pitched ring that went straight through the center of my head.

I went numb.

The man we let into our lives had killed Leo. Maybe not himself, but he ordered it.

I let the darkness that had finally lifted fill me again.

"Grim!" Kenna's voice finally broke through, and I looked down at her wild face. Her eyes were wide with terror. "Please-please, don't do this!"

Terrified eyes were nothing new to me, and I couldn't care less what she wanted. I had a name, a face, a heartbeat to end.

"I know he's a miserable monster, and I can't even begin to process what you're going through." She clawed at my arms. "He's my father, and we need to handle this the right way."

I glared down at her. "Well, he's nothing to me."

Her hands went to her hair, and she closed her eyes as tears streamed from under her lashes. Any emotion I had toward her was quickly replaced with rage and hatred. She was a Tame, after all. She carried the blood of the man who tried to kill me, who killed my brother.

"You need to go." I brushed past her.

"No, no, no!" She whirled, and her hair whipped around her head. "Stop!" She blocked my path and pressed her hands against my chest. "Grim, please listen. A huge part of me hates that man as much as you do. But you're not hearing—"

"Oh, so, now you remember you hate him!" I shouted, and her face flinched at my volume.

"But," she gasped for air like someone drowning, "he deserves the right kind of punishment, not the Gates kind!"

"That's where we disagree." She yanked on my arm when I pulled my gun out and checked the clip. Not that he'd be so lucky to get a bullet.

"You're not listening. I beg you, look how far we've come! One wrong move, and things could get so much worse," she sobbed. "He's my father, and people are watching him, too!"

"Yes, *your* father," I spat, "killed *my* brother!" She cowered at my voice. "A hit that was meant for me!" I boomed throughout the room. "How can you even justify his actions?"

"I'm not!"

I tossed a lamp across the room, and she cringed as it smashed against the wall. "I'm going to break all his bones," her face paled, "savor each snap," I stepped closer, and she stepped back, "and when he begs for mercy, I'll snap his neck."

"Grim!" she screamed and got in my face again. "Listen to what I'm saying. Yes, my father deserves to be punished. I know that. But think about who's watching us. We have no idea if what Jesse just found out will lead you into a trap. This needs to be handled as a family."

I cut her off. "You're not family. You're a Tame." I saw the hurt flash over her face. *Good.*

She shook her head like I wasn't getting it. "Then talk to them!"

"No. This is my kill."

A sob ripped through the room, and I fed off her fear. Suddenly, her eyes moved toward the door. I lunged at her, but she was ready and slipped past me. I stepped back and clicked the button on the nightstand to lock the door.

"Grim!" She yanked on the handle like a wildling, which gave me a moment to grab her arm and yank her toward me. I couldn't have her get to anyone before I could. "What are you doing?" I dragged her flailing body toward the bed. She bucked her legs in the air. "No! No! No!"

I dropped her on the bed, reached behind my headboard, and yanked down the handcuff.

"What? Are you insane? You can't do this!" She had nothing on my strength as I attached it to her wrist. I knew she couldn't get away.

"I just did." I stood back as she took a swipe at me. She screamed obscenities, and I tucked her phone in my pocket.

I shoved my weapon in my waistband and headed for the door.

"Grim," she cried. Her tone made me turn. "Why can't you see I'm trying to help you?"

"Help?" I whirled, spewing venom in her direction. "Where was your help before my brother died? Why couldn't you see what your father was going to do?"

"That's not fair."

"No," I lowered my voice, "what's not fair is your father's here and Leo isn't."

"That isn't my fault," she choked out.

"Isn't it?"

Her face twisted as my words hit her hard. Then I saw her chin rise. "If you leave, that's it, Grim. There's no more us."

Leo's smile faded from my memory, and I nodded.

"I know." I closed the door.

The End

ACKNOWLEDGMENTS

To my mother, for all the spin sessions and listening to me when I do circles with one scene until I get it right.

To Jamie and Elizbeth, for always being there, and for help on "that" scene.

Veronica and Kasey, for digging deep into this storyline and keeping things in check.

To Rachel and Lyle Womack, for always being there when I need you.

To my beta readers, Elizabeth Clark, Jamie Johnson, Rachel Womack, Maggie Saverese Rro, Kasey Griffin, Veronica Nelson, Deb Peach, Mandy Jones-Freeman, Tara Marie,
Jenniffer Bair.

To my editor Lori Whitwam, thanks for always being me eyes.

To my reader group, I just love that you've created a
safe place for me.

To anyone who has taken a chance on my books,

I thank you!

J.L. Drake, born and raised in Nova Scotia, Canada, later moving to Southern California. Though she loves the weather in Cali, she would sell her left kidney for a good rainstorm. Jodi's love of the seasons back home in Canada definitely appear in her books.

When she's not writing, you can often find her sitting somewhere along the coast of Huntington Beach, reading, or at home curled up on a couch with her two children and husband, binge watching a good movie.

AUTHORJLDRAKE.COM

FOLLOW ME ON SOCIAL MEDIA

facebook.com/JLDrakeauthor
x.com/jodildrake_j
instagram.com/j.l.drake
tiktok.com/@authorjldrake
bookbub.com/profile/j-l-drake

Alpha

Tango

HAVOC OF SINS

Grim

Havoc

Sins

DARKNESS SERIES

Darkness Lurks

Darkness Follows

Darkness Falls

STANDALONE BOOKS

Behind My Words

Christmas At The Cabin

Omerta

STONEWALL TRILOGY

Extraction

Embedded

Breached

For the suggested reading order, please scan the QR code: